**When a man of science and a magical woman
clash, enchantment begins. . . .**

JILLIAN HUNTER

A DEEPER MAGIC

PINNACLE BOOKS
WINDSOR PUBLISHING CORP.

PINNACLE BOOKS are published by

Windsor Publishing Corp.
850 Third Ave
New York, NY 10022

The P logo Reg U.S. Pat & TM Off. Pinnacle is a trademark
of Windsor Publishing Corp.

First Pinnacle Printing: August, 1994

Printed in the United States of America

A DEEPER MAGIC *IS DEDICATED*

WITH LOVE

TO

MY VERY DEAR FRIEND AND GODFATHER

GORDON THOMSON

A SPECIAL THANK YOU

TO

DENISE LITTLE, DREAM EDITOR

AND TO MY WONDERFUL, TALENTED FRIENDS:

KATHRYN LYNN DAVIS, JILL MARIE LANDIS, AND

KATHERINE SUTCLIFFE

One

There was a heavy mist off the sea the night that Ian Mac-Neill first met Margaret Rose. Yet it wasn't until almost a half-decade later that he looked back upon their peculiar confrontation as the moment he had fallen in love with her.

Irrevocably, inevitably. But he hadn't known it then.

It was an early October evening, several hours after a rainstorm. Fine drizzling mist wreathed the coal gaslights of Union Street. From the distance came the muffled clanging of a fog bell. Although Ian thought it had a wistful sound, he didn't feel melancholy tonight. He had no presentiment of what was to come, the disappointments, the danger, the desire.

As he walked along the pavement with his vivacious companion on his arm, he glanced back at the interior of the supper room of Dalrymple's Hotel, which he and his small party had just left. The place was still fairly crowded with customers who were friends of his, students, apothecaries, and other young doctors at the Vaccine Institute where he was serving part of his residency.

As of a week ago he was *Doctor* Ian MacNeill, Licentiate of the Royal College of Physicians, qualified in medicine and surgery, and he had just turned twenty-three.

He grinned, for no particular reason, at the young auburn-haired woman walking beside him, Jean Alice Drummond. How she could look so demure he couldn't guess. She'd whispered his new title in his ear repeatedly last night, as if it were an aphrodisiac, while they sat on the sofa in her lodgings above her dressmaker's shop on Exchange Street. It was the closest they had come to sexual intimacy.

He slid his hand under her Inverness cape and squeezed her waist. "Let's get my father home early tonight."

"As if he won't guess why." Jean glanced back at the spry white-haired man who'd just emerged from the hotel doorway behind them. Ian's father, Colin MacNeill, was also a physician but in private practice.

Then something down the street drew Jean's attention. She stared past Ian, her brown eyes widening in anticipation.

"Now there's trouble if ever I saw it." She hopped back onto the pavement to stand beside Colin, murmuring, "Looks to me like someone's borrowed his rich daddy's carriage for the night."

Ian glanced down the street in amusement to watch the elegant green carriage speed toward them, its golden flambeaux burning against the mist in a pair of frosted glass lamps. The driver wore a white silk cape over his evening clothes, and knee-high white pigskin boots. He also had a red rose clamped between his teeth, and was holding the reins in one hand, a bottle of uncorked champagne in the other. A young girl hung head and arms out the window, laughing up at him, tousled dark hair swinging in her face.

Jean pursed her lips. "Shocking waste of champagne, don't you think, Ian?"

But Ian didn't answer, staring with a reluctant smile at the young girl dangling out the window, now singing a bawdy song at the top of her voice.

The driver dropped the rose from his mouth and continued his breakneck speed toward the hotel, heedless of the cabriolet that had just descended the old bridge across the thoroughfare.

The mist obscured the familiar markings of the street, but the cabdriver noticed the approaching carriage in time to swerve in the opposite direction. His abrupt stop startled a stray dog sniffing at a heap of rubbish in the gutter. The animal darted beneath the cab's shuddering body and out into the street.

"No!" Jean cried, her gloved hands flying to her face. "Get out of the way! Oh, Ian—do something."

He started forward only to backstep seconds before the carriage lurched to a stop on the edge of the pavement. Murky water splashed upward from the wheels in a wide arc to splatter him. The dog ran back toward the bridge, frightened but unharmed.

He glanced around at Jean and his father, standing against the ivy-draped granite exterior of the hotel. Jean was trying not to laugh. Then he looked down at his gray peg-top trousers, new from the tailor that morning, and at the fringe of the white woolen muffler Jean had knitted for him, also never worn before. Both articles were spattered with filthy water.

"Of all the irresponsible—"

He waited to continue until the driver took a final swig of champagne and swung down from the box onto the pavement. "You could have your coaching license revoked for this."

"Possibly." Grinning, he clapped Ian on the shoulder. "If I had one."

Ian suddenly recognized the young man as Daniel Munro, an amiable Deeside scoundrel who had recently inherited his father's shipping fortune but none of the senior Munro's diligence or dignity. No respectable person dared be caught in his company. But, for all his reputation, he didn't lack for friends, male or female. As Jean often said, money could make the most glaring fault look endearing.

The carriage door banged open. The folding stepladder fell out with a clatter. A tall dissipated-looking blond man climbed down uncertainly to the pavement, followed by a pale underweight young woman wearing a faded bronze taffeta dress.

Ian saw her eyes lift to his, linger there in slow-dawning recognition, and then lower hastily in shame. He couldn't recall her name, Flora or Fiona something, but he knew she was the youngest daughter of a local clergyman because he'd observed the birth of her bastard child several months ago in the lying-in room of the Poor Ward.

He wondered now, for the first time since that day, what had happened to the small, sickly male infant she'd delivered. Disgraced and disowned by her own family, she had obviously fallen into bad company.

"Why, it's Dr. MacNeill," Daniel Munro said to Ian, as if this were the most cordial of meetings. Then, noticing Ian's father brushing bits of ivy from his coat, he added in amusement, *"And* Dr. MacNeill."

"You've ruined my new trousers," Ian said. "Not to mention almost hitting a cab, killing a dog, and running over three pedestrians—"

"You didn't hit a dog, did you, Daniel?" a concerned female voice called from the carriage.

Both men turned at the interruption, watching in silence as the last passenger descended from the carriage onto the pavement. It was the same girl Ian had seen hanging from the window, but she had obviously remained inside long enough to brush her hair, a dark mahogany swath drawn down over her left shoulder.

She stepped into the light. Despite his irritation, Ian could not help staring down at her. If he had ever seen a more classically perfect face, he could not remember when. The symmetry of her features, high cheekbones and rounded chin, the small, straight nose, the blue-gray eyes that regarded him with such charming self-composure, reminded him of a cameo come to life. Unfortunately the effect was spoiled by the challenging lift of her jaw and an unskillful application of cosmetics, scarlet lip pomade and powder. For God only knew what reason, she seemed to want to alter her appearance.

And her clothing—that ridiculous red silk ruffled gown she wore beneath a sensible woolen cloak—as if she'd changed in the carriage into the daring dress after sneaking out of the house without her parents' permission.

That was it, he realized. She was an exceptionally pretty young girl trying to pass herself off as a woman, and the result was not so much provocative as disturbing.

Her eyes flashed at him in resentment as if she were aware he had seen through her facade. "What's the matter with him?" she demanded of Daniel. "Was it his dog you hit?"

"Good Lord, Margaret, I'm not that careless. He's just upset because I splashed a wee bit of rainwater on his new breeks."

She tossed her hair back over her shoulder. Then with the cool insolence that an adolescent girl can so effectively project, she surveyed Ian from the tip of his uncomfortably tight leather shoes to the top of his black silk hat.

"Perhaps we should take up a street-corner collection to buy him some new breeks." Grinning, she hiked the cloak up over her shoulder where the vulgar red dress had slipped to reveal the fair skin of her collarbone. "Something from this century."

With four sisters of his own, Ian should not have been insulted by her remark or by the playful quirk of her mouth as she spoke. But he was. She's laughing at me, he thought. A rude child of—could she be even fifteen?

Suddenly he felt like rubbing his handkerchief across her mouth to remove the offensive lip pomade . . . and the premature offerings her pouting red lips promised.

He glanced instead at Daniel. "Have you nothing better to do with your time then?"

"Goodness gracious, no, Dr. MacNeill. What could be better than a night out with a pair of pretty young women?"

Jean tucked her arm through Ian's. "There's no real damage done. I can get the stains out if we don't allow them to set." She brushed against his shoulder, whispering, "We'll work on them together on my sofa."

Colin MacNeill came forward to join them on the pavement, slipping his fob watch into his plaid vest pocket. "It's late anyway, and don't think I'm unaware the pair of you were conspiring to get me home."

Jean and Ian stared at each other in embarrassed silence. "I'll hail a cab," Ian said finally, "if they've not all been run off the road."

Colin shook his head. "What for? It's an invigorating night for a walk."

The four younger people had obviously forgotten the incident with the carriage, arguing amongst themselves on their way into the hotel. The lovely yet insolent girl brushed past Ian without a glance; she left in her wake the scent of damp wool and a faint sweetness which he decided was a combination of spilled champagne and her mother's perfume.

"Is that to be the end of it?" he asked after the group. "No apology? Just park your carriage on the pavement and leave the poor lathered horses unattended while you soak up another round of spirits before assaulting innocent citizens in the street?"

The girl named Margaret looked back at Jean with a sympathetic shrug. "It's dreadful when they start getting old, isn't it?" she asked with a grin. "The slightest upset sends them into a frenzy. Perhaps a cup of warm milk and a hot brick against his back will settle him. It always calms my father."

Ian struggled to keep from laughing at her audacity, uncertain whether he was more amused or insulted that she thought him such a prig. "You've a rude mouth on you, little girl," he said, narrowing his eyes. "I've half a mind to call the Charlie on you and your tosspot friends."

She put her hands on her slender hips. "You've half a mind, all right, or maybe even less if you think he'll listen to you. But go straight ahead. You miserable old thing."

She flashed him a defiant grin and followed her friends into the hotel, not waiting until the door closed to break into uncontrollable laughter.

"Do you know what happens to young girls like that?" Ian demanded of no one in particular.

Jean shook her head, hiding a smile in the collar of her cape. His father contrived to keep a straight face by jangling a handful of coins in his pocket.

"What happens, Ian?" he asked, winking at Jean. "We're dying to know."

"They end up in trouble at the Female Benefit Society, that's what, and a sorrier lot of creatures I've yet to see. Are you laughing at me, too, Jean?" he asked, trying hard not to do the same.

"Not me," Jean said good-naturedly, holding his muffler to the lamplight. "I'm sure they didn't mean any real harm. You've been lost in your medical books and lectures for so long you've forgotten what it's like to have fun."

He caught her hand in his, looking into her eyes. "I don't know about that."

Her color heightened at the unspoken reminder of the previous evening, the lingering kisses and tentative caresses they had shared. Lowering her gaze, she pretended to study the muffler more closely.

He released her hand. "What would you do if you caught Alanna out roaming the streets at this hour?"

Alanna was Jean's daughter by her first marriage, a sweet if precocious girl who had still not recovered from her father's death in a railroad mishap two years ago. But she adored Ian, and had confided in him she hoped that he'd marry her mother after he began to assist in private practice.

"Alanna's only twelve years old, and she's too busy helping me to get into any real mischief."

In tacit accord they began to walk down the street where the mist had gathered in woolly drifts. Ian wondered why he had let the incident outside the hotel so annoy him when usually he would have laughed it off.

"It's unfortunate about that young girl," Colin MacNeill said, straggling several paces behind them. "She was a pleasant child, as I recall."

"You knew her?" Jean asked in surprise.

"I did business with her father, the great banker Douglas Rose. With her background, she shouldn't have turned out that way."

Ian grunted. "She should have been turned over his knee."

"He'd have had to care enough to take the trouble," Colin said thoughtfully. "I suspect that's part of the problem. For all practical purposes, he turned his back on the girl when her mother died several years ago."

Jean slowed to allow him to catch up with them. "How could he blame a mere child for something like that? It had nothing to do with her, did it?"

"That depends on whether you listen to a lot of village superstition or not, all the silly talk of water kelpies and a banshee. But och, no, it wasn't the girl's fault. Her mother and—I believe there was a younger child—were drowned in the loch on the family's country estate. I suppose Margaret Rose's crime was to survive the tragedy."

Ian's stern face did not soften once, but already some of his anger was dissipating, to be replaced by a reluctant compassion and curiosity about the girl they'd left behind. "My father always has a defense for everyone," he said, "from the common prostitute with venereal disease to a fat old duchess who's poisoning her family with arsenite wall coverings. There are no true sinners in his eyes."

Colin smiled. "If you live to practice for as long as I have, you'll find yourself treating more broken hearts than bones."

"That doesn't sound very profitable," Ian retorted.

Jean started to laugh. "What a hard case you are."

"No," Colin said. "He may look like a great scowling brute

who scares his patients into unconsciousness before they reach surgery, but he's not really that bad." He glanced at his son. "Of course, he's not that good either."

"Oh, for God's sake," Ian said in disgust, but he wasn't as immune to his father's praise as he put on. Of the two MacNeill boys, he was the one Colin had encouraged to go into medicine.

They parted at the intersection of King Street and the Castlegate. Ian drew Jean into his arms. As the mist drizzled down, they stood beneath a lamppost and watched Colin stride up the block toward his elegant Regency granite villa.

As soon as Colin gave his customary wave from the front steps, Ian steered Jean back onto the pavement. "Your hair is getting damp in all this mist. I should take you home."

"The mist is good for my complexion. But don't pretend it's my welfare you're concerned with, Ian MacNeill. Those blue eyes of yours are full of the devil."

He grinned sheepishly and buried his hands in the pockets of his black cutaway coat. There were disadvantages to courting a woman of Jean's experience. A widowed dressmaker from Inverness, she had left the country to set up a business in Aberdeen. To her credit, she had not only survived but had prospered from the move, adopting the business practices of her competitors, but not yet the rigid Victorian morals of her customers.

When they reached her modest two-story Georgian house, they found Alanna waiting up for them. She had the table set for three with tea, Cheshire cheese, and scones. Before Ian could protest, she'd pulled off his hat, muffler, and coat, and led him across the room. But after only an hour, he found he was ready to leave.

"You're preoccupied with your work, I suppose?" Jean asked as they parted at the door.

"Oh, aye." Ian frowned, looking down at the floor. The truth was, he felt guilty because he hadn't been thinking about work at all. He'd been thinking about that beautiful rude girl he'd met earlier in the night. She'd gotten to him, with her sad eyes and indecently sensual mouth, and her memory wouldn't leave him alone.

Without conscious intent, Ian took the long way home, retracing the earlier route to Union Street even though it meant a leisurely detour. The hotel supper room was still open, would remain so until the wee hours, but the carriage had disappeared. In fact, the only sign of the earlier disturbance was the empty champagne bottle propped between two potted chrysanthemums on the windowsill.

He smiled ruefully, catching sight of his reflection in the steamy windowpane. Jean had forgotten to remove the mudstains from his clothes, and they remained as a mocking reminder of the young high-born hellion he had clashed with earlier on.

The street, deserted and so thick with mist as to be unrecognizable, seemed suddenly lonely and unappealing. Realizing he had to be at the Institute by seven, he stepped off the pavement and headed for home.

Margaret. Margaret Rose. A fine name for an arrogant wee brat, but what a beauty. He wondered if in a few more years she would still be luring men to her like moths to a dangerous flame. He almost envied them the experience. But it disturbed him to think that her fiery spirit might burn itself out in a blaze of self-destructive behavior.

Did her father truly not care that she was ruining her life?

Ian had no idea. But he suspected there would be hell to pay if the illustrious Mr. Rose caught sight of his daughter in that flashy red dress. Not to mention drinking champagne with that fool Daniel Munro.

Still, it really wasn't any of his concern. He didn't know why he couldn't stop thinking about her, and why she lingered, sweetly unsettling, in his mind.

Two

Margaret awoke with a feeling of impending disaster.

The sounds of the kitchen maids working the backyard pump drifted up to her bedroom from the garden. Entangled in her eiderdown quilt, she stared from the bed toward the window. The gray October light filtered through the curtains she'd been too tired to draw the previous evening. Gradually she made out voices in the downstairs lobby.

She recognized the voice of her uncle, the Presbyterian minister Angus Rose. His dramatic Highland baritone when raised in a Gaelic hymn could bring tears to the eyes of his congregation as easily as it could instill terror into its collective heart with his hellfire and brimstone preaching. She had forgotten he'd come to Aberdeen last week from his home in the remote Outer Hebrides. According to her older brother Gareth, Uncle Angus hoped to wangle a loan from her father's bank to repair his little storm-damaged island church.

She got up and noticed the crumpled red silk dress she had thrown across the foot of the four-poster. Suddenly it looked so garish and unflattering that Margaret couldn't remember what had possessed her to buy it in the first place. She'd liked it well enough in the shop, with Fiona assuring her it made her look sophisticated.

But it hadn't. She'd seen that last night on the fiercely chiseled face of the man she'd encountered outside Dalrymple's Hotel. For a frightening instant his blue eyes had seemed to penetrate the mask of self-possession she'd presented. Who was he to judge her anyway, that swarthy dark-haired stranger with his arrogant demeanor and cruel perception that had made her feel tawdry and ashamed of herself? She had only been trying to have fun, to avoid returning home.

She put her hand to her mouth, shuddering at the sour aftertaste of last night's champagne. She had never been drunk before in her life, but last night in the carriage outside her house, Daniel had started to cry because he had no family left, and they had ended up consoling each other with champagne toasts as if that could ease the loneliness they both knew so well.

And if the drinking had not been disgraceful enough, Daniel had become overly demonstrative, experimenting beyond his usual playful embraces to more dangerous sexual demands that Margaret had fought off with far less fervor than was proper.

Today she would turn sixteen. She was old enough to realize that a woman's sexuality could bring her joy or strife, depending on how she used it.

There was a knock at the door and the chambermaid said softly, "Your father wishes to see you in his study, Miss Margaret. Immediately, he said."

Shivering in the morning chill, Margaret slipped on her wool-lined dressing gown and hurried into the hall. She couldn't remember the last time her father had summoned her to his study, but it had been before the accident on the loch. He had never spoken to her privately since then.

"Good morning, Margaret," her younger sister Lilian called from the second-floor parlor. Painfully slim, her blond hair lank around her face, she was recovering from one of her endless colds. "I've a present for you—"

"I'll be back for it in a minute," Margaret said without stopping. "I've been called to Father's study."

"You've what?" Lilian came to the door, her drawn face disbelieving. "What does he want?"

"I haven't an inkling."

But it occurred to Margaret, after Lilian's mention of a present, that this *was* her birthday. And if there were ever a time for her father to make amends, perhaps it had finally come. Yet so many past birthdays had ended in disappointment that she had schooled herself not to expect anything.

Her mother and her two-year-old brother Alan had drowned eight years ago this morning. It was a date better forgotten than celebrated.

She proceeded quietly into the study. Her heart was pounding with a hope she was half afraid to acknowledge before she even noticed the prettily wrapped present on the desk.

It had to be hers.

Her mind raced. Whatever that squarish box contained, be it an assortment of colored thread or chocolates, she would pretend to adore it. If he was willing to take a step, then so was she.

"Margaret," her father said from his immaculate mahogany desk without looking up.

Something in the tone of his voice forewarned her. She stepped forward involuntarily and clutched the hard curved back of a Queen Anne chair. She could remember how once he would push all his documents aside to hold her on his lap.

She looked down at the box on his desk as if it were a talisman against bad things to come.

"It's almost noon." He frowned. "You slept late this morning. I tried to have you awakened earlier."

The cheerful creak of a tea trolley outside the door provided a temporary interruption. The maid knocked, but Douglas did not answer.

Margaret stared harder at the box on the desk. "I didn't realize—"

"You were spotted last night in the company of a notorious rakehell and a woman who has just brought a bastard into the world. Don't bother to deny it. One of my employees at the bank saw you himself."

She was too taken aback to defend herself. She had always assumed that he didn't care enough about her to notice her activities.

"It's my understanding," he continued, "that this is not the first time you've been sighted in disreputable company. You led me to believe that you spent your Sunday evenings at your cousin Audrey's house."

"I told you that once, and it was true—"

She glanced out the window, spotting Gareth sitting on a garden bench with his sketchpad. She could tell by his artificial stillness that he was eavesdropping. Her brother lived in perpetual fear of displeasing their father, and went to the same lengths to gain Douglas's attention with his faultless behavior as Margaret did with her blatant misconduct.

"I didn't think that where I spent my time mattered much to you," she concluded quietly.

"I don't blame you for this entirely," Douglas said. "Perhaps if I had kept you longer in boarding school, but there were reports of your insubordination even then."

The sourness in her stomach rose to her throat. "Are you going to send me away again?"

"I think I should. There's your sister to consider. She's never been associated with any sort of trouble. I wouldn't wish her to emulate you."

"Heaven forbid," Margaret said, momentarily unable to hide how deeply that last remark had hurt and angered her.

Douglas looked up slowly. Their eyes locked, Margaret's suddenly brimming with traitorous tears, his filled with guilt and anguish.

Why don't you come out and say you wish it had been me who'd drowned instead of Mama and Alan that day? Why don't you tell me it was my fault because I insisted we take the boat out onto the loch? I know it's what you think. I heard you admit it long ago to Grandmama.

Her father looked away first, clearly made uncomfortable

by the unspoken emotions between them. "I know that what I am about to propose is not the ideal solution," he said haltingly. "But over the years your behavior has become impossible to control. I am at a loss as to how to supervise you and I—there is no chance, is there, Margaret, that you could right now be in the same unfortunate predicament as that Simmons girl found herself several months ago?"

The question humiliated her beyond belief. "If you mean to ask," she said in a low trembling voice, "whether you will have a bastard grandchild from me, then the answer is no."

"Of course not," he said quickly. "But these things do happen—"

"Where am I to be sent? And when?"

At her interruption, Douglas became composed again, almost detached. "I'm sending you to the island of Maryhead to stay with Uncle Angus and his family. It is our shared hope that a religious influence will temper your tendency toward rashness. He plans to leave on Friday."

Four days. Only four days away. She gripped the back of the chair, refusing to fill the void of silence that followed.

"I'd like your belongings packed as discreetly as possible," he said at last. "There's no point in upsetting Gareth and Lilian. I've tried to keep this unpleasantness from them both."

"May I leave now?" she asked as if she could not wait to escape the room.

He sighed. "Yes. And it might not be a bad idea if you were fitted for some winter clothes that I can forward to the island. I've also made arrangements for a physician to examine you—"

"Cancel the appointment. I'm in excellent health."

"The climate of the Hebrides is harsh. One hears frequent reports of disease brought by foreign sailors—"

She rushed around the desk and dropped to her knees before him, stunning them both by the action. "Daddy," she whispered, her voice thick with tears. "Please." She was asking for so much more than a reprieve—for forgiveness, compassion, affection, and things she could not even name.

Douglas stared down at her, his hands gripping the edge of the desk. Yet it was as if he looked right through her. He did not allow himself to hear her plea, anymore than he really *saw* her pale, hopeful face. He only knew he had to send her away—for her sake even more than his.

In that moment something inside Margaret died. She rose gracefully, stepping back from the chair. "Am I excused?"

Her father shrugged helplessly. "Yes. Yes, go, but Margaret—"

She squared her shoulders. "What is it?"

"This present on the desk—it's a birthday gift from Angus and Isobel. A Bible, I understand. I have deposited the usual amount in your account to be turned over to you on your majority. It is yours, Margaret, on the condition that you do not disgrace yourself."

She clenched her fists, too upset to answer. Then, without a backward glance, she wrenched open the door and rushed from the room, past the young maid who stood watching in unspoken sympathy from behind the tea trolley.

Three

Ian glanced out the door at the small crowd gathered in the stuffy waiting room, mothers in poplin poke bonnets bouncing irritable children on their laps, elderly men fidgeting with dripping umbrellas. He scanned the rows of faces, all made expressionless by the gaslight and dark gray morning. He wished he were back home in bed.

Roger Patton, another young doctor, blond, stout and pleasant-faced in spectacles, entered the hall from a side door behind Ian, maneuvering between tables and stools with two mugs of steaming tea.

"Drink it while you've a chance. God, what a miserable crowd. You'd think the rain would keep them away."

Ian grinned. "What else is there to do on a wet day except get your inoculation? At least it'll give them something to talk about over tea this afternoon."

Roger suddenly noticed the plump middle-aged woman snoring away on the cot in the corner, her muddy feet protruding from the blanket which also covered the basket of white heather she sold in the streets.

"Killed another one, did you?"

"She passed out before I even touched her. She reeks of whiskey and probably won't revive for hours. Poor thing wandered in here by mistake. She was under the illusion this was a library."

"Well, she isn't good for business." Roger went to the door

and curtly called for the next person in line, a woman with two sullen young boys in torn tartan stockings who immediately knocked over a stool and a bottle of disinfectant.

Roger rolled up his shirtsleeves and smiled at the harried mother, pretending to ignore the mess on the floor. "Sir James Simpson is in town to lecture on the proper use of chloroform during surgery."

Ian drew his attention away from the mother who was explaining to her quarreling sons that an inoculation meant they were about to be initiated by blood ritual into a secret gypsy tribe. They quieted instantly, staring in awe at the instruments on the table.

"When does he lecture?" Ian asked Roger distractedly.

"Tonight. Your father said he'd attend."

"I'll think about it."

Ian launched into his standard explanation of what reactions the mother should expect her children to exhibit from their inoculations. But the whole time he spoke, he was thinking about the lecture tonight. If there was glory to be found in medicine, it was in the intriguing new field of anesthetics. Yet so far the potential dangers had kept many doctors from the necessary research.

"There now," he said. "What good boys you are. Leave the sticking-plaster on for the night please, madam. If it should fall off, you may sprinkle a bit of Gregory's powder on the incision and leave it open."

"Where's the gypsy chief, Mum?" one of the boys demanded.

"That's him who cut your arm," the mother answered as she shoved her children out the door. "Did you not notice his swarthy skin and curly black hair? He's the tribal chieftain's son."

Ian smiled and took a sip of tea, glancing at the cot in the corner where the drunken woman continued to whistle and snore. He couldn't afford the time to have her removed to another room, and he certainly couldn't put her out in the rain.

Roger inoculated a young seaman who confessed that he'd only come inside the Institute to escape the wretched weather.

The door opened and closed again. He heard Roger murmur, "Mind the mess on the floor, my dear. We'll have a nurse clean it presently. You may hang your damp cloak on that peg there. What a miserable day this is, and aren't you brave to have hazarded it to get your vaccination?"

Ian had only to hear that solicitous tone as Roger spoke to surmise the patient was a young attractive female. He swallowed his tea and glanced around, mouthing, "I'm going to tell your wife. Anyway, it's my turn again."

Lucy, Roger's bride of only two months, was a pretty petite blonde; possessive, and unbelievably domineering, having convinced her unattractive husband that he was fortunate to have married her and he had better not forget it.

Before Ian could get Roger's attention, he was distracted by the young woman who had just turned from the cloak peg. She stood at the end of the table, noticeably distressed . . . lovely, yet exuding a strange composure.

"It's you," he said in surprise. "The girl from the other night on Union Street."

Even as he spoke, he wondered if he could have made a mistake. This young woman wore an expensive gray velveteen traveling dress, the black lace collar buttoned all the way to her chin. The simple lines of the square bodice and flared skirt drew his attention to her figure, its slender grace and budding curves. Her dark brown hair was pulled back into a severe chignon which on another woman might have been unflattering but only served to accentuate the loveliness of her heart-shaped face.

He'd half hoped that he would see her again and didn't know why—perhaps to prove to himself she couldn't possibly be as beguiling as he remembered. But she was, and he was amazed, amused at his own fascination with someone who didn't know he existed.

She stared at him without a glimmer of recognition. A flush of embarrassment crept up his neck as he felt Roger watching him with a curious smile. Recovering his self-possession, Ian turned to the girl.

"You are—we've not been introduced, but I'm Dr. Ian Mac-Neill, and if I'm not mistaken, your name is Margaret Rose. You've met my colleague—Dr. Patton?"

"Yes," she said in a dismissive voice. "Do I have to remove my dress for this?"

He and Roger exchanged looks. "It isn't necessary, if you can either untie or roll up your sleeve."

She looked down and very slowly began to roll up the cuff of her wide pagoda sleeve.

Roger pulled up a stool behind her, murmuring to Ian, "Not another fainthearted maiden—that's the third today. Get the spirits of ammonia ready, and for heaven's sake, don't look so damned solemn, MacNeill, or they'll move us to the morgue."

Ian smiled reassuringly at Margaret as he seated himself before her. Without the cosmetics she'd worn the other night, her features appeared even more delicately etched, her mouth a soft dark red. There was a small bump on the bridge of her nose, and he found himself wondering what had caused it.

Despite his unwilling interest in her, she seemed unaware of their previous meeting. She sighed and stared past him, at some obscure spot on the wall, twisting an errant strand of hair at her nape around her index finger.

He took her arm and felt an unexpected shock of pleasure go through him, catching him completely off guard in its intensity. Could she have felt it, too? He sensed that her misty blue eyes lifted to his face, but he forced himself to look away, remembering his place and position.

Ian cleared his throat, his voice unusually rough. "I'm merely going to make a small incision in your arm, place a piece of infected thread over it, and then on top of that some sticking-plaster. A smallpox inoculation is a simple procedure, Miss Rose, if you trust an old man like myself to carry it out."

The joke failed, and there was silence. Ian suspected that he could calmly explain he was about to chop off her head and she wouldn't care. What could have possibly happened to her since the other night to so utterly crush her spirit?

"I'm sorry," Margaret said after a moment. "I know you're trying to put me at ease, but I am quite possibly in one of the worst moods of my life today."

His fingers tightened around her arm. "I can't imagine what anyone so young and lovely could have to worry about."

She looked down at his large hand on her arm, her eyes amused. "Do you pay all your patients this much personal attention?"

She was used to men making fools of themselves over her, he realized in embarrassment. It probably happened every day. God only knew where his dignity had gone that he was behaving like an adolescent himself with Roger grinning in the background.

"It's normal to be nervous under the circumstances," he said in his best doctor-to-patient voice. "I assume you do have someone to care for you over the next ten days or so in the event of an adverse reaction?"

She watched him as he made a great show of examining her arm. "Yes. You're very thorough, aren't you?"

He reached toward the tray for a small sharp knife and smiled into her eyes, the blue-gray irises shadowed with a secret pain. She looked at him for a few moments, responding with a smile that was so half-hearted it had faded before he could be certain he'd seen it.

To his astonishment he found himself wishing she would provoke him again, as she had the other evening. Anything except this sad resignation. It stirred emotions in him he could not fathom, an irrational urge to set the world right for her.

"Did you have a row with Daniel Munro?" Ian asked impulsively.

Margaret stared fiercely at the knife in his hand. "Why should you ask me that?"

He shrugged, trying to appear nonchalant. "I don't know. I suppose because you look like someone whose heart has just been broken."

She sighed. "I'm going away," she said as if that explained everything.

"Where to?" It was none of his business, but he found he really wanted to know.

Margaret hesitated. There was something in his midnight-blue eyes that inspired trust. Besides, she had no one else to confide in. "Kinmairi," she said after a long silence. "The island of Maryhead . . . in the Outer Hebrides."

"Good Lord," he said in genuine sympathy. "That's the edge of the world, isn't it?"

She laughed reluctantly. "So I gather. I'm surprised you've even heard of it."

He considered it a minor victory that he'd managed to amuse her if only temporarily. "Well, the government is always trying to send young doctors off to the islands for medical-missionary service. Naturally there's little money in it for the physician, and the islanders rarely come to accept him, but I understand it has its rewards."

Ian studied her a moment, disappointed that the laughter had faded from her face. "This is not a permanent move, I assume?"

"Yes, it is," she said, her gaze turning inward again. "I'll never come back to Aberdeen again. Are you nearly done yet?"

He hesitated at the sudden vehemence in her voice. "Another moment." He could sense Roger hovering nearby with a vial of smelling salts. "You might want to turn your head away."

"What happened to that woman in the corner?"

"Oh, her. That's only Roger's mother. She spends the occasional night here."

He made the incision in her forearm, and she was distracted enough by Roger's snort of indignation that she barely flinched. But before he could reach for the thread, the door opened and a tall, gaunt, middle-aged man in a brown woolen overcoat strode into the hall, shedding rainwater from his broad felt hat.

"I trust I've not come too late, Doctor," he said politely as Ian looked up at him in irritation.

"If you want an inoculation," Ian said, "you'll have to wait your—"

"Uncle Angus." Margaret slipped from the stool in surprise. "I thought we were to meet at the hotel."

He removed his hat. "You couldn't walk in this rain. But I didn't realize you'd come to this place first, or I'd have saved these good gentlemen their trouble." He nodded to Ian and Roger. "You did not complete the inoculation?"

"No," Ian said in annoyance. "I did not."

"Get your cloak, Margaret," her uncle said. "The coach is waiting, and there's a surprise inside for you."

"Now wait a minute," Ian said, rising to his feet. "I understand this girl is traveling to the Hebrides."

"That's correct," Angus said pleasantly. "I'm taking her there myself."

"Are you aware there have been outbreaks of smallpox on the islands?"

"Oh, yes. I minister to the sick and dying along with those well enough to sin."

"And you're willing to risk taking your niece there now when a simple thirty-second inoculation could protect her?"

"That simple inoculation you speak of, Doctor, is the devil's work, no more, no less." Angus's rich voice rose with the passion of his belief. "If we live by our faith, then that should be protection enough. If we don't, then nothing can protect us anyway. You see, I know you mean well, but there can be no resisting God's will."

Ignoring Roger's worried look of warning, Ian caught hold of Margaret's wrist and propelled her back to the stool. "I'll have it done in seconds," he told her under his breath, "before he even—"

Angus barreled his way between them, forcing Margaret back against the table. "No, Doctor," he said firmly.

Ian drew himself up to his own impressive height, his heart hammering. God forbid that he should strike a minister over a girl he'd only just met, but that was what he ached to do.

I have an obligation, as a physician, to protect her.

Obligation, is it? he could imagine Roger asking. *Your obligation is to the Institute, and it doesn't include wrestling with fanatic old fools.*

"This is up to you, Miss Rose," he said in a low voice. "I'll do whatever is necessary to ensure your safety."

Roger's mouth dropped open.

Margaret bit her lip, casting an uncertain glance at her uncle. "I'll think it over—"

"There isn't time," Ian said urgently, leaning around Angus to grip her arm again. "Dr. Patton can inoculate you while I stand guard."

Angus laid his hand on her shoulder. "You're too young, Margaret, to know what's best."

"And you," Ian said to Angus, losing his temper, "are obviously too old."

"Do you both mind not playing tug-of-war with my person?" Margaret demanded, afraid she would make the situation worse by giving in to a horrible urge to laugh.

Angus lowered his hand to grip her upper arm. "I feel the work of Satan in this room."

Ian wrenched Margaret toward him, ignoring the indignant cry she gave as her body pressed up against his, the sudden heat that flooded him. "And I feel like hitting you, Uncle Angus, holy man or not. I really do."

"Steady on, Ian," Roger said, his eyes wide in a mixture of concern and dramatic appreciation for this strange turn of events.

Margaret finally managed to break free, turning angrily to the wall. There was a low rumble of voices, and she realized that the two men were not going to stop arguing until she left. Then all of a sudden she heard a terrific bang, the sound of a fist connecting with something hard, and a man groaning in pain.

She pivoted slowly, afraid of what she would see.

The rough-faced doctor stood cradling his left fist, his mouth pinched white at the corners.

"He's only banged his fist on the table," the other doctor explained at Margaret's disbelieving look. "We do it all the time around here. Especially on days like this."

"Come, Margaret," Angus said, his face somber.

He handed Margaret her cloak and steered her toward the door. Ian watched for a moment, astonished and furious, before he followed them out into the waiting room. He fought a crazy impulse to grab Margaret's hand and run off with her to God only knew where. Dimly he realized that several of his patients had already departed, stirred by Angus Rose's impassioned outburst which touched on a commonly held fear that vaccinations went against the laws of God.

Angus and his lovely niece had also vanished. Presumably that was their black carriage lumbering down the street in the rain, churning up puddles and merging with the heavy midmorning traffic of dray carts, cabs, pony phaetons, and omnibuses. Ian stood in the doorway, gradually becoming aware of the wet slashing wind that penetrated his clothes.

He drew back into the stuffy warmth of the gaslit waiting room. Roger stood beside him, watching from a window.

"Is something wrong, Doctor?" an old man inquired of Ian from a bench along the wall. "They left in rather a rush."

"Everything is fine." He looked at Roger, lowering his voice. "If her father is Douglas Rose, I should think he'd have the final say in this. Perhaps I should call on him."

"That's rather presumptuous," Roger replied. "Not to mention a waste of time. Didn't you see the luggage strapped to that carriage? I'd guess they were for the harbor."

"But imagine that girl scarred for life or worse because of her uncle's religious ignorance."

"Chances are she'll be spared," Roger insisted.

"Do you think that you and Mark could manage for a few hours on your own?" Ian asked obstinately. For some reason, he couldn't put the encounter behind him.

Roger grimaced. "Haven't you heard? Mark resigned yesterday afternoon. It seems the Bengal Medical Society made him an offer to practice in India that he couldn't refuse. I don't suppose the lure of exotic sloe-eyed women had anything to do with his decision. But India . . . I wouldn't dare venture farther than the Highlands or the Islands myself, and not that far if I have any luck establishing a practice here."

Ian shook his head in frustration and walked back toward the hall, avoiding the faces that observed him. He doubted that he'd be so distraught if he hadn't been exhausted from overwork, or if he hadn't met Douglas Rose's daughter a few days earlier under such odd circumstances.

She had made a deeper impression on him than he'd realized. Still, while he didn't believe he would easily forget Margaret Rose, he could not imagine that he would ever see her again. He wasn't certain he even wanted to. Someone like her could so easily become an obsession.

Four

Margaret stared in surprise at the young man seated opposite her in the carriage as it moved briskly away from the Institute. There was something familiar about that straight blond-brown hair and the lively green eyes, but if they had met before, she surely would have remembered someone so attractive. He was tall and on the lean side, lightly tanned, his features so pure and aquiline he reminded her of a prince in one of Lilian's fairy tale books.

"We'll have something to eat at the harbor," Angus said, patting her hand. "Reacquaint yourself with your cousin while I run into the sweet shop to buy Isobel her lozenges."

He launched himself out of the carriage into the gray void of rain and cold. Margaret sat forward, shivering, a tiny shock of recognition going through her.

"Is it really you, Stephen?" she whispered.

He grinned, his dark green eyes glinting. "I knew you didn't recognize me."

"How could I have?" she demanded, still not recovered from her surprise at seeing him. "The last time we met was—"

"Eleven years ago." He shook his head affectionately. "You were a funny wee thing yourself. Scarecrow, that's what I thought, all long skinny limbs and those big eyes. By the book, you've changed."

"For the better, I hope," Margaret said, although secretly she did not think such a thing was possible.

"Indeed." Stephen looked her over keenly, grinning all the while. "You ought to remove your cloak. The wool is starting to smell like wet dog fur."

"Haven't lost your charm, I see." But she was grateful for his light friendly tone. He gave her something to think about besides her own despair.

"Who on the island is there to practice one's charm on?" Stephen asked. "Not my sister Agnes, with her nose always buried in a book. I'm glad to get away to university . . . Kinmairi is a frightful bore."

"Don't remind me," she said, tugging off her cloak.

Stephen stretched forward to help her remove the garment. "I can't believe your father throwing you out of the house," he said in a low, sympathetic voice. "What horrendous crime could you have committed, Margaret, my wretched little cousin?"

To her chagrin, tears sprang to her eyes. "If you asked him, I'm sure he could give you a long list of my many sins. But the truth is that it goes back a long time ago . . . to when my mother and Alan were killed. I've done nothing but displease him since then."

He frowned and eased back against the seat. "Ah, I suspected as much," he said, venting a deep sigh of sympathy.

Margaret stared out the window at the rain, allowing its dreary rhythm to absorb her attention. Gradually she became conscious of a burning sensation on her forearm where the Institute doctor had made the incision.

She pictured his face, craggy-featured with a prominent nose and dark blue eyes that seemed to miss nothing. He looked more like a sea captain or a gypsy tribesman than a physician, and his gentleness had come as a surprise. How humiliating that he had been the target of her uncle's evangelical outburst, although in the end she supposed it didn't matter.

She'd never have to face him or anyone else in this town again after tomorrow, she realized with a stab of adolescent self-pity. Exiled, in her social prime, to the remote Scottish island of Maryhead in the stormy Atlantic sea, she doubted she would ever again have to be concerned with the type of personal impression she made.

"Is it really terribly boring on the island?" she asked Stephen.

"Not if you like cod-fishing and the occasional tragic shipwreck. There's crag-climbing, too, and once in a while an Important Personage comes to see how we heathens live. Oh, we also have our own witch." He snorted. "A wisewoman, she calls herself."

Margaret's eyes widened. "Really?"

"A dreadful creature. She tried to seduce me once in the kirkyard."

Margaret held back a giggle. "How—how awful. You paint a very appealing picture, I must say."

"I'd be a liar if I tried to." Stephen lowered his voice, glancing out the window to the street. "Anyway, I don't think I'll be there for long if I plan well enough ahead."

Margaret looked up at the note of intrigue in his voice, wondering how he could be so unlike Angus and Isobel. "I thought you were studying for the ministry," she said, "to follow in your father's footsteps."

"So I am. But that doesn't mean I'd be content to exist on porridge, herrings, and prayer. There must be more to life, even the spiritual life, than that."

Margaret looked away, her heart leaden. As she gazed out at the rain, she realized with a stab of lonely despair that right now Lilian and Gareth would be playing draughts in the parlor, bemoaning the miserable weather. Did they wonder what had happened to her? And Daniel—had he returned to their meeting place for the past two evenings or had he given up on her by now?

"Porridge, herrings, and prayer," she said with a shaky laugh. "Tell me you're teasing, Stephen."

He grinned. "Now that Maryhead has you, Margaret, life will definitely be more exciting."

Margaret heard the sound of a shopbell, a faint tinkling in the rain. She could see Angus lurching across the street toward them, chin tucked to his chest. His solemn face seemed so unfamiliar, his way of life terrifyingly strange.

"I don't belong here," she said aloud, leaning toward the door. "I can't stay—"

Stephen slid forward and took her hands in his. "My parents are not as bad as they seem. Give them a chance. You need time to adjust, that's all."

"Oh, Stephen," she said with a soft anguished sigh. "You just don't understand. I'll never adjust to what's happened. I don't know if I could even try to."

Five

The Outer Hebrides
November 1848

Margaret drew deeper into the kelp cavern, spumes of cold surf foaming around her laced ankle boots. As she watched the activity on the beach, her common sense told her she would only hinder the rescue efforts. Yet from the moment she'd abandoned her cart on the cliffside path, caught in the storm while on her way home from a Martinmas dinner with the laird at Castle Kinmairi, something stronger than curiosity had drawn her to the scene of the shipwreck.

So far only a few of the island men had actually braved the rough waves to tow the survivors to shore. A shipwreck brought bad luck. And incomers were not welcome on Maryhead even under the best circumstances.

It was twilight. From what Margaret could see in the haze, the schooner lay foundering on her side, water cascading over the port lower yardarms. Her hull was impaled on the submerged rocks which made Cape Rue a deathtrap for incoming ships caught in the northwest gales that so often struck without warning.

"Stephen!"

Margaret splashed through an icy wave to intercept her cousin as he ran past the cave. He came to a breathless halt at the sound of her voice, a coil of rope around his shoulder.

There was a moment of awkwardness as their eyes met; the day before yesterday Margaret had inadvertently discovered him making plans to go to Edinburgh on some mysterious mission he refused to discuss. It was not like Stephen to keep secrets, but ever since his ordination several months ago as one of Maryhead's three ministers, he had changed.

"What are you doing here?" he asked in surprise. "I thought you and Agnes were safe in the castle for the evening."

"We decided to come home early. What happened to the ship?"

"Inexperienced captain, I'd say, snared on a lee shore and unable to beat against the wind. I haven't seen any dead yet, God be thanked. Margaret—" He guided her away from another wave—"are you still angry at me?"

"What do you think?"

A wave broke against their knees, yet neither of them moved. Shivering, Margaret scanned the silver-green billows of water for survivors. Three sailors still aboard the ship were clinging to her swaying bowsprit while waves thundered over them and then crashed against the black cliffs of the cape.

She glanced back at Stephen. "Is there any way to save them?"

"No point in taking out the surf boats in that sea," he said grimly. "Even if the cragsmen could scale the leeward wall of the cliff, we'd not reach them across the rocks."

The cragsmen were a loosely organized club of islanders who, to prove their prowess, regularly climbed the cliffs for sport. Margaret glanced down the beach at the small congregation of men standing around Jamie Shaw, Maryhead's chief administrator and factor to its young laird, Thomas Macpherson.

"We?" she said sharply. "What do you mean 'we' might be able to reach them?"

"Are ye ready, Mr. Rose?" one of the men shouted.

A gust of wind forced Margaret and Stephen apart. Her face

pale, she grabbed his arm. "You're not going to climb in this weather?"

He gave her a tolerant smile. "If I have to. Now be a good lass and see if there are any survivors along the beach to help. Half the island still holds to the old pagan nonsense that it's bad luck to save a drowning man."

Margaret whitened but did not speak as he hurried away, knowing his reference to drowning had been unthinking. Of all people, Stephen knew how deeply the accident on Loch Meirneal had affected her. Perhaps it was for that reason, to atone for her involvement in those two deaths years ago, that she had come to the beach this evening in the hope of saving a life.

"Oh, there you are!" a woman cried behind her.

Margaret whirled, the wind whipping her cloak around her legs. A tall red-haired woman strode like a soldier from the cliffs through the marram grass that grew along the shore. It was Agnes, Stephen's older sister. Margaret had abandoned her on the path with the cart and their two patient little island ponies almost an hour ago.

Agnes waved and shouted again. This time her voice was lost in the frantic ringing of the ship's bell in the wind and the cries of the thousand seabirds—fulmars, gannets, razorbills, and gulls living in the crevices of the cliffs which towered overhead.

Agnes reached Margaret at last. Grimacing, she shook loose a gummy strand of seawrack from the hem of her dimity frock and striped black satin petticoats. "How long did you expect me to wait for you in the cart, half frozen to death and trying to calm the ponies?" she demanded with her typical lack of patience.

Margaret held out her hand to steady her cousin. "Stephen wants me to look for survivors."

"Oh." Agnes's plain angular face softened momentarily.

"Oh, I see. Well, you start searching the shore around the skerries, and I'll return to the cart for a plaid."

Margaret hid a smile. It was so like Agnes to rail against a dilemma and then fling herself without reservation into remedying it. Hitching up her own cloak and skirts, she began to pick her way through the debris that littered the shoreline—seashells, rope, yards, a ship's lantern. After several minutes of studying the treacherous skerries and the sea beyond for signs of survivors, she finally spotted a man floating facedown in the surf.

She hesitated, her stomach knotting with anxiety. She was terrified to even touch him, to turn him over and find him already dead. But she forced herself to wade forward slowly into the waves that surprised her with their powerful undertow.

"Never mind him, Miss Rose." A rough-faced crofter, clad in a pea jacket and thick nailed boots, splashed up beside her to catch her arm just as a wave would have swept her under. "There's another one on the beach who can better use yer help."

"Thank you, Liam."

Shivering with cold and relief, she turned and sloughed through the surf toward the dark-haired man who sat propped up against a lobster boat. She knelt, quietly studying him in the dying light, her skirts and cloak dragging across the sand.

His eyes were closed; his breathing was so shallow Margaret assumed he'd lost consciousness. There was a deep gash on his temple. Several strands of wavy black hair adhered to the blood which had begun to congeal. Across his lap he held a small sea chest and something rectangular, perhaps a book, wrapped in tarpaulin. He had unusual hands, large, with long elegant fingers that, despite his condition, held tightly to his personal treasures.

She leaned toward him and then froze as unexpectedly he opened his eyes and regarded her in silence. She thought in surprise that he looked like a Highland gypsy, his expensive if waterlogged gray flannel suit at odds with his harshly sculpted face and the unruly black hair that curled against the collar of his jacket. But he was an incomer, all right, unlike any other man she had met on the island.

She returned his stare, sensing that he found her attention as disconcerting as she did his.

"I have a concussion," he murmured. "Blurred vision, and I'd wager my pupils are dilated—unless you admit you really are one of the *maighdean mhara* who lure seamen to their death on the skerries. You look like one, with that hair—"

"And you've seen a mermaid before, have you?" she asked with an amused smile.

He smiled back only to wince as he began fingering the painful-looking wound on his head. "No, of course not. I don't even know why I mentioned it unless I'm feverish, too. There was influenza raging aboard ship when I embarked at Skye. I'm telling you this in case I lose consciousness and need medical attention. I shudder to think of my fate should I fall into the hands of one of your local folk healers."

Margaret raised a brow, thinking that he had a rude shock in store when he discovered that was precisely what had happened. "How did you hurt your head?"

"I struck it against a bulwark during a storm."

"Did you have family with you?" she asked.

"Family?" He frowned, staring past her to the turbulent sea. "No. The domestic couple I employed wisely chose to stay on Skye to oversee the ordering of some supplies. I expect them in a day or so . . . if they reach this godforsaken place alive. We were supposed to anchor on the other side of the island— the civilized side with a lighthouse."

Margaret sat back on her heels. She wasn't sure whether she should feel personally insulted or not. "A lighthouse wouldn't have helped much in—"

He cut her off as if she hadn't spoken. "Fetch me a clean

bandage and flask of whiskey so I can help on the beach. There must be others worse off than me."

Certainly not that are more imperious, Margaret thought in amusement. Even with a concussion he managed to order strangers about as if he had the right. Still, she wasn't about to let his lordly airs undermine her own self-confidence. If one thing had come from her years of exile on this island, it was a knowledge of healing skills passed to her from practical Aunt Isobel, who had never consulted a physician in her life. Of course the fact that Isobel and Angus had died eleven months ago of measles could only be attributed to God's will. Isobel, however, would turn in her grave if she knew that Margaret had been openly studying the medical magic of Morag Strong, the island's *banabhuidseach,* the wisewoman who lived in a beehive hut on the moors.

"Will you help me up, miss?"

The man extended his arm, but before Margaret could help him he groaned and dropped his head back against the boat. She frowned, deciding he was in worse condition than he realized. She dug through the sand for a clump of fresh black seaweed and then carefully wiped it across her skirts.

"Chew on this, sir, while I fetch help to transport you from the beach."

He glanced down at her hand and then returned his disbelieving gaze to her face.

"Seaweed," he said. "You expect me to eat seaweed when I've already vomited enough seawater to fill a lake?"

It was all she could do not to laugh at the poor man. Instead, she answered with implacable calm, "Kelp will help to combat the fever."

"At any other time I might be amused by your islander's ignorance of materia medica." He shifted forward, grimacing as he tested his shoulder for mobility. "You'll find several phials of medicine in my traveling chest, assuming it's held tight against the water. Kindly find the one marked Carbonate of Ammonia." He paused to clear his throat. "I assume you are literate—"

"Why, I hardly know, sir," she said with a droll smile. "Could you spell 'em for me please, those big words you nearly choked on?"

He looked sheepish. "I suppose I deserved that."

"Yes," Margaret agreed, her voice cool but not unkind, "and even I, in my profound ignorance, can see you're in no condition to help anyone."

He grimaced. "I'm afraid you're possibly right about that. But at least let me try—"

She glanced around, distracted by the sight of two crofters carrying the inert body of a sailor toward the lobster boat. A sudden blast of wind chased across the cove, but it was not from the cold that she shuddered.

Margaret turned back to the stranger, who was fumbling to unlatch his chest. "You're not from any of the nearby islands," she said thoughtfully. "Are you an apothecary?"

"I'm a physician," he replied, his hands falling still, "from Aberdeen on the Scottish mainland. The government sent me here at your laird's request."

"Thomas asked you here?" she said in astonishment.

He didn't answer, staring past her to the sailor who had been laid out alongside him on a length of canvas. He made to rise, then stopped, dropping back onto his haunches.

"Is he dead?" he asked one of the crofters who had brought the man to shore.

The gray-haired crofter, Margaret's friend Liam, looked up in astonishment. "Bless my soul, ye said ye were a doctor. Can you nae tell whether a man lives or not?"

"Not from this distance," he said indignantly.

"Weel, dinna fash yerself. He's still breathing so far as I can tell."

"Sit back down." Margaret placed her hand on the doctor's broad chest and gave him a gentle shove onto the sand. "I've rinsed my hanky in seawater and can at least wash the blood from your forehead. Once we get you to the farmhouse, I'll dose you up with island medicine."

He was too dizzy to protest, murmuring, "I'll be all right in a few minutes. Just as soon as the faintness passes."

"Agnes is coming down the path now with a plaid. What is your name, by the way?"

"MacNeill," he murmured, closing his eyes as she dabbed at his forehead. "Ian MacNeill."

Ian regained consciousness, briefly, to hear the two women arguing about how they would carry him to their cart on the escarpment above the cove. He could not tell the time, but several stars had appeared in the sky. It was drizzling, and the dampness felt good against his burning skin.

Pain jolted through his bruised shoulder as the taller of the two women positioned herself beneath his armpit and struggled to hoist him to his feet.

"Why did we not ask Liam to help?" she huffed against his chest. "I'm afraid I'm going to do the big lummox an injury."

"The big lummox is afraid you will, too," he said under his breath.

She started, obviously believing him unconscious. He sagged against her, nearly toppling them both to the sand again. She was older than the other woman he had met on the beach and not as pretty either, if he were to judge by his fuzzy image of her strong but sharp-featured face.

"We're trying to carry you up the cliff, sir." She spoke in the tones one might use with an idiot child. "Be a good fellow and let us support you between us."

Ian got to his knees, trying to find his balance without her help and discovering himself incapable of it. "I can walk," he said unconvincingly.

"Let him walk, Agnes, if he wants to be stubborn. But mind he doesn't bring us both down the cliff when he falls."

He recognized the first woman's voice. Even though she had moved away from him to forge her way up the precarious cliff-side path, he had a vivid impression of luminous blue-gray eyes in an angelic face. Which, he thought dryly, would probably turn out to be a combination of twilight illusion and an indication of how feverish he had become.

He hated to admit it, but the young island woman had more accurately assessed the seriousness of his condition than had he. After only a few steps, he was forced to lean on both her and the companion she had called Agnes. It took their combined strength to move him. He stood a full six-feet-two-inches tall, and despite his size, felt as unsteady as a newly birthed foal.

"Please, sir." Agnes spoke in breathless gasps. "Only a few more steps to the cart."

To their credit the women managed to bear him to the summit of the cliff, where the wind blew with a bitter intensity that cut through his sodden clothing. Helpless to resist, he suffered the indignity of being dumped into the springless cart, laid out on a layer of freshly cut peat that would ruin whatever he'd hoped to salvage of his woolen suit.

"There now, that's better, isn't it?" That was Agnes again, roughly tucking around him a plaid that was itself more damp than dry. "We'll soon have you home to a warm fire, and Margaret's secret potions, poor man, if you survive them."

Home. Ian shuddered to imagine it—some primitive stone hut inhabited by two potential spinsters who would spoon-feed him dulse and pulverized bullock's heart as a restorative. He would be the laughingstock of his medical colleagues when the word leaked out, how he had come on a mission of good-will to this unknown island only to succumb to its pagan treatments before his first consultation. It was a humbling experience.

He stared up at the stars. He could hear the wind, distorted as it slammed against the receding clifftops only to be amplified by the low-lying hills ahead. He should not have left the cove. The cart bounced off across the rocky promontory toward a stretch of desolate moorland.

"I should . . . I should . . ."

The cart stopped. The younger woman turned to regard him. Her face suddenly seemed familiar and no less beautiful than his blurred impression on the beach.

"What is it you want now, Dr. MacNeill?"

"I should . . . go back—back to the beach to help . . ."

"And what good would you do, unable to stand on your own two feet or even compose a simple sentence?"

The cart jolted forward again. Ian closed his eyes, swallowing in resignation. He had recognized in her voice the same unthinking condescension he himself used to quiet a troublesome patient. And he knew he was, at least for the duration of his illness, entirely at her mercy.

Six

Rain lashed the single window of Margaret's darkened attic bedchamber as she entered the room. Moving cautiously, she went to the night stand to set down the tray of hot medicinal broth and blue vervain tea she had diligently prepared.

She darted a speculative glance at the large man sleeping in her bed. What a struggle it had been for her and Agnes to lug him upstairs to her room. As if the cliffside haul had not been heart-stopping enough, all three of them had tottered like dominoes at the top of the perpendicular staircase in a near-disastrous moment which Margaret would never forget—primarily because both Ian and Agnes had been laughing like a pair of drunken idiots at the time.

In truth, she could not remember when a patient had caused so much upheaval in the house. But then this man was an incomer and exceptions, however unpleasant, were to be anticipated. Resigned to this fact, she lit a candle to dispel the evening shadows and settled onto the stool at his side.

"And there was light," Ian murmured. He raised his forearm to shield his eyes against the gentle amber glow that encircled them. "I've been trying to figure out where I was. Not the ship—I remember the wreck."

His deep voice so startled Margaret that she half slipped off the stool. "You were supposed to be asleep," she said in mild reproof.

"In and out," he said. "My mind drifts in and out of consciousness like the tide." He lowered his arm to regard her with a look of amused trepidation. "I remember *you*—the sharp-witted mermaid of mercy who came to my rescue. What have you brought on the tray?"

Margaret sat up straighter. You didn't expect that kind of mental activity from a man half out of his senses with a raging fever. "It's something to make you feel better." She smiled reassuringly. "A little broth and tea."

"I'd not mind a taste of broth," he admitted. "My throat feels as if I've had it scrubbed raw with sand."

Margaret leaned toward him, glancing inadvertently from his strong-featured face to his chest, broad, muscular, and brown against her pristine white sheets. She couldn't explain why he should unnerve her when she had coolheadedly tended countless other young men on the island in worse situations. Perhaps it was because of his professional background or because of his association with Aberdeen, where Margaret had prematurely lost her youthful innocence and hope.

As she fussed over him, Ian felt a pleasant lethargy steal over his senses and decided it was a good thing she hadn't asked him to change the bedding. His body, vulnerable from fever and fatigue, would have embarrassed him. She excited him too much, this sweetly serious mermaid who was trying so hard not to look at his naked chest.

Assuming an impersonal demeanor, Margaret said, "Let me prop you up. It's impossible to feed you on your back."

He expelled a sigh. "I'm your obedient slave."

"Not quite," she said tartly. "You're too outspoken for a start. Slaves are supposed to be quiet and submissive."

He made no attempt to respond, his attention drifting to the wind-borne rain that washed against the window in hypnotic monotony.

"Dr. MacNeill?" she said in concern. "Are you all right?"

Ian gave a vague nod, his eyes widening in an effort to focus on her face. With a worried frown Margaret slid her arm under

his shoulders and repositioned the pillow behind his head, surprised that the sudden physical closeness should make her feel
so awkward.

"Your hair smells like flowers," he whispered against her
neck.

She stiffened and drew back from the bed; it crossed her
mind that she should probably call Agnes upstairs to make
sure the doctor behaved himself. But after a moment, her practical nature overrode propriety. He was too weak to initiate
any physical sort of nonsense, and besides, he didn't strike her
at all as such an unsubtle sort of man.

The steam from the bowl on the tray wafted between them
in pungent wisps. Ian wrinkled his nose, but did not comment
on the ghastly odor, touching his temple with his fingertips.

"What have you put on my head, lass, a helmet of mud or
a beehive?" he asked in alarm.

Margaret laughed unwillingly, her eyes warm. "It's a poultice of cobwebs and burnt snail shells, with horsetail for blood
clotting and St. John's wort and wood betony to ease pain."

"Snails, you say. Cobwebs, too. Good God. And this con-
traption around my shoulder that feels like a leather harness—I
suppose it's evaporated adders or something equally appalling?"

"It's a simple gauze bandage," Margaret replied, her tone
clipped. "You complained on the beach of pain, although I
could find no sign of swelling or discoloration."

Ian's blue eyes glinted with gentle humor. "That might be
because it was the other shoulder."

Margaret's cheeks flamed. "I'll change the bandage then."

"Och, no, I'll fix it myself in a bit. You've done a passable
job of wrapping it though, by the way."

"I'm complimented," Margaret said with a wry smile.

"Aye, I thought you might be." He shifted onto his good
shoulder to stare at the night stand, his nose twitching. "The
smell of whatever is on that tray isn't helping my head, however."

Margaret decided then that she would stop at nothing to make him well, not only to get him out of the house, but to prove she wasn't the unschooled bumpkin he assumed her to be.

"I've had great success with my cures," she told him, reaching toward the tray. "Now sit back like a good man and take your soup before it goes cold."

His eyes narrowed as she brought the spoon to his mouth. "Just what ingredients are—"

She slid the spoon between his lips before he could finish, frowning as he turned his face away with an exaggerated shudder. "That," he gasped, "is the foulest, most repugnant—"

She forced another spoonful of the greasy black-green liquid into his mouth, suppressing the urge to smile at his reaction.

"—witches' brew," he sputtered, lifting his hand to the spoon. "Enough! I prefer the fever and the pain. Even death."

Margaret's amusement faded as she noticed the glassy look that had come into his eyes. Physician himself or not, he needed her help. Her voice like steel, she asked, "Shall I have to get Agnes to help me hold you down, Dr. MacNeill?"

"Agnes—she of the flaming red hair and Amazonian strength? No, thanks. Spare me that humiliation at least." He closed his eyes, slumping back against the pillow with a defeated sigh. "All right. I submit—so long as it isn't poison."

"Poison?" she said, insulted to the core. "What a nerve. I spent a solid hour in the kitchen, mixing, mashing, and pounding the proper physic herbs to help you."

He cracked an eye open to look at her. "Not to mention robbing those hapless snails of their homes, you arsonist."

"You're behaving like a little boy," she said impatiently. "And you, supposed to be a doctor."

"Snakes and snails and puppy dog's tails," he said with a rueful smile. "That's what little boys are made of, even the ones who grow up to be doctors."

"Open your mouth," she ordered softly.

She managed to feed him a half bowl of the broth before he drifted off again, his profile stark against the pillow. She touched his lean cheek where a stubble of black hair glinted, satisfied that the feverish warmth had begun to abate. Silently she bent over to blow out the candle.

As she rose from the stool he sighed, slowly turning his face toward her. "You haven't told me your name," he whispered.

"It's Margaret," she said after a pause. But she wasn't even sure he'd heard her, for he made no further response, his breathing slow and even.

Without a sound she lifted the tray and crept from the room, feeling exhausted and at the same time inexplicably invigorated from the encounter. But as she descended the stairs, she wished fervently that she had left him on the beach for another islander to rescue. He was so much more than she'd bargained for.

Agnes was looking out the window that faced across the moor to the windswept coast when Margaret entered the parlor. The hastily built peat fire blazing in the hearth had only begun to counteract the chilly damp that permeated the very foundations of the old stone farmhouse.

"Is there much damage?" Margaret asked in concern.

Agnes drew the yellowed lace curtains across the window. "The apple trees are down, and your herb garden's a sea of mire. If it rains much harder during the night, the burn will probably overflow onto the fields."

"And ruin our lovely crop of chickweed and bog grasses?" Margaret said with a weary laugh.

She set down the tarnished silver tray on the tea table and settled into a chair. "I'm worried about Stephen. It's almost midnight—tomorrow's Sunday, and he hasn't finished working on his sermon for the morning service."

"He's probably returned to the manse and didn't want to disturb us," Agnes murmured.

"There were no lights in his study. I checked when I was upstairs."

Agnes moved away from the window, giving Margaret a look of affectionate dismay. In the few months since Stephen had succeeded his late father to the ministry and moved into the manse that was a short walk from the farmhouse, a strong friendship had grown between the two female cousins that had less to do with a bond of blood than a certain unconventionality of spirit.

The farmhouse belonged to Agnes's husband, Kenneth Alcock, a tweed merchant who spent several months of the year away from home. Margaret thought that this arrangement—long enforced separations interspersed with brief but passionate reunions—secretly delighted Agnes, for it left her with endless hours to write her beloved plays (a pursuit forbidden during her father's life) and to enjoy her first real taste of freedom from her parents' rigid upbringing.

After an initial period of rebellion, Margaret herself had also come to appreciate the island's solitude. She spent misty mornings collecting driftwood on the beach, tending her medicinal herbs, or searching for elf bolts on the moors. And in the evenings she helped Stephen with his parish work, despite Agnes's repeated warnings that Margaret needed a life of her own.

Now Agnes pushed Margaret's ugly one-eyed marmalade cat off her chair and sat to drink her tea. "How is your handsome doctor faring after his soup?"

Margaret chuckled softly, the scene with Ian vividly imprinted on her mind. "He played merry hell with me—accusing me of feeding him a witch's brew, thanks to your little comment in the cart. And I don't know that I'd call him handsome. Put on your spectacles the next time you look at him." She crossed her ankles over the tapestried footstool before the fire. "Masculine, I'll not argue."

"Oh, more than that," Agnes said thoughtfully. "He has what the French call *la belle-laideur* . . . a beautiful ugliness, the sort of man who drives women mad with desire."

Margaret snorted. "As if you'd known hundreds of them."

"Well, I have read—and written—about such men. They can be dangerous, that sort, if you don't guard yourself. That brooding Gaelic face isn't easy to forget."

Margaret smothered a yawn. The cat jumped into her lap and sniffed at the teacup she had just drained.

"Why has he come to Maryhead anyway?" Agnes asked. "Was the schooner blown off course?"

Margaret gazed into the fire. "He's from Aberdeen, of all places. He claims the government sent him as a medical-missionary at the formal request of Lord Macpherson."

"Fancy Thomas not mentioning it this afternoon at the castle," Agnes murmured. "He might—"

"—and brooding Gaelic face or no, he won't last any longer than the last pompous London physician who was determined to save us all from ailments no one on the island had ever heard of before."

"The whooping cough took a terrible toll on the bairns last winter," Agnes said gently. "We could have used a proper doctor's help then."

"He's brought the stranger's cough with him," Margaret countered. "The last time a sailor brought it we were all laid up for weeks in bed, and I thought I would die."

"Influenza. It's called influenza, dear. Stranger's cough makes you sound ever so rustic."

"Well, whatever it is, I'm sure to catch it. He's sleeping in *my* room, in my bed, which reminds me I'll have to disturb him again to fetch my nightrail. What a bother."

"Yet it was your kindness that brought him here," Agnes said with a smile. "Sleep in my room tonight, won't you? There's plenty of room in that big bed."

Margaret sighed. A few minutes later she had reentered her

bedchamber and was retreating to the door with her nightrail over her arm. Resentfully she glanced at the unfamiliar figure in her bed.

He stirred suddenly, flinging out an arm toward her. Hesitantly, she tiptoed to his side. Had his fever risen?

She leaned over him to check and then gasped as he caught her wrist, dragging her down so she sprawled awkwardly across him. For a humiliating instant she could not disentangle herself from their embrace, his knee wedged between her thighs, her face pressed to his firm brown shoulder.

"Stay . . . with me," he whispered, his hand catching in her hair. "Oh, God, I am so hot . . ."

He appeared to have drifted back into a restless sleep. Cautiously Margaret wiggled to the edge of the mattress, only to give a little shriek as he rolled over to entrap her. Murmuring incoherently, he flattened her beneath his powerful body. Then he fell still.

She could barely draw a breath. She could not so much as uncramp her legs, pinioned beneath his solid weight. Breasts, belly, thighs, he pressed her deeper into the mattress until their bodies seemed to meld. Her insides softened, trembling with humiliation and something she dared not name.

"Dr. . . . Mac . . . Neill . . ."

He rolled onto his side, his eyelids fluttering. His unshaven face fell against her neck, abrading her skin. His breath burning her ear, he whispered a name, a woman's name. Jane, Jean—she could not tell.

She eased backward to the foot of the bed, her heart racing. She had to remind herself that he was ill, not in control of his faculties . . . delirious, in fact. But that did not explain *her* response to their brief physical contact, the flickering warmth that had ignited deep inside her, and that lingered still.

Moving quietly so as not to awaken him again, she dipped a cloth into the bowl of water at the washstand and sponged off his forehead, face, and throat.

After a few moments she backed toward the door. Yet even in the hallway, where the thrum of rain on the heather-thatched roof drowned out the sound of his voice, she could not easily forget him.

The mere sight of him in her bed was enough to bring a surprising rush of blood to her face, his muscular arm entangled in the coverlet she had embroidered, that dark head on her pillow. How unsettling . . . to retire at night remembering the sensation of lying beneath him, to even think of sleeping in that room again, undressing there, as if something of him would linger behind like a seductive presence in the shadows.

But she *would* forget him, for he represented all she had left behind: her home in Aberdeen and the bittersweet memories of it she had suppressed, the social behaviors that, on Maryhead, even her uncle had been forced to disregard. It was fortunate that within a few days the doctor would be settled on the other side of the island, and the threat to her peace of mind he posed, whether real or imagined, would be gone.

Seven

Ian had tried to call out to her again as she closed the door, but his cry died stillborn in his throat, and the effort to raise his arm in summons left him trembling. His fever had begun to subside—could that black fishy broth have done some good? He doubted it. He was convinced he'd catch pneumonia in this bleak whistling bedchamber where the damp of rain, mist, and sea air pervaded every crevice.

He wondered whether his mission on Maryhead was destined to failure from the start. A shipwreck did not seem a good omen, and he had doubted all along that his reasons for accepting the position as island doctor would prove adequately altruistic to withstand the demands he'd face.

He'd been embroiled in the middle of a professional scandal when the offer had been made. His longtime friend and associate, Dr. Roger Patton, had been found dead in Ian's laboratory, apparently killed by a self-administered dose of chloroform. The two men had enjoyed an amiable rivalry over who would be the first to perfect the anesthetic. And although the Royal College of Physicians had declared the death accidental in the course of an experiment, the taint had damaged Ian's reputation among his middle-class clientele.

Then there was Jean, who had provided a far more personal reason for his impetuous departure from Aberdeen, a reason so painful he could not bear to think about it, and yet it seemed he did nothing else.

He pushed aside the quilt—it smelled of lavender and lye soap and felt fragile from many washings—and lumbered to his feet, gazing around the room for something of his personal belongings. At the washstand he splashed tepid water on his face and stared at himself in the oval mirror. Pupils normal. Face in the feeble moonlight even more intimidating than usual with that black stubble of beard and bandaged temple.

On the stool he found only his waterlogged calfskin shoes, broken pocket watch, and the undamaged locket miniature he had carried inside his jacket. Shivering, he realized with some amusement that his two female rescuers had stripped him down to his woolen drawers and he was, by dint of his half-nakedness, a prisoner in this damp attic. What a fright he must look, an unshaven monster in his underwear.

He returned to the bed and flicked open the locket, able to see only the outline of the painting of a smiling young girl. In his mind he pictured her clearly. Her expression bespoke such innocent mischief that it hurt to think of the unhappiness that had befallen her.

Margaret Rose.

If it hadn't been for this locket, he'd have probably forgotten the details of her face from their two previous meetings. But he remembered thinking the last time he had seen her how lovely she was, how sad she had seemed. He'd been unable to help her the morning she'd visited the Institute. He'd never thought to meet her again after that strange day. Yet he had never really put her out of his mind.

Where was she now . . . some fifteen years after this portrait had been painted, five years after he had met her? If she had remained on Maryhead, it should be simple enough to find her, unless she did not wish to be found. However, the government hadn't hired him to coax a rebellious young woman out of exile because her ailing father sought to mend a family rift.

He laid aside the locket and closed his eyes. His head felt

hot again, too hot. His thoughts drifted. Ironically, the afternoon he had first met Douglas Rose, Margaret's father, had been the last day he had seen Jean Drummond.

Jean *MacNeill,* he amended silently. Now that she was married to his younger brother Andrew, she had the surname Ian had intended to give her himself.

Over four months had passed since then, and he could still conjure up the dark mood of that day, could still hear their angry voices as they stood in the narrow hallway of his Aberdonian town house. It was the first time he'd seen her since learning that she and Andrew had eloped while he was on a lecture tour in Edinburgh.

She was, by his professional appraisal, a good six months pregnant with his brother's child. His mind almost refused to believe the indisputable evidence of her infidelity. She and Andrew had only been married for five months. How eager they must have been to sleep together.

"Six years of waiting for you to settle down, Ian," she'd said, tears in her eyes. "Andrew and I weren't exactly drawn together overnight. We avoided each other for as long—"

He had interrupted her, unwilling to hear her defense, which in his mind could never justify her deception. "I have a previous appointment, Jean."

She shook her head sadly. "Hate me if you must, but don't let what's happened ruin your life and the medical practice you've worked so hard to build."

"What practice? My career in Aberdeen is over. Roger was found dead in my laboratory six weeks ago. In terms of medical infamy, I rank somewhere just below Dr. Andrew Moir and his bodysnatching students at the Anatomical School."

"Dear God, Ian, no one told me. I know we're isolated in the country, but I honestly hadn't heard."

"Then you're one of the few people I know who hasn't. His wife Lucy spent her every last penny trying to have my medical license revoked. I was barred from the funeral, and she has sworn to ruin me in any way she can, both personally and professionally. I'm late now, Jean, for an appointment—"

"Ian, please, before you go . . . I-I know it no longer matters, but I still . . . I still have . . . feelings for you."

He stood unmoving as if her words had turned him to stone. Then he stepped outside and closed the door on the sound of her soft weeping. The humiliating thing was that he had almost broken down himself a moment ago. For reasons he didn't understand, he had *wanted* to hear her tell him that she still loved him, that her marriage to Andrew was a mistake.

He ran down the steps into the street. Even though rain was inevitable, he decided to risk the long walk to the fashionable Broad Street mansion of the affluent Aberdeen banking genius, Douglas Rose, who with his antecedents had helped make Scotland the world banking center it was today.

A butler led him into a tastefully appointed drawing room where a slender man in his sixties, wearing slippers and a green silk robe, reclined on a chaise longue, his white head resting on the antimacassar.

At Ian's entrance, he put aside the packet of letters in his lap and looked up. There was nothing frail in his face, in the alert gray eyes that seemed to sum up the young doctor at a glance.

The two other people in the room, a young woman on the settee and a slightly older man standing by the window, both blue-eyed and blond, nodded at Ian in greeting. But there was no warmth in their expression, only anxiety generated perhaps by concern over their father, or was it contained disapproval at Ian's presence?

"Would you care for some oyster paté and toast?" the woman inquired stiffly. "Or a glass of port?"

"No, thank you." He hesitated. "I'm Dr. MacNeill, and you—"

"Lilian Rose. This is my brother Gareth, and that, of course, is our father who summoned you."

Gareth came forward to shake Ian's hand. "How do you do."

"Gareth Rose—you're an artist, aren't you?" Ian asked. "I believe a friend of mine bought your sketches at—"

"It's only a hobby." Gareth glanced at his father, his pale features pinched. "I'm too involved in my work at the bank to squander my time painting."

Ian was silent. He'd remembered that it was Roger and his wife Lucy who'd bought those sketches—dark haunting landscapes peopled with witches and warriors, which at the time Ian had privately thought reflected a disturbed mind.

He examined Douglas Rose and found what undoubtedly countless other physicians had diagnosed before him—heart disease and impaired lung function.

"There's nothing you can do for me. I know that," the older man said at the end of the examination.

"May I ask then why you summoned me?"

"I understand you're being sent to the Outer Hebrides by the government—to the isle of Maryhead, to be precise."

"Well, yes—"

Before Ian could recover from his astonishment at the turn of conversation, Douglas went on to explain that he had an estranged daughter living on Maryhead and wanted desperately to contact her. His own letters had returned unopened.

"I have no recent pictures of Margaret," Douglas explained, "just this old locket of my late wife's, but I shouldn't imagine it will be terribly hard to locate her on an island like Maryhead. She is due soon to receive her trust fund."

Ian examined the locket, surprised that he could so easily recall the night he had first met the young girl in the portrait. So she *had* been sent to Maryhead—exiled—after all. Ian had wondered for months after that morning at the Institute what had happened to her, and then, eventually, as time passed, he had submerged her memory along with all his other unfulfilled dreams and desires which had been worn down over the years by the weight of reality.

Ian was privately relieved when the disturbing meeting ended. Yet no sooner had he left the house than Gareth and Lilian Rose followed him out into the street.

"I think you ought to understand the story behind Margaret's estrangement from the family before you exert any effort to locate her," Lilian began with an uneasy glance back at the house.

He disliked the clandestine mood of their approach. "I don't think it's really any of my business."

"It affects my father's health," Gareth said. "My mother Susan and my younger brother drowned when Margaret was only eight. The accident turned Father into an old man overnight, and until recently he blamed Margaret for it."

Lilian looked down at her hands. "It was Margaret's idea to take the boat out that day. She was a willful child."

"Margaret was the image of Mother," Gareth added. "The darkest Rose. I suspect Dad couldn't bear to look at her without being reminded of the accident."

"So he sent her away—he exiled her in effect because his own grief overwhelmed him?" Ian asked.

Gareth frowned. "Well, basically, yes—"

"No," Lilian said, her thready voice gaining force. "She had become incorrigible, running about at all hours with the most disreputable crowd. It was hoped Uncle Angus would save her before she ruined her life."

Ian thought of Margaret as he had first met her that night on Union Street, trying to reconcile his initial impression of the beautiful young hoyden who'd taunted him with the confused child-woman she had actually been beneath the surface. Good breeding dictated that he close his mind to this conversation and firmly discourage a further revelation of family confidences. But the same inexplicable curiosity he had felt about her five years ago had not diminished.

He had not forgotten her, after all. She had always been in a corner of his mind, an elusive shadow, a memory of sadness and defiance and haunting loveliness.

"Why do you tell me all this?" he asked finally. "What has it to do with finding Margaret?"

Lilian fingered the pearl brooch at her throat. "The truth is, Dr. MacNeill, we are not sure whether finding Margaret is in Father's best interest. As you know, he's hardly fit to withstand the strain of an emotional reunion."

"Do you suggest I ignore his request?" Ian asked quietly.

Gareth shook his head. "Of course not. Should Margaret choose to return, well, we'll welcome her, naturally. It will be awkward, that's all. There will be adjustments."

Adjustments for whom? Ian wondered. After Gareth and Lilian had returned to the house, it occurred to him that the pair were probably more concerned with having to divide their father's fortune with Margaret than with what was best for her or Douglas. The Rose inheritance was probably worth fighting for, if you looked at it with a certain cold-hearted subjectivity.

At any rate, he mistrusted Lilian and Gareth's motives, sensing an undercurrent of something between them he couldn't define.

But there was too much on his mind to reflect at length upon the problems of the Rose family. He still had to hire a domestic couple to manage his household on Maryhead. Interviewing at the last minute, he wouldn't have time to check references before the paddle-steamer departed tomorrow.

He supposed he'd be lucky to find any help at all willing to work in the remote Outer Hebrides. God knew he wouldn't be going there himself if he hadn't been driven to it.

Eight

Ian dreamt of death in those predawn hours, of warm heavy waves that roared above his head like thunder, of salty water trickling down his throat. He heard voices whispering through the illusions of his mind, women whispering, witches casting spells . . .

"I think he's had enough for now," Agnes whispered.

"Nonsense. Half of it has spilled all over the bed."

"But you're choking him, dear, and besides, he is a doctor. Wouldn't it be polite to wait until morning to offer him the benefit of his own diagnosis and treatment?"

"His fever has risen."

"Oh, don't put that horrid thing around his neck, Margaret. It makes my skin crawl to even look at it."

Ian tried to cry out to awaken himself, the rational part of his mind realizing that his fever had indeed risen, and that he was in the throes of a delirium. His lungs ached so that he could hardly breathe. He felt something smooth and cold against his chest, an amulet, magic, witchery—

His imagination, fueled by the fever, took flight. God forbid that the islanders practiced the black arts and would lead him prancing naked about the moors with that dark-haired mermaid-woman as their high priestess. He remembered childhood tales of human sacrifices to forgotten druid gods. Worse, rumors of castration . . .

"Human sacrifices? What peculiar fancies the fever has given you, poor man."

He opened his eyes and stared up into Agnes's amused face, realizing in embarrassment that he'd voiced his fears aloud. "I'm Agnes Alcock, Dr. MacNeill. We brought you to my farmhouse from the beach. Do you remember?"

Ian nodded, his head pounding. The woman had raised her voice to speak to him as if he were not only febrile but deaf. "What—what is this thing around my neck?"

Agnes grimaced. "A boiled raven's egg, which my cousin Margaret is convinced will combat your fever."

"But these other—these sharp pointed things?"

"Fox teeth and deer bones," Agnes replied. "Their magical properties are supposed to heal you, according to Morag Strong."

"Who is this Morag?"

Agnes's mouth pulled down at the corners. "Our resident crone of Endor—the charmer. She isn't even a crone really, only a decade or so older than me, but one likes the image."

"But you don't like *her*," Ian guessed.

"Not much."

Ian gathered his strength to ask, "The others aboard the schooner . . ."

"As far as I know, everyone was saved," Agnes assured him. "Now, do try to rest, Dr. MacNeill. At least pretend to be asleep before Margaret returns with more of her vile remedies."

Ian closed his eyes as she left the room. Margaret. The pretty woman on the beach was named Margaret. Was it possible that she and Margaret Rose were the same? He pictured her face as she leaned over him, visualized himself against the lobster boat, clutching his medicine chest and journal.

"Oh, God." He jackknifed from beneath the quilt with such force that the bed jumped across the bare wooden floor. Dear Jesus, his journal. All that water, ruining his work.

He found a pair of man's trousers and a shirt lying over a chair, realizing as he dressed that the pale gray light from the window meant it was already daybreak. Was there any chance of salvaging his personal belongings from the wreck? The bulk of his medical supplies would arrive with Walter and Sybil Armstrong within a day or so. But his journal could not be replaced, not the years of laboriously recorded research and personal observations.

He hurried from the room and down the stairs, intercepting Agnes in the hallway. Her eyes widened at the sight of him, shirt improperly buttoned and hair as unruly as a scarecrow's, but she maintained her composure, remarking calmly: "I see you've found my husband's clothes. Your own are hanging to dry in the scullery. With all due respect, Dr. MacNeill, I do not think you're fit enough yet to be on your feet."

Margaret appeared at the top of the stairs, hastily buttoning her own gown. "What's the matter?"

"The doctor is about, dear." Agnes gestured covertly for Margaret to come down the stairs. "Help me get him back into bed. I fear the fever has affected his senses."

Ian attempted, unsuccessfully, to force his way around Agnes. "You don't understand," he said. "I have valuable possessions on the beach."

"No one on Maryhead would want your treasures," she assured him.

Margaret started down the stairs, and Ian hesitated for only a few moments before trying for the second time to sneak around Agnes. Once again she outmaneuvered him, like a Cornish wrestler, moving to block the doorway, her arms folded across her chest. He wheeled and headed down the hallway to the kitchen. He heard her follow, Margaret trailing behind.

"I think we should try to stop him," Agnes whispered. "He can't run about the island in that condition."

He entered the kitchen and opened the back door onto the cold rainy morning, turning to address the two women who hovered a cautious distance behind him. The one-eyed cat darted in from outside to squeeze between his legs and saunter toward the fire. "Thank you so much for your hospitality," Ian said gravely. "The fishy broth, the amulet, the loan of clothing . . ."

"But Dr. MacNeill," Agnes cried as he ducked outside.

"Just let him go," Margaret said behind him. "Let him do what he wants."

She rushed across the room to close the door before the rain could soak the flagstone floor. "What was he in such a panic about anyway?"

"He's frantic to retrieve his possessions from the shipwreck," Agnes replied. "I don't know what he hopes to do on the beach himself. I doubt he can even walk that far."

Margaret frowned and hoisted the heavy black kettle onto its hook above the fire. "Jamie Shaw brought around a few things last night which apparently belonged to the doctor. I was so tired, I forgot all about them. They're in the parlor."

Agnes stopped to stare at her in the middle of shaking out the rose-knot tablecloth. "You'll have to bring him back then. It isn't right to make him worry."

"I didn't do it on purpose," Margaret said irritably. "Anyway, I don't want him staying in this house."

"Whyever not?"

Because he makes me smile when I know I should be serious. Because I can still feel the imprint of his body on mine. . . .

"Because he's from Aberdeen, that's why, and there's nothing but unhappiness associated with that place for me."

"Even after all these years—"

Margaret didn't answer, inadvertently glancing out the window to see Dr. MacNeill staring across the moor with a look of bewilderment on his face. "Oh, damn," she muttered, shaking her head.

She knelt at the door to put on her half-boots and hurried outside, light rain falling on the irregular stone pathway that led to the moor. Mud splashed onto the hem of her gown, and she silently blamed the doctor. There would be no time to change before Stephen's first Sunday sermon.

She cupped her hands and shouted across the farmyard just as Ian started up the first of a series of rocky hills.

"Dr. MacNeill!"

He turned and stared in every direction except hers, looking so unsteady on his feet that a strong wind could knock him over. He took a step, stumbling over loose stones. Suddenly afraid that he might indeed fall, Margaret ran from the yard and clambered up the hillside, reaching him just as he sank to his knees. Across the moor she could hear the rattle of carts, crofters who would pass directly beneath them on their way to Stephen's little rubble church.

"Let me help you back to the house, Dr. MacNeill."

"Yes," he said, nodding slowly. "It looks like I can't manage by myself."

He took the hand she offered him, breathing heavily and leaning against her until she feared she could not sustain her own balance. The rumble of carts grew louder, rising from behind the hills like echoes of thunder.

"Please hurry, Dr. MacNeill," she urged. "The rain is doing your fever no good."

He nodded, attempting to obey. His shirt had come undone, and from the corner of her eye Margaret noticed several raindrops trickle down the powerful musculature of his shoulders and catch in the black hair that covered his chest. Her face grew warm at the sight.

"Cover yourself," she said under her breath as they half slid to the foot of the hill.

He frowned at her, blessedly regaining his balance without her help. "What?"

"Your shirt," she explained, struggling not to laugh at his bewildered look, "it's completely unbuttoned."

His hand lifted to his chest. "Oh, God. You should have said so before."

She turned away, shivering in the cold to allow him a moment to fasten his buttons. But her hope of saving them both unnecessary embarrassment failed. The few islanders who had braved the elements for the young Reverend Rose's sermon had come into view, a procession of crofters and cattle drivers in their imported Rob Roy tartan finery, farm women in white muslin bonnets and children on sturdy little ponies.

They stared at Margaret and Ian in astonished delight. She could just imagine what they must think—that she, the incorrigible rich girl exiled from Aberdeen was already enmeshed in an impropriety with the newly arrived doctor. And what a remarkably dignified impression he had made for his first public appearance.

"Good mornin', Miss Margaret."

"That would be the new doctor, would it?"

"Yes. I'm afraid—" She nudged Ian with her shoulder, encouraging him to stand apart from her. "Yes, this is Dr. Mac-Neill, sent by the government at Macpherson's request to serve as island physician."

"He's had a blow on the head, has he?"

She glanced at Ian's bandaged temple. "From the shipwreck, yes. It's left him weak, you see. A wee bit weak in the mind."

"Quite so. And he's to stay with you, is he, at the farmhouse?"

"Certainly not. Well, perhaps for a day or two until he's recovered and fit to ride to the castle."

The islanders began to move back down the track toward the kirk, sharing crafty smiles amongst themselves. Ian watched them disappear between the brown undulating hills.

"I resented that," he said. " 'A wee bit weak in the mind.' "

"Well, I had to say something."

"That remark probably set me back several months in earning their respect."

Margaret shrugged and marched ahead of him, rough stalks of broom snapping beneath her boots. "It's your own fault, really, isn't it?" she said without looking back. "You should have shown more sense."

He strode up alongside her, his face flushed with the effort. "My journal—you couldn't possibly understand how important it is that I find it."

"All I understand is that the bloody thing was brought to the farmhouse late last night," she snapped.

"Are you sure—why are you swearing at me?"

"Because you've just made us look absolute fools in front of my cousin's entire congregation. Gossip is ambrosia on this island, Dr. MacNeill. One tastes it so rarely that it is passed around to be savored for as long as possible."

"Gossip?" he said in amusement. "About what?"

A pheasant grouse burst upward from behind an outcrop of rocks, startling them into silence with its clumsy flight. The moor looked bleak and unappealing, the solitary stone farmhouse a refuge against its backdrop of rain-washed hills.

"They'll gossip about us," Margaret said at last. "About you and me."

"About *us?* Why, that's too ridiculous to merit our arguing over it." He caught her by the wrist. "Are you certain my journal was retrieved and that it's still intact?"

She looked down at his hand. "I didn't take the liberty of reading it. I wouldn't presume to violate *your* privacy."

She pulled her hand free and walked briskly to the farmhouse gate. "Meaning what, Miss Rose," he called after her, "that I have violated yours? You *are* Margaret Rose, aren't you, daughter of the Aberdeen banker Douglas Rose?"

She pivoted, her face suddenly white. "What did you say?"

"I merely asked if you were Margaret Rose. I heard Agnes use your Christian name, and though we hadn't been properly introduced, it seemed a safe assumption." He paused to catch his breath. "Douglas Rose asked me to find his daughter."

She released the latch and shoved the gate across a channel of mud, shooing a chicken from her path as she spoke. "Then you may tell him his daughter is dead."

"Dead! You aren't serious—"

"It was a suicide. No one really knew her, and so no one mourned her passing."

With a grim smile Margaret hurried ahead to the kitchen door where Agnes stood waiting with the one-eyed cat in her arms.

"I was about to come out after you both in the cart," Agnes said in an aggrieved voice. "Thank goodness he didn't go in the wrong direction and end up in a bog."

Margaret bent before the fire to wrench off her boots. "It might be better for me if he had," she said, her voice shaking. "He claims that my father sent him here to find me. I told you he was trouble, Agnes. I knew it from the moment I first saw him on the beach."

Nine

Ian's fever broke the next afternoon, and by that evening he was invited down to the side parlor for a supper with the family. Roast mutton, fried eggs and tatties cooked in their jackets, crispy oatcakes, whiskey, and hot tea. Famished, he ate every morsel set before him, too hungry to allow even Margaret's self-absorbed silence and Agnes's polite chatter to dull his appetite. And when he'd finished, imbued by the false confidence of the fine whiskey and wholesome food, he felt relaxed enough to meet Margaret on her own ground.

In a lucid frame of mind for the first time since the wreck, he could not fail to notice how lovely she was.

After supper, he'd had his longest uninterrupted view of her in the light shed by the tarnished bronze candle-sconces above the mantel. He had felt, quite literally, his heart constrict in his chest, as if he had been standing at the edge of a cliff and had taken the first irrevocable step forward. But there was exhilaration in the fall. Her hair was the same rich, dark mahogany he remembered. The heart-shaped face had matured, the lines still strikingly classical, but the blue-gray eyes held more secrets than could ever be portrayed in any artist's miniature.

With an effort he forced his mind back to the question Agnes had just asked him for the second time.

"Will you have more whiskey, Doctor MacNeill?" Agnes asked.

"I shouldn't, but since it is so smooth—"

He glanced up as Margaret murmured something about how chilly the room had become, then rose and left the parlor.

"I assume she told you what happened," he said to Agnes, sensing he might find an ally in her. "I asked her if she was the same Margaret Rose of the celebrated banking family."

Agnes looked down at the book in her lap. "Margaret and Douglas Rose are not—"

She broke off as Margaret herself whisked back into the room, bringing a willow creel heaped with dried peats to the fire. "I told him that Douglas Rose's daughter was dead," Margaret said, her low voice warning her cousin not to contradict her. "A suicide, wasn't it, Agnes?"

Agnes looked horrified. "A—"

"It was a shock to us all, and the poor girl with such a bright future before her," Margaret said with a mournful shake of her head.

Ian was really enjoying this. "A bright future?" he asked.

"As an actress," Agnes said dryly. "I only recently learned myself what a hidden talent she had for drama."

"How unfortunate I could never watch her perform." Ian sighed deeply, wanting to laugh so badly his stomach hurt with it. "I can't tell you how much I looked forward to renewing her acquaintance."

"Renewing?" He noticed Margaret's shoulders stiffen as she asked suspiciously, "You're claiming that you knew her then?"

He scratched his eyebrow, his gaze amused. "I met her twice, actually, on two separate occasions in Aberdeen, but I suspect I didn't leave a lasting impression either time." He paused, looking her in the eye. "In fact, I'm sure of it."

He thought he saw the ghost of a smile pass across Margaret's face, but before he could be sure, she returned to the task of dropping peats onto the fire. "I've been asked to find her as a favor to her father," he continued, glancing at Agnes. "He's in failing health and was concerned about her welfare, what with the death of her guardians almost a year ago and the isolation of the island."

There was a deep and sudden silence. Margaret did not move or betray by any facial expression whatsoever her reaction to his explanation. Yet he could feel her disbelief nonetheless.

Margaret took a sip of the tea Agnes had just given her. "I understand that Margaret Rose was estranged from her family," she said carefully.

Ian wondered how long she would maintain the charade, and whether Agnes would support her by her silence. "I believe that to be true," he replied. "But her father has apparently come to regret the breach and would like to repair it."

"Why should he wish that after so many years?"

"That I could not reveal to anyone but Miss Rose herself."

Margaret put down her tea and jabbed at the smoldering peats with a poker, leaning back as a spume of sweet-smelling smoke wafted into the room. Her heart was racing, her mind a seething circle of sad memories and angry impressions. Why could this wretched man not leave her in peace? It was as if he were determined to prove her earlier misgivings that he'd bring her nothing but trouble.

"I'd heard her father was a prominent banker," she said after a pause. "Couldn't he spare the time to come here himself to find her?"

"Well, as I said before, he's not a well man and hardly in his prime. This arctic cold would hardly help a lung infection."

Margaret came to her feet, indicating that the conversation had reached its end. Ian cast about in his mind for something to say to delay his dismissal, but Margaret seemed determined to banish him back to the attic.

"I'm sorry I can't help you, Dr. MacNeill. I trust you haven't come all the way to Maryhead in the hope of helping Douglas Rose."

He stood reluctantly, regretting not being able to savor one of the finest glasses of whiskey he'd tasted in years. "Of course not. The government sent me to study the feasibility of eventually establishing a hospital here."

"You must be dedicated indeed to sacrifice your skills to our remote island."

"Dedicated or naive, I'm not sure which."

Margaret began to load a tray with the dishes they'd left on the side-table. What awaited him upstairs but his journal and another restless night in that lonely woman's room? Ian wondered. He would far rather sit by the fire and talk to the woman herself at greater length.

"Let me help you with the dishes," he said on impulse, deftly rescuing his own unfinished glass of whiskey.

"Well, I—" She glanced over at Agnes, absorbed in scribbling notes at the hearth. "If you don't mind. But be careful you don't fall over the cat in the hall. He likes to pounce out as you pass."

He followed Margaret into the unlit corridor, carrying on the tray the haphazardly stacked dishes and crystal whiskey bottle. "By the way, where is she buried?"

She swung around. "Where is—"

"The place of Margaret Rose's interment. Her father will require proof of her death."

She looked as if she might like to hit him. "I told you she was a suicide," she said in a quiet voice. "They bury those in unmarked graves, at the crossroads on the moor."

"What a pagan practice," he replied with the appropriate amount of repugnance. "I assume then that it won't be necessary to ask the sheriff's substitute for permission to have her remains exhumed?"

She sucked in her breath. "Do you mean—"

"Forgive me for the gruesome inquiries, my dear," he said, his eyes dancing. "Such frankness is necessary in my profession. I certainly don't intend to upset you with such a macabre detail, but . . ."

She leaned back against the wall, her blue-gray eyes searching his face. "You fraud," she burst out in both anger and grudging amusement. "You audacious, ungrateful intruder. You've known all along who I am, haven't you?"

He suppressed a shrug. "I suspected it from the start. But if you prefer to keep your past private, far be it from me to interfere. Still, you should know that your father—"

"Go away," she said softly. "Please."

"I can't, not until morning. I couldn't possibly find my way across the moors in the dark. But I honestly had no intention of upsetting you. In fact, I'd hoped you would see right away that you could trust me."

"Trust you—when you've just lied to me—"

"I never lied." He sounded deeply affronted.

"You did," she said heatedly. "You told me we'd met."

"We have. Do you not remember that day in Aberdeen, when you came to the Vaccine Institute and your uncle took you away before you were inoculated? I was the doctor who attended you."

She stared at him for several moments, slowly shaking her head. "I can't say you look at all familiar," she confessed. "But then that last week in Aberdeen isn't one I've wanted to dwell upon."

"Well, I remember you wore a velvet dress and that a black carriage took you away in the rain."

She smiled, her voice rueful. "And now here we are—both on Maryhead—at the edge of the world as they say."

It seemed suddenly imperative that she remember him, that Ian prove to himself he'd had a modicum of importance in her past. "Do you know that we actually met before that day at the Institute?"

Her smile became strained, polite. "No. I'm sorry."

"On Union Street." He paused, the memory so vivid in his mind, he could not believe she had forgotten. "You were a passenger in a carriage that nearly ran me down. As I recall, Daniel Munro was your escort."

Her color deepened. "Oh, dear, yes. What a terrible first impression I made on you then."

At the bottom of his heart, Ian was insulted that she'd made the connection to him only through another man. "You were rather young to associate with someone as sophisticated as Daniel Munro, weren't you?"

She laughed with a trace of wistfulness. "Young and undisciplined and on the road to perdition, as Uncle Angus would have said. Yes, I suppose I was."

She turned to lead him into the kitchen. Ian set the tray down on the counter and waited uncertainly while she scraped several plates into a dustbin and then lit the colza-oil lamp on the oaken mantelpiece.

Moving past him as if he were invisible, she tied a muslin apron around her waist and begin to whisk dishes into the deep stone sink. With a pair of brass tongs she deftly removed from the fire several white-hot *dornagan*, smooth stones gathered from along the beach. These she dropped one by one into the sink, bringing the cold water it contained to a steaming boil.

"Can I help?" he asked.

"Pass me the rest of the dishes if you like."

There was something intimate about working beside her at the simple chore, although in his entire life he'd never considered the kitchen to be a particularly romantic setting. Yet when she leaned across him for the heather-bristle brush to scrub the plates, an unexpected impulse to kiss her seized him and did not lessen until he walked to the window and took a deep breath. Even then he didn't trust himself to get any closer to her. She was more of a temptation than he could handle, a tangled mystery of strength, fragility, and sensual enticement.

Margaret glanced around, unaware of Ian's distress. "Can you tell if there are any lights on at the manse? It's the small slate-roofed house up on the hill."

"Yes, I think I see a light," Ian said, relieved for the distraction. "What a lonely landscape it looks at night, and not much better in the day, I expect."

"Yes," Margaret replied obscurely. She bit her lip. "You were on the same schooner that brought Stephen's visitor here, Dr. MacNeill. Do you remember the man?"

"There was a cleric from Edinburgh aboard, but I didn't engage him in conversation. Does his arrival indicate something important?"

"I'm not sure." She pulled off her apron, leaving, he noticed, half the dishes still unwashed in the sink. "But it's almost midnight, and you should get some rest for the ride across the moors tomorrow."

"The ride?"

Margaret lowered the lamp and then went to the door to let out the cat. "Jamie Shaw is supposed to drive you to your cottage on the other side of the island."

"I hope it's not very far from here," he said in a low voice. "I've come to enjoy your company these past two days, and your kindness."

She looked up in surprise. "I did nothing out of the ordinary. Perhaps you're homesick."

"Perhaps." But oddly, he wasn't.

She closed the door against the bracing night air. "Do you have news of my brother and sister?"

It took Ian a moment to realize that she must have been curbing her curiosity about her family the entire time they'd been making small conversation. She *did* care, after all.

"Gareth, I believe, works for your father. I know little more than that."

Except that they are not deserving of one moment of your interest.

"Did you speak with them? Did they mention me at all?"

"Gareth assured me they'd welcome you when you returned to Aberdeen."

"Aberdeen?" He might have issued her an invitation to hell. "I have no desire to ever set foot in Scotland again."

"Your father is sending me a considerable sum of money for your safe return. And I understand that you stand to receive far more on your upcoming majority."

"Keep whatever my father gives you," she said flatly. "Use it as you like."

"But the money is *yours.*"

"It's too late," she insisted angrily. "The rift between us has grown too wide to be repaired."

Ian spoke softly but firmly. "As a doctor, I'll tell you that your father may live on several more years, or he may die before you could make the short sea voyage to visit him."

For a moment he could see the indecision in her eyes, the glimpse of raw emotion that told him she was by no means as detached from her family as she claimed. He hated to be the one to resurrect this unpleasant part of her past, and he wasn't convinced himself she should even return to Aberdeen. But if he admitted that now, there would be no reason to see her again, and suddenly he knew he had to.

Margaret averted her head to cough dryly into her hand. "I'm suddenly tired myself. And I'll be up and gone before you in the morning. I rarely stay up this late."

"That sounds like the start of a nasty cough, Miss Rose." Ian was really concerned.

"Just a tickle in my throat." Disconcerted by all his attention, she folded her apron over the back of a chair. "Can you find your way upstairs?"

"I think so."

"Goodnight then," she said.

"Perhaps I can call on you from time to time for advice on adjusting to life on the island," Ian suggested.

Margaret didn't respond, but instead gave him an absent-minded nod and ushered him back into the hallway to the staircase. There was nothing for him to do but retire to his room.

"I should come back to see you in a day or two if that cough hasn't improved," he called down from the landing.

"We'll see," she said with a noncommittal smile.

She hurried back down the hallway, her movements so final and dismissive that he realized he was already forgotten. He shrugged and climbed slowly to his room, hearing the wind as it swept across the moor. A minute or so later, as he passed the window to light a candle, he saw her again, stealing through the garden to the gate, her cloak billowing out behind her.

A lover's tryst with Cousin Stephen? Well, it was possible, understandable, and yet he felt a jolt of disappointment, a reminder of his own personal frustration underlaid with another unexpected stirring of sexual desire at the thought of her hurrying off to some midnight rendezvous. It explained her haste to dismiss him, her mind planning ahead to meet this other man. And after all, did a minister not eat, breathe, and succumb to temptation like anyone else?

He would not judge them. Envy them, yes, for whatever happiness, however temporal, they had found.

He let the curtain fall back into place, staring down at his journal before finally opening it to record his personal reflections, as was his nightly ritual. But he couldn't concentrate, glancing at the bed, the door, hoping she'd interrupt him. And by the time he'd finished writing, that hope had accelerated into an ache that was almost physical: he wanted her with a passion that frightened him in its primal intensity and sudden irrational emergence. Or maybe that desire had existed inside him for five dormant years, just waiting until they met again to ignite.

Margaret removed her cloak and tossed it on the kitchen table, listening for sounds from within the house. Heaven forbid that the doctor should rise from his sickbed, demanding a nourishing snack. Or even worse, that Agnes would abandon her late-night writing to lecture Margaret on her unseemly behavior—making a midnight foray to Stephen's manse, and for nothing, anyway. Margaret had only managed to glimpse Stephen through his parlor window, entertaining a male visitor.

Although she had been intensely curious about what the two men were discussing, Margaret hadn't felt comfortable spying on them. Reluctantly she'd returned home without speaking to Stephen. Yet she herself had experienced the most peculiar sensation of being watched on the short walk back between the shadowed hills.

Now, from deep within the farmhouse garden came an unearthly yowl that made Margaret freeze until she realized what had caused it.

Cyclops, her cat, had presumably climbed a tree again and hadn't the courage to come down. If Margaret didn't rescue him, the animal would yowl all night, reawakening the doctor who slept upstairs.

Hoping to avoid another encounter with that man above all else, Margaret snatched her cloak from the table and slung it over her shoulders on her march back outside through the moonlit orchard.

"Stop that racket! You'll wake—"

She halted beneath the tall oak and stared up at the cat, balanced on a limb with its back arched, tail bristled, and claws digging into the tree's bark. Turning slowly, she looked toward the shepherd's path on the hill, her eyes rounding at the white cloaked figure who stood unmoving in the mist. Its bony arm was extended, the hand beckoning.

The cat crawled forward on the limb, growling, flattened out on its haunches.

Margaret's heart raced. A banshee . . . No, no, she refused to believe it! The similar apparition she had seen at the time of her mother and little brother's deaths had been an illusion of misty shadow and a child's terror, or so Agnes had repeatedly attempted to reassure her.

But Margaret had never been convinced. Morag Strong assured her that such supernatural visions were very real. And old Simon MacTear, the shepherd who'd lived in the village of Meirneal at the time of the accident, swore he too had seen a banshee that day in the thin woods that overhung the loch.

Now Margaret felt a flash of fearful, adult uncertainty. She had to find out the truth for herself.

There was a rusty shovel leaning against the tree. Surreptitiously, she grabbed it and started up the hill, faltering as the figure emitted a low keening wail—a warning. Its face, enshrouded in a hood, looked dark and devoid of features. And as it turned toward her, she saw the glint of a single white tooth—a fang . . .

She gasped and raised the shovel. The figure lunged forward, striking her with the shovel's wooden handle in the chest. Margaret felt the shovel hurtle out of her hands into the mist, missing its mark. She staggered back down the hill and landed hard on her tailbone in her own herb garden.

For several seconds she was too stunned to move. Slowly, disentangling herself from a clump of rosemary, she sat forward and glanced up at the hill. Nothing moved in the mist. Then suddenly from behind her something pale came flying down to land upon her shoulder, talons ripping through her cloak.

She screamed in panic and pain, and pushed with all her strength to dislodge the cat from her throat. It clung to her in fright, then dropped to the ground as she scrambled back onto her feet.

"Margaret?" Agnes called uncertainly from the kitchen doorway. "Is that you out there?"

"Come here, Agnes," she said over her shoulder. *"Now."*

The cat sat calmly now as if nothing had ever happened, sniffing at the hem of Margaret's cloak as Agnes came running down the path to meet her.

"What is it?" Agnes asked in bewilderment.

Margaret gestured toward the hill. "Up—up there. Something *attacked* me."

"Attacked you?" Agnes looked her over, obviously disbelieving. "It wasn't that doctor misbehaving again, was it?"

Margaret suppressed a giggle. "It was a—a white witchy thing in a bedsheet or some sort of robe."

Agnes's gaze lifted to the darkened attic window. "Well, your sheets are white, dear."

"Oh, for pity's sake, Agnes! This thing had a gleaming white fang and—and no facial features," she finished in a shaken voice.

"Let's have a look then," Agnes said calmly. "I'm sure it was nothing."

By the time they reached the path, Agnes had managed to convince Margaret that one of the local shepherd boys had played a trick on her out of boredom. Either that, Agnes decided, or Margaret had encountered some misguided lass on her way home from one of Morag Strong's horrid moorland sabbats to worship the horned god. Some stupid bint who did not want her identity known.

At any rate Agnes knew there had to be a logical explanation for what had happened, and she openly scoffed when Margaret voiced her fear that the apparition had been a banshee come to warn of an impending death.

$\mathcal{T}en$

Under normal circumstances Margaret would have enjoyed the long walk back to the moor, a creel of kelp strapped to her back. Yesterday's storm had washed ashore a fresh supply, and the cove had been swarming at dawn with crofters' wives filling baskets with black sticky seaweed to fertilize their spring fields. But this morning she felt the cold more than usual, and she regretted not taking the cart for the ride home. By the time the farmhouse loomed into view, she was short of breath, her muscles trembling with exertion.

She slowed as she reached the hill she and Ian had climbed yesterday morning. Remembering how he'd brought them both sliding down the rocks into the mud made her laugh aloud. The big fool. His behavior had provided enough fodder to keep Maryhead in gossip for months.

She hoped sincerely she would find him gone when she reached the house. She didn't like relinquishing her room to a stranger. She didn't like the nervous excitement she felt when he looked at her in his perceptive way.

Stephen was waiting for her in the kitchen, sitting with his head bowed at the black oak table. He rose to help her with the creel, placing it by the fire. Studying his lean brown face, its frame of carelessly shorn hair, she felt the familiar rush of affection and confusion that made her feel so uncomfortable around him of late.

She moved to the fire to unchill her hands. "I was bringing

your supper to the manse late last night, but I saw through the window that your visitor hadn't left. I decided I shouldn't interrupt your conversation. It looked so intense."

"He has to leave tomorrow, and there were details to work out. So many details, Margaret." Stephen could not restrain his excitement.

She sat down at the table, feeling a shiver pass through her. "Who is this person?"

"Anthony Phillips, a representative of the bishopric in Edinburgh. I've been nominated to found a foreign mission in the jungle—my *own* mission, if you can believe it."

"You told him he was mad, I trust." She looked up at his silence. "You turned him down, didn't you?"

"Not exactly."

I don't know him at all, Margaret thought with a shock. How could we have been so close and yet so far apart?

"I understand that the new doctor is from Aberdeen," Stephen said casually. "Agnes mentioned that he was in contact with your father."

Margaret said nothing. She was fully aware he was trying to change the subject.

"Haven't you ever thought, Margaret, that perhaps it's time for you to go home?"

Her mouth tightened. "So that you can indulge in this whimsy with a clear conscience?"

"I've always been interested in Far Eastern religions," he said gently, "in Buddhism and its humanity."

"Buddhism," Margaret whispered in disbelief.

"Buddhism?" an amused deep male voice echoed from the doorway. "This sounds like a fascinating breakfast conversation. May I be allowed to eavesdrop?"

Margaret turned her head, catching her breath at the sight of the dark-haired doctor entering the room, the expression on his face faintly ironic.

If it had been within her power, Margaret would have banished Ian MacNeill himself to some Far Eastern jungle, possibly between the jaws of a man-eating tiger. Instead, she introduced him to Stephen and unenthusiastically invited him to share their pot of tea.

To her annoyance, Ian sat down eagerly beside her, accepting the cup she passed him. You would have thought he could tell by her restrained greeting, the deep silence that followed his appearance, that he had interrupted a serious conversation. But Ian seemed content to sit in the atmosphere of awkward hospitality while Margaret struggled to understand what Stephen had just told her.

Stephen . . . going away. It couldn't be. She put her hand unconsciously to the lace collar of her dress. Earlier she had felt so cold, and now it was as if she were being roasted alive, her throat tight, her head pounding with an exquisite pain.

Ian put down his cup, his blue eyes intent on her face. "You're unwell, Miss Rose?" he asked softly. "The malaise of last night has not abated?"

"I'm perfectly fine," she said, flushing as he continued to stare at her. "Just a mild headache, a little chill."

Ian glanced at Stephen, apparently seeing more than Margaret would have wished. "As you say."

Margaret rose suddenly from the table to fetch a tin of oatcakes from the pantry. Her hair had drifted free from its silver comb, falling about her shoulders. Without intending to, Ian noted the unconscious grace of her body as she returned to her chair. She placed the tin on the table with a jar of coarse marmalade and a crock of unsalted butter.

Ian cleared his throat and drummed his fingers on his teacup, acutely aware his presence was unappreciated. Yet, driven by some perverse curiosity about Margaret's relationship with her cousin, he couldn't bring himself to leave.

Stephen helped himself to an oatcake, then pushed back his chair. "Forgive me for not staying longer, Dr. MacNeill, but

I've a visitor myself back at the manse. By the way, I'd like to talk to you later about tropical diseases."

Ian raised his brows. "Malaria and cholera, I assume?"

Margaret chuckled. "Dr. MacNeill's exotic expertise will be wasted on the simple aches and pains we suffer on Maryhead."

"How long has it been since either of you were attended by a physician?" Ian asked pointedly.

Stephen stopped at the door. "I don't recall that I ever have been. I'll see you tonight at supper, shall I, Margaret? Good luck to you, Dr. MacNeill."

As Stephen closed the door behind him a current of cold moist air rushed into the kitchen. Margaret took a sip of tea and shivered.

"I grow a garden just for medicinal purposes," she told Ian over her teacup. "My herbal infusions and poultices have always taken care of our infrequent ailments on the island."

Ian snorted. "No doubt everyone's terrified of falling ill to avoid drinking that hideous broth you forced down my throat."

"It's an acquired taste, that's all." She kicked off her boots under the table, warming to a debate. "Can *you* cure cholera, Dr. MacNeill?" she asked with an innocent air.

"I have, in some instances, by assiduously hydrating the patient and administering hypodermic injections of saline."

Margaret didn't have the faintest notion what Ian had just said and suspected that he knew it. "But you can't cure every case, can you?" she persisted. Realizing she'd hit a sore spot by his reluctant shrug of assent, she continued, "And at least herbalists don't drain patients of their lifeblood or murder them during barbarically painful surgeries."

Ian flushed. She looked like an angel and argued like the devil, and he was aware of the sexual tension that tightened his body while he stared at her. "There've been a few advances made since you left civilization," he said, his gaze slowly moving over her.

Margaret leaned forward on her elbows, her expression mischievous and challenging. "Such as?"

He sat down on the edge of the table. "The ability to render patients insensitive to pain during a surgical operation—"

"You knock them over the head with hammers, I presume?"

He tried not to laugh. "We use vapors, lass. And there are disinfectants in the operating theaters now to prevent child-bed fever, though I grant you neither practice is yet widespread."

"And why not?"

He paused, aware she'd caught him out again. "Because most of my damned colleagues are still in the Dark Ages."

Smiling, she pushed a plate of oatcakes toward him. "You sound very sure of yourself. Would you like more tea?"

"I'm sure that science and not witchcraft is the path to the healing of human ills. And yes, I'll have another drop."

She refilled his cup, studying him from the corner of her eye. "I don't practice witchcraft. And do doctors not use physic herbs in their compounds?"

"Yes, but we're a century removed from powdered earthworms and horse-dung infusions for pleurisy. Not to mention vipers served up in a human skull and burnt snail shells—"

Margaret's eyes widened. "Perhaps you're in for a few surprises during your residency on the island."

Ian grinned. "Judging from the way it began, I couldn't disagree."

"Let me tell you something, Dr. MacNeill," she said, her blue-gray eyes sparkling good-naturedly. "The last doctor we had on Maryhead used to sneak to the charmer late at night because he didn't have the courage to lance his own boils."

For a moment Ian was distracted from the debate by how vivacious she had become, her lovely face flushed, her eyes so bright they flashed like silver. "Well, Miss Rose," he said slowly, "I remember one of my first cases was an old charmer from St. Kit's Hill who came into the city to have a wen removed from the end of her nose because she wasn't quite clever enough to charm it away."

Margaret gave a hoot of derisive laughter. "Next you'll be claiming you can raise the dead with your science."

"Ah, but I have," he said with a devilish smile. "I've brought back to life a young woman named Margaret Rose. You see, she was a suicide, and yet she's sitting here before me this morning—"

"—arguing with a very silly and arrogant man," she concluded, her manner suddenly subdued.

They fell silent, gazing over the oatcakes at each other with a mutual resentment which Ian vaguely recognized had less to do with their differences than with the abstract similarities they shared. Fortunately, before the debate could develop into a full-fledged quarrel, Agnes appeared at the door.

"Mr. Shaw is here to drive you to your cottage, Dr. Mac-Neill," she announced. "He's making a dreadful fuss about being out in the cold. I daresay you should go to him immediately."

She had evidently been awakened against her will. Her hair had not been combed; the back hook fastenings of her bodice were mismated, and she was wearing a pair of her husband's cowhide brogues, which echoed like slaps against the stone floor as she shuffled to the fire to refill the kettle.

"I see you've found your own clothes," she said over her shoulder. "I washed them myself in boiled rainwater. It makes everything so lovely soft, don't you agree?"

"Oh, yes. Thank you."

Ian got up and reached for the jacket on the back of his chair. It was cold enough that he should be wearing it, but Agnes had unknowingly shrunk the wool so that when he put it on, he looked like a strapping oaf of a schoolboy with overlong simian arms.

"If a chance comes up for me to repay your hospitality, you'll know where to find me."

Agnes smothered a yawn. "You're welcome to visit anytime, Dr. MacNeill, but I fear we're dull company in this house."

"Not in the least," he said politely. "Miss Rose."

She granted him a courteous nod. "Goodbye, Dr. MacNeill."

In the hall he paused to struggle into his jacket, squeezing his arms into the shrunken sleeves. Presumably believing him gone, he heard Margaret ask, "Why on earth did you have to invite him back? He's such a bother, bursting in like that when Stephen was explaining his latest misadventure. Imagine him founding a mission in a heathen land!"

"Siam," Agnes murmured in sympathetic agreement. "I had such a shock myself when he first started making inquiries months ago."

"You knew—it was Stephen's idea from the start?"

"Yes, dear. I assumed he'd told you."

Ian heard the back door slam. Aware he'd been eavesdropping, he hurried outside to the pony cart waiting before the gate. The moorland air cut clean to the bone. The driver, in a glengarry and rough shepherd's plaid, gave him a dour nod.

Ian tugged down the cuffs of his jacket over his wrists. "Sorry about the wait."

"It might not have been so bad, Doctor, had I accepted Mrs. Alcock's invitation to a spot of whiskey." The man pulled off his leather gloves and extended a weather-chapped hand. "Jamie Shaw, Lord Macpherson's factor. You might remember me from the shipwreck, if you remember anything of it at all. By the way, your Mr. and Mrs. Armstrong have arrived."

They shook hands, and then Ian inadvertently glanced back at the farmhouse. He could just see Margaret walking toward the detached dovecote. "Look," he said impulsively, "I'll need another minute to fetch my things. Why don't you take Mrs. Alcock up on her offer?"

"Aye, weel, I might. We've a long ride across the moor, and there's rare fine whiskey in that house."

Ian had made the same observation himself last night, but he barely heard the remark, suddenly intrigued by Margaret's flight toward the dovecote that stood like a lonely sentinel between the farmhouse and the hump of moorland hills beyond.

He glanced at Shaw. "I should remind Miss Rose to have forwarded any of my belongings that might yet wash ashore."

"Yes, sir. A good idea."

A good idea indeed. By the shrewd glitter in his eye Shaw had eloquently informed Ian that he did not believe the awkward lie any more than did Ian himself.

Perhaps it's time for you to go home.

Margaret propped the broom against the wall, a deep sigh escaping her. What a bitter shock to discover that Stephen had secret plans which did not include her when for years she had assumed their sheltered life together would continue.

Stephen alone understood what it would mean to her to return to the man who had rejected her as a young girl and now, on a whim, wished to resume a natural father-daughter relationship. As if the aching years in between had never happened. How many months she had waited for him to call her home.

But Margaret knew she'd never fit back into the tight circles of Aberdeen society; a wayward child who had been openly cast aside by her own family, whose most developed social skills included giving critiques of bawdy unpublished plays and treating the islanders' ills with herbal remedies. What husband would desire a wife who would rather walk on the beach alone than attend soirées and afternoon teas? What father in his right mind would hire her as a governess to his children, learning of her past misconduct, the accident on Loch Meirneal?

And now to lose Stephen to some faraway jungle, the dearest friend she'd ever had. But then perhaps he no longer cared about their relationship, carried away by his ambitions and craving for mystical adventures.

She leaned against the wall until her breathing slowed and the pain ebbed away to a dull ache deep inside her, to a place of darkness she pretended did not exist. She had become so skilled at hiding what she felt.

"Miss Rose?"

Ian slowly pushed open the door, blinking as he entered and his eyes adjusted to the dimness. "Is there any particular reason why you're hiding out here in the damp?"

"I wasn't hiding."

"No?" Ian sounded skeptical.

"I needed to be by myself, if it's any of your concern." In fact, Margaret resented the intrusion. He knew too much about her already.

"I see." He glanced upward, pretending to examine the dusty roosts while observing her from the corner of his eye. She hadn't been crying. In truth, nothing in her outward appearance justified his suspicion that her world had just been shattered.

"I just wanted to remind you that I'm still missing a trunk from the wreck. If it should turn up—"

She exhaled impatiently. "It will be sent to you immediately, Dr. MacNeill."

"Well, then." Ian turned to the door, logic insisting he should leave. "I wouldn't linger in this place overlong were I you. It reeks of dust and mildew, and look at all those cobwebs. There must be at least a hundred wee spiders. Are you not afraid of spiders, lass?"

The kind curiosity in his voice unbalanced her. "Don't . . . don't patronize me," she said dangerously.

She stole a glance at his dark face from under her lashes. She didn't know who he thought he was—obviously he was used to getting his own way. Well, she had no intention of falling prey to whatever devilish charm he possessed. More than once she'd glimpsed a dangerous sensuality lurking in those heavy-lidded blue eyes of his. He might be urbane and educated, but he didn't let her forget for an instant that he was all male. Her visceral awareness of him warned her of that.

She folded her arms across her chest, her face tense. "I wish you had never come here. I wish you'd go away."

"Would it really help if I did?"

She shrugged. "Perhaps." Rebelliously she added in an undertone, "It certainly couldn't hurt."

He suppressed a tender smile. She hadn't known much affection and warmth since her childhood, and he wondered if he could change that. All at once, he wanted to, even for a moment. He hated to see her so unhappy. It aroused protective instincts in him he hadn't realized he possessed, and he wanted badly to touch her, just once.

"No, Margaret," he said, his voice unconsciously rough. "I don't think my leaving would help at all. But this might . . ."

It did not surprise Margaret when he gathered her in his arms and drew her against him. The gesture seemed natural, and something inside her, some secret need, responded without hesitation. Unresisting but not exactly relenting, she sighed, feeling the strong echo of his heartbeat where her cheek pressed against his chest, feeling the latent strength of his body burning into hers.

"Leave me alone," she whispered without conviction, her arms falling to her sides.

"Hush, Margaret," he soothed her. "Let the moment lead us where it will."

His hands moved slowly down her back, the pressure gentle, reassuring, working upward then to the nape of her neck. The tension ebbed like wavelets from her body, replaced by a perilous awareness, a heightened sensitivity that made her feel warm and weightless. Oh, what power he had in his touch. What dangerous, wonderful power. Her head fell back, supported by the cradle of his hands. His thumbs traced the delicate lines of her jaw. Mesmerized and at the same time terrified, she stared up into his dark unsmiling face and could not believe the genuine caring it reflected.

Ian's eyes glinted down at her. Frowning, he bent his head, and she instinctively lowered her gaze, her heart quickening as she felt his cool firm lips skim hers. Pleasure, elemental and unexpected, pierced her to the core.

"No," she whispered, shaking her head in panic.

"No?" he murmured in disappointment, his heart thundering because that single kiss had only unleashed a torrent of white-hot urges inside him, carnal images of taking her right where they stood. Oh, she was damned smart to stop this before he was no longer capable of thinking clearly.

She leaned as far back from him as possible, her voice strained. "I think you've kept Mr. Shaw waiting long enough."

"Yes." Ian turned to leave, his expression shadowed and un-readable. He had meant to offer her comfort, nothing more, but as soon as he'd touched her, his good intentions had been forgotten.

Several moments passed before Margaret herself left the dovecote, and by then the cart had already started across the moors. She put her fingers unthinkingly to her lips. She would never have dreamed a kiss that fleeting could so affect her. Even now the dizzying rush of blood through her body had not yet subsided, and it was evening before she realized that the feverish afterglow she felt had less to do with Ian's kiss than with the full-fledged case of influenza she had contracted.

Eleven

Only six days after she'd fallen ill, Margaret was called to visit an ailing grandmother who lived on the other side of the island. To Margaret's annoyance, she caught herself half hoping, half dreading she would meet Ian MacNeill on the lonely ride across the moor. The incident between them in the dovecote had left her with a curious feeling of incompletion.

On the other hand, she didn't feel strong enough to do verbal battle with Ian quite yet. The long ride had taken more out of her than she'd bargained for, believing herself recovered from the influenza only to realize it had deepened into something more serious. She needed another day in bed and a decoction of lungwort and thyme to ease the congestion on her chest.

She did *not* need a man of Ian MacNeill's presumption and perception to challenge her flagging mental skills. She didn't know if she could even look him in the face again without remembering the primitive need that had gripped her during his kiss. Even now she could feel a tugging ache in the pit of her belly at the thought.

The elderly woman who had sent for Margaret lived in one of the black huts that clustered around the moor, a turf-covered dwelling encircled by muddy pockets of rainwater where ducks floated and splashed. Her basket over her arm, Margaret dismounted behind the hut. As usual, she would leave her pony in charge of one of the numerous children who ran barefoot through the chilly mud to greet her.

"Granny's expecting ye, Miss Rose!"

"And where are your shoes, Nora?"

"Goat ate 'em again, Miss Rose," the girl replied with a mischievous grin.

Chuckling, Margaret entered the hut where she found old Alice Fergusson at the hearth, blissfully smoking a long-stemmed briar pipe. "Ye're pale today, Miss Rose," the woman remarked, exhaling slowly. "I'd not have sent Robbie to fetch ye if I'd known you was poorly yerself."

"I have felt better," Margaret admitted, trying not to cough as a foul cloud of smoke assaulted her. "Hello, Robbie," she said to the adolescent red-haired boy, Alice's grandson, who moved past her into the doorway.

"Mornin' again, Miss Rose."

Alice gave a wicked, raspy chuckle. "Need a doctor, do ye, lass? I heard ye had him at the farmhouse for a time."

"Well, he's gone now, thank God," Margaret said, then surprised herself by adding, "Actually, he might even end up doing some good on the island."

"Not according to Mrs. Strong," Robbie said from the doorway. "She thinks he's an evil influence."

Margaret frowned as she set her basket on the table. "Morag's predictions aside, I think we'll have to give the doctor a chance, if only to please the laird. The Macpherson is often misguided, but he wants to help us."

"Oh, aye," Robbie said, his foxy little face amused. "That's why I went to fetch the doctor to visit Granny—to please the laird."

Margaret's fingers tightened on the bottle she'd removed from the basket. "The doctor isn't coming here now?" she said in a horror-stricken voice.

Robbie nodded. "I expect him at any minute."

"Then I shouldn't have come," Margaret exclaimed. Panic flaring, she began repacking her bottles and herbs into the basket. "Anyway," she said, miffed, "what do you need with *me,* now that you've got a *proper* doctor to help you?"

"Granny and I didn't want to send for him, Miss Rose," Robbie said apologetically. "But the laird's offered a pound of tea to every family that calls the doctor to the house."

"A pound of tea?" Margaret said in amazement. "Well, with such an extravagant bribe I'd be tempted to summon him myself. But there's not enough room in this hut for the two of us, Robbie, do you ken? He's too full of his university-taught treatments to—"

Robbie shook his head in sympathy as she turned away to cough. "Stranger's cough, is it? Sounds dreadful bad."

"It's a nasty dose, Robbie, I confess, but an illness like this has to run its course. Now, I'll be on my way before Dr. Mac-Neill can catch me. I don't want him accusing me of trying to interfere with his work."

"Too late." Robbie's voice rose in excitement, disturbing the baby sleeping in the cradle by the hearth. "He's coming down the hill now—och, and in the wrong direction. Ye'll run into him for certain if ye leave now."

"I'll sneak out the byre door."

"Can't, Miss Rose. Daddie nailed it shut to keep out the cold."

"Just hide yerself in the byre, lass," Alice Fergusson advised Margaret. "I'll soon be rid of the man."

Ian had spent several intolerable nights in the coastal cottage just outside the fishing hamlet that formed the heart of Maryhead's questionable social center. During their endlessly jolting ride from the farmhouse across the moor, Jamie Shaw had neglected to mention that the storm had done considerable damage to the white-limed cottage where Ian was to live and work.

He arrived to find that the barren hills behind the cottage

had unleashed a torrent of mud into the small downstairs parlor he'd intended to use as a dispensary and consulting room. The shingle roof sagged in the middle like a collapsed soufflé. Several windows had been broken, and despite repeated attempts by his housekeeper, Sybil Armstrong, to patch them with brown paper, a chill draught flowed steadily throughout the house.

Until today no one had yet summoned Ian on a medical call. In fact, the few crofters and fishermen who'd passed the cottage had openly eyed him with suspicion.

Ian had hoped Margaret might have called on him, sent a personal message, or at the very least commissioned an impersonal carrier pigeon to check whether he was still alive after her dubious nursing. But he hadn't heard a word from her. Superficially he understood that his behavior in the dovecote deserved a period of socially punishing silence.

Ian regretted that kiss, too, not from any sense of moral conscience, but because it had left him shaken in its lingering intensity. Even now he had only to close his eyes and he could feel her supple body fitting against the hard contours of his, could taste her mouth in all its sweet resentful surrender.

Well, if he'd aroused a similar confusion in Margaret, no wonder she resented him. Yet he sensed that her distress went deeper than the uninvited physical attraction between them. Perhaps she was still in shock over the news that her father desired a reconciliation. Or had she guessed that her brother and sister didn't really want her to return? The secret meeting with Gareth and Lilian Rose haunted Ian. More and more it seemed an air of mystery enshrouded Margaret's past, and now that he'd found her again, he was curious to learn why.

For now, however, he had to contend with more practical matters. Over breakfast this morning, as he was deciding whether to pay a visit to the seaside castle of Lord Thomas Macpherson, Ian's sponsor and laird of Maryhead, Ian had been called to his first case. The scruffy boy at the door had breathlessly explained that his grandmother had a stomach complaint. It sounded like a simple matter, and Ian was glad his only patient would no doubt live to praise his treatment.

If he could find the woman's home, and not make a fool of himself by getting lost in the process.

He heard someone shout his name. Wheeling around the sorrel mare Shaw had left him, Ian saw the young boy who'd summoned him waving from the doorway of his home. As Ian rode toward the miserable black hut, he noticed a horseshoe nailed to the byre.

A protection against evil, it should have warned him of the resistance he was about to encounter.

He followed the barefoot young boy, Robbie, into the soot-blackened interior where a woman, gray hair plaited over her shoulder, sat rocking an infant by the circular hearth. The walls were insulated with peat, coated with smudge, and reeked of the smoke which wafted upward in a thin bluish spume through a vent in the roof.

The boy took the infant from the old woman's arms. "This is the doctor, Granny."

She pursed her lips and clutched together the edges of her shawl, fastened to her blue kelt dress with fish hooks. "No need for ye to fetch the likes of him," she said with a sniff. "Miss Rose's potions or a visit to the charmer would do me better than whatever this fancy London charlatan can concoct."

Ian pulled a stool before her. "I'm from Aberdeen, ma'am, in Scotland."

"Ye don't look it."

"Well, I am nonetheless."

"Don't sound it either," the woman insisted.

"Can you tell me where the colic pains are and how long you've had them?" he asked patiently.

"Where do ye think colic pains would be, young man? Do they not teach doctors such things in London?"

Ian sighed. "I shall need to examine your abdomen, ma'am—that is, your stomach."

"Aye, I kenned that," she said with a snort of disgust.

As he rolled up his sleeves, Ian was distracted by what sounded like a muffled giggle from behind the cow byre. Before he could question Robbie about it, the door behind them opened, and a breath of fresh air and daylight penetrated the sooty gloom. A middle-aged crofter entered, squinting down at Ian.

"Granny saw a woman washing a shroud at the well this morning, Doctor," the man announced by way of greeting. "A white shroud, it was."

The crofter waited in expectant silence for Ian's response, as did the young boy holding the baby by the fire and the elderly grandmother in the crude driftwood chair.

"Is that supposed to be significant?" Ian finally asked.

The man nodded soberly. "It portends a death in the family. Granny fears 'twill be her own."

"Colic is rarely fatal," Ian retorted. "However, worrying over such nonsense never helped anyone's health." He reached into his bag. "I want Granny to take a dose of castor oil three times a day. For the pain I can give her an injection of morphia—"

The man gaped in horror at the hypodermic needle Ian withdrew from his bag. "Great God in heaven. You'll not use that on Granny."

"It will ease the cramping—"

"I'll not have it," the grandmother muttered. "Why, I'd as soon dose myself with Miss Rose's puffin brochan and suffer the consequences."

"What exactly is a puffin anyway?" Ian asked, suspecting that he would dislike the answer.

The young boy looked up. "It's a peculiar little sea bird, Doctor. Do ye not have them on the mainland?"

"Not that we put in our soup."

Something that sounded suspiciously like another smothered giggle rose from behind the crude partition of the byre. Ian narrowed his eyes and tried to look around Robbie to the adjoining cow-shelter.

"Are there children playing in the byre?" he asked quietly.

"That's where we keep our cow, Doctor, not the bairns," Robbie retorted.

"I realize that, but—"

"The charmer predicted ye'd bring trouble," the grandmother said craftily.

That got Ian's attention. "Who is this charmer everyone mentions?" he said, his patience finally worn thin.

"Morag Strong. She warned us against yer practices. Warned us yer arrival would mean the end of peace on the island."

Morag Strong. Ian swallowed over the knot of anger that had risen in his throat. Whoever the woman was, she had imbued herself with a power he would sooner or later be forced to challenge if he hoped to accomplish any good.

"Now, about your indigestion, madam—"

"Bring me back Miss Rose," the grandmother said in a long-suffering voice to no one in particular.

"Back?" Ian's brow furrowed. "What do you mean bring her back?"

Robbie sent his grandmother a warning look. "Miss Rose is sick, Granny, do ye not remember?"

There were undercurrents of conspiracy in the air, which Robbie and his grandmother evidently assumed Ian was too dense to perceive, and he had a strong feeling they somehow involved Margaret Rose. "What's wrong with Miss Rose?" he demanded.

"Stranger's cough, Doctor." Robbie turned the grizzling infant onto its stomach. "Brought to the island by—"

"Strangers," Ian said wryly. "Yes. I'll stop by to see her

later this morning. And you, ma'am, are to eschew cucumbers and fermented beverages—"

"Chew cucumbers?"

"Avoid the damp," he continued, marveling at his self-control. "No rich meals before retiring, and hot flannels applied to the abdomen when the pain is severe. Weather permitting, you might take a brief ocean bath."

"Ye said to avoid the damp, didn't ye? I'll catch my death in the sea, or worse be drowned."

Ian exhaled slowly. "A shallow hip bath will suffice."

"Hip bath? Can't see where my hips have anything to do with the colic."

At that, an unmistakable chortle of laughter, feminine and vaguely familiar, issued from behind the byre. Ian jumped up from the stool, dodging a startled Robbie, and stalked across the room.

"Well, well," he said at the sight of Margaret crouched in the corner behind the cow, her blue-gray eyes bright with guilt. "Is Little Bo-Peep enjoying herself at the new doctor's expense?"

"Hardly." Ashamed at being caught in the undignified pose, Margaret scrambled to her feet, covertly picking out bits of straw from her shawl and skirts.

"Playing milkmaid or spy for professional secrets, Miss Rose?" Ian asked calmly. "If you'd like to learn some proper medicine, I'd be happy to give you a few lessons under more—" he fanned away an imaginary fly "—hygienic conditions."

"Dr. MacNeill," she retorted with as much decorum as a person can muster with a cow chewing at your basket, "if you must know the truth, I was summoned here by Alice herself on a medical matter."

"You?" Disbelief and then doubt flickered in his intense blue eyes. "They sent for you before me?"

"They did."

"Oh," he said quietly. "I see." But what he saw, amazingly,

was not so much the islanders' rejection of him as their acceptance of Margaret. How much it must mean to her, to have earned their affection and respect when her personal life had brought only pain. Why indeed would she want to leave Maryhead for the cruel, remembered loneliness of Aberdeen?

"Are you all right, Dr. MacNeill?" Margaret inquired after a heavy pause which left her wishing she hadn't told him the truth.

"I'm fine," he said gruffly. "What did you prescribe for the old woman's complaint?"

She glanced down at her basket. Despite herself, she found she was eager to exchange healing techniques with Ian, hating to admit she'd been impressed by his orthodox suggestions and gentle approach with Alice.

"For calming the stomach," she began, "I've a bottle of basil in barley water, lovage seed steeped in a silver pot, and a sachet of mullein leaves to place under her pillow at night."

"A *silver* pot?" he said in amusement.

She ignored him. "Peppermint tea is, of course, the sovereign cure for indigestion."

"Of course."

Margaret looked up, realizing he was not examining the contents of her basket at all, but rather was staring at her intently, the amusement slowly vanishing from his face.

"Is something wrong, Dr. MacNeill?"

"Not with me. But you're uncommonly pale, aren't you?" he asked as if just noticing it himself. "And your throat sounds hoarse. Robbie mentioned you were ill."

"I've a little cold." The truth was, she wasn't sure she could even make the ride home, but he didn't need to know that. "As I understand it, Dr. MacNeill," she continued, eager to divert his attention away from her, "an infusion of angelica is helpful for easing cramps."

He reached for her arm. "Let me have a look at you in the light."

"Don't be silly." She edged around him and the cow, put out that he hadn't even remarked on her remedies. "I don't need your help, your hypodermics and hip baths, thanks very much, but the best of luck in your practice, anyway."

"Afraid I might be able to teach you something, Miss Rose?" he called after her.

She stopped dead at the partition, half turning to give him a small tight smile. *"Afraid?* Little Bo-Peep lost her sheep, Dr. MacNeill, not a cow. And as you seem unable to tell the difference between them, I hardly think you're qualified to be giving me lessons in anything."

Ian grinned as she whirled around. So her spirit hadn't been extinguished after all, only dampened. There was hope indeed for the resurrection of Margaret Rose.

Feeling foolish standing alone with the cow, he hurried out of the hut after Margaret, snatching his bag from the floor on the way. His face burned at the sniggering which followed his exit. As a physician in the Highlands, his own father had often met with ignorance and superstitious refusal to take treatment, but had it been this frustrating? He doubted it.

Margaret and her pony were slowly receding from sight by the time he skirted the procession of ducks, children, and goats outside. Well, he wasn't about to chase after her to apologize, for what offense he wasn't sure anyway, him being in his opinion the injured party.

He began to walk toward his horse.

"Wait, Doctor!" The boy named Robbie came pelting after Ian, splashing through the mud to hand him a dirty canvas sack. "Ye've forgotten yer fee."

"It's all right. The laird will see to it."

"Daddie insists."

"What is it?" Ian asked, his nostrils flaring at the fishy odor emanating from the sack.

"Puffins, sir. My father caught them fresh five days ago. He said I should tell you they have healing properties."

Despite intense reservations, Ian slung the sack over the saddle of the sorrel mare he had left grazing in the grass. With luck he could "lose" the pungent offering somewhere on the moors. That was if he decided to visit Margaret on the other side of the island to further investigate her illness. It would probably mean hours of dreary riding just to face more rejection and frustration.

He decided on impulse that he would not call on her unless she sent for him.

He was only ten minutes on the western cart road, lulled half to sleep by the monotonous jogging of the mare, when Robbie rode up beside him on a tough little island pony.

"Dr. MacNeill! You're wanted again, sir."

"Not Granny's stomach—"

"No, sir. Over at Cape Rue."

"Cape Rue?"

"Where you was shipwrecked. Black William's fallen off the cliff and hurt his leg, and my brother is frantic to fetch help for him. He's in horrible pain, sir, and the family depends on the income he brings."

Cape Rue. Well, it was an apt name, and it looked as if he might end up seeing Margaret again whether either of them wished it or not. Yet when he reached the cape, feeling the invigorating salt air sting his face as he took the cliffside path, it was Agnes and her brother, the Reverend Rose, he noticed, talking alone on the promontory that looked out to the sea.

"Good afternoon, Dr. MacNeill," Stephen called to him, his blue cassock flapping in the breeze. "I trust you've enjoyed your first week on Maryhead."

"It's challenging in some ways, fascinating in others," Ian said as he dismounted.

Agnes pushed a strand of hair from her cheek. "What brings you to our side of the island, Dr. MacNeill?"

"I'm looking for a shepherd called Black William who took a fall from the cliff path."

Stephen frowned. "We noticed no one on our walk from the beach. Just a ram caught on one of the ledges and putting up a fearful racket. Broke its leg, I suspect. The cragsmen will have to be sent for to rescue it."

"Excuse me for a moment," Ian said. "Robbie—" He strode up to the boy still mounted on the pony. "Black William is a ram? You summoned me across the island for a bloody sheep?"

"He's not just any sheep, Doctor. He's my uncle's best stud, and he's in awful pain."

Ian turned and found Agnes studying him with an expression of unbridled delight. "You've found your patient?" she asked.

"I believe so. It's a sheep."

She smiled broadly. "Then perhaps when you're finished with him you could pay a call on Margaret."

"Is she very ill?"

"Mending. It was the influenza, but the cough that remains is troublesome," Agnes said. "She isn't expecting you, though. I'm afraid you won't get a very warm reception."

Ian grinned. "I'm afraid you're right. But I'll be at the farmhouse anyway, Mrs. Alcock, as soon as I'm done here examining Black William."

Twelve

Margaret stood frozen in the parlor doorway, staring at the tall man who moved about in the twilight shadows which only emphasized his swarthy skin and blue-black hair. Him again, she thought, and would have successfully escaped upstairs to bed had a sudden fit of coughing not given her away.

Ian half turned, his hands clasped behind his back. "I dislike the sound of that cough, Miss Rose," he said quietly. "If you'd disrobe, I will listen to your chest."

She stared at him in mute astonishment.

He stepped back to the window, his face once again in shadow. "In place of an examining table, we'll use the sofa. Mrs. Alcock was kind enough to provide a plaid for your modesty. By the way, do you have a mortar and pestle I could use to pulverize some pills?"

Margaret did not answer, embarrassed by his offhanded request that she undress, furious that Agnes had brought him back into the house against her wishes.

"I don't need examination," she said firmly after catching her breath.

"I think you do. Influenza is often fatal among populations unaccustomed to its ravages. And it would reflect on my skills if the first woman I met on Maryhead perished from medical neglect."

Ian came around the table, frowning at her. "Your face is

drawn, your cheeks flushed. Have you ever had a severe examination?"

"No," she answered tightly. "Uncle Angus had a deeply ingrained distrust of physicians. He referred to them as frauds, quacksalvers, sawbones—"

"—charlatans, humbugs, and mountebanks," Ian finished for her, unmoved by the string of insults. "You don't have to disrobe. Simply loosen your garments at the shoulders, and I'll make do."

When Margaret didn't move, Ian picked up a long wooden cylinder which had a hollow tube at its end. If she hadn't felt so horribly weak, if she hadn't herself witnessed several cases of influenza leading to death, and if Ian hadn't been so damnably self-assured about treating her, she would have demanded he leave the house.

"A stethoscope," he said. "It enables me to check the condition of your lungs. Unfortunately my thermometer was broken in the wreck, but if you'll allow me to touch your forehead. . . . Yes, you are slightly feverish." He grinned, his eyes meeting hers. "Or is that your temper indubitably rising, Miss Rose?"

Margaret pulled away with a nervous little laugh and sat down at the very edge of the sofa, staring out into the gathering shadows of the garden to avoid making further eye contact with him. Reluctantly she began to unfasten her gown and work it off her shoulders, gripping the coarse plaid to her chest. She stiffened as he drew a footstool close.

"This is silly," she grumbled. "I truly doubt I could die of a cough."

"Of course you could. Why, you could keel over at any moment."

She saw the amusement on his face, and it only increased her agitation. She could not believe she was submitting to a "severe" examination. She had no idea what such a thing could possibly entail, but she decided it would be humiliating and painful and that she would be better off dying a hundred deaths from pneumonia than to find out.

Ian pulled a black leather glove onto his left hand, then slid the stethoscope beneath the plaid, his craggy face turned away in concentration. Sudden heat flooded Margaret's body. His leather-clad fingers were gentle and alien against her skin. The sensations they aroused as they skimmed her breasts mortified her beyond words. Yet it was as if she were entranced. She could only sit in horrified silence, conscious of the painful palpitations of her heart.

"Breathe in slowly for me, Miss Rose, and then exhale. Now again, and not so fast this time. There's no need to be nervous."

Her face was so near his that she could see the blue-black highlights in the hair that waved around his neck. The pleasant scent of woodruff shaving soap and powdered herbs filled her senses as she inhaled.

He drew back and peeled off his glove, running his hand lightly up each side of her throat. Not once had he looked Margaret in the face, and when he did it was with an impersonal glance to note the brightness of her eyes. Drawing a watch from his vest pocket, he took her wrist to feel for her pulse.

He touched her forehead and frowned. "The fever and your cough concern me."

"All that rigmarole—the poking, the gloves, the funny stick, just to tell me that?"

"You have bronchitis." He rose from the stool. "And you're damned fortunate it hasn't advanced into pneumonia."

"May I get dressed then, before it does?"

"No. Lie on the sofa, please."

Margaret stared at him in alarm. "Whatever for?"

"I'm not quite finished."

She yanked the plaid up to her chin. He was too self-assured by half. "I haven't forgotten that you kissed me that day," she said.

Ian didn't glance around from the table. "Nor have I."

"I won't let it happen again."

"Really? Well, what makes you think I'd want to repeat that unfortunate moment myself?"

Margaret had no answer for that, and strangely, instead of feeling reassured, she was surprised and a little stung by his retort.

She watched with mounting trepidation as he rifled through his bag to withdraw a pewter ring, with three prongs resembling a candelabrum, several strips of clean linen, and three greyish rods that looked like charcoal. These he lit with a match and waved through the air to produce pungent streams of smoke.

He glanced at her. "Moxae chinois—what little was not damaged by the saltwater. I'm going to burn them near your chest to—"

"I know. It's Chinese moxa, an ancient herb, and highly effective in healing the lungs. I read about it in one of Stephen's books on Oriental green medicine." She dropped back on one elbow, inhaling the faintly acrid fumes. "I'm surprised *you* would rely upon an Eastern method."

"Would you prefer I used the leech?" he asked. "My collection of the wee bloodsuckers survived the shipwreck well. In cases such as yours the suggested amount I'm to draw is at least three palettes of blood. That's twelve ounces—an application of two dozen leeches on the chest." Somehow he managed to keep from laughing aloud at the growing horror on her face.

"You wouldn't—"

Margaret broke off, bolting upright to shove her arms into the sleeves of her dark green bodice jacket. Ian turned in surprise at her sudden silence. Stephen stood in the doorway, looking surprised and hesitant to enter until he saw the instruments on the table.

He moved to turn up the wall lights. "Well, Dr. MacNeill, is my cousin a good patient?"

"She's a pain in the neck, actually," Ian answered. "Tell me, have you suffered no symptoms of the influenza yourself?"

Soft golden light flooded the parlor, highlighting Stephen's chiseled features. "Nothing so far, but then I'm rarely sick. I do, in fact, wish a word with you, Dr. MacNeill, in private."

Ian placed his stethoscope back into his bag. "All right—if I can trust Miss Rose to rest quietly for the time it takes the moxae to burn down."

Margaret made a face. "Only if you promise to tell me later what this private conversation is about."

"It doesn't concern you, Margaret," Stephen said smoothly. "Island affairs, that's all."

The young reverend had lied.

Ian stood in silence on the seaside bluff, freezing in his cashmere vest and jacket. Stephen rubbed his hands together in unabashed pleasure, his face lifted to savor the arctic blast.

"You wished to speak with me . . . something about island affairs?"

"The island? Oh, yes, well, it's actually about Margaret. My sister tells me you've been enlisted by Douglas Rose to send her back home."

"Yes," Ian said cautiously. "But Margaret is vehemently opposed to the suggestion."

"Then perhaps you could change her mind, convince her she doesn't belong on Maryhead."

"I hardly think it's any of my affair, or that Margaret gives a damn for my opinion."

"She'll never have a normal life here," Stephen said pensively. "We who live on the island belong to a very unreal world, which is in part why I'm choosing to leave."

"To your jungle mission?"

"Yes." Stephen faced him, his voice subdued. "The Orient. I've failed here, in my work, my personal life."

Ian glanced back across the hills to the farmhouse. The moxae would have extinguished itself by now. He had to remember to leave Margaret some medicine for that cough. Tincture of squills. Oil of aniseed. The prospect of losing her to pneumonia, all too common in such cases, filled him with an anxiety he could not attribute wholly to medical concern.

"I don't believe she likes me very much," he thought aloud. "I'm not sure why."

Stephen laughed. "I'm amazed that she let you examine her at all. My Margaret is usually so much more reserved." He started down the bluff. "Come on, friend. You're turning blue, and I've made my point." He started back down the bluff. "You're settling in to your new home, Dr. MacNeill?" he asked over his shoulder.

Ian hurried after him. "What the storm left of it. The place is a mess."

"Really?" Stephen slowed for Ian to join him. "May I place the manse at your disposal then until repairs are made? I'll be spending the next month or so in Edinburgh for my official indoctrination, and until a new minister can be found, the manse will be empty."

"Well, I—"

"Of course, you'd have to contend with Margaret and Agnes for neighbors. Think about it, Dr. MacNeill. You don't have to decide tonight."

"Yes, all right. I'll give you an answer tomorrow."

But Ian had already made up his mind to accept the offer, and his decision had nothing to do with the leaky stone cottage that he had come to equate with the lonely shambles of his life.

Thirteen

She'd hoped the dreams had stopped. Almost eleven months had passed since the last one now, and they had to that point been occurring with far less frequency than during her first years on Maryhead.

It was always the same. The long walk up the gangway to the steamer, someone jostling her so that she stumbled against the guardrail and pitched into the water. She saw a hand extended, a man's hand, and thought at first he was trying to save her. But the receding glimpse of his face revealed only a cold gray void, and she fell, endlessly, into darkness and damnation, realizing it was her own father who had pushed her.

As always there was a figure waiting for her in that darkness, a white cloaked creature with its clawed hand extended, and in that hand was an invitation to death.

A banshee, the bean sith.

But for the first time ever there also appeared in the dream another person . . . the dark stranger she had rescued on the beach. He caught her as she hurtled into the darkness. He caught her and then rolled her beneath him, his body covering hers. Shocked, she realized as the cool air caressed her skin that they were both naked . . . in her bed.

"Stay with me," he whispered, but now, instead of drawing away, she arched upward against him like a wanton, unresisting, inviting. His mouth grazed her throat, her shoulder, moved back and forth between her breasts until she whimpered, helpless to control the trembling of her body. His pelvis pressed hard against hers. His hands slid down her sides to grasp her hips.

She groaned, in pleasure and protest . . . some distant part of her mind trying to awaken her before it was too late, but the sensations were too intense, the desire to draw him deep inside her too powerful. . . .

"Damn it. Damn him," she whispered, shoving the blanket to the floor. She was sweating, and shivering, not just from cold, but with anger and self-contempt, a terror that she would never break free of the past.

Ian MacNeill had reopened the old wounds.

She blamed him for the dream tonight, for reawakening memories of home and family. She did not believe he had meant to hurt her, but the fact remained he had sought her out at her father's behest, and she resented him, irrationally or not, for that.

She got up and quickly dressed. It was just dawn. Her chest ached with every breath. Her head felt hot and pounded dully. If she weren't determined to see Stephen before he set out on the mail packet, she might have slept all day.

She walked him to the bluff. She did not complain of feeling unwell, and Stephen was too self-absorbed to notice. He spoke of establishing a mission in the Siamese province of Chiang Mai, of holy men and hillside shrines inhabited by giants and genii.

It sounded to Margaret like another world.

"You should leave Maryhead too," he said softly. "There's nothing here for a beautiful young spirit like you."

"I could go with you to Siam," she said impulsively, but in her heart she knew it could never happen. She was as attached to the island as Stephen was to his work—she was afraid to leave.

"Och, Margaret," he said wistfully. "I'd never subject you

to such hardships." He pulled away from her as a shepherd approached the bluff, raising his staff in recognition. "Be a good girl, and think about Dr. MacNeill's offer to send you home—"

She drew back angrily. "Oh, that man. If anyone doesn't belong on Maryhead, it's him."

Stephen gave her a curious look. "I found him reasonable and plain-spoken. Why do you allow him to antagonize you so?" He picked up his valise. "Anyway, it would be simple Christian charity to make him feel welcome in the manse. He's supposed to move in this afternoon, and I've left the pantry bare."

"He looks capable of feeding himself."

"Come, Margaret. What do you have to lose by offering him your friendship? You're both interested in healing."

"Our methods are a universe apart."

"Perhaps not," Stephen said, his face pensive. "Perhaps you're more alike than you realize."

"Now there's a frightening thought," Margaret said with such conviction that they both began to laugh.

"Well," he said, his voice deceptively light, "now that we've made each other laugh again, I suppose I should be on my way."

"Let me know about forwarding your things."

"I have to come back at least once before I leave for Siam, assuming the bishop approves of me. One last Christmas together, I promise."

"Calm seas, Stephen," she whispered, the wind stirring her long hair.

He grinned, eager to go. "You'll stop at the manse—"

"Yes," she agreed reluctantly.

He hesitated as if he wanted to say more. Then he turned, hurrying down the twisting path to the sea. Margaret kept him in view until he reached the bottom of the cliff where he paused to wave up at her. She raised her hand slowly in return, fighting the impulse to run after him.

She turned, her throat constricted, and stared down at the manse. Alone, alone, alone . . . the waves below seemed to murmur in sympathy as they crashed against the cliffs.

Margaret decided to visit the manse that same morning, to restock the pantry and leave a supply of fresh linen. The doctor could fetch his own supply of peat from the cleit, the little stone storehouse on the hill. Too lightheaded to bother with it herself, she wished to be well away from the manse before he arrived that afternoon.

But when she let herself into the cottage, there was a cheerful fire crackling in the parlor, and on the stone hearth before it an assortment of water-damaged books had been spread out to dry.

She glanced around the sparsely furnished room. To her surprise the house already seemed to vibrate with the disturbing energy and presence of the dark Scotsman whom she still regarded as a stranger.

"Dr. MacNeill?" she called quietly from the door.

There was no reply. Suddenly self-conscious and worn from the emotional strain of Stephen's departure, she retreated back into the parlor to wait.

When Ian entered the room minutes later, she was sifting through the stack of anatomical plates that he'd left on the tea table. She glanced up, feeling an unexpected thrill go through her at the sight of him in the doorway, dark, tall, dominant.

"Miss Rose," he said in obvious surprise, "I hope this is a pleasure call and not a sign that your condition has worsened."

She frowned. He looked even more impressive than she remembered, his brooding face so masculine it might have been carved from marble.

"It's neither actually," she answered. "I didn't expect to find you here." She looked down distractedly at the drawings she'd been leafing through, cardiovascular veins and arteries. As she placed them back upon the table, she realized that her hand was trembling.

"The graphic detailing of a human heart upsets you, Miss Rose?"

"What? Oh, so that's what it was. No, it's quite fascinating, and I'm not on the squeamish side."

"But your hand was shaking."

Damn, did the man miss nothing? "My cousin left this morning, as you must be aware," she said.

He lifted his brow. "You're taking the medicine I prescribed?"

"No," she said with a touch of irritation. "No, I'm not."

He smiled faintly. "Well, at least you're honest about it." He walked to the fire, staring into the flames. "There was an open Bible and a plate of oatcakes on the kitchen table when I came in from the stable. As I understand it, that's the traditional Gaelic welcome." When she didn't respond, he glanced around. "Was it you who left them?"

Her heart gave an unaccountable lurch. "Yes, I did."

His swarthy face inscrutable, he removed a bottle of camphor from his pocket. "Is it safe for me to assume that you're personally welcoming me to Maryhead?"

"It's safe to assume that I observe tradition," she said with a little smile.

"An evasive answer, and very unsatisfying." He returned her smile, turning the green glass bottle back and forth in his fingers so that it caught the light. "I remember your mentioning you grow a medicinal herb garden. Perhaps you'd be interested in the orthodox pharmacopeia."

"I might," Margaret said archly, "if I had a notion what the devil it was."

He laughed in delight. "My medicines, lass. I've decided to

use Stephen's study as a dispensary and perhaps later a laboratory. Do you think he'd object?"

"No." She swallowed, thinking of Stephen, the void in her life his leavetaking would make. "I don't think so."

He narrowed his eyes. "Is something wrong, Miss Rose?"

"Not at all. Yes, show me this dispensary. Let me admire this modern science you're so determined to bring to Maryhead."

They left the cozy warmth of the parlor and walked to the small cold study where Margaret had once helped Stephen write his sermons. Aside from a few books on Oriental philosophy and folklore there was little left to remind her of her cousin. She stared at the bottles that now lined the shelves: ARGENTI NITRATIS, TINCT. CASCARILLAE, INF. DIGITALIS, TREACLE.

Ian crossed his arms across his chest. "Well, what do you think? Will Stephen have a shock when he returns?"

She watched him bend to retrieve a carton of pamphlets from behind the desk, an impressive figure in his crisp white shirt, black vest, and nankeen trousers. He seemed almost too vital, too masculine for his surroundings.

"Stephen isn't coming back," she said quietly, "at least not to stay."

Ian straightened, his face alight with understanding. "Ah, so that *is* the heart of the matter. I suspected as much."

"How could you?" She had little patience with him suddenly, this perceptive stranger who had no place in her life. "How could you even pretend to understand?"

"Because I want to understand you."

She ran her fingertips down the nose of the plaster bust of Hippocrates on his desk. "You're wasting your time."

"Well, that's nothing new."

Margaret glanced at him, taken aback by his answer. His dark blue eyes, so adept at probing *her* secrets, gave away little of what he really thought.

He looked at her levelly for several moments and then ducked behind the desk to collect an armload of books from the floor. "I have a dinner appointment with the laird and need to stow these away upstairs before I leave," he said. "There's a bottle of medicine in the top drawer here which you're to take, three ounces at a time, every four hours daily."

She noticed he avoided using his right arm and remembered he'd bruised that shoulder in the shipwreck. She felt guilty suddenly, not only for trying to hurt him but for succeeding at it. "Would you like help carrying up the other books on the floor?"

Ian hesitated. "Perhaps with that crate over there—it's only pamphlets and paper, nothing too heavy to lift. If you're up to it yourself—"

"I can manage," she said. "I'm used to carrying peats."

She hoisted the crate into her arms and followed him to the narrow staircase, thinking of the last time she had climbed these stairs, when her aunt was dying. She thought of Stephen, out to sea by now, and she slowed, leaning against the handrail.

Alone, alone, alone. The word echoed an aching refrain, fading as Ian glanced around to see what had detained her.

"Shall I have to carry you up the rest of the way, Miss Rose?" he teased her. "I remember you did the same for me once and almost killed us all in the process."

She smiled wryly. There wasn't time to dwell for long on her private misery. It took all her wits to stay one step ahead of this unusual man.

"I assume it's all right to use the attic for storage," he said a few moments later as he opened the door onto a garret that smelled of must. "I've placed some of your family's things here which Stephen left behind, along with the supplies brought by the Armstrongs that I've yet to unpack."

She lowered the crate to the floor. "The Armstrongs?"

Ian nodded. "The domestic couple I took on at Aberdeen. An odd pair, Walter and his wife, but the best I could do under the circumstances. No one else wanted to come here, and they did have previous experience with another doctor."

She gave him an appraising look. "I'm surprised *you* came here." And for the first time she was truly curious about his personal life. "Did you leave a scandalous past behind?" she asked half seriously.

"Actually, I'm here because I have a contract." He looked around the room. "Perhaps you'd like to sort through your aunt's belongings."

Aware that he hadn't answered her, Margaret walked past him to the window. Rubbing her knuckles across the grimy lozenge-shaped pane, she murmured, "The light is poor, but I suppose it should be done. Agnes will never find the time for it."

"There's a lamp in the corner," he said behind her. "I'll light it if you like, and I'll fetch the chaise longue from the bedroom for you to sit in comfort."

He started past her at the same instant that Margaret turned from the window. Their bodies brushed in unplanned synchrony, an accidental embrace that made her catch her breath. For an unguarded moment, as Ian automatically slipped his arm around her waist, she was tempted to savor the physical closeness. Then, giving a soft laugh to hide her disconcertment, she edged around him, as if putting distance between them would enable her to pretend she had felt nothing.

Ian stared at her, slowly backing away. "Let me fetch the chair."

"No—"

But he was already out the door, returning moments later with a faded gold brocade chair balanced on his shoulders like a hermit crab's shell. Margaret knelt and hastily pushed a pile of books from his path. He swung the chair down easily, sending papers and dustballs scattering across the unvarnished floor.

"There." His gaze flickered over her. "Now the light, and I'll leave you alone."

As Margaret straightened, something akin to anticipation shivered over her nerve endings. Ian had removed his vest to bring her the chair, and the simple lines of his shirt and trousers emphasized the broadness of his shoulders and long muscular frame. As he leaned forward to light the lamp, the flame threw his face into stark relief, the rough-hewn features and angular planes. If he could not claim Stephen's aristocratic beauty, Ian had a dark, intensely male appeal of his own, a magnetism so compelling and yet subtle that it shocked Margaret to realize how attractive a man he actually was. Why had it taken her so long to recognize it?"

"Safe," she said uncertainly. "It occurs to me that were we in Aberdeen a woman's reputation wouldn't survive even this innocent encounter. I wonder—am I safe with you?"

He gave her an enigmatic smile. "A defenseless young woman lured by the careworn older man into his garret for a clandestine seduction—is that the tableau?"

"Something like that," she said, unable to resist a smile herself at his phrasing.

"Well, I wouldn't worry. I choose the time, place, and object of my amours with both deliberation and discretion, and they are rarely happenstance. Nor are they numerous."

Margaret felt suddenly stupid, her face growing warm at the unexpected rebuffal. As if *she'd* brought him up here for some cozy rendezvous!

He motioned to the chair, his voice amused. "Sit. I'll bring you up your medicine."

"I don't need it."

"You'll take it anyway, and I'll help myself at the same time to another wee dram of your cousin's whiskey."

She lowered herself into the chair only to rise from it abruptly. "Whiskey. Oh, dear. How could I possibly have forgotten it's Friday?"

"Friday?" Ian smiled. "Is it holiday on the island? Puffin day or something like that?"

"It's just an errand I'd forgotten to run," Margaret said hurriedly. Too preoccupied to take any notice of his joking, she moved past him to the door. "Please store my aunt's belongings until I have time to sort through them."

"I've made up a prescription especially for your cough," he said, puzzled by her erratic behavior. "And why have you brought nothing heavier than a shawl in this weather?"

She bristled. "I'm almost twenty-one years old, Dr. MacNeill, and not in your custody, no matter my father's instructions nor promises of reward."

"Very well. Catch another chill if you like." His face annoyed, he lifted from the floor a hatbox crammed with letters, receipts, and papers. "Take this nonsense with you, too. It invites a fire."

With an impatient sigh, Margaret held out her arms, then recoiled as her gaze fell upon a yellowed newspaper clipping that had floated to the floor.

The headline above the faded print turned her blood to ice: WIFE AND YOUNG SON OF PROMINENT BANKER DOUGLAS ROSE DROWNED ON FAMILY ESTATE.

It was a clipping from one of the penny-a-line scandal papers that had circulated in Aberdeen at the time of the accident on Loch Meirneal and that still fed on the gossip hunger of the populace to this day. Margaret remembered that her father had forbidden them in the house, but the servants had read them belowstairs anyway.

She knelt and picked up the clipping, her voice unsteady. "I suppose you've read this?"

"I've never seen it before," Ian answered, watching her in confusion and concern. "It's an article from an old newspaper, isn't it?"

She straightened, her blue-gray eyes dark and stricken against the sudden paleness of her face. "Yes. It's about me—and the accident twelve years ago, when my mother and little brother drowned."

His craggy face softened. "Shall I get rid of it for you?"

"No," she said quickly. "I'll do it. It—it's half-truths and horrid lies. I can't believe it even found its way into the house."

"It was among your aunt's things," he reminded her gently.

"It was on top of them," Margaret countered. "As if some-one had recently read it."

"Well, it wasn't me," he assured her. "And if it's any con-solation, I myself have also been the victim of vicious broad-sheets which did irreparable damage to my reputation."

She took a breath. He was only trying to make her feel better, but how could he possibly understand the shame that surrounded her, the unspoken accusations that she had lived with for so long? She realized that she hadn't wanted Ian to associate her with the accident, but it was probably too late anyway. Her father must have told him of the family tragedy.

She retreated to the door, needing suddenly to get outside, the paper crumpled in her hand. "I'll leave you to your work. The pantry has been restocked, and if you need peats—"

He strode forward to reach the door a second before she did. He couldn't let her leave in such obvious distress. "What-ever is in that article is long past and best forgotten."

She shook her head, white-lipped and too upset to allow his logic to penetrate. "But I'll never forget my mother and Alan, and there are times when I search for answers that I start to believe the rumors about that morning myself."

"Rumors? No one could be blamed for an accident."

"Well, I was." Margaret lifted her head, unconsciously chal-lenging him to accuse her, too. "Don't you want to read the article for yourself?"

What he wanted to do was to hold her in his arms and restore the intimate mood of a few minutes ago. Instead, he said: "I'll read it only if it helps me understand you better."

"I don't need your understanding, Dr. MacNeill," she said in a cool voice. "As you said, the past is best forgotten." When he made no comment, she felt compelled to add, "I don't need *your* help at all."

He studied her for a moment, then backed away from the door, his face resigned. "I'd hoped you would accept me as a friend, Miss Rose. I'd hoped to overcome the bad feelings of our first meeting. However, it seems I've deluded myself. Go then. Go about that mysterious errand you mentioned."

He didn't go downstairs until he heard her leave the house. In the study he collected his bag and coat, then sat at the desk to make an entry in his journal. But he couldn't keep Margaret from his mind. If she only knew how close he'd come to living up to all her fears about enforced seduction. If she only knew how their accidental embrace had pitted all his self-possession against a raw desire he could feel like a drug in his system even now. And he felt frustrated, not just because of her emotional withdrawal, but rather because it had become inordinately important that he make a favorable impression on her.

Thank God he had his work.

He couldn't remember a time when he had not known he would be a doctor, even as a shy young boy whose rugged looks had belied his intellectual curiosity, and he had accompanied his physician father on countless medical calls in the country village of his birth.

Strange that he and his younger brother Andrew had been so different. Failing at a law career, the congenital lameness in his left leg keeping him from military service, Andrew had no interest in medicine and cheerfully admitted he had no other intellectual aptitudes either.

As Andrew, brown-haired and boyishly handsome, had often said with typical unconcern, "I like to hunt, to fish, to muck around in the garden, share a pint with the old shepherds and lend a hand at eweing. I'm a farmer at heart."

It was that conversation which had prompted him to offer

Andrew the position of factor on Taynaross, Ian's Highland estate. With his practice in Aberdeen demanding all his attention, Ian couldn't maintain the estate himself, and he hated to sell his cherished country retreat where he and Jean, along with his entire family, had already spent several holidays together and planned to live.

And now Andrew and Jean lived in that large stone house with their unborn child because Ian had been too disheartened over their marriage to even bother finding another agent.

He missed them all suddenly, his parents and his sisters, their fond bickering and the warmth concealed behind their well-meaning criticism. And, unexpectedly, he felt a pang of regret over his alienation from Andrew, over the betrayal that had overshadowed the years of closeness, the only two sons allied against the aggressive femininity of the four MacNeill girls.

He looked up distractedly, the past fading, as a chunk of peat shifted in the fireplace. Glowing in the grate were the charred embers of the newspaper clipping Margaret had evidently intended to burn on her way outside.

He sat forward, hesitating. Then slowly he got to his feet. What right did he have to probe the past of Margaret Rose, a past possibly haunted by memories more painful than his own?

He walked to the hearth and swiftly knelt, snatching the burning remnants from the fire. He felt like a thief, an impostor, a liar, stooping to retrieve from the grate what he hoped would provide him with some clue to Margaret's character. She'd despise him if she saw him now, after his sanctimonious profession that he never read such rubbish, and he could not believe it himself, behavior beneath the contempt of even a parlormaid.

He spread the charred clipping across the hearthstone, glancing back once into the doorway. For all his trouble, singed fingertips and uneasy conscience, the last paragraph was the only legible portion that remained of the article. There had been an artist's sketch, too, of the two victims, but it had been torn away or had disintegrated over time, leaving only the right side of Susan Rose's delicate face.

As he began to read, Ian felt an unexpected sadness at the thought of such a young woman dying, her daughter a witness to the horror of how it had happened.

And so this writer is left to wonder whether it was indeed an accident, or whether there was, as the old village shepherd denies, foul play involved. Unless an eye-witness comes forth, it seems unlikely that the truth of the tragedy at Loch Meirneal will ever be revealed. Certainly one must at least consider the possibility of supernatural involvement, as is widely believed in the village of Meirneal. The castle overlooking the loch has a long history of murder and violence, and on its grounds have been reported numerous ghostly apparitions. Alas, the truth seems destined to remain locked forever in the mind of the eight-year-old girl, Margaret Rose.

Fourteen

Margaret was not in the mood to brew whiskey. For one thing, she hadn't fully recovered from her illness—her carefully prepared yarrow teas, the poultices of beeswax and black pepper had not helped. For another, she missed Stephen already and could not imagine the empty days ahead without him.

But even worse, she couldn't stop thinking about her meeting with Ian that morning, the newspaper article which reminded her she was tainted, an outcast from ordinary people, and a murderess in her father's eyes if not in actual fact.

She carefully set aside another measure of barm, the yeast that would be added to the barley piled in canvas sacks against the stone walls of the hut. Fresh water from a nearby burn clanked in the iron pipes attached to the still-room, and the aroma of malt filled the air. In the glen outside, crofters loaded pony carts with casks destined for shipment from seaside caves.

On Maryhead everyone from the laird to the resident gauger drank or participated in the production of illegal liquor. Without the income it brought, starvation would finish off the dwindling population.

"Ye look peaked, Margaret," one of the crofter's wives remarked. "Go outside for a breath of air."

She nodded gratefully and pulled off her muslin apron, making her way through the tangle of dogs, children, and maltsmen gathered about the small glen. At the burn behind the bothy, she knelt to rinse her hands. Without warning the headline of the newspaper clipping she had glimpsed earlier flashed into her mind. She drew back onto her heels, sighing in despair. It had been twelve years since that morning at Loch Meirneal. Would she never be free of the past?

The devil take Ian MacNeill anyway. The man seemed destined to bring nothing but trouble into her life, whether intentionally or not.

From the beginning he had threatened her in a way she did not understand, assuming an intimacy that probed too deep for comfort, that reawakened too many emotional needs. He knew more about her personal affairs than was proper. He remembered her from the days when she'd run with a fast crowd, when she had insulted him in the street, dressed like an adolescent strumpet who so desperately craved attention she would command it by any means. He had met her again in the bewildering days following her father's banishment. He knew about the accident on the loch, that the drownings had been her fault.

Yet these shameful facts about her life that Margaret herself cringed to remember had not repulsed Ian. Rather, he seemed drawn to her. Or was that only the physician in him, the compassion that came as second nature?

It might have been easier to tell if he hadn't kissed her. Each time she'd met him since then had only served to remind her of how eagerly she'd responded, parched for even the smallest drop of affection.

"Don't linger too long in the open, Margaret," one of the men called down to her from the hillside. "A pretty girl like you doesn't want to take any chances."

She smiled grimly and splashed her face and wrists with icy water. No, she didn't want to take any chances, never again. Not where her heart and Ian MacNeill were involved.

* * *

Riding along the ancient coastal road to the castle, Ian passed a row of dwarf rowan trees on the clifftops, twisted into weird shapes by the wind and bedecked with colorful tatters of tartan—offerings to the gods of ancient times. He might have been amused by the superstitious symbols had he not realized that such deeply ingrained beliefs would hamper his own work on the island.

He slowed his horse as he noticed a small gathering of men, women and children ahead, all staring at some as yet unseen object against the cliffs below. He recognized the crofter's boy Robbie in the congregation.

"Not Black William again, is it?" he called out.

"Oh, no, Doctor." Robbie ran over to greet him. "It's my cousin's betrothed—down there on Wedlock Ledge."

Ian's stomach turned over. "Is he still conscious?"

Robbie gave him a queer look. "I should hope so, walking the ledge blindfolded as he is."

Ian dismounted, pushing through the crowd with Robbie at his side. He could see the man tentatively edging barefoot across a narrow needle of rock that with one misstep or gust of wind would lead to a fatal drop into the sea.

"Why didn't anyone try to stop him?" Ian demanded of the crowd. "The man must be mad."

"Mad in love," a woman in a white-frilled cap said laughingly. "He's proving his bravery as a cragsman in order to marry Mary Hay. It's the custom here on Maryhead."

"Then pray God I remain a bachelor," Ian said with a shudder.

His head swimming from vertigo, he drew back from the edge of the cliff and returned to his horse. He could only hope the poor bugger didn't fall, and that no one would ask him to perform the postmortem if he did.

"We'll see ye walking the ledge in a month or so, Doctor," the woman in the white-frilled cap cried from the clifftop as

Ian remounted. "Wearing the blindfold to win Miss Rose's favor, I should guess."

"I wouldn't count on it, ma'am," he said politely, riding past her. "I value my life a little more than that." Amused, he spurred his horse back onto the road.

A half-hour's ride down the coast, he spotted a revenue cutter at anchor in a secluded inlet. The sight took him up short. What possible interest could the Crown have in this strange little island?

Then, glancing shoreward, he saw a dozen officers, excisemen, swarming the beach, their blue coats a blur of color in the misty grayness of the afternoon. Curious, he slowed his horse and watched as the officers climbed the path to the road, like so many toy soldiers with their helmets and bayonets. The captain arrived first, his portly figure huffing from the climb.

"Good afternoon," Ian said, leaning across the saddle pommel with an amicable smile. "On government business, are you?"

The captain looked Ian over, apparently deciding he was a man who lived on the right side of the law. "Yes, sir," he replied. "Our monthly run of the lesser islands."

"For the purpose of—?"

"Catching out illicit whiskey distillers, sir, what else?"

"Of course," Ian murmured, feeling an unexpected empathy for the captain's potential victims. "But brewing dew isn't such a serious business to engage a man of your obvious importance, is it?"

"You condone criminal activity, sir?" the captain asked shrewdly.

"No. But I do condemn the poverty that drives a man to it." His curiosity satisfied, Ian dug his heel into the mare's side. "Well, good day to you, captain. Unfortunately, I'm not enough of a hypocrite to wish you luck in your work."

Disturbed by the encounter, Ian decided impulsively to cut across the moor to save time. Shortly afterward he regretted the choice as the desolate landscape began to reinforce his sense of personal isolation. It would soon be Christmas, and then the Daft Days leading to Hogmanay. He'd never spent the New Year holiday without friends and family surrounding him.

He thought of Margaret, wondering when he would see her again and where she'd had to hurry off to this afternoon. And he cursed himself for caring when he should be grateful for his lonely single life and its safety from emotional entanglements.

Still, their lively arguments invigorated him. Her cool reserve excited him. It had become a challenge to make her laugh. And though he told himself that this mild obsession was only a symptom of his overly analytical mind, an intellectual exercise, privately he had grave doubts. Goddamnit, he wanted her.

A brown hare darted across the track. As Ian leaned forward to reassure the horse, he detected a distinctive aroma in the air, deliciously nutty and familiar. There were no crofts in sight, but he recognized that tantalizing smell. It reminded him of the breweries of Aberdeen which he had once passed daily.

Then suddenly it all made sense, the excisemen and Margaret's mysterious errand, remembered only after he'd mentioned taking a glass of whiskey.

The banker's daughter, the minister's cousin and island witch's pretty apprentice, was brewing illegal whiskey for reasons he had yet to understand. But one thing in Ian's mind was certain: Unless he could forewarn her, Margaret would be arrested and taken into custody by the officers who could only be minutes behind him on the moor.

Fifteen

Margaret leaped to her feet as a pair of Liam's collies bounded past the burn and up the hillside, barking furiously at the lone rider who had appeared at its summit. Panic erupted in the glen. Several pony carts set off at a jarring trot for the moor. Children and women ran after them to conceal the loaded whiskey casks beneath hastily pitched blankets and layers of peat.

Apparently oblivious to the chaos his appearance had created, Ian reined in his mare. "Would somebody call off the dogs?" he shouted down into the glen. "They're frightening my horse."

Unable to restrain a smile at Ian's utter lack of awareness, Margaret strode forward, almost colliding with Liam as he burst out of the bothy. "Who the hell is that dimwit on the hill?" Liam demanded. "The excisemen weren't due till next week. I'll brain that bloody gauger for misinforming me."

Margaret tossed her head. "That dimwit isn't a revenue officer. It's Dr. MacNeill."

"The doctor?" Liam said in disbelief. "Has the man lost his wig, giving us a scare like that? They're pouring out precious tubs into the burn this verra moment."

Liam's wife, having overheard this conversation, called off the dogs and passed along the word that it wasn't an exciseman in their midst, only the doctor. One by one the maltsmen halted their activities to stop and stare. His face impassive, Ian proceeded down the hill into the unfriendly silence, dismounting as he reached Margaret and Liam.

"What in God's name are you doing here?" she demanded in an amused undertone.

He pushed a gloved hand through his windblown black hair. "I thought you might like to know that the excisemen are en route to disrupt your operation." He glanced around the glen. "Very tidy it is, too."

Margaret stared at him, trying unsuccessfully to suppress a shiver as his horse nudged him against her. "How do you know about the excisemen?"

"Saw the cutter off the coast, and officers on the beach."

"I'm murdering the gauger," Liam said calmly, then pivoted on his heel, shouting toward the bothy, "To the caves! Salvage what the hell ye can!"

Margaret spun about to follow him, freezing as Ian caught her arm. "Where do you think you're going?" he asked.

"To help, of course." She stared at him over her shoulder, her face challenging. "Well, are *you* going to make yourself useful or not?"

His fingers tightened around her forearm, sending a current of warmth all the way up into her shoulder. "I have to risk my neck in your illicit venture to win back your favor?"

She tugged her arm free. "Suit yourself."

His smile faded. "It crossed my mind—well, I didn't want you to think that *I* brought that article into the manse, or that your father gave it to me."

She considered him for a moment and then motioned to the mare. "If you want to help, hitch her up to the cart and load the tubs that are outside the bothy."

Ian's brow furrowed. "We'll run straight into the revenuers on the coast road."

"Not if we cut through the glen to the caves."

He hesitated. "I'm only doing this to impress you, Margaret."

She thought about that remark as they rode shoulder to shoulder in the cart through the glen. It was quiet, except for the croaking of hooded crows above the hills and the occasional tinkling of a burn. They hurried around a few crofter children scraping gray-green lichen off rocks to use in the dyeing of tweed, and several black-faced sheep scrambled up the steep wooded slopes at their approach.

Margaret believed him when he said he hadn't brought that newspaper into the manse. But would her aunt or Stephen have kept that clipping after so many years? Strange, how it had suddenly reappeared. It seemed to reinforce her theory about Ian causing her trouble.

"Margaret, about this morning—"

"I don't wish to discuss it again." She stared straight ahead, feeling Ian watch her, sensing he could see through her indifference. "Can't you make your horse go any faster?"

"Certainly," Ian said coolly, "if you care to wait while I unhitch the cart and dispose of your illicit merchandise." He glanced over his shoulder at the hills behind. "That cold-eyed captain would probably take perverse delight in arresting a doctor as an accomplice."

"Not to mention the great Douglas Rose's daughter," Margaret said with a bitter smile. "That might change my father's mind about a reconciliation, proving he was right about me all along."

Ian gave her a long penetrating look. "He really hurt you, didn't he, lass?" he asked softly.

She shrugged, not bothering to answer. And for the remainder of the ride she made a pretense of ignoring him until, with relief, she reined in the cart before a small hillside cave concealed beneath a tangle of denuded bramble.

Liam hurried out to greet them, grinning at the sight of Ian with a cask over his shoulder. "Weel, weel. Good thing we didn't let the dogs take ye down, Doctor."

Ian swung the cask into the arms of another maltster emerging from the cave. "I'm doing this under protest, you understand."

"Aye." Liam winked at Margaret. "I kenn'd that. Never mind the rest. The men will unload it—we'll hide the cart in the cave. Best ye set off to wherever ye're going, and take Margaret with ye before the excisemen arrive. She made the mistake of insulting the captain last time he was here."

Ian brushed off his trousers. "I don't find that difficult to believe."

"I'll go back to the bothy with you, Liam," Margaret said.

"I dinna advise it."

"But the doctor has a previous appointment," she persisted, deliberately not looking at Ian.

"Only to visit the laird," Ian said. "Miss Rose is more than welcome to accompany me—for safety's sake, of course." He glanced across the moor. "Anyway, I'm good and lost now. Someone will have to show me the way."

Liam's black eyes narrowed. "We canna have him wanderin' about lost. He's liable to lead 'em straight back here in his ignorance—"

"In my what?"

"In yer innocence, sir. I meant innocence."

Margaret glanced sidelong at Ian, feeling an unwilling smile form on her lips. He looked so smug, upsetting the entire operation and then playing the hero. She might even have suspected he'd fabricated the story of the excisemen except for the young island girl in pigtails who suddenly came bouncing wildly on a pony down the hill.

"Revenuers!" the girl shouted at the top of her voice. "They've just left the bothy and are marching across the moor!"

Liam started forward to stop the lathered pony, shaking his head in chagrin. "Weel, if the excisemen didna know where to find us before, they'll know it after that racket. Margaret, get yerself out of here, lass. You and the doctor are worth more to that bastard captain than all of us combined. And take an anker of dew for the laird. Fergus, strap a couple of half-ankers to the doctor's horse."

"Now, wait a minute," Ian began.

"Och, be quiet and do as you're told," Margaret said lightly.

He grinned at her, and suddenly it seemed to Margaret that everyone, everything else faded into the background.

Her heart skipped a beat.

"Let's go then," he said, his deep voice quizzical as if her face had revealed that instant of powerful awareness.

Confused, she looked away as he moved behind her to boost her onto the horse. As he swung up into the saddle in front of her, she leaned back to discourage the least physical contact between them. But after the mare took her first unsteady steps up the hillside, Margaret had no choice but to cling to him or slide backward. Gradually, in the hope he would not notice, she eased her hands from her lap to around his waist. The nubbly texture of his tweed jacket abraded the side of her face, smelling pleasantly of the moss and heather used to dye the fabric.

"That's very nice, Miss Rose," he murmured. "Far better a way to keep a man warm than an old blanket smelling of peat."

"Perhaps you'd rather I had left you alone on the beach that day."

"Och, no. I'd not have missed your soup for the world." He shifted around to look at her, letting his hands rest briefly against hers. "Are we going the right way? I'd hate to ride straight into the revenuers."

She stared across the treeless moor, wondering why she did not feel relieved when he lifted his hands away. "Do you see the circle of standing stones in this distance?"

"Ah, yes. That would mark the remains of an ancient cere-monial meeting-place. I trust no one on the island has revived the age-old cults which required snake-worship and boiling a man's head in oil."

"Not so far as I know, Dr. MacNeill," she answered with a smile. "However, with enough provocation I'm sure the latter practice could be revived."

He chuckled quietly. "But a few heathen beliefs linger nonetheless, don't they?"

Was he making fun of her? Margaret wondered. Him with his medical degrees and fancy Latin phrases that put her boarding-school lessons to shame. Or did that warm lilt in his voice signify something else entirely?

She frowned, disturbed at the inappropriate turn of her thoughts when their safety was at risk. "As I was about to explain before you sidetracked me with your silly remark, the path veers down into the hamlet of Maryhead proper and then climbs the cliffs again to the castle. There's a loch in between, which we'll pass in a few minutes."

"Do you not ever get lonely here, Margaret?"

Unexpected pleasure rippled through her at his use of her Christian name. Did she get lonely?

"I suppose I did at first," she admitted. "But after awhile you grow accustomed to the solitude."

Ian shook his head. "I wouldn't. I'm too used to having people about me all the time. I find my own company rather wearing, I'm afraid. Too much time for reflection reveals more dark tendencies than I care to contemplate."

"I'm sorry you find us so boring on Maryhead."

"Boring?" He looked out across the small larch-pine forest that hovered just ahead and laughed. "A shipwreck, and then evading excisemen in the company of a beautiful young woman? Oh, no, my dear. This is quite heady stuff for a man who considers himself a country doctor at heart."

He slid to the ground, drawing the reins over the mare's head. "I'll walk for a spell to give the horse a rest—in case we have to make a daring escape."

Margaret let him lead her only a few paces before dismounting to walk beside him. To her surprise he turned and caught her as she would have slid to her feet.

"That wasn't necessary," she said in embarrassment.

She sensed the suppressed power in his hands, swinging her easily to the ground and then lingering at her waist. "But I enjoy playing the gentleman," he said. "And you have to admit I'll have few enough chances on Maryhead."

Margaret smiled. "There's a lawyer who lives here with two eligible young daughters—and a sea captain's widow with a pension and penchant for handsome young men."

"Well, I'm by no means handsome, and certain people have even called me old." He pulled her against him. "Do you remember that night, Margaret? You made a remark to the effect that I was old enough to be your father."

She flushed. "I've forgotten—"

"I felt every ache and creak in my joints magnified a hundredfold for months afterward." He slid his hands up her shoulders. "And you didn't even remember me—"

From the corner of her eye Margaret noticed that the horse had wandered off to crop at a patch of moorland grass. "Dr. MacNeill . . . the excisemen might see us—standing out on the open moor—"

"Hang the excisemen."

"I believe it's supposed to be the other way around," she said laughingly.

She looked up into his brooding face, her amusement fading at the subtle but unnerving change in his expression. His hands tightened around her shoulders with unmistakable urgency, and she knew he was about to kiss her. Her heart began to drum in a mixture of awakening desire and dread. She felt her body strain forward as if worked by invisible strings which he controlled.

"Close your eyes, Margaret," Ian instructed her huskily.

He lowered his head, raising one hand to cup her chin. Her body rigid, she stared up into his rough-gentle face and tried to suppress the little shivers of anticipation that shot through her. His eyes narrowed, midnight-blue to burning darkness.

"Margaret," he said, his breath warm on her cheek. "I want you so very much."

He drew her forward. Her lips parted on the soft exhalation of her sigh. The endless wash of violet-gray sky that rose above the hills shifted before her vision like a kaleidoscope, a reflection of her own bewildering emotions.

She closed her eyes.

He kissed her, his tongue outlining the fullness of her lower lip, slowly penetrating her mouth. A pleasurable languor pervaded her from shoulder to toe, and she felt herself sliding, drifting without anchor into waves of velvet warmth. She welcomed the oblivion, the violently sweet sensations that made her shudder and blindly lift her hands to his chest. She welcomed the escape from thought, and even more so from emotion.

His face reflective, Ian ran his thumb against her mouth and then drew back so that they stood apart. "Why now and not that morning in the dovecote?" he whispered roughly.

Opening her eyes, she stared up at the sky. "I'm not sure."

He wanted to pull her back into his arms and reawaken the urgent response she'd tried to resist. But when he reached for her again, she twisted away from him, the rising breeze stirring the fringe of her Paisley shawl. The horse ambled up to butt against her shoulder, and she patted it absently, trying to pretend nothing had happened.

"There's rain in the air." He glanced up, so physically aware of her his body ached with it. "Perhaps we should remount, after all. And if you want my advice—"

She moved around to the opposite side of the horse, her eyes flashing with resentment. "I *don't* want your advice," she cried. "There's no point in it, and I'm no longer a wayward child who needs the benefit of one of your lectures either!"

He leaned across the saddle to address her. "Well, it's clear to me you need someone's advice—distilling illegal whiskey and allowing men to kiss you against your wishes. *Someone* needs to take you in hand."

"You might have shown some self-control yourself," she said indignantly.

"I was in perfect control." He turned aside to untangle the reins. "I *wanted* to kiss you—and have ever since I woke up in your bed and found you spooning your foul soup into me."

There was a long silence, and Ian looked away in consternation before he caught the slow smile that lit Margaret's face. She glanced up at his profile, at his broad forehead and strongly carved chin, at the dark gypsy hair stirring in the wind. It pleased her somehow that he'd thought about kissing her, but it was a waste of time.

She began to walk toward the loch, feeling warm from the inside out. "You're a very smooth talker," she said without turning around.

With a wry smile Ian trailed after her, leading the mare toward the dimly lit stand of larch trees. "Actually," he said, "my mother claimed that that was God's way of making up for my rough looks."

The odd thing was that he didn't look rough anymore to Margaret, only dark and mysteriously attractive. She stopped and gazed down at the small peaceful loch, watching its wavelets ripple against the brown-pebbled shoreline. As she heard Ian walk up behind her, she closed her eyes and welcomed the moist assault of wind on her burning face. She could almost pretend he was holding her again, kissing her, until his startled voice broke the spell.

"Dammit, Margaret, is that what I think it is? Look behind you—"

She opened her eyes and glanced back reluctantly toward the low-lying hills they had climbed. From her vantage point she could just make out the outline of a half-dozen officers on the track, bayonets balanced on their shoulders.

"The captain and his men are well-armed, but I don't suppose they'd shoot us," Ian said, as if to convince himself.

"The dirty bastard killed two crofters last year and claimed it was an accident," Margaret retorted.

Ian looked suddenly alarmed. "What was it you said to insult the captain anyway?"

"He told me I should be ashamed of myself, a well-bred young woman associating with criminals."

"But what did *you* say to him?"

Margaret folded her arms across her chest. "Only that he should be ashamed of his stupid fat-arsed murdering self for intimidating harmless people in their homes."

"No wonder they've followed us," Ian exclaimed. He pulled the horse into the dense hazel underbrush of the little forest. "Help me unload the whiskey and roll it into the loch."

She trailed him only a few yards into the tangled stand of trees. "I'll do nothing of the sort. I see absolutely no need for such a drastic measure."

He half turned, his voice ironic. "Well, as I see it, they've got weapons to our whiskey, and we've just broken the law. They'll spot us with their binoculars in another minute, if they haven't already."

"The laird's boathouse is on this side of the loch." Unruffled, Margaret picked up her skirts and began wending a path through the hazel shrubbery. "We'll have to hide in it until they pass."

Incredulous, Ian stared after her. "With the horse?"

She didn't answer, leaving him to guide the mare down the slate-littered incline to the shore. Ignoring his complaints, she led the horse into the boathouse and concealed the whiskey beneath a tarp she'd found on the floor. Between the mare, the laird's rowboat, and fishing tackle, there was barely room inside for her or Ian to even turn around.

"Now what are we supposed to do?" he asked her, his neck

twisted at an awkward angle so as not to hit his head on the ceiling.

"Wait here until they pass overhead." She pulled a musty plaid from a peg on the wall. "I don't suppose you've anything to eat in your little black bag."

"No," he said. "But I have some medicine for you."

"No, thanks."

"You're taking it nonetheless, or I'm turning you in."

He helped her right the boat and spread out the plaid inside it so that they had somewhere to sit. The horse stirred, moving restlessly to the door which Ian had left cracked open to watch for movement on the hill.

"You certainly lead an eventful life for a gently reared girl from Aberdeen," he commented as he sat down beside her, watching the door, his legs stretched out across the thwarts. "I can't imagine the laird will be pleased with us, using his property to conceal stolen goods."

She grinned. "Macpherson is the mastermind behind the operation. Brewing dew was his own idea to save the island from starvation."

"Surely things weren't that bad."

"Failed crops, poor fishing, mass immigrations of our able-bodied men to Canada and Australia. The older islanders can't exist on Maryhead's scanty harvests, and Macpherson can't afford to feed us all from his own purse."

"The Relief Boards don't help?"

"Not enough."

"Aye," he sighed. "It's never enough."

It began to rain. The boathouse grew close and uncomfortable, errant raindrops trickling in through numerous leaks in the roof where the moss chinking had begun to disintegrate. Ian's long torso and legs refused to conform to the confined space.

"Margaret," he said after awhile, "about that kiss—"

"Don't you dare start that nonsense again." She scooted

away from him to the stern, cringing as a cold shower of rain-drops plopped down from the ceiling to the back of her neck. Silently, avoiding his amused eyes, she edged back to the bow beside him.

He grinned. "Lovely day to become outlaws, isn't it? We'd have done as well to sail around the loch in the rain at the risk of drowning."

Margaret lowered her head, not responding, her face suddenly pale and tucked into her knees. Ian exhaled softly when he realized she was reacting to what he'd said.

"God, Margaret. I wasn't thinking when I made that joke. I'm so sorry."

"You *did* read the article," she said, hurt and accusing him in the same voice.

"I'd heard the story before. Forgive me for being an insensitive fool."

"I'm no longer afraid of the water as I once was," she admitted slowly. "Living on the island I've been forced to overcome that fear. But I avoid boating unless it's necessary, and then I have nightmares for days afterward."

"I can imagine," he said, studying her face.

"When I saw the shipwreck—"

"Hush a minute." Reluctantly breaking the rare moment of closeness, he stretched forward on his knees to pry open the door another inch. A smattering of rain blew in upon him, molding the front of his shirt to the well-defined muscles of his chest. Margaret swallowed, aware again of the attraction she felt for him, resisting it.

"Is it them?" she whispered, raising her head.

He nodded, drawing the door shut without a sound. "They're sending two men down here. At least the rain washed away our tracks."

"Dr. MacNeill, I have a horrible urge to cough."

"Well, don't. Oh, damn. Wait." He began to rifle through

the black leather bag strapped across the saddle. "Chew these wafers, but be forewarned they'll make you drowsy."

"How drowsy?" she asked suspiciously.

He grinned slowly. "Not enough for you to worry about."

"It's not that stuff you mentioned . . . that renders a person unconscious?"

"It's safer than puffin soup."

"You're an evil man, Ian MacNeill," she said with a grudging smile. And that, she realized, was part of his dangerous charm, the way he could draw her out of a despairing moment to make her smile.

"And you, Margaret Rose—"

He fell silent, sinking down beside her as masculine conversation sounded outside the door. Margaret held her breath and reluctantly placed in her mouth the wafers Ian handed her. Their bitter taste made her eyes water, so she concentrated on listening to the curt exchange of voices outside recede until the steady droning of the rain absorbed them.

She sat up slowly. "Do you think they're gone?"

He gave her a warning headshake and leaned forward, listening for so long Margaret could have screamed to break the suspense. Then, without a word, he nudged open the door, arose, and went outside, returning a minute later. He towered in the doorway, the gray afternoon glare creating an aureole around him, rainwater glistening on his hair.

He crawled back into the boat beside her. "What a load of trouble for a drink we can't even taste to keep us warm."

"When we get to the castle," she said with a drowsy yawn. "We may as well wait out the rain."

Closing her eyes, she tried to concentrate on the rhythmic patter of rain on the roof . . . anything except the large muscular body pressed next to hers. His obvious strength, the heat and private scent of his skin, made her feel both protected and insecure at the same time. She realized that she should at least move so their bodies did not touch. But the strain of the day, the humid closeness, and the incessant rain lulled her, reducing thought and inhibition. She was half asleep when Ian began to sing.

"I will lift up mine eyes into the hills," he began in a deep lilting voice.

Margaret shivered with pleasure.

The psalm so beloved by her mother, sung by Ian as an old Scottish hymn, took her back to another time and place, to the hills of white heather where she had been raised. Sometimes she thought that the years before her mother and Alan had died could not have been as magical as she recalled them nor the dark years that followed as wrenching.

Still, there were days that stood out starkly in her mind above the others, marked by memories so painful she could never forget them.

Sixteen

On the morning of Margaret's eighth birthday, her father had given her a rose-cut diamond pendant, a shocking extravagance for a child, his wife Susan had said. But Douglas retorted that he could afford it, no man had ever had a more delightful daughter, and Margaret was priceless in his estimation.

She had been wearing that pendant when, after breakfast, she'd pleaded with her mother to take the children boating to the island that sat in the middle of Loch Meirneal. It was an enchanted place, the island, half mysterious dwarf-rowan woods, half bare rock littered with the debris of the merlins and swans that sheltered in its shadows. Margaret wholeheartedly believed the village folklore which claimed that the sith, the wee ones, lived there. According to legend, a very good child would be allowed to actually see the fairies on her birthday if she delivered them gifts.

Her younger sister Lilian had cried because she had a cold and wasn't allowed on the boating adventure. Gareth had stayed home sulking because it wasn't *his* birthday, he wanted to play Turkish pirates, and he didn't care about silly fairies anyway.

So only Margaret Anne, her pretty brunette mother, and two-year-old Alan Rose had set out for the loch that morning, singing ditties and carrying a picnic lunch to share with the swans.

Margaret could remember her mother's voice as she de-

scended the footpath from the glen to discover the loch enshrouded in mist.

"What a miserable day to go boating, Margaret. You can
barely see your wee island from here. Is your heart really set
on this folly?"

Margaret was silent, pondering the cold sinister stretch of
water they must cross to reach the island. Even the old ruined
Castle Meirneal high upon the hill, where she and Gareth
played, had an unappealing look without its fairy-tale backdrop
of woolly blue clouds.

There was a bad feeling to the place that morning, a feeling
that made her stomach twist. Perhaps she felt guilty over her
mother's eagerness to please her, knowing that Mama hadn't
quite recovered her strength from a bout of pneumonia last
spring. Or perhaps she could sense that the *Each Uisge,* the
water kelpies, were lurking about in the loch, waiting to do
their mischief.

"Och, no, Mama. We'll go next year."

Her mother smiled and ruffled Margaret's hair. "What—wait
another year with that moping face to haunt me and you staying up past midnight every night to glimpse the fairies in the
garden? I couldn't stand it."

"Do you think we'll see them today then?" Margaret asked
eagerly, her unease forgotten. "I've brought the acorn cups for
their tea and foxgrass to weave their beds."

"We'll see. Now mind your brother while we get into the
boat, and Margaret, he's your responsibility while I'm rowing."

"Boat," Alan shrieked mirthfully as Margaret hefted his
squirming body into her arms to position them both in the
boat. He had been dressed by his nursemaid for the occasion
in a green bonnet and black velvet doublet with a plaid like
a little prince.

"Hold still, you naughty wee worm," Margaret said, "or I'll
give you to the Gille Dubh—the black fairy—for breakfast."

"We shouldn't have brought him," her mother said with a worried frown.

"I'll mind him, Mama."

True to her word, she occupied Alan with nursery rhymes and games of peek-a-boo until her mother begged them to stop and enjoy the peaceful silence of the loch.

"Do you ever pretend you're the Lady of the Lake, Mama, the enchantress Merlin loved? Or what about Lady Forbes of Castle Meirneal, whose husband hanged himself when she drowned?"

"What an imagination you have." Her mother smiled fondly, leaning forward in rhythm with the oars. "Look under the canvas for the life-belts. We're almost to the birches."

She spoke of the shadowed birch copse on the shore to her right. The family used the trees in summer to mark how far out the older children could wade. There was a dramatic drop-off after that point, or sooner if it had rained.

Margaret peeled back the canvas tarp folded across the stern, dividing her attention between Alan, the island, and the cork life-belts that her father had insisted be worn since a trout fisherman's child had drowned in the loch last summer.

"There's only one belt here."

"One? That's odd. Well, put it on your brother and be very careful as you do."

"Fith," Alan said. He waved his hazel fishing rod at the metallic glimmer of movement beneath the dark-blue waters. "Fith, Maggie mine!"

"Sit down, Alan," Susan said firmly. "Margaret, don't let him play so near the side."

"I am trying to get this damned belt undone. Someone's put it in a horrid sailor's knot."

"You'll not use such language, Margaret Anne, else I'll send you straight back to the house, birthday or no. And that's the end of playing with the village children for you."

"Well, I cannot untie the stupid knot, Mother."

"Then give it to me."

"Here—"

"Margaret, watch your brother!"

Margaret swiveled around at the waist just as Alan leaned over the side of the boat to dangle his fishing rod into the water.

"No, Alan," she cried. She lunged for him as he bent even farther forward and then hit the water with an outraged scream.

The unbalanced boat veered back toward the shore at the sudden shifting of weight. Alan sank, beyond her reach, a white swan feather from his bonnet floating on the loch.

"Oh, God," Susan said. She flung down the oars and scrambled forward. "Oh, God, help us. No. Oh, God."

Shaking uncontrollably, Margaret threw aside the useless life-belt and poised to dive overboard. But her mother was faster, though her heavy woolen cape and gown billowed out around her to impede her efforts.

"Scream for help, Margaret! Scream for old Simon on the hill. Look, that's him up by the castle now—"

Margaret shouted until her throat was raw, all the while watching her mother dive clumsily beneath the water. But there was no response from the mist-swathed hills, and she thought frantically that her mother had imagined seeing Simon by the castle. The old shepherd had failing eyesight and poor hearing anyway.

The boat had drifted toward the island. In horror, she realized it had been too long since her mother and Alan had disappeared beneath the loch. Her mind numb with dread, she scanned the placid surface for the slightest hint of movement and then jumped into the loch. The shock of cold convulsed her whole body. She swallowed a mouthful of water, coughing, choking. She was so dazed she wasn't sure whether the white cloaked figure standing on the shoreline was real or merely an illusion of the mist against the trees. It looked hauntingly unreal, its arm outstretched in silent supplication. Or was it a birch limb that stretched outward from the shadows?

She ducked and swam downward with all her strength. The cold so stung her eyes that she couldn't see whether the nebulous object which waved tauntingly before her was her mother's cape. She tunneled toward it and grasped in blind desperation, her fingers closing around a swatch of water grasses. There was said to be a beast living in the depths of the loch, and cruel, carnivorous water kelpies. . . .

She remembered little after that. Somehow she had resurfaced to cling to the boat, too heartsick and weary to bother climbing aboard, and the current had washed her ashore where an hour later Simon MacTear had found her flung out on the sand in a state of shock.

What stood out in her memory then were the low-voiced villagers who arrived in droves to comb the loch, led by her father, gray-faced and silent in helpless grief.

They sent her back home with her nursemaid, but as evening fell, she returned to the loch to hide in the copse and watch, by the light of bog-fir torches, the grim efforts to retrieve the two bodies.

There was a hoarse cry from one of the villagers, but Margaret could not watch as her mother was lifted from the loch into a rowboat.

No one had noticed her presence. No one noticed the little girl stumbling back to the house, sobbing until her face was bloated and her empty stomach heaved spasmodically along the way against the shock.

It was as she climbed the stairs of the silent mansion to her room that she remembered the ominous figure who had stood on the shore that morning and so impassively watched the accident. Margaret felt a fear squeeze her chest that was so profound she almost fainted. The figure could only have been a banshee, the woman of peace, patiently waiting to claim the souls of the mother and child who had lost their lives in the loch.

Seventeen

Ian had almost fallen asleep himself when she began to stir, her hands pushing at the plaid he had drawn over her.

"You're dreaming, Margaret," he said, touching her cheek. "I should have warned you that the wafers have that effect."

She stared at him for several seconds before exclaiming indignantly: "You're holding me—you've got your arm around my shoulders!"

"Well, you fell asleep with your head on mine," he said calmly. "It was the only way I could get comfortable myself. What were you dreaming about anyway?"

Margaret closed her eyes, shaken by the vivid and horrifying memory of that morning. "It—it wasn't a dream. Not exactly. I wish it had been."

She wriggled around in an unsuccessful attempt to dislodge his arm. His hand drifted down her shoulder to the small of her back, drawing her onto her side against him.

Her voice shook. "Ian—"

"Be still a moment, Margaret. Just be still a damned minute and let me hold you."

Ian felt her hesitate and then gradually relax, closing her eyes as she laid her face against his chest. Please God, he thought distantly. Don't let me fall in love with another woman who's going to put me through hell. At least not yet.

Countless moments passed before either of them spoke or

stirred, experiencing the quiet exhilaration of an attraction at last recognized if not accepted.

"It's stopped raining by the sound of it," Margaret whispered awkwardly.

"Has it?" he asked in a voice which said he didn't give a damn about the weather.

His heart began to pound. It occurred to him that he could kiss her again—there was no resistance in her now, but he had glimpsed a window of vulnerability beneath her usual cool reserve. He glanced downward. She rested against him in a sort of awkward grace, her hair tangled around his wrist, her arms positioned at a peculiar angle between their two bodies, to serve as a physical barrier, he supposed. He noted the six unfastened pearl buttons of her bodice, looked lower still to the curve of her stockinged calf visible below the eyelet lace of her drawers where her gown had ridden up, muslin embroidered with roses and red moorland mud.

That inch of lace intrigued him, tormented and flooded him with forbidden urges. He imagined pressing her beneath him on the plaid, exploring the secret places that were hidden by the layers of her clothing. The force of his desire, so sudden, so ungentle, took him by surprise. His hand closed around the curve of her hip. His fingers crushed the soft fabric of her skirts in his frustration to touch her.

She lifted her head from his chest. He heard her gasp softly, as if she sensed his violent fantasies, his battle for control. He wedged his knee between her legs, breathing hard, at war with himself.

She looked soft, sensual and defenseless, her cheeks flushed like a child's. His own clothing seemed suddenly to smother him; the air around them too thick to draw into his lungs. Without warning, she lowered her left arm, inadvertently brushing the constriction in his trousers.

"God, Margaret . . ."

She leaned back upon his arm, her pose lazy, languid . . .

provocative without design. Her hands lifted to push impatiently at her hair, the movement thrusting her breasts against the partially unbuttoned bodice. His throat closed and he could not look away.

Something of his thoughts must have shown on his face. Her eyes darkened suddenly to slate. Her hands lowered to her sides, her fingers curling into her palms. He saw her lips part on a quickened inrush of breath. He smiled, torn between tenderness and reckless male triumph.

"Ian?" she whispered, her voice almost inaudible.

He lowered his head and kissed the hollow of her throat where a bluish vein pulsed against the paleness of her skin. She did not move, not a muscle. She did not move or seem to breathe and he was unsure how far he dare press his advantage.

He brought his hands sliding across her shoulders, dragging her bodice and chemise down. He cupped her partially exposed breasts and rubbed his face against her, against muslin and scented female skin.

She gasped and twisted to the side. He knew he should stop. He knew so much better than she how a single act of passion could alter a life, but his mind disregarded the warning. He closed his eyes, his heart beating as if it would burst. He caught a nipple in his mouth and suckled hard, his lips moving against her.

"Ian . . ."

There was a sufficient measure of panic in her voice to bring him back to his senses. He sat forward abruptly, with his face to the door, breathing in uneven spurts. He could feel her staring at him in bewilderment. He couldn't believe himself how close he had come to physical anarchy. Waves of heat shuddered down his entire body, ebbing away to an uncomfortable flush.

"What were you dreaming about?" he asked her . . . anything, any subject, to detract from the animal force of his own lust.

She drew herself upright. "My family. The past."

He exhaled slowly. They were going to pretend nothing had happened. Bury that dangerous spark of passion beneath polite conversation. He did not think he could bear it. He wanted to run outside and jump into the cold numbing waters of the loch.

"Sad memories?" he asked her.

"Yes," she said, her voice remote, so cool he could kill her, and then she glanced around. "Have you ever heard of Castle Meirneal—Castle Merlin in Aberdeenshire where the infamous Lord Forbes hid Charles II from Cromwell and later committed suicide after his wife drowned?"

"No." He looked at her over his shoulder, murdering Charles II, Cromwell, Lord Forbes in his mind. "Was it a special place for you?"

"It overlooked the loch."

"The same—"

"Yes." She smoothed her fingers over a snag in the plaid. "Before my mother and Alan drowned, Gareth and I played there almost every day . . . King Charles and Cromwell's men, Lord and Lady Forbes. We were forever chopping off Lilian's head or hanging her from the ceiling beams."

He smiled at that, thinking of his own childhood, of the horrors he'd inflicted on Andrew and his sisters as he'd played physician to treat their imaginary woes. He realized how fortunate he had been in his life, until recently, and he could not help wondering how deeply her family had damaged her, Douglas with his prolonged grief and blame; Angus, the missionary, whose zealous morality had probably exceeded even the rigid Victorian code.

"There were some good memories then," he said, encouraging her to continue.

"It was a special place, before, a fairy-tale castle in the clouds," she said. "And then everything changed. The last time

I saw it, it seemed no more than a cold lonely ruin, a sentinel to death and sadness, and I couldn't bear to look at it from the carriage. That was the day we left our country house to move into Aberdeen."

"Our perspective changes over time. Who knows what you would feel for the place if you returned there now?"

She shook her head. "I never could. I suppose the castle has always had an unhappy history—it's said heather will not grow in soil that has absorbed blood spilled in violence. But as children we never noticed the absence of heather on the battlements where we played."

She smiled and began to refold the plaid. "You inspire confidences, Dr. MacNeill."

He was flattered, but he didn't have much chance to enjoy the feeling. He could tell by her sudden silence, by how she edged away, that she'd already begun to withdraw. Undoubtedly she regretted that she had revealed so much to him. He felt disappointed and even cheated, allowed a glimpse into her soul and then shoved back before he could begin to help her. Never mind the physical indiscretion of only minutes ago. This rejection was far worse. Intolerable.

Yet even so he wished he could restore the childhood faith she had lost, and in the process perhaps hasten the healing of his own broken dreams.

"Perhaps it's time to let go of the painful memories, Margaret, to stop dwelling on what happened so long ago."

He saw instantly that it had been the wrong thing to say. She rose, ducking around the horse to the door.

"It has stopped raining," she said, self-conscious. "It should be safe to go."

Ian rose to his feet. His face troubled, he restrapped the whiskey casks to the mare, then pushed open the door for Margaret, pretending not to notice how she fumbled to refasten the half-dozen buttons at her throat. His fascination with seducing her seemed laughably pathetic, and he considered it a perversity of human nature that she could so easily recover her composure from an experience that had left an unforgettable impression on his mind.

He opened the door, feeling a wave of cold moisture against his face. The air smelled of decaying bracken and wet sand. He saw Margaret's hand freeze at her throat, the look of guilty surprise on her face.

A shadow fell across their path, the shadow of a man, but it was not Stephen. Instinctively Ian stepped in front of Margaret, too late noticing the firearm pointed at his chest.

Eighteen

"Of course I wouldn't have shot you, Margaret. I'd just bagged a grouse on the moor when I noticed the boathouse door ajar."

Thomas Macpherson, university-educated, effeminate, and Edinburgh-born, was the last person on earth Ian would have pegged as a typical Laird of the Isles. The slender sandy-haired man's embarrassment at intruding upon what he clearly assumed to be the denouement of a lovers' tryst embarrassed both Margaret and Ian in turn. Stuttering profuse apologies for his ill-timed appearance, Macpherson made Margaret blush and Ian almost believe that there had been more than an accidental romantic twist to their interlude in the boathouse.

Almost. The ungracious remark she made under her breath as Ian helped her into the laird's trap neatly squelched that little fantasy: "Stop hovering about me so, Dr. MacNeill. Thomas is the worst gossip on the island. He'll assume there's something between us."

Disgruntled, he followed on horseback behind the trap as it took the winding seaside road to the castle. The terrain seemed friendlier here, stone hedgerows bursting with colorful rowanberries, crofts with curling wisps of smoke rising into the dark November sky. Margaret too seemed on friendly enough terms with the young blond laird, laughing at his description of a castle party, chiding when he mentioned the deer hunt he had arranged to attract business to the island. Clearly she enjoyed a close relationship with Macpherson, and she made herself quite at home once they reached the castle, kneeling to play with the leggy deerhounds that came bounding out to greet her from the great hall.

"Get down, you big stupid things," Macpherson shouted from the doorway.

The dogs, in an orgy of bad manners, completely ignored him. Sighing, he strode into the hall to the blazing fireplace, unintentionally posing beneath an oil painting of himself in the garb of an ancient island chieftain: spear, winged helmet, and chain mail, standing with his disobedient dogs against a cairn.

Ian turned away to hide a smile. Presumably Macpherson, who had purchased and not inherited Maryhead, felt compelled to play the role of the laird to the hilt.

"I was worried when you didn't arrive earlier, Dr. Mac-Neill," he explained as he lit his pipe at the driftwood fire with a twig. "I'd not have worried, naturally, had I known Miss Rose was your escort."

Margaret looked up from the hearth, her face flushed from the heat. "I shouldn't stay. Agnes will be concerned."

"You'll have to stay for an early supper—cock-a-leekie soup and fried scallops, with apple tarts for dessert."

She smiled, relenting.

Ian watched her while pretending to examine a rusty suit of armor on the wall. It intrigued him to witness this spontaneous facet of her character, and strangely it made him jealous, realizing how she had deliberately kept *him* at a distance when she could so easily relax with another man.

His jealousy overshadowed what would have been an excellent supper served in the drafty hall.

"Well, Dr. MacNeill, how do you find Maryhead so far?" the laird asked him over dessert. "Did the islanders embrace you with their usual Gaelic warmth?"

Ian fished a dog hair from his glass of sherry. "Not exactly."

Macpherson laughed. "As warm as an arctic wind off the Atlantic is their welcome. I know. I'm an incomer, too. They'll never accept us, you understand, no matter how many of them I support and you heal. They've only taken to Margaret because she's young and pretty . . . and fey. She understands their superstitions."

Margaret slipped a piece of scallop to the dogs slavering under the table. "They've not all accepted me."

"I had hopes of building a hospital," Ian said to Macpherson. "The previous physician here had mentioned it in his reports as a possibility."

"Aye, when Maryhead had a population, before the lure of sheepfarming in Australia and New Zealand stole our young blood away. We're a dying breed, we islanders. That's why I turn a blind eye to the illegal distilleries—the crofters have to eat. That's also why, despite Margaret's lovely pouting, I've decided to open the island as a resort for holidaymakers from the mainland."

"I do not pout," she said, taking what Ian noticed was her second glass of wine.

He put down his glass. "Holidaymakers—here? What a ghastly notion. Who in their right mind would visit Maryhead for pleasure?"

Before Macpherson could reply, the carved oaken doors flew open and Jamie Shaw, so distraught he forgot to doff his hat, barged into the hall like a cannonball.

"Forgive the intrusion, my lord, but we've had trouble again on the cliffs."

Macpherson dabbed at his sparse beard with a serviette and rose. "What sort of trouble?"

"Another boatload of those thievin' bastards from across the channel have carted away a half-dozen ewes as bold as you please. Euan Bruce took it upon himself to go after them with his staff. They beat him something fierce, m'lord, about the head and then—then they shoved him off the cliff."

Macpherson looked sick. "He's dead then?"

"No, m'lord. He managed to land on a ledge and his wife got the cragsmen to rescue him. They've carried him here in the cart, but—"

Ian left the table. "Where is he now?"

"His wife had him taken round to the kitchen. She didn't want him bleedin' on the laird's carpets."

"Oh, for Christ's sake, the silly besom," Macpherson said, then, "Dr. MacNeill, is there anything I can bring you?"

"Yes. I'll probably need clean straw—chaff, some sheets. Miss Rose, if you could heat some water and lay out several towels."

"Of course. I'll take you to the kitchen."

Macpherson stopped him at the door. "Now listen, Dr. Mac-Neill, this is your chance. Euan is a popular man on the island. If you save his life, you'll be a Maryhead hero for eternity. If you don't . . ."

It wasn't as grim as Ian had feared. The man had sustained fractures of the right collum femoris and tibia, a dislocated ankle, and a brain contusion, but not the compound fracture that would have surely caused a fatal infection. Ian ordered the kitchen cleared of crofters who had filtered in to watch, only Macpherson and Euan's wife, rough-faced and silent, re-maining by the fire.

From the corner of his eye, he noticed Margaret move to-ward the door. "I could use your help, Miss Rose."

She revolved slowly. "What would you have me do? I didn't wish to interfere."

He edged away from the table where Euan rested, chalk white and silent but for an occasional gasp of pain. "All you have to do is administer the stuff in this inhaler until I stop counting. The mask is laid over his nose like this, the tube is placed inside his mouth."

She stared down at the canister of chloroform while he un-hooked the velvet face-piece to demonstrate its application.

"What a strange apparatus," she remarked. "What will it do to him?"

"Put him unconscious while I cauterize his wounds and set the fractures."

"Unconscious?" Mrs. Bruce turned from the fire, her plain face anxious. "Euan, should I not fetch the charmer and ask her advice?"

"What for?" her husband said with mild scorn. "It was church bugs for the dysentery she gave my cousin's child and put him in the grave."

"But she said—" The woman glanced at Ian, her voice dropping to a frightened hush. "Did she not warn us about *him?*"

"Who knows what Morag's blether means, all her talk of ghosts and evil spirits?" Euan said, pain making his voice impatient. "Doctor, how long will this queer device keep me down?"

"For several minutes," Ian replied. "Please, is there anything I should know about the condition of your heart?"

"It's still beating, Doctor," Euan joked, grimacing. "Why do you ask?"

"Inhalation can be dangerous to a patient with a weak heart," Ian explained, then lowered his voice as he removed a square of gauze from his bag. "Margaret, I'll have to bleed him without benefit of leeches. Have Macpherson take his wife outside, and ask him for a needle and thread for you to use."

She gazed down at the jagged lacerations on Euan's face and arms, feeling perspiration begin to gather between her breasts. From experience she knew that even to set a dislocated ankle could cause excruciating pain.

"Am I to stitch his wounds?" she asked Ian, biting her lip.

He shook his head. "I'll do that, but you can sew the sheet around the foot stirrup he'll need to support his leg."

She prayed suddenly, for his sake and not just Euan's, that he would succeed. "How will you know when he's unconscious?"

"You can tell by the movements of the eye," he replied. "The pupil should be contracted." He smiled. "Failing that, I usually pull a hair from the eyebrow or beard for a reaction."

Margaret smiled unwillingly, impressed by his confidence.

He proceeded in silence, dimly conscious of her watching him as he cauterized Euan's wounds, then swiftly set, bandaged, and splinted the unconscious man's fractures. Not once did she mention amulets or superstitious remedies to rival his medicine. But only moments after Euan Bruce had been anesthetized, Ian noticed there appeared on the table a rowan branch fashioned into a crude cross, the universal Scottish charm against evil.

He glanced up and Margaret shook her head in silent denial, which in a strange way reinforced his self-confidence. She trusted *him* above her magic. If only for a moment, if only for the duration of the operation, it was enough to make his spirits soar.

It was late when he finished, slumping in the ladder-back chair by the fire while the servants went quietly about scrubbing the stone floor. Euan Bruce slept on a pallet in the corner. Margaret, standing over him with his wife at her side, stared down at the rowan branch, at her tidy stitchery on the stirrup, and then at the inhaler Ian had designed.

"He felt no pain," Mrs. Bruce marveled. "I cannot credit it, that devilish device—"

Emotion deepened Margaret's voice. "It's a gift from God, the greatest blessing to mankind that has ever been invented," she said quietly.

"We'll see, won't we?" the woman said under her breath.

Margaret frowned. "What do you mean?"

"Well, Euan's not awake yet. Who can say whether he's been blessed or cursed?"

Blessed or cursed.

Margaret glanced over at Ian, her heart heavy with an uncomfortable influx of emotion: admiration, envy, awe. She would never be able to look at him in the same light again after what she had just witnessed. In fact, she was really seeing him for the first time, seeing past his superficial arrogance to the most fascinating person she had ever met.

Lord Macpherson brought Ian a glass of whiskey, unable to contain his enthusiasm. "It was fantastic, Dr. MacNeill, that stuff you used to put him to sleep. If they'd had that a few years ago, my father wouldn't have been afraid to have the operation that might have saved his life. He suffered from the stones, as I understand, but he feared having himself cut open."

Ian sighed. "Anesthesia has benefits we haven't even begun to discover."

"And dangers, I imagine."

Ian thought suddenly of Roger with sharp regret. It saddened him that the memories of their friendship had been overshadowed by Lucy Patton's reaction of wild anger and accusation when Ian had explained to her about the fatal experiment in his laboratory, that Roger's sacrifice might save untold lives.

"Yes, there are dangers. It is after all a new science." He took a drink and stretched his stiff neck, noticing that Margaret had left the kitchen. "Where is Miss Rose?"

"Oh, Margaret." Macpherson leaned forward to retrieve the whiskey bottle from the floor. "She asked to be taken home in the trap. Nothing could induce her to stay the night in the castle."

"The proper Miss Rose."

Macpherson laughed. "Yes, but that's not why she won't remain here. She believes we're haunted, the castle inhabited by the spirits of the bloodthirsty clansmen who so enjoyed depopulating the neighboring islands. Fortunately, MacNeill, you and I are both so exhausted from this afternoon's ordeal that we could sleep through a summer of supernatural occurrences. Your bed and bath are being prepared."

Ian nodded and subsided into silence. How could she leave without so much as a farewell, an acknowledgment of what they had shared in the course of the afternoon? Disgruntled, he drained his glass and stood. Halfway to the door, Macpherson called him.

"By the way, Margaret reminded me about the annual Hogmanay Ball we hold at the castle. You might want to escort her and Agnes across the moors for the occasion. We celebrate the New Year in grand fashion."

"Did Miss Rose suggest you invite me?"

"Oh, no, dear fellow. That was my idea—can't have the hero of the hour a wallflower on Hogmanay now, can I?"

Ian glanced at Euan Bruce lying in the shadows of the kitchen. "You'll do something about the sheep stealing?"

"What can one do, MacNeill, against thieves and ruffians? The sheriff's substitute has promised to investigate, but we are as defenseless as were the original inhabitants of Maryhead to repel their Viking invaders. There are some things one must accept."

"Accept no adversity," Ian said unthinkingly. "That's my personal motto."

"One could perish on one's knees, my friend, mouthing those words. One could expire . . . simply awaiting the favor of Miss Rose, for example."

Ian's fatigue temporarily lifted. "You speak from experience?"

"No, she and I both enjoy our solitude, and I have always been too selfishly fond of her friendship to encourage a love match between us. Poor Margaret. Poor wounded mermaid. I would not wish to see either of you hurt. Guard your feelings—if it isn't too late."

His face expressionless, Ian began to rebutton his shirtsleeves. "Of course it isn't. I barely know her."

But it was a lie, a rueful lie. It had been too late from that very first evening in Aberdeen, and Ian knew it.

He fell asleep that night aware he had begun to deceive himself, and when he awoke less than an hour later, it was with a sense of panic that his life was slipping out of control.

He got up from the bed, restless, and went to the window, opening the shutters to admit the brisk sea breeze. From the tower he could see the winding coastal road and on it a lone cart rolled away from the castle gates.

Euan Bruce's cart. Ian could make out the man's figure in the back; the white sheet of his stirrup, and the lumpy outline of his wife as she drove the ponies. There was a woman he did not recognize beside her, small, raven-haired, a woman silhouetted against the moonlight. And at the fork in the road to the moor, she turned and looked up at the window, raising her hand to Ian in a salute that might have expressed triumph or acknowledgment.

Morag Strong. He knew it without being told. The charmer who had apparently taken his presence as a personal challenge to her power. Would she fight him over possession of Margaret, too? he wondered.

It was war.

After the incident in the black hut with old Alice Fergusson, it had become common knowledge on the island that Margaret Rose and the new doctor had declared professional war. The truce they had called in the laird's castle over Euan Bruce had been soon forgotten.

Their second minor skirmish occurred a week before Christmas, when Ian was called to the crofts to treat a young farmer who had burned his hand on a griddle. His distressed wife had immediately summoned Margaret, and then, as an afterthought, Dr. MacNeill.

Ian ordered an application of linen rags soaked in cold water until the pain lessened and then a bandage using carbolized zinc ointment.

Margaret suggested holding the burned hand in St. Bridget's well for three hours and seven minutes and then a poultice of honey and crushed comfrey leaves.

The poor young farmer looked bewildered, asking Margaret, "Should I burn the other hand, Miss Rose, to be fair to you both?"

Ian glanced at Margaret, holding back a smile. "That's a rather original interpretation of Solomon's wisdom. No. Just follow my advice, lad, and you'll be fine. St. Bridget's well, seven minutes—that's a load of nonsense, for lack of a more appropriate word that I can't use in front of the women."

Outside, Margaret marched right past Ian to her cart, her nose high in the air.

"You'll walk into something like that, not watching where you're going," Ian said, folding his arms across the fence where he'd tethered his horse.

She ignored him.

"And," he continued with a lazy smile, staring admiringly at the sleek stockinged calf she displayed as she rearranged her skirts on the seat, "you might seriously hurt yourself and require the services of a doctor."

She shot him a frosty look and clucked to the ponies, glancing back in disbelief as he vaulted onto his horse to follow. Pretending to be unaware of his presence, she drove directly to her next patient, a young nursing mother whose baby was not thriving. Margaret recommended fenugreek tea, an amulet of moonstones, and putting the child to the breast more often during the night.

Ian prescribed sulphate of iron for the baby and a nightly tonic of ginger beer for the mother.

The mother nodded and privately decided to wear the moonstones, drink the beer, and wean the baby.

"She didn't trust you," Margaret told Ian with a smug smile as they walked together from the cottage.

"Me?" Ian said, his confidence unshaken. "It was you and that silly necklace. And St. Bridget's water for a burn."

He tsked insultingly and strode past her.

Margaret stopped in her tracks, resisting an impulse to throw a stone at his head as he paused at the gate. "That well water is the coldest water on the island," she retorted, sweeping through the gate he opened. "It's as cold as—as—"

"—as cold as your lonely bed at night?" he asked softly, coming up right behind her.

"No." She turned slowly, smiling, and poked him in the chest with her forefinger. "As cold as the heart of a physician who treats patients and not people."

Ian frowned.

"Good day, Dr. MacNeill," she said cheerfully. "I'm on to my next case."

He pretended to look alarmed. "And I wasn't called?"

Margaret sauntered away and climbed into the cart, her smile broadening. "It's a case of the evil eye on a milk cow. Rather out of your realm, wouldn't you say?"

"Rather more in Morag Strong's, actually," he retorted.

She shook her head in good-humored chagrin.

Ian broke into an amused grin and watched her drive away, tempted to ride after her, for the sheer pleasure of her spirited company, for the dangerous exhilaration he felt when they were together.

Still, he could afford to bide his time. This was a small island, an intimate if weird world, in which he and Margaret would inevitably meet again, and again.

Nineteen

Christmas morning dawned gray and cold, hoarfrost riming the eaves of the secluded stone manse. On the doorstep outside, Ian scraped a wedge of icy mud from his bootheel and let himself into the house, listening to the grandfather clock ticking in the silence.

He drew off his gloves and dropped them onto the hallstand.

Walter Armstrong materialized from the rear of the house. Pot-bellied, bandy-legged Walter, in baggy blue tartan trousers and a lambskin cap, he was a dismal Yuletide companion.

He pulled off his cap and took Ian's cloak and scarf, his cadaverous face without expression. "Are you ready for your tea, sir? Fresh barley bannocks, kippered herrings and eggs."

"Yes. Lovely. But I thought you and Mrs. Armstrong had gone to kirk." Despite his aversion to spending Yule alone, Ian would have preferred solitude to the bony-faced Walter and his annoyingly inquisitive wife Sybil.

"We are leaving, sir. But Sybil thought she should wait to learn the outcome of the delivery you just attended. The father is rumored to be a great drunkard and the mother a wee sloven. Pity the poor bastard born to them, I say, sir."

Ian paused. "Is anyone in the child's family a personal friend of yours?"

"Why, no, sir."

"Then why should your wife care about the details of the child's delivery . . . or its conception?"

He did not look back to see Walter's reaction but continued up the stairs to wash and shave. The familiar ritual took the edge off his anger and made him regret his impatient outburst. He usually didn't take out his temper on his inferiors, but Walter the butler had become superfluous in a house where there were never any callers, and his wife's faultless housekeeping seemed wasted on an employer who spent all his time writing medical treatises. The only good thing he could say about them was that they did seem to understand a doctor's life.

He sighed in relief as a door downstairs opened and closed. With a freshly laundered shirt slung over his bare shoulder, still toweling off his face, he hurried down the stairs for the late breakfast which would compensate somewhat for Sybil Armstrong's scandalmongering ways.

Margaret stood in the entrance hall. Willowy, striking Miss Rose in a dark blue velvet dress with a sculptured bolero jacket, which he admired as she unselfconsciously stripped off her cloak. She had no idea how beautiful she was, the sensual power she had over him, and that was part of her appeal.

He broke into a delighted smile. "Hello."

She swiveled around toward him, her eyes widening at the sight of his naked chest. In silence she looked up at his grinning face and then began to fuss with the cloak and basket draped over her arm. He finished buttoning his shirt, feeling a surge of desire for her overcome him, raw and filled with forbidden promise, the most irreverent Christmas morning fantasy he could imagine.

"Is this a social call, or am I being summoned to resuscitate a goat who's had a Yule accident?"

"And Happy Christmas to you." She smiled primly and took from her basket a small package wrapped in a flour cloth. "Shortbread for your tea. You have a spot of soap on your chin."

He put his hand to his face. He felt faintly embarrassed, but also pleased by her personal attention. "Did I get it?"

She came forward to take the towel from his shoulder. "The other side. Aren't you cold?"

"Not in the least."

He caught her hand as it brushed his cheek, drawing her toward him until their bodies barely touched. Then slowly he inhaled, the creases at the sides of his mouth deepening in an unconscious smile. Margaret's lips parted a little and she leaned back, dropping her basket to the floor.

"What are you doing?" she whispered, her voice both curious and uncertain.

Ian stared down at her face, his eyes riveted to hers, wondering if what he saw in their blue-gray depths—confusion, exhilaration, desire—reflected Margaret's churning emotions or only his. It was almost agony, the teasing way her body touched his, the sweet pressure of her breasts against his bare chest, the warmth and fragility of her hand in his. For a dangerous moment, his mind went blank.

"What are you doing?" she repeated, more forcefully.

Not now, he warned himself. Don't make an amorous ass of yourself on Christmas morning. He sighed heavily, releasing her hand. "Why did you come?"

Every muscle in Margaret's body seemed to quiver with the release of coiled tension. Why had she assumed he was going to kiss her again—because deep inside, she'd been willing it to happen?

"I came to invite you to Christmas dinner," she said in a deceptively casual voice. "Agnes is burning a goose—possibly the kitchen, too—and I've made some perfectly sodden plum pudding. We're in a celebrating mood. Kenneth has just come home for a month."

"Kenneth?" Ian looked puzzled.

"Agnes's husband. After dinner we're all walking to Clootie Hill to watch the Yule bonfires. It's good fun, and we've a load of driftwood to contribute. Anyway, it's up to you, if you care to join us."

She broke off, her hand lifting to her hair. Ian took notice of the feminine gesture, of how animated she had become.

"If you have other plans," she began again.

"No. No. Well, actually I had been invited to dine with Martin Twaddle and his family. You know, the lawyer with the eligible daughters."

Her eyes glinted. "Ah. Mary and Barbara, the twittering Twaddles, as Agnes uncharitably calls them. I trust they don't still suffer from that dreadful dyspepsia."

Ian frowned. "Dyspepsia?"

"Nothing that should bother a doctor, just an indiscriminate belch now and then. They practically live on my peppermint tea and comfrey. Mary believes it could possibly correct her bowed legs." Margaret turned to the hall mirror, draping her cloak around her shoulders. "Well, I've delivered the invitation. Shall I tell Agnes you're coming or not?"

Ian watched her reflection, fascinated. "I have no presents for anyone. Unless I brought pills. Do you think a gift of pills is inappropriate?"

She smiled, refastening the frogs of her cloak. "We've nothing for you either. By the way, Stephen is back. He'll probably drop by to see you before dinner."

"He's come back—"

She went to the door. "Only to say goodbye."

Stephen again. So that explained her good spirits. "I'm sorry," he said, but he wasn't. "On your account, that is."

She shrugged, her hand on the latch. "He mentioned that he wanted to sort through the books he'd left behind here. Oh, in case you'd wondered, he denied any knowledge of that newspaper article."

"Yes. I had wondered."

"He said—he believes there won't be another minister coming to the island for several more months, so the manse is yours to use until then."

"I'm grateful," he said politely. "I've already set up my laboratory."

She glanced past him to the parlor, and Ian wished suddenly that she would leave. That beguiling glint in her eye, the pretty dress, had not been for his benefit after all. Agnes had probably put her up to the supper invitation, too.

"I saw Euan Bruce a little while ago," she said after a distracted pause. "He seems well enough."

"Except in spirit," Ian agreed. "That beating took the heart out of him."

"Well, he isn't a young man," Margaret said. "Anyway, I'm going to call on Peggy Kerr now. Just to see how she and the new bairn are faring. I thought I'd give her some shortbread and fresh milk."

"She could use the nourishment," Ian said. "And some rest. When I left her, a gaggle of women had formed a circle around the cradle and were waving some sort of stinking herb in the air."

Margaret nodded. "It's to protect the child from being stolen by fairies and will continue until its christening."

"It's a ridiculous custom. Surely you don't believe in changelings, Margaret?"

She frowned. "No. Well, until later then." She opened the door, then looked back at him, her eyes dark and troubled. "I wouldn't try to challenge the beliefs of the islanders though, were I you. There is so much we can't understand."

"There's a rational explanation for everything."

"I wonder."

He stood alone after she had gone, disconcerted by the stirring of desire he had felt. On principle he decided he wouldn't accept the supper invitation. Not to sit back like an unwelcome guest. He would work instead in his laboratory. Fueled by his own frustration, he would work to discover what had gone wrong with Roger's experiment, and if he anesthetized his own emotions in the process, well, so much the better.

He heard Margaret's footsteps receding, and had just remembered the breakfast awaiting him, no doubt cold by now, when he heard her scream from beyond the stone wall that surrounded the manse.

Margaret jumped down from the cart in horror, uncaring that she'd landed in a puddle of icy mud. Her first reaction, as she spotted Ian running from the house toward her, brandishing his walking stick as a weapon, was to burst into laughter. She hadn't even realized she had screamed.

"What happened?" he demanded, scanning the hills behind them as if he might find an answer there.

She bit her finger to stifle another surge of nervous laughter. "I'm sorry. There—there was a rat under the plaid on my seat. A big wretched thing with black shiny eyes and claws."

He raised his stick. "Sounds like a veritable monster."

"You're not going to bash it with that stick?"

He looked solemn. "Not unless it attacks me first."

She looked away as he lifted the edge of the plaid with the stick. Several moments passed, and when she didn't hear anything, she turned in hesitation, glancing down at the flattened plaid. She was not squeamish by nature; the sight of a rat in the barn would ordinarily not even have caused her to blink. But there had been something about the way it had been positioned under the plaid, something suggestive of evil. . . .

"Is it gone?"

"Only in spirit." Frowning, Ian held up the rigid gray body by its tail. "Rigor mortis has already set in."

She recoiled, keeping her eyes on Ian's face. "It's dead?"

"Quite."

"Oh, well," she said in a rush of relief. "I suppose Cyclops—that's my cat—hid it there. He's been following me around all morning, hoping for a bit of cheese."

He smiled faintly. "Yes. A perverse feline Christmas present, perhaps."

"Or perhaps a crow dropped it into the cart and it crawled under the plaid to die."

"It's been dead for several hours," Ian said guardedly.

"Oh, dear." She noticed all of a sudden that he seemed preoccupied, pensive. Had she annoyed him with this silly interruption? After all, it was Christmas morning, and he probably had calls to make, as did she.

"Thank you, Dr. MacNeill." She brushed past him to climb into the cart. "I'll not detain you any longer."

"I'll dispose of this, shall I?" he asked, holding the rat away from him.

She shuddered. "Yes, please. And Happy Christmas again."

She picked up the reins and clucked at the two ponies, steering the cart onto the heavily traveled peat-cutters' path. It was a half-hour drive to the croft where Peggy lived with her aging parents, and the shabby little community had just come into view when Margaret realized she had forgotten her basket of foodstuffs. She had dropped it beside the hallstand at the manse, distracted by the sight of Ian clumping down the stairs bare-chested, and on Christmas morning.

She slowed the cart and closed her eyes, as if by doing so she could blot out the image of Ian so obviously glad to see her again, charmingly self-conscious, Ian defending her from that disgusting creature with his cane, his ugly-handsome face amused.

Well, she had no choice but to return to the manse, even if it meant interrupting his morning, or threatening her own inner equilibrium again with the emotional tug-of-war she'd come to associate with their encounters.

She turned the cart around, guiding the ponies back between the hills. At the manse she dismounted and hesitated at the gate, remembering again with distaste the rat she had found. She hurried to the front door and knocked. After waiting al-

most five minutes in the cold for an answer, she decided Ian
would understand if she let herself in to retrieve the basket.

She wondered where he had gone. An emergency call to the
crofts, perhaps? But surely she'd have passed him on the path.
She had pounded at his door to raise the dead.

As she entered the hall, she was assailed by the sharp smell
of chlorine and an unidentifiable fruitlike odor. She picked up
her basket but couldn't bring herself to leave. There was no
sound from the back of the house, nothing out of the ordinary
but that unpleasant combination of odors.

Yet something was not quite right. She put down the heavy
basket and headed decisively down the hall. As she approached
Stephen's former study, the air became thick with condensed
steam and that sharp mixture of smells; she could hear water
bubbling furiously from somewhere inside the room.

"Ian," she said hesitantly, stepping inside the door, "are
you—"

She broke off, glancing down with a grimace at the shallow
pan on his desk which contained the rat she had found in her
cart. Attached by thread to its tail was a tag labeled in Ian's
untidy handwriting.

She backed away from the desk, gasping as she stepped on
the shards of a broken glass globe strewn across the carpet.
The room looked as though a madman had run amok through
it. Microscope and glass slides, dry bones, bottles, and the
bust of Hippocrates in pieces on the floor. Copies of *The Lancet* and *London Medical Gazette* strewn everywhere. She knelt
and picked up a pamphlet entitled: *On Chloroform and Obstetrical Procedures* by Ian MacNeill. Beneath it a newspaper
headline announced:

*Animal Magnetism! Brash Young Aberdonian Physician
Practices the Dangerous Science of Anaesthesia!*

She heard a faint groan from the back of the room. Rising
quickly, she spotted Ian partially reclining beneath the table,
his head and arms entangled in the floor-length tartan cash-

mere curtains. There was an inhaler lying against his throat, the twisted metal tube still attached to his mouth.

He lifted his head and stared at her blankly, then fell back against the tasseled cushions propped beneath his shoulders. His face was flushed, and a series of convulsive shudders had seized him, a terrifying sight to Margaret.

"Ian—"

Take . . . my . . . pulse. . . ." He gestured weakly toward the desk. "Pen . . . paper, to assure . . . accuracy."

He leaned forward to put his head between his knees. His breathing sounded strained, peculiar. Margaret stared at him in concern, sidestepping hesitantly to the desk.

"Four fluid-drachms far too much," he muttered. "Make note of—"

He broke off, gazing in horror at the table where a Florence oil flask was kept boiling in a water-bath and lighted by a spirit lamp. The flask hissed and then emitted a thin whistle. Spurts of scalding vapor began to erupt into the room like a miniature volcano.

He lunged to his feet, shouting toward Margaret, "Get the hell out of here!"

She dropped the pen she had just picked up, too terrified to disobey. Out of the corner of her eye she saw Ian lean against the windowframe, clawing the curtains for support. He looked as if he might collapse at any moment.

She sprang forward automatically to help him. Then suddenly the flask heating on the table exploded, releasing a geyser of glass, boiling water, and foul gases into the air. Tongues of orange-violet flame raced down the table, igniting the wads of blue litmus paper Ian had discarded.

He tore off his jacket to beat at the flames, but his movements were so slow and uncoordinated that he only succeeded in fanning the fire. He glanced up and stared at Margaret, his blue eyes unfocused. Billows of smoke rose like a barrier between them.

"Save yourself," he said faintly, staggering back against a chair. "Take my . . . journal. . . ."

The fire had by now reached the carpet. The odor of singed wool, the smoke, the pungent gases, made Margaret's eyes water until tears streamed down her face. In blind panic she snatched the first beaker of liquid she could reach from the table to hurl at the flames on the floor.

Ian came up from the chair like a jack-in-the-box. "Not that—alcohol solvent—"

She dropped the beaker. There was a glass bowl of water on the chest against the wall, and on its surface floated a lifeless goldfish. She was about to heave the bowl when she saw that Ian had kicked up the carpet, smothering the flames that had threatened to ignite into an unstoppable fire.

Shaking with fright and anger, she opened the window and knelt to help him up from the floor where he was scrambling to retrieve his notes. "You—you killed the poor goldfish with your horrid s-science. . . ."

He frowned, falling against her as they stood up together. She bumped back against the table. "It's . . . dead?" he said in confusion.

The small of her back arched awkwardly from the strain of supporting his weight. But then gradually she became conscious of an enervating warmth where he rested against her lower body, her cloak a flimsy barrier to the heat that flowed between them. She gripped him by the shoulders to hold him steady and felt his muscles contract beneath his shirt. What was wrong with her that she could be so physically aware of him when only moments ago they might have died?

He groaned and turned his face into her neck. Unable to move, Margaret forced herself to concentrate on easing the discomfort in her spine, although it seemed preferable to the nameless ache that had begun to undermine her composure. Then suddenly he swayed back and she could breathe.

It was a relief, to be free of his weight, a relief and strangely a disappointment as that ache slowly faded away.

"Dr. MacNeill," she said sharply, surveying the devastation of the room. "I think—"

He had gone to the chest, tickling the inert goldfish with his fingers. Margaret wiped her streaming eyes with the back of her wrist and watched him in annoyance, aware he had already forgotten her in favor of his experiment. A flash of orange-gold fin caught her attention. The fish began to circle the shallow bowl.

Ian sighed in obvious relief. "So," he murmured, "we both survived, though barely."

Margaret, curious despite herself, came up behind him. "You used that—that—"

"Nitric ether—"

"You used that . . . on a *fish?*"

"On both of us." Wincing, he pressed his fingers to his right temple. "God, what a headache, and my stomach—" He moved around her to the desk, quickly downing a drink he had apparently prepared earlier. "Opium and red wine," he explained. "It combats the aftereffects of the anesthesia."

"Doesn't the goldfish get some?" she asked dryly. "It seems only fair."

He sat down heavily in his chair, shuddering as the drink hit his stomach. "Very amusing. Actually, the fish work as well as the canaries."

"Canaries?" Margaret repeated as if he had taken leave of his senses.

"Roger and I used to experiment with birds. Oh, never mind. You wouldn't understand anyway—you have the same look on your face as my former housekeeper when she found the canaries in the water closet. That experiment even made the papers."

"It can't have been pleasant cleaning up this sort of mess," Margaret said, visibly shaken.

"This rarely happens," he said calmly. "I overestimated the dosage. Now explain to me exactly what you noticed—" He had reached for the pen, but he froze suddenly. "I *am* sorry, Margaret. I didn't even think, but are you all right? You didn't burn your fingers in the fire, or suffer from the fumes?"

"I'm fine." She drew a deep breath as if to reassure herself. "But the carpet is ruined, and Stephen's study—"

"—shall be replaced."

"You almost killed yourself," she burst out angrily.

He shook his head. "My colleague *did* kill himself experimenting with nitric ether, failing to use a controlled dose. But I'm beginning to suspect he had a bad heart, a congenital condition, that proved the fatal link. Poor ambitious Roger."

He stared down at the desk in silence, playing with his pen. To her surprise Margaret felt sorry for him, for his private anguish. "I didn't manage to take your pulse," she said. "But I can tell you that your behavior was very unsettling. You were racked with tremors and lurching about like a drunken lunatic, and your breathing—"

"Delirium cum tremore." He looked up keenly. "And the breathing—"

"Shallow, irregular."

He began to write, using his left hand, she noted. "You might have burned down the house, Dr. MacNeill."

He shook his head to silence her. Piqued, she bent to pick up a piece of the shattered oil lamp from the floor. When she straightened, she discovered Ian had left his chair and was examining the inhalation apparatus he'd left on the floor.

She could not believe his behavior, his reckless disregard for his own safety in the name of science. At Castle Kinmairi, when she'd seen how he had helped Euan Bruce, she had thought him the most brilliant, the most compassionate and enlightened man she'd ever met. And now, today, after this terrifying mishap at the manse—

"I think you're an idiot," she said aloud, her heart racing

against her ribs as she realized what might have happened had she not returned in time. "An utter idiot."

"What?" he said absently.

"I'm going now, Dr. MacNeill. I only returned to fetch my basket."

"Yes. What was that again? Oh, your basket."

She turned to the door, then glanced back at him in annoyance. "It is Christmas, you know. Hardly the sort of day one would spend blowing oneself to kingdom come."

"No? You wouldn't think so," he murmured.

"I'll go home now, sprout a pair of gilded wings, and jump off a cliff, shall I?"

He looked up with a faintly puzzled frown, then turned to the table. Margaret realized he hadn't heard her at all. She picked up her shawl from the desk, shuddering at the grim sight of the dead rat in the metal pan. There was writing on the tag it bore, and this time she could read it quite distinctly: Perform Post-Mortem on Miss Rose's Rat.

"A post-mortem?" she said, disbelievingly. "Why would you possibly—"

She looked over at Ian, too absorbed in salvaging what remained of his experiment to respond. And then she realized she did not really want an answer, not on Christmas morning. She did not want to think of rats at all.

Still, her gaze fell upon the stiffened rat's corpse once again before she left the room. And the sense of foreboding that she'd felt on first discovering it in the cart returned, casting a cold shadow upon the day.

Twenty

When Stephen arrived at the manse, Ian was formally dressed in a black worsted wool suit and savoring a glass of whiskey by the fire, delusory strength for whatever the evening would bring. He poured a second glass and handed it to Stephen, standing stiffly by the window like a guest in his own house.

Stephen looked down at the glass, his face disapproving. "I don't drink," he murmured. "Nor did my father, though I'd understand your taking a dram after the scare today in your laboratory."

"I apologize for the damage to your carpet. Fortunately the fire was confined to a small area."

"What is fortunate, Dr. MacNeill, is that neither you nor Margaret were hurt."

Ian looked past Stephen. A robin had landed on the windowsill outside where earlier Walter had sprinkled some shortbread crumbs. "I forgot to thank her for her help."

"There's tonight for that." Stephen put down his untouched glass. "Agnes thinks you're nurturing more than a passing fondness for our cousin. I told her it was surely her playwright's imagination."

Ian laughed softly to hide his surprise at the other man's perception. "What *I* might feel for Margaret seems irrelevant considering the fact that she happens to dislike me so intently."

"I wouldn't take it personally."

"What do you mean?"

Stephen stared at the bird on the windowsill. "I've often wondered if she isn't afraid to fall in love."

"You've obviously given the matter great thought. You know her well."

"Yes," Stephen admitted. "There was a young British naval officer who used to visit the island. He wished to marry her, and I think even my father would have approved of their courtship, but Margaret wanted nothing to do with him. The young man was refined, attractive, lighthearted. Yet Margaret kept rejecting his romantic overtures until one day he went away and never came back. I don't think she ever noticed."

Ian finished his drink. He could hear faint sounds coming from the kitchen, Walter and Sybil making their own Christmas dinner.

Stephen turned from the window. "It strikes me that you've solicited a lot of information about my cousin."

"But it was you who brought her name into the conversation," Ian said smoothly. "And as for my probing, well, perhaps it is professional habit."

"But your interest in Margaret has nothing to do with your profession, does it?"

There were footsteps in the hall and then from the door Walter announced that the doctor's horse had been saddled. Ian rose to his feet to face Stephen, grateful for the interruption that saved him from answering.

"By the way, Mr. Rose," he said on their way out the door, "does Mrs. Alcock ever use arsenic about the farm . . . to kill vermin, for example?"

"Agnes use arsenic? I wouldn't think she'd bother. Why do you ask?"

Ian glanced toward the kitchen. "Margaret found a rat under the plaid in her cart. A dead rat, which she assumed had found its way there itself. However, I suspect it had been poisoned, and—and there were peculiar markings on its abdomen, a sort of charcoal hieroglyphics. Well, here, see for yourself—"

They were in the hall where a pair of candles burned in brass sconces at either side of the door. Ian paused to pull a scrap of paper from his vest pocket, passing it to Stephen.

"I copied them as clearly as I could. I wondered if perhaps they were Oriental characters. I read only Latin and English myself, but I thought you, a Far Eastern scholar by the look of your extensive library—"

The blood drained from Stephen's face. "Witchcraft. These are the runic markings of the ancient Wicca alphabet. There is indeed a book on the subject in my library by an Elizabethan astrologer, but the origins are possibly Greek or Germanic, arguably even Viking, but not Oriental."

"Do you understand these . . . runes?"

"Not at all," Stephen replied. "Did Margaret see them?"

Ian took back the paper and refolded it. "Presumably she was too repulsed by the rat to examine it closely enough to even notice. I suppose it's not implausible, a poisoned rat finding its way under the plaid where it might have remained undetected for several hours. But the markings—"

Stephen nodded grimly. "I'm afraid the ancient gods are remembered here as often as is the Almighty. For all I know, the rat was intended for *you,* Ian, a sort of warning from the local witch that she doesn't appreciate the competition. She lives off the income from her healing charms."

Ian opened the door onto the frosty starlit evening. "Perhaps I should visit her then, to let her know I don't appreciate the ghastly calling card. Agnes has mentioned her name—"

"Morag Strong." Stephen shuddered, striding ahead of Ian to the hillside path. "I wouldn't go anywhere near that woman if I were you. She's had the most profoundly disturbing influence on the inhabitants of this island. And on Margaret—"

"The herbal brews and nasty soups?"

"Even more damaging than that, I'm afraid. She's convinced

Margaret she can commune with spirits, that it's possible to summon the dead from the netherworld."

Ian frowned, remembering Margaret's sad past.

"I'll see you at supper, Dr. MacNeill," Stephen said, his face drawn. "The evening should be pleasant, but I'd be personally grateful if you wouldn't bring up the subject of Mrs. Strong again. She has been my nemesis, you see, in my battle to save souls on the island."

"I understand."

But Ian didn't, not really, and as he walked toward the stable where the saddled sorrel mare awaited him, he decided that the time had indeed come for him to visit the strange woman who lived on the moor.

The Christmas tree, the intimate if sumptuous dinner party that Gareth Rose had hoped would please his ailing father had failed, and by nine o'clock Douglas had retired to his rooms. No one missed him. He had spent the evening complaining to Lilian, her husband, and Gareth, that the holiday would be meaningful to him only if Margaret were home. Bringing her back to Aberdeen had become an obsession with Douglas, and his family suffered for it.

Obsession was a word Gareth had only recently come to understand himself. It described the dark passion that drove him later that same night to the sandstone villa where Lucy Patton lived. They'd met a few months earlier at a private auction, and she had not only bought all his work on sight, but had commissioned him to paint her portrait—in the privacy of her home.

She had seduced Gareth the same day he'd begun to sketch her, and in the weeks that followed, they had shared their deepest secrets. Her husband, a brilliant young doctor on the verge of making medical history, had been murdered by an envious rival, Ian MacNeill. Did Gareth know of him? She hoped not,

Jillian Hunter

because she was dedicated to destroying the man who had stolen her husband's professional research and had not paid for his crime.

Gareth told her about his own unhappy life, the accident on the loch, about how he had spent years trying to earn his father's love. At first he thought Lucy understood his pain and why he did not want Margaret to come back to threaten the relationship he'd built with Douglas. Yet before long he realized Lucy understood only revenge. But by then it was too late. Gareth had told her too much. His body craved hers and his soul, his tortured soul, craved the solution she had offered to his problem.

"I'll help you keep your sister away if you'll help me ruin MacNeill," she'd said the second time they had slept together. "With the 'Devil Doctor' about to be exiled to Maryhead, it shouldn't be hard for us to devise a plan."

Drained, his shoulders throbbing where she'd scratched him, Gareth flung himself across the bed and longed for a bath to wash her perfume from his skin. "I don't want to hurt Margaret—"

She cupped his flaccid member in her hands, whispering, "And if there is no other way?"

He shuddered, aroused, repulsed, afraid. "I have to be at the bank early tomorrow . . ."

"But you loathe the bank."

"My father needs me."

"You need this. . . ." She kissed him deeply, pulling him against her, and as always when they made love, he ignored his misgivings, the mild revulsion overpowered by desire.

Afterward, while he dressed and prayed his father wouldn't find out about this affair, Lucy sat in the middle of the unmade bed with a surgical scalpel and stack of old newspapers, meticulously clipping articles about the infamous Ian MacNeill and his mad experiments.

"Look, Gareth," she said, her voice excited as she scanned

one of the old publications she'd found in his makeshift studio, the small parlor she let him use because she no longer entertained. "It's an article about your family—"

He whirled around, his shirt hanging open, and ripped the paper from her hand, gasping when he realized he'd torn a sketch of his own mother in two. "Damn you! I told you I didn't want you in my things!"

Her face became pensive. "It's about the accident, isn't it? About your sister?"

He turned back to the dresser, shaken, feeling her stare at him while he brushed his hair. She put on her Chinese wrapper and got up to pull the bellcord, leaving the scalpel on the bed.

"I had MacNeill sent out of Scotland," she said quietly, coming up behind him. "And I can help keep your sister away, too."

He stared at her candlelit reflection in the mirror. "How?"

She smiled as a soft tap sounded at the door. "Fear, Gareth. We'll frighten her to death." And before he could respond, she began to back away from him. "I'll have Walter bring your carriage round. Think over what we discussed."

The memory of that conversation faded. The carriage climbed the drive to Lucy's villa, familiar now, the crunch of hoofbeats on gravel bringing Gareth back to the present. Christmas night. Several months had passed since he and Lucy had decided to help each other, and not a day had gone by that he did not agonize over what he might be forced to do if Lucy's plans to keep Margaret away failed.

Twenty-one

After a quiet supper, they played Substance and Shadow in the farmhouse parlor, then walked up to Clootie Hill to watch the bonfires in progress. From the start, the mood of the evening had been subdued with an underlying current of tension. Agnes, in an uncharacteristic outburst of emotion, tearfully apologized for the burnt goose. Ian gallantly joked that burning the main course wasn't as bad as almost burning down the manse. Wasn't it fortunate that Margaret had saved him?

"You didn't seem very grateful at the time," Margaret said as she spooned scorched custard over her plum pudding, every bit as sodden as she'd promised. "In fact, you were perfectly horrible to me."

Ian frowned at the pudding. "Preoccupied," he amended. "I was preoccupied."

No one mentioned the rat. It was hardly a suppertime topic. From Margaret's point of view, it need never be discussed again, and why Ian should have kept it was beyond her understanding. Besides, she wanted to enjoy the few hours of Christmas that were left.

But the tension that Margaret had sensed earlier only seemed to mount during the walk to Clootie Hill, a subtle menace in the air. She was also acutely conscious of Ian's presence, even though he spoke little and stayed a few self-conscious steps behind her and Stephen. And at first Stephen grumbled that he wouldn't go—the hill was named after Black Donald, the devil himself, and it was unseemly for a minister to dignify a pagan festivity with an appearance, especially on Christmas night.

But Margaret coaxed, and Stephen relented, even carrying the tin hand-lantern needed to light their way through the fog.

Agnes lagged far behind with Kenneth, her tall blond giant of a husband whose gap-toothed grin belied a sharp mind. Margaret wouldn't have been surprised if the pair of them disappeared for the night; they had been exchanging amorous looks for hours. She supposed that such embarrassing behavior was to be expected when married couples reunited after a three-month separation.

They had climbed high enough now to feel the waves of heat that radiated from the bonfires. The flames danced higher and higher into the sky, orange-gold undulations that threw shadows upon the stone Celtic cross crowning the hill. The families of crofters and fishermen formed a circle around the fire. Driftwood, heather twigs, bramble and herring barrels, any combustible item saved over months for the occasion contributed to the blaze. The night marked the beginning of a week-long celebration, Burning the Old Year Out, a festival of pagan origins held to bring good fortune for the upcoming year.

"Mind where you're walking," Margaret called back sharply to Ian, just steps behind her on the path.

He poked at a pile of rocks with his stick. Silhouetted against the firelight with his caped greatcoat and walking cane, he looked to Margaret to be even taller and darker than usual, elegantly menacing, if she let her imagination run wild. She was astonished that he'd accepted the supper invitation, especially after the disaster in the library. She had hoped to spend the evening alone with Stephen, a final attempt to dissuade him from his intended spiritual venture in Siam. And yet she had felt a powerful thrill of pleasure when she had opened the door to find that dark figure standing beside Stephen, a pleasure that had fleetingly outweighed her sadness over Stephen's imminent departure.

But Stephen was avoiding her; ruefully she stared up the hill to where he stood with his former parishioners. With Agnes and Kenneth lost in their impassioned oblivion, she alone bore the responsibility for entertaining Dr. MacNeill, who seemed determined not to leave her alone.

"Why do you carry that cane about anyway?" she asked as he reached her side. "You look pretentious walking with it on Clootie Hill."

Ian smiled, refusing to take offense. "It's a weapon."

Margaret strode past him to the circle of villagers at the top of the hill, half hoping he wouldn't follow her. She could no longer pick out Stephen amidst the crowd of familiar and unfamiliar faces, but there were enough people she knew from Cape Rue to distract her from Ian. She caught her breath as she felt him shoulder a place beside her. He wasn't about to let her forget him. His presence insisted upon a response.

"The children loved the shortbread, Margaret," someone called across the bonfire. "Where are Agnes and her husband then, as if we don't know?"

"Is that the good doctor you've brought along, lass? Is he going to throw that fancy stick into the fire?"

An elderly man chuckled. "Don't tease the puir man so, Mrs. Leach, or he'll put us all unconscious like he did Euan Bruce. His wife says the old fool still isn't right in the head."

Margaret glanced up curiously at Ian. He didn't seem to mind the good-natured joking as he pitched into the bonfire the handful of heather twigs Agnes had given him earlier. "That's my sacrifice to keep Clootie quiet for the year," Ian said, "but I'm not giving up my cane. It's ebony topped in real gold."

Someone passed around a flask of whiskey. Ian took a swig and handed it down to Margaret, raising an eyebrow at the long draught she took. A crofter bumped up behind them, and

Margaret shook her head in chagrin as the whiskey splashed over her cloak.

"This is to thee, O mighty Ocean," a voice chanted across the fire, "that thou shalt bring us another year of your bounty."

"Sulphur and brimstone, the devil's breath," Ian mused quietly. "Do they realize why they've come together to burn a load of rubbish on a hill?"

Margaret, having just decided to join Stephen on the other side of the ring, gave Ian a distracted look. "I don't think they really care so long as they're having fun."

Ian started to say something more, but she had moved too far away to hear him. Still, she could feel him staring after her as she pushed through the laughing crowd of islanders to reach the opposite side of the hill. In her haste she attempted to walk through the short bristly scrub instead of taking the well-worn footpath. It was a mistake.

She caught her heel in a tangled heather root and started to slide down the hill, into the darkness and quiet of the heath below.

That's what I get for drinking whiskey from a flask, she thought wryly. But she wasn't drunk, only nervous, as she had been ever since the afternoon's excitement at the manse, the dead rat, the fire. She straightened and brushed off her cloak, then turned her head slowly to stare down the hill into the misty shadows.

A shiver chased down her spine. Something had moved.

"Maggie mine," a child's voice whispered.

Every muscle in Margaret's body tensed. "Who is it?" she called out uncertainly. "Is someone there?"

A young boy of about two or three materialized from behind a peat cart. He was too well-dressed to be a crofter's child, overdressed, in fact, in knee breeches with a ruffled white shirt and black velvet doublet. A blond curl fell across his forehead beneath the green bonnet he wore, a bonnet jauntily decorated with three white swan feathers.

Margaret felt as though the earth had opened up beneath her feet and she were falling.

He held out his arms, his voice playful and plaintive. "Maggie carry Alan."

"Alan. It can't . . . be."

He darted back as she began to move toward him, impeded by the dry twisted bracken between them. "Don't run away," she said frantically. "Darling, Alan . . . whoever you are, don't be scared—"

She watched him disappear behind the peat cart and then reemerge to run around to the other side of the hill. The glow of the bonfire illuminated his figure as it proceeded along the path, the white feathers in his bonnet.

There was a moment when something inside her cautioned against following him. But her emotions overrode the warning, and she hurried around the cart to the hillside path, pleading with him to stop. Unexpectedly a drunken crofter materialized out of the mist before her, weaving from side to side.

"What's the hurry then, lassie?" he asked with a friendly chuckle. "Auld Clootie canna be that eager for yer offerings."

"Get out of the way," she said impatiently. "My brother— oh, *move*—"

Looking more puzzled than insulted, he stepped aside to allow her passage and then, to her irritation, caught her arm to hand her the bundle of heather twigs she must have dropped. During the delay she had lost sight of the boy; he could only have merged into the tight ring of revelers on the hill.

She pressed her hand to her heart as if to still its painful drumming. It couldn't be her brother. What had come over her? But there were only a handful of children on the island whose parents could afford a costume like that, exactly like the one Alan had worn the day of the accident. And he had called her by name, his pet name for her.

She couldn't locate him, nor anyone who even resembled him in the small bands of children playing around the perimeters of the bonfire. So frantic was she to find a rational explanation for his appearance that she walked straight past Stephen without recognizing him.

He ran after her. "Is something wrong?" he asked over the din of voices around them.

"Stephen." She whirled and tugged him away from the circle, her face desperate. "I saw Alan. He—he called me by name and asked me to play with him."

"Alan? Alan who?"

"My brother. My younger brother."

"Your—" He stared at her, his mouth tightening. "You know how I feel about women drinking whiskey, not to mention brewing the stuff, and this only goes to prove my point."

"I don't have time for one of your sermons. Just help me find him—"

"If you're looking for me, I'm not lost," Ian said behind them.

Margaret glanced around, her nerves so taut she did not think she could even pretend to be polite to Ian. "This is a family matter, Dr. MacNeill."

His smile froze as he glanced from her to Stephen. "Well, I was only coming to say good-night anyway, and to thank you for the supper."

He started to turn away, his cane tucked under his arm, when suddenly Margaret, in a moment of desperation, took his wrist. "Wait, please. You must have been watching me to know where to find me now—did you see a small boy approach me, about so high in a black velvet suit and a feathered bonnet?"

"No. I'm sorry."

"You saw me fall—on the hill?"

"No." Ian looked at her in concern. "Did you hurt yourself?"

She dropped his hand, turning away in frustration. "Stephen, help me look for him."

"It couldn't have been Alan," Stephen said gently. "You know that."

She nodded, looking unconvinced. "I just want to see him up close, to put my mind at peace."

"What does he look like again?" Ian asked her. "I'll cover one half of the hill, and you the other."

Stephen shook his head in annoyance. "You don't understand, Dr. MacNeill," he said in a curt undertone. "We're talking about her brother."

Ian glanced at Margaret. "But I thought—not Gareth Rose?"

"No," Stephen said tersely. "Wee Alan Rose, who could not possibly have made an appearance, and if I may take the opportunity to say so, I do not appreciate either your encouraging Margaret to imbibe spirits or to smuggle them for that matter."

Ian frowned. "Are you implying that she's drunk?"

"She reeks of whiskey." Stephen's nostrils flared as he turned to Margaret. "I don't know how you could miss it, unless you'd been drinking heavily yourself."

"She spilled more on her cloak than either of us drank," Ian said slowly, "and she could not possibly have taken enough from the flask to cause hallucinations."

Stephen fixed him with a sanctimonious look. "I realize you want to defend her, but—"

He did not finish the sentence. Margaret wouldn't allow it. Grasping Ian's hand, she drew him back into the circle of revelers, where she had just glimpsed a small boy sitting on a young woman's lap.

Ian, towering a head above nearly every island man present, used his size to shoulder a clear path. "Is that him, the wee lad eating a biscuit? He's just run off after a dog, if it is, but he's not wearing a bonnet."

"He could have taken it off," Margaret said, struggling to keep up with him. "What about his clothes?"

"I couldn't tell," Ian replied. "We'll find out in a minute." She was too distracted to mind when his fingers closed tightly around hers. All that mattered was finding the boy, and that Ian was helping her, that he, not Stephen, took her seriously enough to become involved. She knew she could not possibly have talked with a child dead twelve years now. But she also knew what she had heard, and seen.

Ian squeezed her hand, imbuing her with a surge of strangely welcome warmth. "There's the laddie playing with his brothers at the bottom of the hill. Is that your apparition, Margaret?"

She bit her lip and stared down into the shadowy depression, lit by pine torches secured on a few scattered carts. Her cheeks burned from the bonfire's heat and from the sudden onslaught of cool mist off the moor.

"I can't tell from here. It could be him."

"Let's have a look."

He took her arm and guided her down the perpendicular footpath to where the children fought their torchlit battle of vanquished chieftains and Vikings.

She stopped short on the path, drawing a painful breath. She could not possibly have seen her brother. What had she been thinking? "It's not him," she said tonelessly.

"You're sure?" Ian said.

"Yes. He's not even—" She edged forward, distracted by the sight of a single peat cart rolling across the moor. On the crude plank seat were a man and a woman, and in the bed, sitting on a bale of hay, a young child wearing a bonnet. "Ian, do you see them—the cart traveling inland?"

"Well, yes, but only barely, and we could never catch up with them without my horse."

She worked her arm loose and started past him. "We could borrow another cart."

"But they'd be a mile away by then."

"Maybe not."

She had reached the bottom of the path before she realized he hadn't followed her. She knew suddenly that she would not find the child, that even if she did catch up with that cart it would not be carrying the same boy in the bonnet.

She glanced back at Ian but saw that he had turned away to watch the small dark-haired woman who had materialized on the path. Margaret stared at her in surprise.

"Morag!" She clambered upward to greet the other woman, noting curiously the frown of disapproval on Ian's face.

The woman, looking far younger than her forty years, picked up the skirts of her linsey-woolsey gown to descend the path. "Merry meet, Margaret. How is that cough, my dear?"

"It's gone. Morag, I have to talk to you—" She broke off, aware of the tension emanating from Ian as he stood staring down at her friend. Morag's reaction to him, her faint smile, the intense silence, was equally striking.

Puzzled, she witnessed the personal exchange between them, an unspoken assessment such as might have passed between old friends. Or adversaries. There had been a time when Margaret had been passionately jealous of Morag Strong, for although the woman was not now and never had been beautiful, hers was a character that combined unabashed sensuality with a maternal warmth that made her appealing to men and women alike.

But Morag also had a dark side, and it came unexpectedly to Margaret's mind now. "You remember I spoke to you of Dr. MacNeill?"

Morag's hazel eyes glinted with private amusement. "His name has come to my notice of late."

"I return the compliment," Ian said evenly, "or was that an insult, Mrs. Strong?"

Margaret did not like the feeling that she was not privy to this mysterious communication between them. "I saw Alan on the hill," she said quietly to Morag. "At least it looked like him, and he knew his pet name for me."

"Alan?" Morag's dark eyebrows drew into a frown. "Where did he come from?"

"We were wondering the same thing ourselves," Ian said in a brusque voice that bordered on rudeness. "You'd not be able to answer that, would you, Mrs. Strong?"

She smiled. "I think it's time you and I discussed our differences at length, Doctor. Would tea tomorrow at my cottage be convenient? Four o'clock, shall we say?"

"I look forward to it," Ian said without enthusiasm. He turned to Margaret, his face concerned. "Are you ready to go back to the house?"

She looked across the moor, aware he had spoken but not really hearing what he'd said. "There must be an explanation," she murmured.

Morag patted her hand. "Let Dr. MacNeill take you home."

"Coincidences do happen, Margaret," Ian said. "In the morning everything will make more sense."

"I suppose so."

"Tomorrow then, Doctor," Morag called after them. "Mine will be the black house with a broomstick against the gate and henbane in the garden. And do not step on the toad I keep under the doorstep."

He glanced down at Margaret with a wry smile. "You keep charming company—no pun intended."

Margaret smiled but deep inside her a sense of uneasiness grew. For the second time that day she felt as though she had passed beneath a shadow, a shadow which concealed a malevolent presence.

Twenty-two

Ian and Margaret returned alone across the moor to find the farmhouse in darkness. Margaret spoke little, preoccupied by her memories of Alan and by thoughts of the man who walked beside her, accepting her need for silence.

His presence, dark and masterful, kept at bay the fears that might have overwhelmed her had she been alone. For that reason only was she willing to tolerate his prolonged company. Or so she told herself.

The admitted physical attraction between them did not threaten her because she believed she could control it. There could be no danger of emotional involvement with Ian. The self-protective scars of the past which bound her heart allowed no soft places for trust and love to grow.

He saw her into the house. In the hallway she removed her cloak and glanced upstairs as a floorboard creaked. "Kenneth and Agnes must have gone to bed," she whispered. "Can I offer you something before you leave?"

"Well, I—"

She put her hand on his arm. "Stay—for just a few moments. I have too much on my mind to sleep just yet."

Common sense urged Ian he should politely refuse. But he ignored that warning with reckless disregard, as he had previously ignored all logic when it came to Margaret. Nodding, aware of a spark of anticipation in the air, he allowed her to take his greatcoat from his shoulders. She led him into the parlor and went straight to the whiskey bottle on the sideboard, pouring two glasses. As he moved to turn up the lamp, she shook her head.

"Don't bother." She handed him a glass. "The light from the fire is all we need."

He frowned, taking the glass and replacing it on the sideboard. "I don't particularly want another drink."

"Nor do I then." She sat down on the hearthstone, leaning forward to gaze moodily into the dying fire. "It's said the gypsies can read the future in the flames."

"So I've heard." He stared at her, wishing for the drink he'd refused.

She glanced at him with a wry smile. "But *you* put no stock in soothsayers. Not the methodical-minded doctor. And yet you helped me tonight when I asked you to. You helped me without questioning my sobriety . . . or my sanity."

He made a dismissive motion with his hand.

Margaret hunched forward, her smile fading. "Tell me, good doctor, were you merely trying to placate me earlier or did you actually believe I saw my brother?"

Ian came up behind her. Her hair shone in the firelight, dark brown shot with amber-gold threads, and he caught himself just as he would have brushed a strand from her shoulder. There was a change in her tonight, a restless, mercurial energy that was as intriguing as it was disturbing.

It was Margaret caught off guard again, exciting in her human failings which she struggled so hard to conceal. He swallowed dryly, temptation tightening his throat.

"I believe you saw a small boy who looked like your brother—"

"But not that it was him?"

He sat down opposite her, looking into her eyes. "How could it have been?"

She stared at him for several moments, the usual antagonism, the caution, absent from her expression. The ormolu clock ticked loudly, a counterpoint to Ian's heartbeat. He felt the heat of the fire burn through his clothes, and something warmer yet, from inside him. As if she dared not acknowledge the dangerous mood that had fallen, she looked back pointedly at the fire, her eyes downcast and distant.

"Be careful with Morag," she said after a moment.

"I thought she was your friend."

"I suppose she is, but Agnes and Stephen despise her." The clock chimed out the hour above them, and she frowned. "It's late."

He stood, reluctant to leave, knowing that he couldn't fight the desire pulsing between them much longer. His self-discipline had never come up against such a relentless need. "I have a surgery early in the morning, on the other side of the island."

She looked up in surprise. "Someone is actually letting you cut him open?"

"A crofter—it's only a carbuncle, actually, but I half expect Morag to convince him to refuse the operation."

"A carbuncle is not such a serious thing that it can't wait, is it?"

He reached the door. "It could wait, I suppose," he replied hesitantly.

He heard her rise, heard the alluring swish of her skirts and petticoats as she came up beside him, and he gripped his hands into fists to keep from touching her. "Do you think she's pretty?"

He had trouble enough mastering his animal instincts without her standing so close to him, he could almost taste her. "Morag? She's pretty enough. But she doesn't hold a candle to you, Margaret."

She smiled and looked down at the floor, her expression at once innocent and seductive. He wished fervently to read her thoughts . . . to find she wanted him as much as he did her so that he could rationalize staying longer.

"I'll fetch your coat," she said, crushing that hope.

She strode ahead of him into the hall. In the darkness he strained to fit on the arm-length cape which Margaret held behind him, managing to strike her twice in the arm with his cane.

"God, I'm sorry—"

"It's all right. You did say it was a weapon."

He put down the cane. "Let me see if there's a bump—"

"There isn't."

"—or a bruise."

She was caught in his spell from the instant his hands touched her shoulder, easing up her throat to her face. Unmoving, not breathing, she murmured, "There is one more thing I should mention about Morag."

His thumbs brushed her temples. "Which is?"

"But you don't believe."

"No, I don't. Well, not in witches."

She lifted her eyes to his. "She predicted we would become . . . lovers."

He drew a deep breath at that, a dark smile playing at the corners of his mouth. "Perhaps there's more to Mrs. Strong's magic than meets the eye," he said softly. "Perhaps I have something to learn about the otherworld after all."

"You think it's a joke—"

"Oh, no. Not if it concerns you . . . and me." He lowered his hands to rest on either side of her shoulders. "And now I am intrigued, Margaret. Too intrigued to sleep tonight."

He pulled her toward him in a fierce embrace. As their bodies met, he felt a violent quiver go through her and then a soft, soul-deep sigh of unwilling surrender. Her head dropped back. Her eyes glistened like pewter, a subtle enticement in their depths so that for an exhilarating moment he did not know whether he was more the captor or the captive.

"Don't go yet," she whispered.

He stared down into her face. "If I stay . . ." His voice faded, questioning.

She smiled, her gaze shifting away from his.

He did not return her smile.

She backed away from him one step at a time, shyly breaking free as he continued to stare. He couldn't help it. He didn't believe it would happen. It had been a day of fires and phantasms, all of it unreal.

"Ian," she whispered uneasily. "You look so intense."

He removed his coat, dropped it on the floor, and stumbled after her like a sleepwalker, returning to the parlor where the fire had burned down to embers. If he looked intense, it was nothing compared to what he felt, arousal like a fever in his blood.

In the middle of the floor they collided awkwardly, and he caught her against him, sliding his hands down to her hips and kissing her hard on the mouth. In the rationally functioning part of his mind he realized she was using him, using desire as a distraction. But he wanted her. Oh God, he wanted her anyway with a hot reckless hope that burned through all his reason.

He sank backward onto the sofa, pulling her down on top of him. She landed in a provocative barmaid's sprawl, too stunned to resist, and he kissed her throat, his left hand working at the hooks of her gown. The bolero jacket fell loose, revealing her rounded shoulders, the lawn chemisette secured with ribbons he untied with an impatient tug.

She gave a soft muted cry. Her hair tumbled forward, casting her face into shadow. He sensed that she was terrified. He sat up slowly and lifted her into his lap, his voice ragged.

She touched her tongue to her upper lip. "You frighten me," she whispered.

Ian stared into her eyes, the bewitching slate-blue of the winter sea. The dark tumult of her hair over her shoulders, her seductive innocence, reminded him of the nubile village May

queens of his youth. Unattainable, those fey maidens of his
adolescent fantasies, whom he'd been too shy to pursue.

He was no longer shy. His eyes moved over her face, studying her, feature by feature, lingering on her mouth.

He smiled slowly. "No matter how long it takes, no matter
what I have to do, you're going to be mine."

She looked away, and he watched the rise and fall of her
breasts in fascination. "I warned you, Margaret," he said
thickly. "This is a very daring proposition—"

She leaned back against the sofa, her hair spilling over her
naked shoulders. He traced the tip of his forefinger along the
underside of her breast, circling the nipple until it puckered
like a rosebud. She went absolutely still, her voice an unsteady
whisper when finally she spoke.

"I feel daring tonight."

"Daring or in need of distraction?"

Her eyes flashed with a hint of the reckless fire he had
never forgotten. "Why should it matter to you?"

"It matters," he said intently.

He captured her just as she would have wriggled off his lap,
pressing his face between her breasts, silky brown hair and
faintly perfumed flesh. Margaret's mouth went dry, and she
could not summon the words to stop him. She was unsure she
wanted him to stop, and though she had turned to him initially
in confusion, this terrifying passion between them had raged
beyond her control. Perhaps she needed him, the sweet bewilderment, the reprieve from conscious thought that could only
be found in his arms.

She closed her eyes. His arms swept up and gripped her,
forcing her back against the tufted cushions. His mouth
brushed hers in a slow erotic kiss. Then he lowered his head
and she felt his tongue teasing the tip of her breast, drawing
it between his teeth until the sweet ache in the pit of her belly
grew so intense, she found it difficult to breathe.

She arched against him, panic rising. "Ian," she whispered, "if someone wakes up . . . Agnes or her husband . . ."

He laughed hoarsely. "I'll marry you in the morning."

His mouth found hers in another heart-stopping kiss that she should have resisted. Instead, she heard herself laughing along with him, twining her arms around his neck, her lower body draped over his lap like an offering to a pagan god.

Yet she did not feel ashamed. Confused, exhilarated, embarrassed. But the turbulent sensations that inundated her did not make her feel ashamed. And then he slid his hand beneath her skirts, touching the insides of her thigh. Staring directly into her eyes, he rubbed the silk of her pantelettes against her raw skin. Her stomach muscles clenched. A sweet lethargy stole over her limbs, immobilizing her, body and mind.

"Your skin is so soft, Margaret," he whispered. His fingers pressed against the opening of the undergarment, separating the wet silk that adhered to her skin. "Let me finish undressing you."

Margaret pulled herself upright, her entire body trembling, singing with a sudden onslaught of sensation. "Ian, please," she whispered, her eyes embarrassed.

He smiled, placing his hand against the cleft of her thighs. "Please what?"

She was afraid to look at him, afraid of what he'd made her feel. "Please stop."

Slowly he drew back, looking wild himself and breathing as if he had just climbed one of the cliffs on Cape Rue. "Another moment and it would have been too late," he said huskily. "You realize that, don't you?"

At her silence he flung his forearm over his eyes. Margaret frowned and stared down unseeingly at her lap, fumbling to fit the bodice back into place. Her hands shook. After several moments Ian cursed softly and stretched toward her, sliding his arms around her shoulders to refasten the hooks.

"Don't," she said in a bewildered voice. "Don't make it worse than it already is."

"Look," he muttered, "I'm only trying to help you. I care about you, Margaret. Isn't that bloody obvious—" He broke off, lifting his head. It took her a moment to realize that he had directed his attention to some point behind the sofa. She looked around unthinkingly to the window and saw a short figure flit behind the lace curtains into the darkness of the garden. When she turned back to Ian, the look of fury on his face was frightening.

"What is it?" she whispered.

"That was my housekeeper." He sprang up from the sofa and strode to the door. "The dirty, nosy bitch—"

"Don't make so much noise!"

With a final tug at her bodice, she jumped up and hurried after him into the hall, snatching his coat from the floor along the way. "Ian, please, you'll wake up—"

He was beyond hearing her.

He wrenched open the front door. As she peered around him, not knowing what to expect, she glimpsed an attractive middle-aged woman with curly red-gold hair standing on the step. The woman put her hand to her mouth at the sight of Ian glowering down at her, his face so darkly fierce that even Margaret flinched.

"What the hell do you think you're doing?" he demanded. "Do I pay you to spy on me, Mrs. Armstrong?"

The woman paled but stood her ground, her cunning blackcurrant eyes darting with interest to Margaret. "Spy on you indeed, sir! You had an emergency call from the crofts, and I have spent half the night trying to track you down. My poor husband, sir, has climbed Clootie Hill a half-dozen times, and him with a game leg."

She paused to collect her breath, her ample bosom huffing in indignation. Ian glanced back at Margaret, a smile twitching at the corners of his mouth.

"Mrs. Armstrong," he said, turning back to the housekeeper, "to search for me is all very well, but I don't understand why you didn't knock at the door—"

"I did knock, sir! I knocked as loud as I deemed polite, but no one answered."

"And then you just happened to pass by the window—"

She drew her white woolen shawl over her shoulders with a faint smirk. "I was hoping to see a light abovestairs, so that I might throw a stone against the attic window to awake Miss Rose. You did tell me, sir, numerous times, that I was to fetch you when a child took ill."

He frowned, nodding in appreciation to Margaret as she passed him his cane and greatcoat. "What's wrong with it?"

She sucked in a deep, dramatic breath. "Smallpox, sir."

He and Margaret exchanged shocked looks. "Smallpox—how do you know this, Mrs. Armstrong?"

"By the description of the symptoms, sir, and because I heard rumors of the smallpox on the island of St. Kilda. I keep abreast of news, you see."

"Yes," he said dryly. He pulled his gloves from his coat pocket. "Good night, Margaret. Thank Agnes again for supper."

She lifted her skirts to step down beside him. "Is there anything I can do? I'd like to help . . . well, normally, I *would* help."

"I'll let you know—" He stopped short, staring at her so intently that she took an involuntary step backward. "You have been inoculated against smallpox, haven't you, since that day in the Institute?"

She twisted her hands. "My uncle didn't believe in doctors. He said modern medicine was the work of the devil."

"I remember him," Ian said grimly, moving onto the flagstone path. "But devil or not, *you'll* be vaccinated as soon as possible. Until then, you're not to leave the farmhouse or receive visitors."

"Oh, I—"

She fell silent and watched him stride toward the barn where he had stabled his horse, Sybil Armstrong marching with breathless self-importance at his heels.

"Is everything all right, dear?" Agnes called down the staircase into the hall.

Margaret drew back into the house. "I don't know," she murmured. "After tonight, I just don't know."

Twenty-three

Three cases of Chicken-Pox (not Smallpox, God be thanked) reported so far. Prescribed the usual saline purgatives. Cold baths and paintings of gutta percha to affected areas.

Autopsy on Margaret's rat inconclusive. Lungs, stomach congested. Blood vessels of heart and brain coagulated. Noted a faint citrus-like odour—ask Margaret if she had oranges (imported) in her basket. Peculiar this.

Cause of Death: Asphyxiation from Margaret's plaid???

"Your horse is ready, sir," Walter said from the doorway after giving his customary little cough to announce his presence.

Ian put down his pen, nodding wearily. His muscles ached from stooping over sleeping children and riding hunched, half awake, in the cold. "Just give me a moment, Walter."

"Yes, sir."

He'd slept only two hours or so since leaving Margaret last night, after rushing down into the crofts. His relief at not finding a single case of smallpox had made him shake. By dawn, after a hot bath and wolfing down a gargantuan breakfast, he was relaxed enough to sleep, but then the memory of what had happened in the parlor had come flooding back.

He had lain in his cold uncomfortable bed, naked beneath the sheets, his body burning, angry, aroused.

The scent of her still lingered on his mind: rose water and female musk. God, he wanted to devour her.

And just as he'd drifted off to sleep, the door handle had
turned. He had sat up slowly, hoping against logic that *she*
would appear in the doorway, it didn't matter for what reason.
But he would seize the advantage and bring her to his bed,
ravish her within an inch of their lives, and then sleep in her
arms until he was rested enough to seduce her again.

Unfortunately it had been Mrs. Armstrong, not Margaret,
ogling his bare chest for several irritating moments before
she'd recovered sufficiently to speak.

"Breech birth in the fishing village, sir. Walter's got your
things ready."

It was Walter's nasal monotone now that stirred Ian from
his fatigued trance. "Shall I expect you home for supper, sir?"

"Probably not." He got up from the desk, glancing tiredly
around the room. "I'll be taking tea at Mrs. Strong's cottage
if you should need me."

Walter hovered behind him in the hallway. "I wanted to ask,
sir. Well, actually, my wife said to inquire whether you'd mind
our using the leftover suet and stale scones to make a meal
for the birds. It being winter and such."

"Do what you please with the table scraps . . . so long as
they're not left around to draw vermin."

"Good heavens, no, sir."

As Ian left the house, he could feel Sybil peering at him
from the kitchen window, shocked no doubt that he had agreed
to consort with that lewd practitioner of the black arts, Morag
Strong.

He laughed quietly as he set off up the track, his breath
fogging in the bitter cold. On the shoulder of the hill he looked
down from his horse at the farmhouse nestled in its neglected
fields. He slowed pace, his blood warming at the thought of
Margaret sprawled across his lap in that cozy parlor, her
breasts exposed, skin gleaming like gilded ivory in the firelight.

Aroused, yielding, delectable—Margaret as he had dreamed

of her, but surely in his imagination he had exaggerated her response. Certainly he hadn't made the emotional connection with her that continued to elude him.

She was still on his mind almost an hour later when he reached the moor, staring down for several minutes at Morag Strong's strange little cottage before he actually saw it. Capped by a conical roof of twisted heather and bog turf, which sprouted grass in gentler weather, it resembled a fairy abode more than a place of human habitation.

"Ye look weary, Doctor."

Morag's voice, with its underlying mockery, startled him. Swinging around, Ian watched her slowly ascend the hill on a fat piebald pony. In the dying afternoon light, he noticed the silver-grey threads in her hair. Still, she was a striking woman, her figure lush, her features dark and vibrant.

"It was a long night," he said. "There was panic in the crofts at the possibility of smallpox."

Morag smiled slowly. "Come into the cottage and take a bowl of soup."

He shuddered. "I've yet to develop a taste for your puffins, even with the lovely Miss Rose spoon-feeding me the ghastly stuff."

Morag gave a rich, throaty laugh that sent an unpleasant chill up Ian's spine. "Oh, *Margaret's* broth. No, there's nothing medicinal in my kettle today."

She urged the plump spotted pony forward, guiding Ian down the hill to a byre which adjoined her cottage. Inside he found the single-room dwelling surprisingly clean and comfortable. A spinning wheel sat in the corner, and the bed-loft was laid with a freshly laundered quilt.

"Sit down." She indicated a rough pine table and two crooked driftwood chairs.

Ian complied, glancing up surreptitiously at a wall shelf on which a human skull, used to cultivate moss, stared at him from empty eye sockets. He thought of Margaret's warning and chuckled inwardly.

"Are you very hungry, Doctor?"

He tore his gaze from the skull. "That depends."

She untied her shawl and hung it behind the door, turning slowly with a smile to face him. Her heavy breasts strained against her worn brown woolen gown, and her hips swayed as she walked toward him. Whether she intended sexual provocation in her approach or not, Ian was afraid to conjecture.

A moment later, he was sure.

She laid her brown hand on his shoulder, the fingernails ragged, embedded with garden soil. Her clothes smelled faintly of peat smoke and perspiration. "I watch you sometimes, when you ride alone across the moor," she said softly. "I could not believe a man with a face so brutal could dedicate his life to helping others."

"Mrs. Strong—"

"And then I realized that in coming here you had run away from something on the mainland," she went on thoughtfully. "What would ye want to escape, I wonder?"

"I came here to talk, Mrs. Strong. To call a truce with you."

Morag released a quiet sigh and moved to the cupboard. In silence she set the table with tea, brown bread, and bowls of hearty broth—carrots, leeks, potatoes, and chicken. She tore off a hunk of bread, slathering it with sweet unsalted butter, and passed it to Ian on a wooden trencher.

"Go on then, eat," she urged. "One shouldn't have a serious discussion on an empty stomach."

His face suspicious, Ian dipped his horn spoon into the bowl. As he raised it to his mouth, he noticed a Bible on the bench by the fire.

"Considering a religious conversion, Mrs. Strong?" he asked with a grin.

Realizing what had drawn his attention, Morag began to

laugh. "Stephen left it for me last night. He had it blessed by the bishop and brought back from Edinburgh."

Ian swallowed the spoonful of soup; it was delicious. "I suppose it's difficult for Stephen to leave you on the island, knowing he's failed to save your immortal soul."

"It's difficult for him to leave Margaret."

Ian put down the spoon. "What do you mean?"

"Ah. Now I have yer complete attention." She poured their tea into two mugs, shaking her head. "Stephen is afraid she'll become like me. Of course, with you here to protect her, I don't think he need worry."

Ian took the mug from her hands, shaking his head. "What makes you think I'm trying to protect Margaret?"

"I watched ye with her last night on Clootie Hill. When a face as severe as yours softens, it is quite a remarkable transformation."

He snorted and stared past her to the fire. Against his will, images from the previous evening at the farmhouse stole across his mind. He took a sip of tea and scalded his mouth, almost welcoming the pain as a diversion from the disturbing memory of Margaret.

Morag raised her own mug to her mouth but did not drink. "Like Stephen, ye'll soon be gone."

Ian stared at her across the table, suddenly tired of her taunting. "Is that a threat?"

"I've seen your future, Dr. MacNeill," she said with a shrug. "It simply isn't meant that ye should stay on Maryhead."

"And Margaret?" Ian asked before he could stop himself, not believing at all in the prophecies of love-starved spaewives, but wanting, just the same, to hear that he and Margaret would have a romantic future together.

Morag's eyes gleamed. "Would you like to buy a love charm to carry with you on those lonely rides you take? I warn ye, the price for Margaret's affection would be very high. I'm so fond of her, ye see."

He finished his tea, annoyed with himself for carrying the conversation this far. "Mrs. Strong, I didn't come here today as one of your misguided clients. The fact is that you're doing the people of this island a great disservice by discouraging them from seeking proper medical attention."

"Your attention. Proper is a matter of opinion."

"Smearing horse dung on an umbilicus to prevent a wicked fairy from spiriting away a newborn's soul is a dangerous heathen practice—not medicine."

"You believe in only what yer senses report," she countered. "Has it never occurred to you there exists a world beyond what ye can see?"

"A world from which dead children might be summoned to revisit grieving relatives?" he asked sharply. "Do you realize the painful memories Margaret was forced to relive believing she saw her brother last night?"

Silence closed around them.

"You speak of wee Alan Rose?" she asked softly. "I know nothing of that."

He began to feel unpleasantly warm and dizzy. "Why did you warn the islanders that I would bring trouble to Maryhead?"

"Everyone knows an incomer brings a spell of bad luck to the island." She smiled, her dark eyes shining. "Would you care for more tea, Doctor . . . to clear your head?"

Ian inhaled slowly, wondering if he had complained aloud of the lightheadedness. "You'll not be easily rid of me, Mrs. Strong," he said, noting with vague alarm that her face seemed blurred; the faint smirk no longer mischievous but malevolent.

"What makes you think I want to be rid of ye?" she asked coyly.

He reached into his vest pocket and extracted the paper on which he'd copied the runes inscribed on the rat's abdomen. As Morag took the paper, her smile vanished.

" 'The past returns to haunt you,' " she translated slowly. "Well. What does it mean, I wonder?"

He stared at her intently. "I thought you might tell me."

"I'd do nothing to frighten Margaret." Her voice was solemn. "I do care for her."

"Do you really?" he asked, his tone cynical.

She shrugged and reached for his empty mug, three times swirling it around clockwise and then placing it upside down on the trencher.

"Tea leaves," he said. "How mundane. I expected at least a crystal ball."

She did not react but picked up the mug and studied the configuration of leaves. "A broken heart," she murmured. "How well ye've hidden it behind that hard face. Will Margaret be the one to heal ye, I wonder. I've taught her so many of my secrets."

He was afraid suddenly that if he didn't leave the cottage straight away, he would pass out. He shoved back his chair and stood, swaying against the table. "What did . . . you . . . put in my . . . tea?"

She raised her work-reddened hands to her neck and untwined the thick knot of hair at her nape. As it tumbled down her shoulders, she began to loosen the leather thongs that strained across her bodice.

"You don't look at all well, Doctor," she said with soft mockery. "Perhaps ye should lie down."

His head spinning, Ian managed to step back from his chair and reach the door. As he pushed it open, he sucked a draught of fresh air into his lungs and heard soft laughter behind him.

"The past returns to haunt you, Dr. MacNeill. What does it mean, I wonder?"

Twenty-four

"And you're positive there's no mistake—I really am expecting a child?" Agnes asked, struggling into a sitting position as Ian reentered the room. After examining her, he'd left her alone to absorb the news while he washed his hands in the kitchen. But she was still in shock.

"There's no mistake, Mrs. Alcock."

"A bairn—this summer. Well, Kenneth will have to stay on the island now, won't he?"

Ian smiled; sharing happy news like this seemed a good way to start the New Year. "I'm not overly concerned about the slight bleeding you mentioned, Mrs. Alcock, but to be on the safe side, I suggest you limit your activities."

"Then I won't be able to accompany you and Margaret to the Hogmanay Ball at the castle tonight. All the jolting in the cart can't be good for the bairn."

"Probably not, Mrs. Alcock."

She gave him a wicked grin. "Who's going to act as your chaperone then?"

His dark eyebrows arched in amusement at the prospect of impropriety with Margaret in a peat cart. "My conscience, perhaps?"

She got up from the sofa, smoothing her skirts down over her stomach. "No doubt it's impending motherhood that makes me uneasy, Dr. MacNeill, but I do wish you and Margaret would reconsider and stay home tonight instead."

He frowned. "Why is that?"

"I don't know. The lonely ride across the moor in the mist, the trouble with the sheepstealers, the Hogmanay revelers. Traditionally this is a night when murder and mayhem are in the air."

"On Maryhead?" Ian asked in surprise.

"We're not isolated from human emotions here, Dr. MacNeill. To be sure, trouble isn't commonplace, but it happens."

"I promise to take good care of Margaret," Ian said with a self-assured smile. "I'll carry my cane and hitch my horse to the cart. Don't worry, Mrs. Alcock. Our journey will prove uneventful."

Ian had never been more wrong about anything in his life.

For a start the cart broke an axle on a rock, not a half hour from the house. With the long ride ahead, Ian suggested they return home on his horse. But Margaret refused, having promised Lord Macpherson she would bring some hops to make a poultice for his lumbago.

"The cold weather makes his pain worse," she explained.

"Then send one of the crofters to the castle with the stuff."

"I can't," Margaret said. "Thomas needs *me* to apply the poultice."

"Hops indeed," Ian said, disgruntled at the thought of her touching another man. "It's a sharp purge he probably needs, possibly hot cushions or tincture of actaea racemosa taken in water, and a thorough exam. Anyway, he's supposed to set an example for the rest of the island by summoning me for proper medical care."

"Jealous, Dr. MacNeill?"

He scowled. "Och, look at the filth on my hands from trying to fix that wheel."

Margaret, pacing impatiently on the path, stopped behind him. "That's just the problem with doctors, unpronounceable words and exams for a common backache. And I told you that wheel couldn't be fixed. We'll be late now for the music."

He got to his feet and stared at her, tempted to point out that he wasn't responsible for the condition of the roads. But the sight of Margaret stopped him cold. You didn't argue with a woman who looked that good.

She wore a rose silk brocade evening gown under her cloak, with a black velvet boned bodice, the embroidered collar low on the shoulder. When Ian had walked into the farmhouse parlor to see her standing by the fire, gilded in hues of pink and gold, her hair twisted into an elegant coil, his mouth had gone dry and he had stared so hard that behind him Agnes had started to giggle.

And the frustrating part was that he wasn't seeing the dress at all—he would stare at Margaret if she were dressed in sackcloth. He was remembering instead what had happened in that same room between them just a few nights ago. He was remembering her in such delicious detail that even now his teeth ached with that desire.

He sighed in exasperation. "I didn't realize you cared that much for music."

"I adore it." Her brows drew into a frown. "Well, what little one hears on the island. Why—why do you keep staring at me like that?"

"I apologize, Margaret," he said, amused. "You look exceptionally nice tonight is all."

She studied him covertly as he wiped his hands on his handkerchief, feeling an unwanted flutter deep inside her. Exchange his elegant broadcloth suit and ebony walking cane for chain mail and a battle-axe, and Ian might have passed for an ancient warrior chieftain. For certain his fiercely molded face conjured up shockingly delightful images—of a pagan warlord who would fight to the death for his woman, a man whose unrestrained passion for her overrode his finer instincts—

He dashed the absurd fantasy with his next remark, bringing

Margaret crashing back to earth. "Damn axle grease won't come off my hands. I don't suppose you've got any witch hazel in your bag of potions and nostrums?"

"If that rude remark is in reference to my reticule, I have in it only my dancing shoes, the hops, and a small phial of lavender water."

"Lavender water?" Ian grunted. "Everyone within smelling distance would be calling me a fancy London lad like old Alice Fergusson."

"I doubt anyone would question your masculinity," Margaret retorted without thinking.

Ian looked up slowly, his eyes narrowing. "I'll take that as a compliment to my manhood, coming from you."

Her face burned—that wolfish gleam in his eyes told her all too well he hadn't forgotten the other night. Unfortunately, neither had she. Well, the situation would never be repeated. She didn't need the kind of temptation Ian offered. In fact, she'd come to the conclusion she wouldn't see him again on a personal basis after tonight. It would be her Hogmanay resolution.

As Morag had warned the islanders, he was a dangerous man, too good at making Margaret laugh, making her yearn for the kind of life she'd accepted could never be hers. If she ever married, it would be to an uncomplicated island man, someone predictable and safe.

Sooner or later Ian would leave Maryhead; you either became part of the island or you left it. And Ian would never belong here, not with his innovative mind and impatience for the old beliefs. Margaret couldn't see him changing. But she could see him breaking her heart.

She drew deeper into her cloak. "We'll have to abandon the cart and continue on horseback."

Ian hesitated. He knew he should refuse, but he couldn't resist the thought of spending the evening alone with Margaret, and she could probably talk him into anything. Besides, they'd reached a crucial point in their relationship. He was ready to make a lasting commitment. He'd been half serious the other night when he had offered to marry her.

"Steady the mare for me then while I unhitch the cart," he said. "You're sure you don't want to go back to the farm-house?"

"Yes. I'll go mad if I watch Agnes eat another fried herring dipped in oatmeal to make the baby's brains grow." She took the reins to hold the horse, lifting her free hand to touch the pendant suspended from the black velvet ribbon around her throat.

Ian frowned. "What's that thing around your neck you keep touching?"

"White quartz—a fairy fire stone. It's supposed to bring me luck."

"Has it?"

She glanced back at the cart with an ironic smile. "Apparently not."

"It's silly," he could not resist remarking, "if you want my opinion."

"I don't, and so is your cane. Now are you taking me to the castle tonight or not?"

Five minutes later they'd left the cart and set off riding the mare westward across the moor, fine mist touching their faces. A huge yellow moon glowed above the hills and shimmered on the infrequent glimpses of black-gold sea beyond.

Suddenly Margaret twisted around and stared back at the brooding landscape. "What is it?" Ian asked, sensing her unease.

"I'm not sure. I had the most unpleasant feeling someone was following us. But there's nothing there."

"Perhaps it's the headless shepherd of Kinmairi Moor."

"What headless shepherd?" Margaret asked suspiciously.

"I don't know his name," Ian said, managing to keep a

straight face. "But every Scottish moor worth its salt has at least one."

"You might pay more attention to where you're going and less to foolish remarks," Margaret admonished him. "Many of the roads on Maryhead end in the middle of nowhere."

"Margaret, I have the sense of direction of a moor fox hunting a hare in the mist."

A few minutes later Ian stopped at the crossroads, staring in astonishment. From behind a hill a parade of middle-aged and elderly men wearing muslin tablecloth togas and carrying bog-fir torches suddenly appeared. The leader sported a horned headdress and was shooting an ancient musket into the sky at irregular intervals. Margaret's friend Liam brought up the rear, a rusty spear on his shoulder.

"What in the name of all that's holy is that?" Ian asked as the raggle-taggle procession marched past them with absurd dignity.

Margaret giggled. "It's Maryhead's Parliament . . . our august governing body as it were. They make an annual parade across the moor every Hogmanay to keep the evil spirits at bay."

"And the good ones, too, I'd imagine. What a din."

He urged the horse forward, conscious of her body pressed to his. "So Margaret Rose likes music," he said over his shoulder. "All modesty aside, I've been told I sing passably well myself."

"Aye. I heard you in the boathouse." Hesitantly she added, "You do have a lovely voice."

"Shall I sing for you now?" he asked, encouraged by her praise. " 'Auld Lang Syne' is an appropriate selection for the evening."

The mare stumbled over a few loose stones. Margaret grabbed hold of Ian's waist before she could stop herself. He angled his head to stare down at her, and she thought she saw a lazy smile flicker across his stern face.

"They always sing 'Auld Lang Syne' in the castleyard after Thomas makes his dreadful yearly speech," she said, pointedly placing her hands against his broad back. "It makes me cry."

"What—the yearly speech or the singing?"

"The song, you joker."

"I should never want to make you cry," he said lightly. "What about 'Proud Margaret' instead?"

"I don't mind."

As Ian began to sing the amusing ballad in his deep baritone voice, Margaret found herself once again immersed in waves of pleasure. Darkness had descended in earnest, shreds of silver mist drifting alongside them like companionable spirits. Every so often you could see a bonfire flare to life on a distant hill, and small processions of islanders swinging fireballs made of oil-soaked rags and wood shavings.

Margaret had just closed her eyes, enjoying the song's final chorus, when Ian broke off abruptly and slowed the mare.

"Margaret."

She stirred, loath to break the spell his voice had cast. "What is it?"

"The mist is coming in thick and fast. I'm afraid we've wandered a bit off track."

She opened her eyes. To her astonishment she couldn't distinguish a single familiar landmark in the white-shrouded terrain. "A bit," she said in dismay. "Oh, Ian, you might have a lovely voice but you've absolutely no sense of direction."

"I know," he said with a sheepish grin.

"Fox indeed."

"A wee white lie." He paused. "Which way should we go?"

"I don't really know," Margaret answered grumpily. "Give the horse her head and see what happens. And watch for the torches."

For a full half hour they tried to follow a taunting glimmer of orange-gold torchlight in the distance. Yet every time they neared it, the flame eluded them until finally it faded away.

"I never venture this far into the moor," Margaret murmured. "But I've heard of crofters landing in the bog and people wandering out at night never to return."

"There's a cheerful thought."

"What if that light we saw was a will-o'-the-wisp?" she asked worriedly. "It's said such a light lures you to your death."

"What delightful company you're proving to be, Margaret Rose."

She grinned, despite her growing apprehension. "We'll miss all the fun at the castle, the stories by the fire and the dancing." She glanced up at his dark profile, an involuntary shiver going through her. "Do you dance, Ian?"

"Oh, aye. Like a chained bear with two left feet. Or is it paws?"

She laughed openly at that, but her amusement swiftly turned to confusion as she caught herself lifting her hands a second time to his waist. More and more she seemed to forget herself in his compelling presence. Like a hypnotic flame he drew her out of the darkness in which she'd hidden for so long. But she was terrified of being burned. To love again, to lose again, was too painful to risk.

She sat up straighter, struck again by the unsettling sense of being trailed. But why would someone follow them, as lost as they were?

"What is that ahead, Margaret, on the hill? A croft, do you suppose?"

"I'm not sure. I see no lights there anyway."

The horse stepped forward reluctantly at Ian's coaxing, muddy loam sucking at her hooves. Something about the place pricked unpleasantly at Margaret's memory. She'd been here once, with Morag Strong.

"It smells damper here than before," Ian said. "Are we near the sea?"

"Very near, but there's a burn running through those rocks,

which makes the soil damp." She touched her necklace, shivering. "Allt na Caillache . . . the Hag's Stream. Ian, I don't like this place—"

"God, Margaret," he said in alarm. "The horse is starting to sink. She's fetlock deep—"

"Don't panic. I'll get off to guide you both up the hill."

He grasped her wrist as she poised to dismount. "I'm far heavier than you. Besides, you'll ruin your dress."

"Never mind the dress. I'm afraid you'll lead us off a cliff."

She heard him jump down into the mud a moment after she'd dismounted, hovering behind as if he could bodily prevent her from disappearing into the bog. Threading through the tall sedge grass they guided the horse up the hill toward the ruins of a prehistoric tower whose stones glistened in the mist.

"Not a croft," Ian said in disappointment. "You were right."

"Yes." Margaret's voice was low. "I've been here once before."

It stood on the summit of a steep hill that overlooked the sea. Called a broch by the islanders, it was a three-storied primitive structure with numerous subterranean galleries. Once, in pre-Christian times, when warfare and magic were interwoven into the drudgery of daily life, the broch had served as a lookout tower to shelter the islanders.

Now peat and bog moss covered its weathered stone walls, and mist floated into silent chambers where forgotten clansmen had gathered to await attack.

Ian and Margaret stood in silent contemplation, letting the horse water at the burn. "We could wait inside until a crofter passes by, or the mist clears," Ian suggested. "I've never explored a broch before, have you?"

Margaret frowned. "A long time ago. When I first arrived on the island. It wasn't much fun that I recall."

"Ah, Margaret." He flashed her a boyish grin. "You weren't with me then, were you?"

Before she could think of a retort, he'd walked to the burn and knelt to take a drink. But just as he cupped his hands into the cold sparkling water, Margaret rushed up beside him and fell to her knees.

"You're getting your gown wet," he exclaimed, the water running through his fingers.

She pushed his hands away from the burn. "You can't drink here."

"Why not? The horse did."

"It's an evil place," she said quietly. "Those stones in the water—there's a legend that a nearby abbey was ravaged during a Viking invasion. Nearly all the nuns were raped and murdered. It's said that the abbess's tears formed the burn, and that her heart hardened and broke into a thousand pieces, those red-veined stones you see in the water."

Ian looked dubious.

Margaret continued, "It's said that having no heart, she sold her soul to the devil in exchange for vengeance on her enemies. When the Vikings returned the following year, they were slaughtered on this very spot."

Ian wisely held his tongue. He liked the way her eyes shone in recounting the silly story. He liked how the mist made the fine hairs around her temples form into wispy curls.

"I've heard that if a person impure of heart touches those stones," she added, "he'll be badly burned."

That was a challenge Ian couldn't resist. Grinning at her horrified gasp, he plunged his hand into the chilly water and extracted three smooth stones. "Well, well." He showed her his unblemished palm. "So much for legend—I confess to having some very impure thoughts about you on the ride here."

She jumped up in disgust and walked away.

He followed, chuckling to himself. "Come on, Margaret. It's bloody cold out here. Let's look around the broch."

He started forward, only to stop with a startled laugh, swaying from side to side on the rocking-stone of the broch's causeway, which had been positioned to creak in warning of invaders. A moment later he had regained his balance and vanished into the gloomy chasm of what might have once been a hallway. Margaret's breath caught in her throat with unaccountable fear for him as his tall figure disappeared into darkness.

"Don't go any farther!" She had to fight the urge to run after him, the image of his dark sardonic face imprinted on her mind. Impure thoughts, indeed. She should let him fall into an ancient dungeon.

But bereft of his company she felt too alone and uneasy, aware of the tension in the air, the sense of being watched intensifying. Still, she didn't venture any closer to the broch, gazing instead to the sea. Through the mist she could see distant smudges of flame from the traditional procession of torchlit boats which circled the island to warn away witches for the upcoming year. To her right a series of windswept ridges rose like a dragon's tail against the vaporous darkness of the moor.

"Come on, Margaret!" Ian called, his voice muffled by the broch's heavy walls. "I'm too afraid to go in by myself."

She smiled reluctantly, turning her head to shout back, "I am *not* coming in!"

"Why not?" He returned to the entrance, poking his head through an archway of stones. "I haven't run into any boggles or brownies as yet."

She walked carefully across the causeway, standing outside the broch. "It's not a good place, Ian."

"Look, it doesn't have the luxuries of home, I admit. But what do you expect from a bunch of people who ate with their fingers and sat around boiling oil in anticipation of the next Viking attack?"

"Oh, you fool," she said softly. "This is Morag's covenstead."

Ian didn't appear to have heard her, vanishing from view into an underground gallery. Margaret waited for another minute, listening uneasily to the burn rush over the stones, the waters where desperate petitioners made pacts with the devil, and Morag's husband had been found dead six years ago, presumably too drunk to save himself from drowning after he had fallen face down in the burn.

Reluctantly she entered the low archway and followed Ian into the dank-smelling depths of the broch, giving a little shriek as suddenly he popped out before her from behind a crumbling mortar partition.

"Quiet as a grave in here," he announced with a grin.

"It *is* a grave," she retorted, staring behind him into the stagnant gloom.

"A living history lesson. Come along, lass, let me stimulate your latent intellectual curiosities."

She swallowed the nervous laughter that threatened. "That—that sounds entirely vulgar. Anyway, what can we see in the dark?"

"I've got a candle and matches in my pocket. Give me your hand."

She did, feeling warmth rush through her veins as his strong fingers closed protectively over hers.

They proceeded deeper into the underground gallery, silent as the tunnel parted and the collapsed walls revealed the ruins of a Celtic temple. Beheaded statues of once revered pagan deities sat upon a low altar between the skeletal remains of a sacrificial goat and a collection of smooth white stones. Moldering silk hangings shed disintegrated threads of fabric as their passing stirred the air.

A shaft of moonlight that found entry through the ceiling shone upon a chalice of beaten copper and an athame, a ceremonial black-hilted knife. Ian lit a match, and before Margaret could look away, her eyes fell on the altar, covered with candlewax, bloodstains, and ashes of uncertain origin.

The match died, leaving a hint of sulphurous smoke in the air.

"I want to go back outside," she said.

Ian poked his cane into a broken urn. "You'll get lost without me."

"Ha." She was picking a careful path through the dirt. "Look who landed us in a bog in the first place."

He crept up behind her and reached for her shoulder, lowering his voice to a stage whisper. "Margaret—Margaret Rose. The spirits command you to turn around."

"What spirits?"

She glanced back reluctantly and saw that he had pulled his evening jacket up over his head and was waving his arms and moaning like a headless specter.

"The spirits of ammonia?" he suggested, grinning at her through his jacket.

"The islanders would certainly be impressed by your demeanor if they could see you now," she said coolly. "I know I'd feel confident placing my life in the hands of a man who acted like such a moron."

He drew the jacket down, chuckling appreciatively. "My sisters would adore you, Margaret."

She left the gallery, wondering why that remark should please her. "Are you a close family?" she asked when he caught up with her.

"Yes." He hesitated. "At least we were."

"Were?"

She reared back suddenly before he could answer, straight into his arms, her gaze fixed on the small white skull glimmering in the dirt. Ian bent to examine it, then stood again, shaking his head.

"It was a fox or a deer. Definitely not human."

"It reminds me of death, nonetheless," Margaret shuddered. "Stay if you like. I'm going back outside."

He threw down the skull and caught her hand, lacing their fingers together. "This place inspires me, Margaret. It puts me in a mind to romance you ancient Pictish style."

She arched her eyebrow. "And what precisely does that entail?"

"God help me if I know," he replied, his smile wicked as he drew her against his chest. "I never studied ancient Pictish courtship in university."

His face was dangerously close to hers, his wide sensual mouth only a whisper away from her own. She felt her lips part in anticipation, her heart quickening with the heady rush of blood through her body. No, she thought in panic as he pulled her harder against him. No, no, *no.* And then she closed her eyes, expecting his kiss, confused when she finally looked up and saw he had turned his head, an alert expression on his face.

Something had disturbed the silence. From outside the broch came the sound of footsteps splashing through the burn. A sheep's plaintive bleating.

And the silence again . . . a profound unnatural silence that throbbed in the shimmering drifts of mist outside.

Margaret stared up at Ian, his blue eyes warning her not to speak. Then, silently, he edged around her and climbed the corner staircase that led to a round lookout tower, the arrow loops giving a sweeping view across the moor.

"What the devil?" she heard him mutter, and without warning, he nearly knocked her down in his rush to get out.

"Someone's trying to steal my horse," he said angrily. "Stay here. I counted three of them."

"Three of what?" she asked in bewilderment.

He didn't answer but hurried from the broch, his cane clutched in his hand. Margaret wavered for only a fraction of a second before she ran after him. She far preferred to face whatever physical danger might await outside than to remain alone in this oppressive tomb where God only knew what unholy pacts had been made.

Twenty-five

It took her several anxious moments to spot Ian moving about in the mist. She was able to pick him out because he towered over the two younger men who were slowly advancing on him. A third man, with a long wiry build, sat smoking a cigarette in a peat cutter's cart; Ian's horse had been harnessed alongside it with a skittish island pony. In the cart bed itself a half-dozen sheep stirred and bleated, resisting the rough hempen ropes that bound their legs.

Ian's coldly furious voice made her jump. "I'll give you thirty seconds to unharness my horse and release the sheep you've stolen."

Margaret inched forward across the causeway, swooping to snatch a few heavy stones from the bank of the burn. Only as she held them did she remember the story of the abbess, but the stones remained cold in her hand, and she was so afraid for Ian, she couldn't worry about anything else.

The two younger men closing in on Ian had blatantly ignored his demand. Pinpricks of fear ran down Margaret's spine at their boldness, to challenge a man of Ian's size.

But who did he think he was anyway, fending off three men with his city walking stick? He had to remember Euan Bruce's battered body, that the aging shepherd had been unmercifully beaten and then tossed off the cliff by his attackers to die.

Murder and mayhem in the air.

Agnes, uncharacteristically emotional, perceptive in her pregnancy, had tried to warn them before they'd driven off.

The man in the cart, his hair scraped back into a queue, leaned forward to address the two men on the hillside, his voice bored. "See if he has any valuables—and then kill the bloody bastard."

"Kill him, Mungo? Jesus, that wasn't part of the plan."

Margaret froze, clutching the stones in her cloak. "Mungo Bruce," she said without thinking. "Why, you're not from across the channel at all! You're Maryhead born and bred, you little swine, and you're stealing food from the mouths of your own people—not to mention beating your old uncle senseless."

Mungo swung around in surprise at her voice, straining to identify her in the mist. "What would ye know of hardship, you who've never had to toil a day in yer pampered life?" he shouted back at her. "It takes money to survive on the mainland. What sort of life do I and my family have to look forward to on this miserable plot of mud?"

A breeze had blown up from the ocean and was stealing across the moor to disperse the mist. Margaret shivered. "The laird won't take this lightly, Mungo," she said. "Whatever little money you've made selling stolen property across the sound won't compensate for the punishment you'll have to face."

"The laird," Mungo said with a derisive laugh, "that simpering fop . . ." He jerked his head toward the two men on the ground, and, as Margaret watched in horror, they swung together to converge on Ian, dirks gleaming in their hands.

"Ian!"

"Stay there, Margaret!"

She rushed forward automatically, unable to distinguish him in the sudden blur of bodies behind the cart. A faint metallic click, a sound she could not identify, and then a startled cry. Her stomach knotting, she heard the soft crunch of a fist connecting with flesh and bone, a man gagging.

Mungo vaulted down from the cart to block her path, his

long arms swinging at his sides like an ape. "What am I to do with ye, Margaret Rose, she who was too good to dance with me at the castle last Hogmanay?"

"You idiot. I wasn't even at the castle last year."

"Dance wi' me now then," he said, his eyes black with menace.

"Get out of my way!"

"Ye look right through men like me," he muttered, wiping his nose on his wrist, "lusting after yer own cousin."

She glimpsed a body lying beneath the cart and realized, with profound relief, that the homely plaid and woolen trousers did not belong to Ian. She raised her chin, hiding the stones in her skirts. "What will you do with me, indeed?" she said angrily. "If your mother knew—"

It was, apparently, the wrong thing to say.

His eyes wild, Mungo lurched forward, stalking her like an animal until she had to backstep across the burn in self-defense. Her damp skirts brushed the rough edges of the rocking-stone. Her heart pounded so hard it hurt to breathe. She had lost sight of Ian, and suddenly it was as if she and Mungo were trapped alone in a nightmare world where shadows breathed and unseen forms stirred in the unhallowed surroundings of the broch.

There had been so many violent deaths on this very spot. Margaret felt her palms grow moist against the cold stones she held. It wasn't only her fear of what Mungo intended to do that unnerved her. But there was something in the air, a collective presence, an energy.

"Margaret?" Ian called to her from what sounded like a mile away. "Where have you gone?"

"Over—"

"Shut up," Mungo said, raising his big hand to her face. "I've never killed a woman before," he went on as if to himself. "Ye should have stayed home tonight, Margaret Rose, working yer spells."

Margaret was beginning to wish she'd done just that. The

stones she clutched seemed suddenly warm, pulsing with a force she could not control, searing her dampened palms. Her hand lifted of its own volition. Then before she realized what was happening, the stones were spinning the short distance across the burn, striking Mungo in the face.

He threw up his arms and screamed, a high-pitched squeal of agony disproportionate to the force she had used. Then the stones dropped into the burn, hissing like hot coals.

In horrified amazement, Margaret raised her gaze to Mungo's face and saw on his cheek the red-hot brand the stones had burned. She stepped back gingerly onto the rocking-stone.

"Ye . . . witch . . ." he said in a strangled whisper. "It is true . . . what they say . . ."

He leaped across the burn toward her. The rocking-stone teetered crazily at the added weight. Not daring to look back, Margaret scrambled across the causeway, wondering if it was her imagination or if she could see a pony slowly climbing the hill.

What the hell had happened to Ian?

As she fled, the rope that Mungo held, fashioned into a noose, struck her hard on the side of the face. She faltered, forcing herself to ignore the pain that radiated from her cheekbone. The black mouth of the broch gaped open, exuding the breath of death and decay. There was nowhere else to hide. She ducked inside, hoping Mungo would be too afraid of the shelter's dark history to follow.

"Margaret," a familiar voice whispered from the pool of blackness at the bottom of the stairs.

She started as Morag began to climb toward her, her white robes brushing the dank steps. "Hurry, Margaret. There's a secret passageway from the temple to the coast path."

Margaret slowly descended into the darkness. "What about Ian?" she whispered.

"Where is your faith, Margaret?"

"It's not in your pagan altar and ashes, I can tell you that," Margaret retorted shakily.

The rocking-stone outside creaked. As Margaret strained to listen, she heard heavy stumbling footsteps, the unrhythmic sounds of a scuffle in the impenetrable shadows of the entryway. Then Ian's voice floated down into the broch, unnaturally terse.

"Go with her, Margaret."

He was alive.

Her heart leaped in relief. Glancing upward she could just make out his figure at the top of the stairs, lean-hipped, long powerful legs planted apart in a conqueror's stance. His face looked like stone, unreadable from where she stood, but she could see that he'd lost his evening jacket, and his ruffled white shirt had been ripped open from his collar to his waistband. His cravat, however, looked absurdly unaffected above his half-bare chest.

Then she looked down. Mungo Bruce lay sprawled on his back like a turtle at Ian's feet, held prisoner by the tip of Ian's walking-stick sword—that cane concealed a *sword,* and it was poised not a centimeter from the straining arch of Mungo's throat.

Margaret and Morag walked the pony along the cliffside coastal road, not talking until the castle came into view, shining white against the sea. The outer courtyard was jammed with ponies, dog-carts, a carriage or two, the usual Hogmanay madness. In the interior court revelers drank whiskey and toasted red herrings over barrel bonfires. From deep within the great hall drifted the foot-stamping strains of a reel, fiddlers and violins.

Margaret stood facing the sea, so upset by her last glimpse of Ian she scarcely felt the brisk ocean breeze on her bruised cheek. "Do you think he's all right?"

"Mungo or Ian?" Morag said, her tone ironic.

Margaret turned, frowning. "Both of them, actually. Ian had a killing look on his face. Maybe we should go back to the broch. He looked so—"

"Primitive? Protective?" Morag suggested, her eyes sly. "I always thought his face hid some interesting secrets, but apparently it took you to bring them to the surface. Anyway, I wouldna worry about yer warrior. I sent my son to fetch help for him."

"What were you doing at the broch anyway?"

"I had a special petition." Morag's eyes shone like a cat's. "A love spell. Are you interested for yer doctor?"

"Definitely not." Margaret pulled her cloak around her. "Are you coming with me to the castle or not?"

"God, no. Thomas and I aren't speaking since he brought the doctor to the island." She paused. "Do you know ye haven't come to visit me once since that man arrived?"

Margaret was a little shocked to realize it was the truth. "I've been busy at the crofts, what with all the illnesses that winter brings."

"There are many things yet I have to teach you," Morag said softly. "Do ye still want to learn from me, or do you prefer to take lessons from your doctor?"

"I want to learn about healing," Margaret said succinctly. "He knows so very much more than I do, Morag, even though I'd sit on a hot peat before admitting it to his face."

"I warned ye he'd bring you danger. Tonight was only the start of it."

Margaret looked away, burying her cold hands in the folds of her cloak. She was shaking; she couldn't clear her mind of the image of Ian as she'd last seen him, the violent energy that charged the very air around him.

"Tonight is the end of my association with Ian," she said faintly.

"D'ye really think so?" Morag asked, her voice smug. "Aye, well. He'll leave the island soon anyway."

Margaret shrugged. "I realize that."

"He'll go away just like Stephen," Morag added, trailing slowly behind in her ghostly white gown. "Do ye ever think of your cousin now, I wonder, or has the doctor already replaced him?"

"I'll always have the greatest affection for Stephen."

"But great affection isn't love, is it, Margaret, or passion?"

They stopped outside the castle gates, the breeze blowing up harder now from the sea. Morag's face looked cynical in the torchlight that spilled onto the road.

"Thank you for your help tonight," Margaret murmured, turning toward the castle.

Morag caught her hand for a moment. "Ian MacNeill is a dangerous man. I did warn ye, Margaret."

"The superintendent tense," Ian continues. His closing his eyes. "It is this large vein which conveys the blood from the superintendent..."

Twenty-six

Breathing hard through his teeth, Ian closed his eyes for several seconds to clear his mind of the blood-red rage he had felt when he'd seen Mungo Bruce chasing Margaret into the broch. He was dangerously tempted to murder the man who writhed under him like a worm exposed to sunlight. In his opinion, Mungo deserved a slow painful death.

He shifted back and slightly lowered his sword arm, a low groan of pain escaping him. The fight with the two other little bastards on the hill had reinjured the shoulder ligaments he'd torn in the shipwreck, and he suspected he had at least one black eye, possibly a broken rib. His Hogmanay heroics were going to take a hell of a toll in the morning.

Mungo, apparently sensing Ian's lapse in attention, heaved himself upward in a burst of desperation only to collapse back on the steps as Ian jammed his elbow into Mungo's sternum. "Ugly bastard," Mungo grunted, his eyes bulging in defiance. "Think ye're such a big bloody hero in front of them two weird women." He raised his egg-shaped head, taunting through chipped yellow teeth. "Go on. Kill me then."

Ian laid the sword blade across Mungo's sweating throat and allowed himself a chillingly detached smile before he spoke.

"Lesson in Anatomy: Lecture on Surgical Anatomy of the Blood-Vascular System. Veins of the Neck."

An involuntary shiver went through Mungo's wiry body. "Ye're not scaring me with that fancy blether."

"The internal jugular vein," Ian continued, half closing his eyes. "It is this large vein which conveys the blood from the brain—assuming, of course, that you have one, which in your case I doubt. The severing of this vein will generally result in mortality." He paused a moment, his voice soft. "That means death, Mungo."

Mungo arched his neck, his eyes stark with horror. "Christ help me."

Ian leaned back, his gaze impersonal. "It is so bad, so very bad for a man to physically threaten a woman. Violence against the weaker sex brings out the beast in me, Mungo. It always has—"

He glanced up, distracted by footsteps from above. The slight well-dressed figure of Jamie Shaw appeared in the broch's entryway. "Liam and his men are right behind me, Dr. MacNeill. I assume you can use their help?"

"Aye. If they don't mind interrupting their parade."

All of a sudden Mungo shot to his feet, greasy hair whipping in his eyes as he flung Ian a final look of horrified defiance. "Doctor, he calls himself. He's a lunatic, that's what he is. A bloody lunatic butcher wi' a license."

Three of Liam's toga-clad companions, supervised by Jamie Shaw, climbed down the stairs to take Mungo outside.

"Are ye all right yerself, Dr. MacNeill?" Liam called down.

"I've been better. What happened to Margaret?"

"She and Morag walked ahead to the castle. Ye'll come along with us, too, Doctor? The mist has cleared, but I must admit, I'd nae feel right leaving you to find yer own way."

"Let me wash at the burn first. I'll catch up with you on my horse."

"Aye, weel. Don't lag too far behind. The moor is haunted, ye ken."

"The abbess and her ravaged nuns?"

"Och, no. The headless shepherd."

* * *

For several moments Ian didn't move, wondering how he was going to explain all this to Agnes. Then slowly, his body protesting, his sword again retracted, he got up and climbed the stairs to emerge onto the moor.

A forgotten sheep bleated in protest from the abandoned cart. As Ian knelt, the burn rushed across a bed of submerged stones, bearing its secrets down the hillside toward the sea. What irony, he thought, that in the same evening he discovered he harbored a capacity for murder in his soul, he also realized he had fallen in love with Margaret.

Love and murderous urges. He rinsed off his face and hands, imagining what he would tell her later tonight, testing the words in his mind.

I love you, Margaret.

I met you at a time in my life when life still held hope and I believed dreams could come true. Perhaps they do, after all. Because here we are together, disillusioned by the past, struggling toward the future, but together all the same. Do you think it means anything? If I asked you to take the chance, would you be willing to find out?

He walked slowly toward his horse, grinning. It was a nice little speech, but as he glanced down at his clothes, he decided it might have greater impact if he asked Thomas for the loan of a decent shirt first.

Twenty-seven

As Ian entered the castle's vast candlelit hall, the energetic music of the fiddler's reel died into a deep silence. The dancers broke apart, women in tweed skirts, men in tartan. He felt like Moses parting the Red Sea, the lines of islanders drawing back from him in whispering little eddies. Their eyes burned into him, black coals of mistrust in hostile faces.

The tall grandfather clock in the musician's gallery above rang out the twelve strokes of midnight. Trust him to time an entrance.

A ripple of dismayed whispering went through the hall.

"Misfortune, now, for an entire year," said a fishwife. "Has he nae heard a doctor is an unlucky first foot on Hogmanay?"

"Morag Strong says he's really Iain Dubh. . . ."

Iain Dubh. Ian scowled as he walked slowly forward, recalling some idiotic island lore about Black Jock, reputedly a thirteenth-century warlock with incredible powers.

"Aye, and does he nae carry about a wand and book of magic?" someone else whispered.

My cane. My journal, Ian thought. Great God, now my journal is the devil's grimoire.

An enormous driftwood chandelier suspended from the ceiling burned a hundred fish-oil candles, to sting the eyes and offend the sensitive nose.

He felt the islanders examining his bruised face and damaged evening attire, his mud-stained calfskin shoes, tsking among themselves with unbridled disapproval. Farmwomen, crofters, tacksmen. Normally he might have laughed off their reaction, but suddenly he was tired and seized with impatience to find Margaret, to be alone with her and share his thoughts.

Before he could search for her in the crowd, Thomas Macpherson appeared, dressed absurdly as the Abbot of Unreason in a green felt cap with tiny bells and a green velvet robe, the cuffs trimmed with gold lace.

He shook his head at Ian's bizarre appearance, bells tinkling, and handed him a mug of traditional Athole Brose—whiskey with cream, oatmeal, and heather honey. "You look as if you could use a cauldron of the stuff," he said, whistling through his teeth.

Ian frowned and took a drink as the fiddlers resumed their sword reel. "Where's Margaret?"

"In the kitchen," Thomas said. "She wanted to wash the bog mud from her stockings. I'm still not clear on what happened to the pair of you tonight on the moor."

Ian drained the mug and grinned. "Ask me later. You'll notice I'm not fit to be standing in mixed company."

"I like you, MacNeill," Thomas said, grinning back. "Do you remember your way to the kitchen?"

"Aye." Ian had already begun to back away. "The incident with Euan Bruce wasn't all that long ago. I wonder how he'll feel when he finds out I almost murdered his nephew tonight."

"Pity you didn't," Thomas called after him.

As Ian strode down the torchlit corridor, the pair of scullery maids who were bearing trays of drink to the hall exchanged startled glances and darted apart to let him pass.

He walked between them, shrugging his shoulders. "I thought it was a costume ball," he said, and they scurried away, their giggles echoing down the hall.

Through the partially opened black oak doors of the enormous stone kitchen, Ian could see Margaret at the fire, holding her freshly washed stockings to the heat with a pair of tongs, one bare slim foot propped on a stool, the other balanced on the hearthstone.

Seeing Margaret engrossed in the personal task made Ian forget the pain in his shoulder, his rib. Such a feminine thing, stockings. And she was alone—they could have a private conversation, the start of a New Year, of an intimacy between them.

He sneaked up behind her, whispering against her neck, "You'll burn your pretty toes."

She spun about, startled, lowering her arm so that the stockings came into contact with the flames just long enough to ignite.

"Oh, dammit." She dropped the tongs, the smoldering silk into the fire. She'd been so deep in thought about Ian, about how to curtail their friendship, that she hadn't heard him approaching. Tears sprang to her eyes, and they had nothing to do with the loss of her stockings.

"Oh, Ian, you idiot. Look what you've done."

He flushed and knelt to retrieve the charred stockings, but she shoved his hand away, her eyes widening as she looked him over closely in the firelight.

"Dear God. Your face is a mess."

"I prefer to think of it as character," he said, flinching, then shivering with pleasure as she touched the discolored skin beneath his swollen left eye.

"This looks terribly painful, Ian."

"It's nothing compared to my rib—" He sucked in his breath in sudden anger, for the first time noticing the bruise on Margaret's own cheekbone. "God almighty! I should have filleted him. I think I will tomorrow."

"No, you won't," she said, lowering her hand. And as he stared at her, his face furious and frustrated, she backed away from the stool and covertly pulled down her skirts. "Sit at the table so I can tend to your wounds. I need to talk to you anyway."

"Do you indeed?" he asked softly. Wouldn't it be something to tell their grandchildren they'd realized they loved each other on the exact same evening?

Margaret gave him a nervous look. "I'm not sure how to begin."

He grinned as if he knew a great secret and followed her to the table, refraining from any insulting remarks about her medical treatments as she poked around in the tall cupboard beside the sink. He was aching to carry her upstairs to a private room. "I wanted to talk to you, too, Margaret," he said. "I had a revelation about us at the broch."

She turned slowly, frowning, and brought a bowl of vinegar and a clean linen cloth to the table, murmuring, "I couldn't find any comfrey."

"Never mind then." He noticed how she avoided his eyes and felt a stab of foreboding threaten to deflate his high spirits.

"What did you want to tell me?" he asked quietly, but he thought he already knew, and he began to ache all over, his eye, his shoulder and rib, his heart.

She took the chair next to his. Her movements precise, she dipped the cloth into the pungent vinegar, squeezed it out lightly, then lifted it to his face. "In view of all that's happened between us," she began, choosing her words carefully, "I've decided, well, I think it's better if we don't see each other again. On a personal basis, that is."

Ian closed his eyes for a tense moment, his self-control threatening to shatter. His shoulder muscles tightened in a spasm he could feel all the way to his fingertips. He was positive now he had cracked his rib. The vinegar-cloth burned like bloody hell on his eye, as did the lacerations on his upper lip. Everyone on the island thought he was the reincarnation of a warlock. And Margaret had decided they should not see each other again.

"You've decided," he said in a low, angry voice, forcing his eyes open to stare at her.

We've got your authors!

If you seek out the latest historical romances by today's bestselling authors, our new reader's service, KENSINGTON CHOICE, is the club for you.

KENSINGTON CHOICE is the only club where you can find authors like Janelle Taylor, Shannon Drake, Rosanne Bittner, Sylvie Sommerfield, Penelope Neri and Phoebe Conn all in one place…

…and the only service that will deliver their romances direct to your home as soon as they are published—even before they reach the bookstores.

KENSINGTON CHOICE is also the only service that will give you a substantial guaranteed discount off the publisher's prices on every one of those romances.

That's right: Every month, the Editors at Zebra and Pinnacle select four of the newest novels by our bestselling authors and rush them straight to you, even *before they reach the bookstores*. The publisher's prices for these romances range from $4.99 to $5.99—but they are always yours for the guaranteed low price of just *$3.95!*

That means you'll always save over $1.00…often as much as *$2.00*…off the publisher's prices on every new novel you get from KENSINGTON CHOICE!

All books are sent on a 10-day free examination basis, and there is no minimum number of books to buy. (A postage and handling charge of $1.50 is added to each shipment.)

As your introduction to the convenience and value of this new service, we invite you to accept

4 BOOKS FREE

The 4 books, worth up to $23.96, are our welcoming gift. You pay only $1 to help cover postage and handling.

To start your subscription to KENSINGTON CHOICE and receive your introductory package of 4 FREE romances, detach and mail the postpaid card at right *today*.

We have 4 FREE BOOKS for you as your introduction to KENSINGTON CHOICE To get your FREE BOOKS, worth up to $23.96, mail card below.

FREE BOOK CERTIFICATE

As my introduction to your new KENSINGTON CHOICE reader's service, please send me 4 FREE historical romances (worth up to $23.96), billing me just $1 to help cover postage and handling. As a KENSINGTON CHOICE subscriber, I will then receive 4 brand-new romances to preview each month for 10 days FREE. I can return any books I decide not to keep and owe nothing. The publisher's prices for the KENSINGTON CHOICE romances range from $4.99 to $5.99, but as a subscriber I will be entitled to get them for just $3.95 per book. There is no minimum number of books to buy, and I can cancel my subscription at any time. A $1.50 postage and handling charge is added to each shipment.

Name _____

Address _____ Apt. # _____

City _____ State _____ Zip _____

Telephone (____) _____

Signature _____

(If under 18, parent or guardian must sign)

Subscription subject to acceptance

KC 0894

We have
4
FREE
Historical
Romances
for you!

Details inside!

"Before it's too late," she said, suddenly flustered.

He caught her hand, drawing it and the damp cloth against his half-bare chest. "It *is* too late," he said, his blue eyes fierce. "That's what I wanted to tell you tonight, but all of a sudden it seems absurdly inappropriate."

"I don't know what you mean," she said unsteadily.

"Yes, you do, dammit." His face suddenly tired, he released her hand. "It's always been too late for me. I've loved you for years."

Margaret stared at him in utter disbelief. "Oh, Ian," she said, lowering her eyes.

"What about Christmas night?" he demanded, and he was angry enough to shake her now. "What did that mean?"

"I don't know." She shrugged and gave him a despairing little smile that broke his heart for the loneliness inside her he wanted to banish, for the loneliness he would feel himself without her in his life. "I don't know what came over me," she went on, drawing a steadying breath, "but I do know it's something we both have to forget."

"I don't want to forget it," he said, and he felt like some big wounded beast who was too stupid to avoid the next blow.

"You have to," she said softly.

A silence heavy with suppressed feelings filled the room. Ian stared hard at Margaret, hurt and furious, not just at her, but at the cruel surprises of life that had destroyed a young woman's trust and turned her into a virtual prisoner of her own tangled emotions. He raked his hand through his hair, struggling to understand how to reach her.

"Oh, Goddamnit," he said. "Trying to figure you out is hopeless."

"Perhaps you shouldn't try."

"And perhaps you should," he fired back.

She leaned back in her chair, staring past him to the fire where her stockings smoldered in acrid-smelling ashes. She was deeply moved by his obvious sincerity, and for a moment her resolve wavered and she wished he would refuse to give up on her. What would happen if she followed the urging of her heart to allow him closer? Just thinking about it filled her with such joy, she almost changed her mind. But before that joy could hold, a cold terror welled up from the deepest recesses of her being where all the unhealed wounds of her young life, her fear of intimacy and abandonment, clamored to warn her what would happen if she let herself love this man.

"It's impossible, Ian. We've been touched by disaster from the start."

Ian swallowed over the constriction in his throat. "Perhaps that was part of the appeal. So far we've always managed to come through."

She stood, placing the cloth carefully on the edge of the bowl. "Isn't someone waiting for you back on the mainland?" she asked softly.

"Not anymore."

That gave Margaret pause. Despite her determination to end their association, she felt a contrary pang of jealousy at the idea of Ian involved with another woman. "Why aren't you with her now?" she asked, curiosity overwhelming her.

Ian rose from the table. Picking up the cloth, he dipped it into the vinegar, then lifted it to Margaret's face. "She wouldn't have me. Perhaps you could contact her though, and form a social club. Unfortunately I don't have another brother for you to marry."

She had no idea what he meant. Ian pressed the cloth to her bruised cheek. She blinked as the vinegar stung her skin, then looked down at the floor, tears gathering behind her lowered eyelids. Oh, damn everything. She hated his tenderness. It broke through her defenses and stirred her emotions like nothing else. It made it so much harder to push him out of her life.

She jerked her head away from his hand. "I think you've confused physical desire with love."

"And I think you're confused," he said softly, aching to wipe away the traitorous tear that was rolling down her cheek, "if you've never realized the two are meant to be combined."

"Oh, I am confused," she admitted. "I'm totally bewildered by what happens when we're together, and the only thing I'm sure of is that it can't go on."

"For God's sake, Margaret, at least give me a good reason why."

But she couldn't. She couldn't explain her fears to him because she had always avoided analyzing them herself. She didn't understand why she was afraid of the kind of closeness he wanted. It was something that lay beneath the surface of conscious thought; she just accepted it, and lived her life the best she could.

And now Ian had raked up all the old yearnings for love and happiness she had taught herself to pretend didn't matter.

There were servants hanging back in the doorway. Ian watched Margaret walk back to the fire, barefooted, her head bowed. She looked as miserable as he felt, but he was starting to feel so sorry for himself, he didn't have much sympathy left to share.

"I'll look the other way if we should run into each other," he said, backing toward the door. "We'll have to take turns treating patients to avoid chance encounters. After all, it's a small island." He hesitated, unable to keep the hurt anger from his voice. "And by the way, have a good New Year. I know I'm very grateful that I've started it by having my heart thrown back in my face."

She flinched and closed her eyes, standing before the fire until she could no longer hold back the tears that had been gathering. She had driven him away, the best thing that had ever happened to her. By the time she had composed herself enough to look around, Ian was gone.

Twenty-eight

It snowed for an entire week after Hogmanay. Margaret thought she would lose her mind, cooped up in the farmhouse with Agnes and Kenneth, who was eating as if to compete with his wife's expanding waistline. There was no way to escape the couple's cozy intimacy, which unintentionally excluded Margaret, reminding her of how alone she really was, how happy life could be. For other people.

She had expected to feel relieved after ending her relationship with Ian. And in a way she did. She didn't have to worry about him leaving her. She didn't have to worry about him criticizing her natural cures. And she didn't have to hurry home to Agnes after seeing Ian to ask the definition of one of those long unpronounceable Latin words he loved to throw around. Life was definitely easier.

But if she'd banished Ian from her life, she found it far more difficult to do so from her mind. She thought of him constantly, and suddenly her days had become longer, darker, lonelier, without anticipating their spirited meetings, his teasing, his compelling face, his strong arms to hold her.

She realized too late she really liked being held in those arms.

She was a little surprised she hadn't heard from him. If he cared for her as much as he said, wouldn't he have pursued her harder? But this, she argued to that doubting inner voice, was what she'd wanted. Unthreatened peace. Solitude.

As another week passed and the snow drifts melted, she fell
back on her former ways, the old habits of filling in her time
by doing for other people. Waiting on Agnes and Kenneth.
Distilling rheumatism cordials and herbal tisanes for the in-
variable winter complaints. She spent endless hours at the
crofts, especially with Peggy Kerr and her thriving infant son.
But the ache inside Margaret did not ease.

She half expected to meet him by accident at the crofts. She
knew he still visited Peggy to check on her son's progress.
Then Peggy herself explained one morning, "The doctor's
taken up at the castle, Miss Rose, what wi' trying to have us
all e-knock-yew-lated."

Margaret, holding young David in her lap, looked up
quickly, her eyes betraying the interest she tried to deny. "E-
knock . . . oh, then he's started to give the smallpox inoculations. I didn't realize the vaccine had arrived."

"Came on the last mail packet," Peggy said. "Ye should
have seen the puir doctor, standing there wi' his skin-prickers
and string and no one to prick. Everyones afraid to go to him
because Morag warned them they could end up like Euan
Bruce if the doctor had his way."

Her smile fading, Margaret handed David back to his
mother. "What do you mean end up like Euan? Has he had a
relapse then?"

"Relapse?" Peggy snorted. "I'll say. He took sick and died
two days after they caught his nephew Mungo and deported
him to the mainland."

"Oh, God, no. No one told me. I can't believe Morag being
so irresponsible—this will kill Ian's reputation on the island.
But what about you, Peggy? Have you had an inoculation yet?"

"Me, Miss Rose, as healthy as I am?" She gave Margaret
an impudent grin. "What about you?"

"Uh, not yet. But I mean to very soon."

"How soon?" Peggy challenged her.

Margaret reached down for her basket, her eyes gleaming "I'll have one if you will."

Peggy put her son to her breast, rubbing the back of his bald head as he latched on lustily to her nipple. "I suppose," she grumbled, "but only if you go first. I don't know why ye'c want to do it, though, go against Morag's advice, I mean."

Margaret got up and tugged on her mittens, her fingers suddenly clumsy with impatience. "Morag is wrong this time, Peggy."

"But she's taught ye so many of her secrets, Miss Rose."

"And so has Dr. MacNeill," Margaret said with an unwilling smile of acknowledgment. "More perhaps than I realized. I'll have Kenneth drive us to the castle in the cart." She didn't want to give Peggy a chance to change her mind. "Be ready in an hour, and I'll see if I can persuade some of the others to come in the meantime."

As Margaret walked outside to the cart, she realized her heart was already pounding in anticipation of seeing Ian again. It would be just this once, she told herself. A brief impersonal visit. Suddenly she laughed out loud, knowing she was a liar, her laughter frightening a goat who had ambled up to sniff at her basket.

"Here." She tossed the scrawny goat a handful of caraway biscuits that a crofter had made, feeling reckless and irrationally happy. "They were for Agnes, but she'll never know if we don't tell her."

Ian shook his head, his voice weary as he spoke with Lord Macpherson across the long banqueting table in the castle hall. "Don't waste your time and money on any more bribes of tea and crofting rights. They won't come if they're afraid."

"Devil Doctor," Thomas murmured, staring out the tall mullioned window. "They're saying you're a warlock whose power is greater than that blasted Strong woman's."

Ian plowed his fingers through his windblown black hair, more frustrated than angry. "I've been called that before in Aberdeen, before I ever met Morag, by the way, because of my experiments. But here on the island they think I'm the reason Euan Bruce died. They're afraid of me."

Thomas glanced around, absently patting the pair of hounds who panted at his knees for attention. "But Euan's death didn't have anything to do with you, did it? It wasn't related to your surgical operation, or that stuff you used?"

"The anesthesia was completely unrelated to his death," Ian snapped. His face perplexed, he folded his arms across his chest and sat back in Thomas's Hepplewhite chair, a damned delicate thing of such Lilliputian design that Ian felt like a giant. "I suspect Euan suffered internal injuries from the beating. But I'll never know. The family's refused me an autopsy. And now no one on the island will have anything to do with me."

"Including Margaret?"

"Especially Margaret."

Thomas frowned. "Vaccinations have been done since before either of us were born."

"Try to convince the islanders of that."

Ian didn't hear Thomas's reply; he was thinking about the good laugh Margaret would have over his predicament.

He'd tried so hard not to think of her since the decision she'd made on Hogmanay. He'd tried so hard that he had almost succeeded in shutting off all his other emotions, too, and he was beginning to not care if this whole ignorant island sank to the bottom of the sea, himself included.

He sighed in resignation and pushed away the glass of brandy sitting in front of him. The truth was that he did care about Margaret, far too much, and he cared about this soggy little island. If he managed to protect it from a smallpox epidemic which could wipe it out, he'd be satisfied that he'd accomplished something. And if he left here tomorrow he'd have at least that to console him.

But even then he would still want Margaret. He missed her so much now that he'd spent the last three evenings in a row, standing for over an hour each time on the hill outside the farmhouse. It was insane, him acting like a voyeur who would have been humiliated if she'd caught him, and he'd half frozen off his ballocks to boot. But he couldn't stay away, he couldn't even sleep at night for the violently erotic dreams he had about her that made him wake up shaking and struggling to breathe—

"Is it necessary to have made a prior appointment?" a soft impish voice asked from the doorway, and Ian wondered in amazement if he was indeed part warlock to have conjured Margaret from his thoughts.

An unconscious smile lit his face as he watched her enter the hall and stop at the end of the table. From the corner of his eye he noted with surprise the small crowd of islanders standing in the doorway behind her. But he couldn't tear his attention from Margaret, drinking in the sight of her, his elusive mermaid.

"How can I help you, Miss Rose?" he asked politely, when the feelings roiling inside him were anything but polite.

She began to unfasten her cloak, feeling a strange tingle along her spine at the warmth in Ian's eyes as he watched her. She glanced back at the anxious faces in the doorway, deliberately keeping her own voice calm. "We've come for our"— she smiled faintly—"our e-knock-ewe-lations."

Ian stood, forcing back a grin. He realized the sacrifice to her own reputation she had made coming here, an act of faith in the "Devil Doctor." He wanted to leap across the table and kiss her in front of everyone. He wanted to rebuff her openly as a retaliation for ending their association. Instead, he motioned for her to take the chair beside him.

"Do I have to remove my dress for this?" she asked, her

voice soft with a secret amusement Ian did not immediately understand.

Ian glanced down at her face. The same affectionate exhilaration he had always felt when he looked at Margaret came back to him in a rush. But the moment was made bittersweet by the distance she had put between them. They had come full circle since that long-ago day in the Institute. And she was still as emotionally beyond his grasp as she had been then, despite all that had happened between them on the island.

"Just roll up your sleeve, please." He raised his voice so the islanders could hear the standard explanation. "Now, a smallpox inoculation is a simple procedure, Miss Rose—"

"If I can trust an old man such as yourself to carry it out," she mischievously interrupted. "For heaven's sake, Ian, haven't you changed that speech in five years?"

He stared at her in disbelief, his fingers resting on the rapid pulsebeat of her wrist. "What did you say?"

She glanced down at his hand. "Do you pay all your patients this much personal attention?"

He leaned toward her, oblivious of Thomas, of the islanders intently watching the exchange between him and Margaret. "I thought you didn't remember."

She pulled her wrist away and began to roll up her sleeve, a faint smile playing on her lips. "It's begun to come back to me recently."

He picked up his knife from the tray, speaking in a low voice that only Margaret could hear. "The last time we tried this, I didn't see you for five years afterward, and then it took a shipwreck to bring us back together. I'm furious at you, you know, for coming in and out of my life like that. And for what you've put me through"—he stared into her eyes—"and don't bother to deny you felt something for me, too, even if it was against your will."

She leaned back against the table. "Ian, please."

He made the small incision in her arm, saying huskily, "It won't work. We belong together."

She looked away from the table, forcing a broad smile for the benefit of Peggy and the others who observed the procedure in suspicious silence. "It's practically painless," she said in a loud voice. "I barely felt a thing."

"You wouldn't admit it if it were bloody torture," Ian said quietly. Torn between exasperation at her stubborn nature and admiration of her courage in coming to him today, he finished the procedure and glanced up at the crowd in the door. "Next please!"

Margaret rearranged the sleeve of her gown and got up from the table, trying not to show how he had upset her. Why had she thought she could face him today and remain unaffected when she'd never succeeded at it before?

"I hoped you were a physical obsession that would pass, Margaret," Ian said quietly as she turned away. "I'll see you tomorrow at the farmhouse."

She glanced back, but before she could speak, he added, "The inoculation will likely make you ill. It's a professional call. Nothing more—unless you want it."

She swallowed, suddenly not knowing what it was she wanted. "I'll stay to help you here," she said slowly. "To prove to everyone you haven't killed me with your e-knock-ewe-la-tion."

He smiled, but his heart wasn't in it. In two weeks he had missed her more than he would have believed possible. And the sad part was that he knew Margaret had missed him too but she would never admit it.

Twenty-nine

For five days Margaret was too ill to leave her room. But during the entire time, she was aware of Ian beside her, reaching for her in the feverish shadows, although she was unable to acknowledge him except for a few incoherent words.

She had dreams of him, too. And in her restless sleep, she confused those dreams with the increasing moments of lucidity when she would awaken to find him sponging her down, his blue eyes reassuring. "It's all right, Margaret," he would say. "I'll take care of you."

Then early one evening—she had no idea of the day, she woke up and saw Ian at her desk, writing in his journal by candlelight.

She struggled to sit up. Ian stood at once and hurried to the bed, his face so haggard she felt guilty for the sleep he'd obviously lost over her. "Margaret, there now. That's much better, isn't it? The worst is over."

She studied him in silence. There were dark circles beneath his eyes, a black stubble of beard on his jaw. "You've killed me," she whispered, her voice rusty from disuse. "It's revenge for my soup, isn't it? I feel like the farmhouse has fallen on my head."

He smiled in relief and sat down on the edge of the bed. "You're fine. Not a mark on you anywhere."

"Anywhere?"

He gave her an unabashed grin. "Well, five days is a long time, and I am your doctor."

She fell back against the pillows with a helpless laugh. "You haven't been here every night. Agnes wouldn't allow it."

"No," he lied. "Of course not."

He took her wrist, smoothing his thumb across the delicate bones. His touch electrified Margaret, sent a jolt of white heat through her whole body. "Erratic pulse," he murmured, raising his brow. "You're either not completely recovered or you're excited about something."

She pulled her hand free. "It's probably hunger."

"Maybe it's loneliness," he suggested, his voice seductive.

He was leaning over her, his large body pressing against hers in such a way she couldn't have thrown him off if she'd had the strength. His hair had grown longer in the past few weeks, shaggy black tendrils falling on his collar. She felt his eyes on her face, dark, searching for the opening she was terrified to give.

"How many people have you inoculated?" she asked conversationally, hoping to break the spell he'd cast over her.

He moved his hand up her forearm to her shoulder. Margaret's heart hammered in her chest. "About two hundred. I think there were some who came back twice when Macpherson started giving out chickens as an incentive."

"Two hundred," she said in admiration. "That's nearly the entire population."

He lowered his hand to brush her hair from her shoulder. Margaret held her breath, then exhaled, arching her throat involuntarily as he drew his hand down her arm. "Don't you ever give up?"

"Not when it matters to me as much as you do."

Their gazes met. He brushed his fingertips across her breasts, and Margaret felt her stomach muscles tighten in a purely instinctual reaction that must have shown on her face to judge by the slow knowing smile he gave her.

Yet that smile hid a myriad of primitive impulses of his own. Their enforced separation had only sharpened Ian's need for her, and if she weren't still weak, he'd peel back that old quilt and slowly undress her, dedicating the night to making sure she knew she belonged to him. But the heaviness in his groin had become such a sweet ache he had to leave her bed and leave it now.

He knew she wanted him, too. Her erratic heartbeat, that thready catch in her voice, couldn't be put down to any lingering physical ill. She wanted him, and he was going to take full advantage of that wanting the moment she was well enough to withstand all the raw passion he could barely hold in check.

Margaret swallowed at the intense hunger on his face. His desire for her was obvious, charging the air between them, and she wasn't sure she had the resolve to fight him anymore.

"Have I ever told you how much I love your mouth?" he asked quietly. Her eyes widened as he rubbed his thumb across her lower lip. "Even from that first night we met."

"And my sharp tongue?" she said with a grin, aware it was a dangerous moment. "I want a bath," she added softly, "and something to eat. I'm ravenous."

"I'll have Agnes come up to help you." He rose from the bed, his hand brushing her cheek in a possessive caress that made her shiver. "I have to be back at the crofts early tomorrow anyway."

She sat up slowly, biting the corner of her lip to suppress a wild impulse to ask him to stay. Secretly she touched the side of the quilt where the imprint of his body remained, and the swirling excitement in her stomach tightened into a longing that almost made her beg him to come back to her side.

But he looked haggard himself, and there were others to help, families Margaret would have to visit the first thing tomorrow—after she'd checked on Ian at the manse to make certain he wasn't driving himself to the brink of exhaustion.

And as for her resolution to end their friendship, well, she told herself that perhaps this wasn't the time to make any more rash decisions.

"Lock the door after me, Margaret," he warned her. "I'll be back in the morning."

"Why—"

"Just lock it," he growled, his face darkening as she started to leave the bed and the candlelight shone through her nightdress, emphasizing every sweet curve and hollow of her body.

She moistened her lips. "You look like you need some rest."

"Oh, I need something, Margaret, and I'm going to take it if I don't leave now."

When he'd closed the door behind him, he heard her scurry across the floor, throwing the bolt with such force that he could only laugh, knowing it was only a matter of time before he breached her defenses. He couldn't last much longer otherwise.

Thirty

To Margaret's astonishment, she slept until past noon the next day. By the time she'd dressed and had tea, listened to three dreadful scenes from Agnes's new play and packed a hearty cold supper for Ian, it was almost four o'clock in the afternoon. She didn't have time now to visit the crofts before dark.

"He doesn't need it, you know," Agnes remarked with a small frown as she watched Margaret fasten her cloak.

"Doesn't need what?" Margaret asked, glancing around.

"All that food. He has a housekeeper." Agnes lowered her eyes to the notebook in her lap. "Unless of course you've a personal interest in seeing he's well fed."

Margaret stared down at the heavily laden basket, nudging Cyclops away from it with her foot. "He looked so haggard, Agnes. I think he's been too busy taking care of his patients to eat properly."

"He was busy enough taking care of you," Agnes said archly. "It was almost indecent, the amount of time he spent in your room."

Margaret bent to pick up the basket, her face warm as she remembered waking up to find Ian at her bedside.

"Have a nice evening, dear," Agnes murmured.

"Oh, I'll be home before evening."

Agnes raised her brows. "As you say."

The cat followed Margaret to the door and squeezed out onto the steps beside her.

"You'd better not come along," Margaret warned him laughingly. "If Ian gets ahold of you, he'll drag you into his lab and knock you out with the goldfish."

But the cat followed anyway, and Margaret let him, in a good mood as she walked the short distance to the manse. Then on the hillside path she spotted Walter Armstrong in his tatty old cap and tartan trousers, the pair of field glasses he held trained on some spot in the farmhouse orchard.

"Hello, Walter!" she shouted with a wave of friendliness toward the world in general, and although she didn't particularly like the man, if he worked for Ian, he must have some good qualities.

The birds Walter had been watching took flight from their resting place on the fence. Walter lowered the field glasses, working his thin lips into a dour imitation of a smile. "Miss Rose."

"Anything interesting on the wing today?"

"There were some green piper swallows from Greenland, miss, before you arrived."

"Oh, dear," Margaret said. "All that way. Well, don't let Cyclops near 'em."

Walter looked down in horror at the overweight cat sniffing at his boots. Surreptitiously he gave the cat a little kick, and Cyclops hissed, streaking back to the safety of Margaret's skirts.

"It's bad luck to kill a sparrow, Cyclops," Margaret said.

"Bad luck for the sparrow," an amused masculine voice added from the path behind her.

"Ian!" She glanced around to see him grinning down at her. "I was on my way to the manse to give you supper."

He looked her over approvingly, noting the healthy color in her cheeks. "And I was just at the farmhouse to check on you. Come on. We'll walk together to the manse so you can feed me. I'm starving." He took the basket, adding as an after-thought, "How's the bird watching, Walter?"

Margaret didn't give Walter a chance to answer, her eyes sparkling as she and Ian fell into step together. "I think he's annoyed at me for scaring them away," she whispered.

Ian just laughed. Walter and his disturbing peculiarity were the furthest things from his mind; Margaret, the fact she'd come to see him, consuming all his interest.

When they reached the manse, Ian sensed Margaret hesitate before following him inside. "You'll share the supper you've brought with me," he said firmly as they stood in the hall.

"Well, if you like."

"I like." He set down the basket for a moment and helped her remove her cloak, his large hands lingering on her shoulders. "In fact, I insist. Why don't you set the table in the small parlor and I'll open a bottle of wine?"

After they'd eaten a cold beef-and-onion pie and three tartlets of dried apples, they sat by the fire and sipped the rich burgundy in silence, Ian not bothering to hide the sexual interest in his eyes as he stared at Margaret.

"I should go," Margaret murmured, "to let you sleep."

She set her glass down on the table and stood to leave, but before she could move, Ian jumped up to block her exit. She was afraid to meet his eyes, staring instead at his strong brown throat, at the pulse beating at its base.

"I should go. I really should."

"But you won't because I'm not going to let you."

"Ian—"

"I want you, Margaret," he said hoarsely. "Do you intend to torture me forever?"

She smiled self-consciously and finally looked up at him, but Ian wasn't smiling, his dark blue eyes so stark with love and desire she didn't even resist when he took her by the hand and led her to the door, grabbing the unfinished bottle of wine and their two glasses on the way.

In the hall, Margaret felt a second of uncertainty. "Won't the Armstrongs—"

"Don't worry," he said, his fingers gripping hers. "They know to knock."

They climbed the stairs together, Margaret starting to giggle at their furtive escape. "You're not very good at this sort of thing, are you?" Ian asked, but he was laughing quietly, too, having a damned awkward job not banging the bottle of burgundy and two glasses against the banister.

Margaret looked indignant. "It's my first time."

"A good thing, too."

"And I suppose sneaking up and down stairs with women is second nature to you?"

He thought of Jean, of the few but memorable sexual misadventures he'd had before they'd met.

"I notice you didn't answer," Margaret pointed out as they reached his bedroom door.

He smiled and ushered her inside the sparsely furnished room, setting the bottle and glasses on the dresser. Margaret went immediately to the window and closed the curtains. Ian watched her with his eyebrows raised, leaning against the wall.

"What do you think you're doing?"

She turned, looking embarrassed. "You know, Walter and the field glasses."

"He'd have to climb a pretty tall tree to get a view inside this room."

"Or a hill."

Ian laughed softly and came forward to draw her away from the window, guiding her to his bed. As her gaze lifted to his he added gently, "Oh, God, you're so very sweet. Don't worry about anything."

He brought his hands to her shoulders, then down her back, unfastening the impossibly tight row of buttons on her rose chintz gown. Margaret stood unmoving, her breathing suspended as she felt his fingers deftly untie the ribbons of her chemise.

"You're a little too good at that," she whispered.

"Raise your arms, love," he said, smiling down at her.

She did, mesmerized by his deep seductive voice, allowing him to remove her petticoats, her drawers, the puddle of clothing on the floor rising to her calves. Then finally he knelt to take off her garters and stockings, sliding his hands up along her flanks as he stood to take her into his arms.

Margaret closed her eyes, feeling very fragile and cherished and frightened as he held her. "Ian—"

"It's all right, Margaret."

"You're sure?" she whispered.

"Oh, aye."

"I—I feel a little peculiar."

He stared down at her. "You're not well?"

"A little faint is all."

"Och, that's normal. I feel the same."

"And my heart is beating to burst—"

"So is mine."

They smiled at each other. Then Ian swung her into his arms and laid her beneath him on the bed. Something protruded into Margaret's hip from under the heap of rumpled bedclothes, and her eyes widened, a puzzled laugh escaping her. "Ian, what on earth . . ."

His own look of confusion gave way to a chuckle. "It's only my journal. Just push it on the floor. And you'll pardon the unmade bed. Mrs. Armstrong is afraid to come in here anymore."

"Maybe we should wait."

He shook his head. "I can't.

"But—"

He silenced her with a deep, leisurely kiss, his arms enfolding her, urging her back against the bed. She ached to touch him and wasn't sure if she should, uncertain of his reaction.

From deep in her belly melting sensations spread, and she was breathless when Ian broke the kiss, his blue eyes unreadable in the dimness. Her heart in her throat, Margaret watched him take off his shirt and waistcoat. What little light penetrated the drawn curtains cast into relief the angular planes of his face, his desire for her etched into every feature.

She began to pull a sheet up over her breasts and Ian shook his head. "Don't cover yourself. I want to look at you."

Her hand fell to her side, but she felt very embarrassed, both hot and cold all over as his eyes slowly swept over her.

At the side of the bed he unbuttoned the waistband of his trousers. His clothing fell to the unvarnished floor on top of hers. Margaret moistened her lips. She should have looked away, but the unexpected beauty of his male body stole her breath—his muscular shoulders, wide chest, and lean brown torso, the triangle of black hair that tapered down from his flat belly to his erection. She pressed back against the headboard. Their gazes met, and arousal flooded her at the unashamed sexuality in his eyes.

"It's all right," he said again.

He lowered himself onto the bed beside her. With a shock of pleasure Margaret felt his bare chest crush her breasts, his leg burrow between her thighs. His body heat burnished her skin, and the position felt exciting and peculiar. He bent his head to suckle her breasts, and Margaret arched like a bowstring, her insides trembling with a pleasure so intense, she had to force herself to breathe. As his mouth encompassed one sensitive tip at a time, his tongue circling the dusky areola, she shuddered and twisted down into the tangled bedding.

He rested his face between her breasts, his eyes closed as he regained his control. "Oh, Margaret. It seems like I've waited forever for this to happen."

"Five years anyway," she teased him.

She touched his crisp black hair, stroked his cheek, feeling shy as she did so. She couldn't let herself care this much. She couldn't let herself be swayed by his tenderness when there was a risk he wouldn't become a permanent part of her life. And maybe it was wrong to be here with him now, but she'd never have a chance like this again to experience lovemaking with a man like Ian, a man she could so easily love forever if she'd allow it. Her heart twisted at the thought.

He eased his head back and stared at her, his eyes searching hers. "What's the matter?"

"What if you have to go away?" she whispered.

"Leave the island?" he asked in surprise. "I've no intention, especially not after today."

He ran his hand down the side of her hip to her belly, between her thighs where she was already moist with excitement. She tensed as he slipped his little finger inside her, separating the silken folds and flicking gently at the hooded nub of sensitive skin beneath.

"Do you like this?" he whispered, the hoarseness of his voice betraying his own pleasure.

Before she could answer, something scratched against the door. Margaret tried to sit up, her face alarmed. "Did you hear that?"

"Relax. It's only the cat. Anyway, I locked the door."

Smiling down at her, he lowered his head back to her breasts and drew a taut pink tip deep into his mouth, working his tongue across it in rhythm with the teasing of his fingers. Sensations, overwhelming and erotic, streaked through Margaret.

"Well, do you like it?" he asked again, her fragrance driving him wild.

"I wouldn't admit it if I did," she whispered, a catch in her voice.

He smiled lazily, murmuring, "I already knew the answer anyway. Your lovely body betrayed you."

She flushed, but her embarrassment was nothing compared to the aching compulsion growing inside her. With his low growl of encouragement, she began to rock against his hand, her movements so sensual that Ian couldn't stop himself, dragging his face between her breasts to her belly, to the fragrant core of her where his fingers were sparking unbearable impulses through her lower body.

"Ian," she said, her hands clutching his shoulders. "Oh, please . . ."

Then as his mouth touched her there, tasted her musky essence, she surged upward from the bed only to subside with a whimper of shock at the intimate thrust of his tongue inside her.

Ian smiled at her surrender, his heart beating in swift violent strokes. He curled his arms around her hips, caught her hands to hold her down on the bed until he took her past shame to sheer delight.

Her self-conscious gasps of pleasure punctuated the silence, aroused him beyond the bounds of rational behavior. As she began to quiver, spasms racking her slender frame, he slowly raised himself to kiss her again, letting his lower body nestle against hers. Margaret stiffened, pressing her forearms to his chest in an instinctive effort to delay the final intimacy.

"I'm afraid," she whispered.

"Don't be," he whispered back as he brought his own two hands between him and Margaret to interlace their fingers in a gesture that would foreshadow the intimate joining of their bodies. "Do you know what I'm going to do to you?"

She smiled, drifting in a haze of awakening sensuality. "Not another inoculation?"

He gave a strangled laugh. "That's one way to describe it, I suppose." He hesitated. "Oh, Margaret, I wish you would touch me."

"I wanted to, but wasn't sure how."

"Just try," he whispered.

Their gazes locked, Margaret raised her hands to his neck and twined her fingers in his hair. Ian closed his eyes for a moment, moving against her, his thick shaft slipping between her thighs. Following her instincts, Margaret allowed her hands to drift down the ridged muscles of his back, to the hard contours of his hips. Ian arched his spine at her touch, a shudder of animal pleasure rippling through him. Then, tentatively, Margaret brought her hands around to his groin, closing her fingers around his sex.

"When you touch me . . . I can't breathe . . . can't think . . ."

He kissed her swiftly, hard, his eyes almost black with mindless need. She whimpered softly beneath him, her legs parting. Then with a groan, he came to his knees and positioned himself between her thighs. Her breathing quickened. Her body raised upward in instinctive capitulation.

His entry seared her, robbed her of breath and speech. At her muted cry he kissed her again, a kiss of comfort as well as male possession. Although intellectually aware of what the sexual act entailed, Margaret was unprepared for the hot tide of feelings that flooded her, dark waves that concealed dangerous whirlpools of sensation and emotion, desire drawing her deeper and deeper into unknown channels. And it was Ian who had unleashed them from a secret well of longing hidden inside her.

Too late for regrets, recriminations. Too late for anything except the sweet agony, the straining for the penultimate that claimed them.

She arched upward and he responded, sheathing himself slowly in the sweet depths of her body, pressing past the fragile barrier. Margaret tensed, her eyes searching his face for reassurance. But Ian couldn't have stopped now if he'd tried.

"I'm sorry," he said hoarsely. "Am I hurting you very much?"

She gave a slight shake of her head, her shoulders dropping back against the bed. Ian released a terse sigh, then began to rock inside her again, faster, the muscles of his face hardening until suddenly he looked like a stranger. But he was not. He was closer to Margaret than anyone she had ever known. She squeezed her eyes shut and locked her hands around his neck. Closer than she had ever imagined it possible for two people to be.

"Look at me," he said in a tight voice. "Margaret, look at me, love."

She did, and the coiled pressure in her belly, the unbearable tightness, seemed to spread through her body until she thought her heart had stopped beating.

"Raise your hips," Ian said roughly. "Higher. Oh, God, you feel so good."

She slid her hands down to his buttocks, and as Ian thrust deeper, the trembling began inside, release overtaking her in a burst of sensations so powerful she was not immediately aware that Ian had also stiffened, his head thrown back, a groan breaking in his throat.

"Ian," she whispered.

"Oh, God. Margaret . . . so good . . ."

An interval of incredible magic, bodies fused together, hearts beating in wild harmony. Ian could not speak, his heart soaring with a happiness that surpassed anything he'd ever experienced. And when he withdrew from her to fall onto his side, he felt bereft, drawing her against him, kissing her face in its frame of tangled hair, cradling her against his damp chest.

Margaret laid her face on his shoulder, contentment stealing over her, her shivering body absorbing his warmth. He'd break her heart if she wasn't careful. But she had tried so very hard to deny what he made her feel. Just for tonight she had lowered her defenses. Just for tonight, perhaps, she could elude the ghosts of the past.

Thirty-one

She stirred in Ian's arms, inhaling the tangy scent of his skin, the fading perfume of lovemaking on the sheets he had drawn over them. "What time is it?" she whispered, nudging him in alarm. "Ian, I have to go."

He slipped his arms down her back, cupping her hips to mold her against him. "Umm. No." His voice was thick with sleep, and satisfaction. "Can't go. It's too late."

She wriggled out of his arms. "You don't know how Agnes and I were raised. Anyway, what would you think of my behavior if I were one of your sisters?"

"I'd have a damn shock waking up naked in bed with you for a start."

"This isn't the time to joke," she said crossly, ignoring his sleepy grin.

"I know." He twisted onto his side and forced her down beneath him, his blue eyes intent on her face. "It's time to make love again."

"I can't stay," she whispered, her stomach quivering. "Let me sneak home while it's still dark."

His grin faded. "I love you, Margaret."

Her lips parted on an involuntary breath. "I suppose you feel obligated to say that now."

"Only because it's the truth." He studied her face, his heart sinking at the way she seemed unable to accept the love he wanted to give. "I don't suppose you feel obligated to say the same?"

She tried to sit forward, her hair falling over her breasts like a mantle. "Ian, I *have* to leave."

He bent his head and captured her mouth with a slow bruising kiss, his fingers anchoring in her hair. Margaret groaned, her resistance melting. She needed time away from him, to think over what had happened. She was terrified.

He drew back, pushing a hand through his hair. Margaret sat up slowly, her breast brushing his arm, and Ian briefly closed his eyes, forcing himself not to touch her again. "I'll walk you back," he said reluctantly.

"Why?" she asked. She stretched over him to retrieve her clothes from the floor, tempting Ian again with her shapely sheet-draped derrière, positioned at a provocative angle across his lap. The sight instantly aroused him.

"Why?" He frowned, trying to remember what they were discussing, her slender body too distracting to his train of thought. "Because I want to be with you for as long as I can."

He got up as she dove over him like an otter. Smiling down at the sight of her tangled in the discarded clothes on the floor, he lit the candle on the nightstand. Then, still naked himself, he moved to the fireplace, leaving Margaret to pick out her stockings from his trousers while he knelt to rekindle the coals. A glance at the clock told him it was only midnight, and Margaret was taking an inordinate amount of time to get dressed.

All of a sudden his own clothing came hurtling through the air to hit his back in an overtly hostile attack, boots, underwear, trousers, shirt. He leaped up with his trousers over his arm. "What the hell was that for?" he asked in astonishment.

She stood, half-dressed, pushing her arms into the sleeves of her gown. "I've just been reading your journal."

"You haven't."

She tossed back her hair. "Very interesting, too. Especially the part about Jean, wondering if she'd be jealous because you were sleeping in my bedroom."

He hopped into his trousers, his face dark. "Damn it, Margaret. That was an invasion of privacy."

"Well, you've pried enough out of my past."

"Because I care about you," he said.

She came forward into the firelight, looking so vulnerable that his anger began to fade. "Why didn't you marry her?" she asked.

"She left me," he said, reaching down for his shirt. "For someone else—my younger brother Andrew. I told you before."

He brushed past her to pick up the journal. "I shouldn't have read it," Margaret said in a low voice. "But I saw my name, and I—do you still love her?"

Ian thought of his last meeting with Jean, of how they had parted, so much bitterness between them. "No. I don't love her anymore."

"And you came to Maryhead because she broke your heart?"

He came up before her, catching her chin in his hand and tilting her face to his. "I didn't know what a broken heart was until Hogmanay, when you told me you didn't want to see me again."

She smiled wanly. "So much for my resolve."

"I do love you, Margaret," he said softly. "I wish you'd believe that."

She pulled back a little, her gaze drifting to the rumpled bed. "What are we going to do?" she whispered.

"We'll walk across the moor tomorrow and talk after I visit the crofts. Now turn around and let me button up your dress, although I have to admit taking you home in the middle of the night goes against my instincts. You belong in my bed."

Margaret repressed a shiver of pleasure at his proprietary manner and gave him a defiant grin over her shoulder as she turned to present him her back. "I'm going to the crofts myself in the morning," she announced, a challenge in the air.

He smiled, his fingers refastening the buttons, but his mind was troubled. He, having known a family's acceptance all his life, had a limitless measure of love from which to share. Jean's betrayal had been a deep wound, well on its way to healing. But Margaret's emotional scars were so deeply buried, he was afraid his love alone could not soften them.

Her healing, perhaps, depended on something beyond his skills, and he didn't know exactly what. He only knew that he loved her, and he would move heaven and earth to have her feel the same way about him.

Thirty-two

The parliament of Maryhead convened every Tuesday morning at seven o'clock, in front of Conacher's Tavern on The Street—deliberately unnamed because it was the island's only actual thoroughfare. As usual, the twelve male members sat in their herring-barrel pews, the primary issue on their agenda, the only one in fact, the problem of what to do about the island doctor.

It was unusually somber for a session.

A newspaper from the mainland, examined and reexamined so many times it had begun to disintegrate, passed from hand to hand. More than half the men present could not read, but the information in the headline article had been repeated so often over the morning ale that every self-respecting M.P. knew it by heart.

The scandal of it. The shock.

The sheer delight of at last discovering the skeleton in the incomer doctor's closet, and hadn't everyone suspected something like this from the start?

"To think I let him prod puir Granny's innards," Lamont Fergusson lamented between leisurely draws on his pipe. "Something must be done now, to protect Miss Rose, what wi' her about the island at all hours, and no man in the farmhouse, and the young reverend in China."

"What am I, then, if not a man?" Kenneth Alcock asked, looking deeply offended. "And it's Siam, not China."

Fergusson held up his hand diplomatically. "Ye're rarely home, Kenneth. No offense was meant to yer manhood, but ye'll have to agree from this article that MacNeill is a monster."

Kenneth pretended to scrape a chunk of mud from his left shoe. No, he didn't agree, rather liking Ian himself, but he wasn't inclined to defend an incomer to parliament. Except that Agnes would kill him if he didn't, and he was more afraid of his red-haired pregnant wife than all these men combined.

He cleared his throat. "He seems a pleasant enough sort, actually—"

"Pleasant?" Owen Macbean snorted. "Murder is bad enough, God rest Euan Bruce's soul, but this—this—" He nodded contemptuously toward the newspaper.

"Rather clever though." The oldest man on the island at 103, Artair Robb, looked up from the naked woman he was whittling into a pipe stem. "Grant the devil his due. The doctor is a clever laddie to get away wi' what he did."

"A monster he is."

"Crafty bugger."

Only Liam seemed willing to follow Kenneth's lead in defending the doctor. "What if the article isna even true?"

"Of course it's true," Owen retorted. "It's in the paper, isn't it? Ye read yerself what that woman claimed he did to her."

Liam's weathered face took on a troubled look. "Let's take our concerns to the laird before making any rash decisions."

"The laird?" several skeptical voices echoed in unison.

"Weel, just to make Macpherson feel as if he's a part of things," Liam added. "He's such a sensitive lad, ye ken."

Thomas handed the newspaper to Ian, his brown eyes bright with anxiety. "I'm sorry," he said, giving a helpless shrug. "This doesn't look good for you."

Ian took the paper and stared down at the faded newsprint,

expecting to read that Maryhead had been declared nonexistent by the Crown. But as the forgotten headline finally penetrated, he felt his face darken to purple, the blood creeping up into his neck, roaring in his ears.

WELL-TO-DO WIDOW ACCUSES YOUNG ABERDEEN PHYSICIAN OF RAPE UNDER ANESTHESIA!

Mrs. Marjorie Dodd of Trinity Quay, who came to Dr. MacNeill's practice at the recommendation of a retired college professor, has charged the popular young doctor with sexual misconduct while she was held helplessly unconscious by chloroform in his armchair.

"Jesus God," Ian said. "Where did this come from? It's over three years old."

"I noticed," Thomas said, rubbing his chin. "And I only know it turned up in Mrs. Bruce's hands—I tried to tell everyone it was nonsense."

Ian turned, pacing between the deerhounds stretched across the carpet. "God. Roger's death causing concern I could understand, but *this*. Did you even read the whole thing? A month after this paper came out, the bloody woman retracted her story and said her dentist had impregnated her. The Privy Council investigated and found no cause to even bring it before the board. She was never pregnant, not by me, her dentist, even her dead husband's ghost."

Thomas smiled unwillingly. "Of course, Ian, *I* never believed—"

"The world is full of lunatics," Ian continued angrily. "And I seem to attract more than my fair share of them."

"I know this is ridiculous. But that isn't the point—the islanders don't. They've always been afraid of incomers and proper medicine, and this just serves to prove them right."

Ian turned, almost diving into a chair to avoid stepping on the deerhounds as they rose for a scratching session. "I have a copy of that stupid woman's retraction somewhere in my things. You can read it in the castle yard to the entire island, for God's sake."

Thomas sighed. "You don't understand."

"No? Explain it to me then."

"They have no faith in you, Ian, no matter what I or Margaret know to be true of you. I can't *force* them to accept you. They don't want you here!"

Ian's mouth tasted suddenly sour. "What exactly are you saying?"

"I have to ignore my personal feelings, and do what's best for the island," Thomas said, his thin face apologetic. "You can't stay here. It's a waste of your skills. Dammit, man, I've seen what you're capable of doing."

Ian's fingers tightened around the newspaper. "I see."

"They're like children, Ian. They don't know what's good for them."

Ian was numb. "When do you want me to leave?"

"Och, there's no rush." Thomas hesitated. "However, the first spring steamer arrives in a fortnight. I wouldn't blame you if you were on it when it left."

Thirty-three

After Ian had walked her back to the farmhouse, Margaret managed to sneak back into her room for the few remaining hours of night. When Agnes knocked quietly on her bedroom door the following morning to ask if she would have a cup of tea with her, Margaret pleaded a headache and practically hid under the quilt to avoid her cousin's inevitable questioning.

She felt horrible, racked with remorse over what she and Ian had done—in Stephen's bed, no less.

She felt wonderful, vibrantly alive, smiling to herself because the sun was actually shining, her herbs would relish the rare warmth, and for the first time in years, she was filled with hope for the future.

She needed distance from Ian, to sort out her feelings.

She needed to see him again, the sooner the better. Alone. This afternoon.

She swore she wouldn't let him touch her though.

She couldn't eat breakfast for reliving every glorious detail of last night, every sensual touch they had shared.

As soon as she'd washed and dressed, she packed up the cart with her basket of herbal medicines. Most of the crofters had suffered only mild reactions to the inoculations and were back to their daily routine, so she paid more social calls than medicinal. By midmorning she was both surprised and disappointed that she hadn't run into Ian.

"Perhaps he's busy on the other side of the island wi' an

emergency," Peggy Kerr said. She was ladling watery porridge into horn bowls on the table. "Here. Eat up. Ye've gone thin in the face from the fever."

But although Margaret forced herself to take a few spoonfuls, she had no appetite. And when after another hour, Ian had still not shown up, she made a quick visit to the black huts bordering the moor to ask if anyone had seen him. She couldn't shake the feeling that something was wrong.

She passed Morag walking on the moor, and the knowing glitter in the other woman's eyes reinforced her fears.

"Out and about so soon?" Morag looked Margaret up and down. "I'd have thought the doctor would keep ye in bed for another day."

Margaret reined in the cart, angry at the implication. "What are you talking about?"

"Why, the inoculation of course. What else could I possibly mean?"

"Do you know where he is?" Margaret demanded, in no mood for Morag's taunting.

"And how should I know?" Morag replied. "Although if I had to hazard a guess, I'd say he was on his way . . ."

"To where?" Margaret's voice was sharp with the worry that had become overwhelming.

"I told ye he didn't belong here—"

Margaret didn't wait for Morag to finish. Her throat tight, she urged the ponies forward, taking a detour through a stretch of bog. During the ride, she tried to calm herself. Ian wasn't the sort of man to make love to her one day and disappear the next. Anyway, where on the island could he disappear to?

No one came to the door when she finally arrived at the manse. Remembering the near disaster the last time this had happened, she ran around to the back of the house and peered in the window of Ian's makeshift lab.

Her gaze lifted to the bedroom window. She'd been insulated

from this sort of emotional turmoil before Ian had come into her life. Why had she let herself begin to care?

She tapped on the lab window. In spite of the fact that she was acting like a peeping Tom herself, she had the most unpleasant feeling that she in turn was being observed.

And then she heard a faint noise from within the darkly curtained laboratory. The sound of something dragging or being dragged across the floor, a person breathing heavily.

"Ian!" She banged on the window.

No response. But *something* was going on.

She flew back around to the front of the house and let herself in, rushing down the hallway. The house was quiet, and as she shoved open the door to the laboratory to stare into the dim shadows of the room, a feeling of cold engulfed her.

He had brought the passion, light, and laughter back into her life. What would she do without him?

"Ian?" Her voice anxious, she walked slowly into the room.

There were no boilers lit. In fact, the table itself was bare. The desk, the bookshelves had also been stripped, dust leaving ghostly outlines where his possessions had stood. Margaret touched a pencil, her breathing painful.

He's gone, she thought in disbelief, gripping the edge of the desk for support. Then she glanced down and saw the long unmoving figure on the floor, draped in a bedsheet.

Lord God. He's killed himself.

She knelt swiftly. Her hands trembling, she tore back the sheet.

A human skull leered up at her, the jawbone clattering as she flung the sheet back over it in horror and jumped up. Her foot caught in the sheet's tail, undraping the rest of the skeleton that lay across the carpet.

"Oh, God," she said, taking such a violent step backward that she hit her hip on the corner of the desk. Then as she whirled around, she saw Walter in the doorway, his gaze moving past her to the floor.

"That—that thing under the sheet," she choked out. "I thought it was the doctor."

Sybil squeezed past Walter into the room, her round face reflecting a split second of what appeared to be cruel amusement at Margaret's stupidity, mistaking that skeleton for a man.

"The skeleton belongs to the doctor, Miss Rose," Sybil explained, releasing an almost inaudible sigh of impatience. "Such things are used for anatomy. Dr. MacNeill asked my husband to bring it out for the voyage."

Margaret inhaled deeply, recovered enough from her fright to realize what the woman had just said. "Dr. MacNeill is planning to leave the island?" she asked slowly.

The front door opened and slammed. Standing beside her husband, Sybil said in a disapproving undertone, "I'm sure Doctor will explain everything to you himself, Miss Rose. Seeing as that you're on such intimate terms with each other."

Ian stared at Margaret from across the room, then gave her a slow intimate smile that showed nothing of his own confusion. His first impulse after leaving the castle had been to find her. Being with Margaret was possibly the only thing that could counteract the blow Macpherson had just dealt him.

He strode toward her, studying her serious heart-shaped face and wondering if she'd already heard the news about him.

"That will be all, Mr. and Mrs. Armstrong," he murmured as he reached the desk. "Miss Rose and I are going to have a private conversation."

Margaret took a deep breath, trying to work through her shock to interpret the strange expression in Ian's eyes. Then as the door closed, she said quietly, "Your housekeeper just told me—"

She broke off as he pulled her against him. "I've been looking for you since you left the crofts," he said roughly.

The urgency in his voice was uncharacteristic of his usual

calmness but understandable to Margaret in view of her own frantic attempts to find him. Having become lovers had obviously altered the rules of their behavior. But gradually, as Ian held her in a grip that almost hurt, she began to realize that the roughness in his voice had less to do with passion than a sign of his distress. Something *was* wrong.

"God, Margaret, I missed you." He brought his face down to kiss her, murmuring against her mouth. "I couldn't sleep after you left last night. I almost came to get you."

For an instant Margaret forgot everything: her doubts, that horrid skeleton, Sybil Armstrong's revelation. She merely closed her eyes and responded to the kiss Ian demanded as if after last night he had the right. But when he drew back and she saw that the usual gentle humor in his eyes had been replaced by a quiet torment, her misgivings returned in a rush. She felt suddenly cold with fear, conscious of the empty room, the empty bookshelves, what that emptiness meant.

"Your housekeeper told me you're going away," she said, waiting for him to deny it when the truth was so painfully written on his face. And as the silence deepened, she shook her head, whispering in disbelief, "Oh, no, Ian. It really is true."

"Yes," he said flatly. "Macpherson asked me to leave this morning." He sounded as stunned as Margaret felt. "I didn't expect this, Margaret."

"Neither did I," she said softly.

Ian released her, leaning back against the desk with a look on his face that was more weary than resentful. "Well, you've won, my love. You and your charmer will be able to cast spells and burn snail shells into eternity. Here. Look at this for a laugh."

He removed the folded newspaper from his vest pocket, watching her face whiten as she scanned the article. "I told you the press had tried to ruin me, Margaret."

She shook her head, unable to speak. Rape. Ian accused of

raping a middle-aged woman he had anesthetized for an operation on her ear. "It's ridiculous," she said at last, not doubting his innocence for even a second.

"She recanted the entire story a month afterward," Ian said slowly. "The newspaper neglected to print that. She was a pathetic creature, really. I honestly felt more sorry for her than anything."

Margaret frowned. "How did Thomas get hold of the paper?"

"I don't know. I don't suppose it really matters."

"I'm so sorry," she said softly, her throat tight.

He shrugged, taking the newspaper from her and tossing it on the floor. "My days here were numbered anyway, I suppose."

"What will you do now?"

"Return to Aberdeen, I expect. With any luck the scandal over Roger's death has died down, and anesthesia is becoming more commonplace. Perhaps I'll even try the country, but there's the problem of Jean and my brother. They're living in my Highland house, you see."

He was leaving her. It seemed he had only just arrived. They had only last night surrendered to the attraction that had been building between them from the start. What happened in Stephen's room should have been a beginning, not an ending. But he was leaving, to return to Aberdeen.

"It's what you wanted, isn't it?" he asked, and if Margaret hadn't been so numb, so enmeshed in her own emotions she would have heard the undertone of hurt beneath his sarcasm, the opening for her to tell him how she really felt about him going away.

"That's unfair," she said quietly. "I never wanted this to happen."

He pushed away from the desk, lowering his voice as he faced her again. "Come with me when I leave."

A silence swept down upon them so profound Margaret

could hear the ticking of the clock in the hallway. She lifted her hands to her face, the implications of what he suggested filling her with hope and panic, opening up a universe of sweet dreams or nightmares; she didn't know which.

"I didn't expect any of this," she whispered at last, while he waited for her answer. "It's impossible," she said aloud as an afterthought. "We'd both regret it later. Oh, God, Ian, it's too complicated."

He watched her intently, refusing to give her up when she was the only thing that made this situation bearable. "It's not impossible at all," he stated. "Or complicated. I love you and want to marry you. Come with me, Margaret."

She pressed her fingertips to her temples, trying to suppress the inner voice that told her to accept him without a care for the consequences. And then she thought of the crofters, of their needs, of her insulated life on the island. "How can I possibly leave here, Ian?" she asked in confusion. "This island has become my life."

"It isn't a life," he said angrily. "Even Stephen had the sense to realize that. I love you, dammit, and no matter what you say, I know you feel something for me."

Margaret had never felt so torn in her life. On the one hand her every instinct urged her to grasp the happiness he offered her before it was too late. But her fears, so deeply ingrained in her nature, held her back like invisible bonds that were impossible to break. To return to Aberdeen with all its painful memories was a sacrifice she wasn't sure she could make for anyone.

His deep voice jarred her from her thoughts. "I'm going to take you with me. I'm claiming you for my own." He drew her back into his arms, his breath warm on her face as he whispered coaxingly, "Trust me to protect you from whatever you're so afraid of."

"Oh, Ian, stop it," she whispered, breaking away from him.

"You can't protect me from something that's already happened. No one can."

Ian fought a moment of panic at the thought of leaving without her. No. He couldn't. Not even if it meant giving up medicine to raise sheep on this unholy little island.

He cupped her chin in his hand, his voice fierce, resentful. "I can't imagine life without you."

She shivered, closing her eyes, and with a rough exhalation of breath, he kissed her soft, trembling mouth. "Do you really think we could live without each other?"

She sighed. "I don't know. Oh, Ian, last night was so wonderful . . ."

He smiled slowly as she opened her eyes. "One more time then, shall we? I'll convince you why we belong together. Jesus, you don't think I'm going to give you up again?"

She knew she should refuse, pretend reluctance. But she didn't, her heart racing against her ribcage as he scooped her up in his arms and carried her to the door. She was ashamed, confused, so consumed with her own desire for him that she could only grin at the horrified gasp that came from down the hallway where Sybil stood, her hand to her mouth.

"I won't be needing you again until morning, Mrs. Armstrong," Ian said with a roguish wink that made Margaret close her eyes in mortified amusement. "I believe you and your husband have enough packing to keep you occupied."

"For heaven's sake, Ian," Margaret managed to whisper between a series of uncontrollable giggles, grasping a fistful of his shirt as he took the stairs in long impatient strides. "Sexual compatibility is hardly enough for us to build a life upon."

"I agree," he said with a complacent smile. "But we've always had so much more than that, haven't we, Margaret? It's just the icing on the cake."

Thirty-four

Margaret stretched luxuriously across the bed, affording Ian a tantalizing view of the firm body that he had come to know intimately in the past twenty-four hours. Nude, her milky white skin like polished ivory in the room's fading light, her mahogany hair as vibrant as strands of dark fire on his bed, she exuded such a mysterious blend of innocence and sensuality that Ian could have studied her all afternoon.

"We can't stay here forever," she said with a wistful sigh, primly tugging the sheet from under his muscular thighs to cover her nakedness. "Agnes and Kenneth will be scandalized. I'm ruined now, you realize."

"Ruined for another man?" he asked with a wicked smile. "Oh, I hope so." Casually he peeled back the sheet from her shoulders and lowered his face to her breasts, capturing first one delicious pink tip and then the other between his teeth. His hand slipped between her legs, his fingers playing, caressing the warm moist flesh. "If you're too sore," he whispered, "I could love you again with my mouth."

"You're very decadent," she breathed, her body arching helplessly in reaction, "for a doctor."

He reared back, giving her a wolfish smile, and slid down between her thighs. Margaret closed her eyes, her body taut with anticipation. "We still haven't talked," she whispered, "about your leaving—"

"Our leaving," he corrected her, his voice deceptively soft, but in his mind, the decision had been made.

Margaret sighed, aware of the erratic pounding of her heart, arousal and her conflicting feelings making a mockery of her attempts to think clearly. Then, by increasing degrees, she became conscious of a strange cacophony of sounds from the hills beyond the manse, the jingle of harnesses, the clatter of cartwheels on the rutted path.

Ian, stroking her belly with the flat of his hand, looked up and met her puzzled gaze. "What the hell was that?"

"I've no idea." She twisted deftly onto her elbow. "But I don't like it."

Ian reached for his trousers and shirt with one hand, tossing her the chemise, drawers, petticoats, and crumpled gown they had strewn across the floor in their impatience to make love. It was the first time anyone on the island except Margaret had called on Ian at the manse, and the timing could not have been more painfully inconvenient.

He watched, trying not to laugh, as Margaret struggled into the complicated layers of feminine attire, hopping from one foot to the other to put on her stockings. Grabbing his comb from the dresser, he tugged it over his scalp, then attempted to restore some order to Margaret's disheveled hair, spilling like a soft cloud around her unlaced bodice.

The brass knocker at the front door resounded through the manse like staccato gunfire. His face terse, Ian listened for a few seconds, hearing Walter answer the door and valiantly try to keep the unannounced visitors at bay. Voices rose in anger; it was definitely trouble.

Ian sighed, kissed Margaret on the forehead, then gently pushed her away from the door where she stood listening.

"Stay here," he said quietly. "Don't come down until I call you. It probably has to do with the inoculations."

He tucked his wrinkled muslin shirt into his trousers and slipped on his calfskin shoes, emerging from the room and into the upstairs hallway as the small crowd of island men on the steps outside broke their way through the flimsy barricade of Walter Armstrong's bony outflung arms.

"What is all this?" Ian demanded. Frowning, he hurried down the stairs, suddenly afraid, not for himself but for Margaret as he surveyed the hostile faces of the men crowded into the narrow entry hall below.

It was, he soon realized, Maryhead's laughable pretense of a parliament, the ragtag body of shepherds and crofters who had decided he did not fit into their old-fashioned world. Well, perhaps he didn't, but neither did Margaret, and he felt a stab of possessive anxiety for her, for her good name and her deep involvement with these people who had undoubtedly come here on some mission of misguided retribution for whatever sins they believed Ian had committed.

Fine then. They could reject Ian, insult him, detest him, but he wouldn't let their narrow-mindedness hurt Margaret.

To his astonishment, he recognized Kenneth Alcock in the doorway, an awkward blond giant who towered above his companions with a look of genuine misery on his face.

"What does this mean?" he asked Kenneth directly, his voice cutting across the silence that had fallen.

Kenneth wet his lips, clearly not relishing his position as spokesman for the angry band. "Just tell them Margaret isn't here."

Ian would have easily given the lie, anything to save her from an ugly situation, had she not opened the bedroom door at that precise moment and walked calmly, defiantly, to the top of the stairs.

A murmur of disapproval went through the hall. Margaret looked very pale as she stared down in silence at the men who over the years had come to accept her as one of their own.

Kenneth's mouth tightened. "This is not good, Dr. MacNeill. You ate at my table and enjoyed my wife's approval and hospitality. I did not expect you to seduce my cousin-in-law in return."

"I'm old enough to make my own decisions," Margaret said with a composure she didn't feel as she descended the stairs, the disappointed faces that watched her making her ache with shame for herself and anger at the islanders for this unnecessary intrusion.

"Dear God, Margaret," Kenneth said, his voice shaking. "In the manse. In Stephen's room. Have you no shame? Have you taken complete leave of your good senses?"

"Did he use medicine on ye, Miss Rose?" Owen Macbean asked in a luridly sympathetic voice. "Did he put ye unconscious to have his way wi' ye?"

Ian rolled his eyes.

For a horrifying moment, Margaret thought she would laugh.

But she could really only blame herself. She had broken her own rules, made herself the focal point of unsavory gossip on the island, and no one would ever look at her with the same respect again, forgetting all the sleepless nights she had spent with feverish children in the crofts, forgetting her home-brewed medicines and teas.

"Who sent you here?" she demanded of the men grouped in the hallway. "The laird isn't small-minded enough for this. Who gave you the authority to try and judge us this way? Surely not you, Liam?"

"It was not," he answered without hesitation, then cast a shamed look at his peers. "It was the charmer if ye must know. I'm what ye might call an impartial party."

Margaret felt as though she had been kicked in the stomach, betrayed by the woman she had so fiercely admired and defended. "But why?" she asked, feeling naive because she really didn't know. "Why would Morag want to do this to me?"

Ian smiled darkly. "Competition, I'll warrant. You were getting too damned good at your work, my dear."

Several of the men looked up expectantly at Kenneth Alcock. There was a definite procedure to be followed in situations such as this. Perplexed, his voice faltering, Kenneth forced himself to meet Ian's ironic gaze. "Well, Doctor. It hardly matters who sent us here, in light of the damning evidence." His eyes dropped to Margaret's bare feet, peeping out from beneath her hastily donned gown and petticoats. "What are you going to do to rectify the situation, Dr. MacNeill?"

"I'll marry her, naturally," he said easily. "It's what I'd intended all along, although I'd have preferred to propose under more romantic conditions."

Kenneth released a loud, relieved sigh, and a few men even chuckled, humor returning as honor was upheld. "Well then. Everything's all right, isn't it?" He looked to Margaret for confirmation, finding little to reassure him in her white uncertain face. "Margaret, is it all right?"

She straightened her shoulders, aware of Ian watching her, his face intense, expectant. "I don't know," she said quietly.

Of course she could refuse to marry Ian. In a year the scandal would die down. She would settle into young spinsterhood, engaging in open battles with Morag over healing supremacy on the island. She would serve as nursemaid to Agnes's child. She would lead a busy, selfless life, helping others. The sort of life she had begun to believe she desired.

Until now.

She looked up slowly at Ian, his blue eyes amused, afraid, in the almost brutal face she had learned concealed such a complex, passionate nature, and hope stirred in her heart.

How could they make a marriage work when she would enter it with so many misgivings? She had never intended to return to Aberdeen. Ian wouldn't insist on it if he really understood how she felt about her father.

"Don't decide anything now," Ian warned her, afraid that if she were pushed into marriage, she would never be able to trust him.

She nodded, her shoulders relaxing. Then, glancing over at

Kenneth, she announced with quiet dignity, "I'm going upstairs to fetch my shoes. I expect all of you to be gone by the time I come back down."

Ian watched her climb the stairs to his room, hoping she wouldn't blame him for what had happened. But he couldn't help thinking it was his fault, his uncharacteristic indiscretion and impatience to take her back into his bed. What would he do if she refused to leave the island with him?

Suddenly unable to control his feelings, he turned on the now-deflated group of men who had retreated to the doorway. "Are you satisfied?" he asked, his voice soft with sarcasm.

No one answered. No one dared.

Then Liam said tentatively, "Weel, we'll be on our way, Doctor. Now that we're assured everything is all right between ye and Miss Rose."

"Is it?" Ian inquired coldly, afraid to even face Margaret alone after this humiliating scene. "You're all relieved that she's to wed a rapist rather than just sleep with him, is that it?"

"Dear Jesus," Kenneth said, his face as white as snow.

"I *am* going to marry her." Ian turned, his gaze lifting to the landing. "That is if she'll have anything to do with me after today. Now get out of here, all of you, before she comes back down. Get the hell out of this house."

The small crowd drew back, then a bespectacled crofter standing behind Liam boldly raised his voice. "Ye'll take the wedding challenge then, Doctor? Ye'll prove yerself a man to Miss Rose?"

Ian glowered. "What bloody nonsense are you on about now?"

Liam nervously fingered his cap. "Wedlock Ledge, sir. 'Tis customary on the island for a prospective groom to prove his manliness on the crags."

"It's suicide," Kenneth blurted out. "I never did it when I married Agnes."

"Aye, Alcock," Owen Macbean mumbled. "And we all know who wears the trews in yer house to this day."

There was laughter, and Ian was about to impolitely tell them where they could put their custom when Margaret reemerged from the bedroom, her brown hair loose on her shoulders, her delicate face clearly distressed.

His heart tightened at the thought of losing her. "I'll take the challenge," he said offhandedly.

She'd reached the foot of the stairs. Maryhead's members of parliament spilled outside the manse's foreyard, Kenneth hastily closing the door behind them. For an awkward interval Ian and Margaret looked at each other, mesmerized by a barrage of intimate memories so fresh, so fragile, that neither of them could move. Then Margaret glanced down and began to walk past him, catching her breath as he rushed forward to block the door.

"I won't leave here without you," he said, putting his hand on hers, his face so determined that Margaret realized there would be no easy answer to her dilemma. "Will you come with me?" he asked, his blue eyes vulnerable.

"I don't know," she whispered. "I can't decide anything until I talk to Agnes and have a bath."

Ian grinned, but his blue eyes remained intent. "If you can joke about it, then there must be hope."

"We'll see."

"By tomorrow morning?"

She laughed quietly. "You're quite impossible."

Reluctantly he moved away from the door. "Tomorrow afternoon?" he said as she reached the first step. "The evening then—before supper?"

She ran down the path, then paused to give him a little wave before continuing to the farmhouse. As he watched, it was all he could do not to follow her, cringing at the memory of how the afternoon had ended in disaster and hoping that the damage done could be repaired.

Thirty-five

Margaret knew that she wanted to marry Ian. What she didn't know was if their marriage would work, with Aberdeen their home and honeymoon. She was desperately afraid to take the chance.

She even sought Thomas's advice, sitting with him on the cliffs while the sea breezes battered them with stinging salt spray.

"You're a fallen woman," he said with a rueful smile. "Now I can't introduce you to my mother next year when she visits."

"And you're absolutely no help at all." She sighed and looked out at the sea. "He wants to marry me."

Suddenly aware by her tone of voice that she was seriously considering leaving the island, Thomas sat up and frowned. "What did you tell him?"

She tried not to smile. "I told him I needed to talk to Agnes and have a bath."

Thomas looked hopeful. "Not exactly a burning commitment on your part. How did he react?"

She sighed again. "I'm not sure. He made a few silly remarks."

Thomas was silent, wrenching up a handful of pearlwort by the roots and flinging it off the cliff only to grimace as the breeze tossed it right back into his face. "Tell him to go to hell."

Margaret drew her shawl over her shoulders. "I can't stay

here now. Morag will turn everyone against me. Kenneth and Agnes are starting a family."

Thomas frowned, for Morag was even more a part of Maryhead than he, and long after he left, she or her type would probably still hold sway.

"You do want to marry him." It was not a question, but a fact. "In spite of your hesitation, Margaret, you've already decided to go back to Aberdeen with him."

"If—if I don't go, I'll lose him forever."

"Then nothing else matters, does it?"

"But I'm afraid," she whispered.

"Of what?" he asked gently.

"Of loving him," she answered miserably. "I know it doesn't make sense, but I'm so afraid if I really care about him and I lose him, I'll be utterly destroyed."

He stretched back and gazed up at the sky. "You could stay and marry me," he suggested reluctantly.

She turned her head to stare down at him. Then simultaneously they started to laugh at the absurdity of a marriage between them.

But when their laughter faded, there was a heaviness in Thomas's heart that would take a long, long time to lift. He'd been contented to have a close friendship with Margaret, but he had never counted on losing her either, the island's mermaid. And he was unselfishly afraid of the pain she would encounter when she left Maryhead for the mainland, of the world's ugliness she would face when she gave up the protection he liked to think he had offered her.

They were married on a blustery February morning in the island's main kirk by an elderly Anglican minister. In the white poplin gown she saved for christenings, Margaret had left the farmhouse to find the first spring snowdrops thrusting their heads through the cold earth of her garden. The discovery almost made her cry, her herbs and flowers soon to be abandoned to the careless tromping of that family of Titans, Agnes, Kenneth, and their unborn child.

Her husband. Mrs. Ian MacNeill. Oh, God, it was true. The plain gold band resting heavily on her finger, bought by Ian at a cattle drovers' fair only yesterday, was a physical reminder of their union.

The Gaelic ceremony in the drafty church, the reception afterward in the farmhouse had been so awkward and rushed, it had had an air of unreality about it. She could barely remember repeating her vows. But she did remember Ian's face as he'd slipped on the ring, that dark face reflecting joy, fierce possessiveness, and a relief so obvious that Margaret giggled when he kissed her.

"Mrs. MacNeill," he whispered softly against her mouth, "I really thought you were going to change your mind and leave me in the lurch."

"Aye," she admitted mischievously. "I almost did."

Maryhead's parliament honored the newlyweds with an hour of pipes and toasts of illegal whiskey. Thomas, the best man, got a little drunk and maudlin, giving a speech that didn't make any sense at all about the marriage of tradition to progress.

Margaret was certain as she covertly observed her husband from across the room, his tall dark figure dominating the other guests, that their marriage was a mistake.

And Ian, openly staring at his lovely wife, was convinced they would find happiness together.

"It's time, MacNeill!" someone roared good-naturedly, and Margaret made a face at Agnes over her whiskey glass.

"Time for what?" she whispered. "Don't tell me they're going to escort Ian and me upstairs in some ancient nuptial ceremony?"

Agnes looked worried. "I don't know. Kenneth, what's this about?"

Kenneth didn't answer, abruptly abandoning her and Margaret just as Ian downed his glass of whiskey and nodded silently in some sort of prearranged signal, allowing the tide of island men to bear him to the door.

All around Margaret the small party of guests collected caps and shawls, calling back benedictions and cryptic remarks in their rush to follow Ian outside.

"Come on, lass, look sharp."

"This is in yer honor after all, Margaret."

Margaret, her mouth suddenly dry, pushed through the departing guests to reach Thomas in the crowded hallway. "What exactly is Ian doing in my honor, Thomas?"

He was pulling on his woollen overcoat, his face averted. "He's going to walk Wedlock Ledge."

"And you didn't try to stop him?"

"I just found out myself. You'll need a heavy cloak if you're coming. Pray God the wind doesn't rise."

She ran back into the parlor, her face like chalk as she looked out the window to see Ian striding ahead of his enthusiastic followers. "He's lost his mind," she said to Agnes, staring over her shoulder. "He's going to kill himself on our wedding day."

Ian narrowed his eyes and pressed his cheek into the abrasive cleft of the cliff's uppermost crag. "What is that thing down there that looks like a stone grave marker protruding from those rocks?" he ground out, not even daring to glance up at the eager audience that watched him from above.

" 'Tis a stone grave marker, sir," Robbie Fergusson called down from the overhanging bluff where he lay flattened on his belly, a front-row seat. "It marks the final resting place of Sir Alfred Barnes, a Professor of Botany from the mainland who was the last incomer to take the challenge."

Liam clucked sympathetically. "Once ye've pulled down your blindfold, Doctor, ye'll not notice it."

"Don't worry, sir," Robbie added. "The professor only missed the ledge by a wee bit."

"A wee bit or a mile. I can't see how it matters," Ian retorted grimly. He stared out across the sea where a blue shark cut lazy circles in the choppy waters. "Perhaps we should wait for a calmer day," he suggested in a hopeful voice.

Liam moistened his calloused thumb and raised it to test the breeze. "Gentle as a babbie's breath. 'Twill nae disturb a hair on yer head, sir."

Peggy Kerr grinned down at him. "Here's yer bride coming now, Doctor. Look alive then."

"Look alive," Ian murmured. "One can only hope." His senses reeling as he surveyed the awesome drop to the rock-strewn sea, he clung with one hand to the crag while reaching up for the blindfold with the other.

"Don't." Margaret's voice cut through the whispering crowd like a whip. "Ian MacNeill, I don't know what it is you're trying to prove, but I'm not impressed."

Kenneth put his arm around her, his voice low but firm. "Ye'll not interfere here, Margaret. There comes a time when a man has to prove his mettle, if only to himself."

She glanced down once at the three-hundred-foot drop and felt nausea rise to her throat. "Ian, please."

He stared up at her, his face inscrutable. Then, with a terse sigh, he slowly tugged the blindfold down over his eyes and lowered his other hand to his side. His bare toes curled into the cold moist ledge, seeking a secure hold before he began the walk to the narrow point that overhung the sea. A wave of salt air washed over him as he took the first tentative step forward. And then, unexpectedly, instead of fear there was freedom.

He'd started out unsure of why he was risking his life for a handful of islanders who'd rejected him, for Margaret, who even by marrying him was achingly unattainable, always a heartbeat from his grasp.

And then he understood.

He'd lost nothing for his efforts, but had gained strength, experience. He had done his best. To save two hundred people from smallpox surely could not be called a failure.

And there was Margaret. To marry a woman who couldn't admit she loved you was asking for a fall. But the risk, the challenge, of making a life with her was worth every terrifying second.

Thirty-six

Two days later the small iron-paddle steamer chugged into Cape Rue, smoke rising from her topmost decks. Margaret stood unmoving in the small crowd of cattle drovers, wool merchants, and island families waiting to embark. She was pretending not to see the white-uniformed steward who motioned from the taffrail to the gangplank.

"It's time, Margaret," Ian said gently.

The last bell rang, the sound dying in the breeze to the accompaniment of a gull's distant screech.

Panic gripped Margaret. Her eyes blurring with the tears she'd tried to suppress, she looked back over her shoulder at Agnes and Kenneth waving from the bluff, two distant endearing dots in her memory.

"Oh, goodbye," she said softly, biting her lip. "I'll miss you so."

She blew her nose on the handkerchief Ian gave her and gazed fiercely at the black cliffs of the cape. Grey seals dove from the skerries into the chilly waves, and the sails of the island's fishing boats glinted in the sunshine. She was leaving this, her refuge, a leap of faith . . .

"It's time," Ian said, grasping her hand to guide her into the throng of people hurrying up the gangway. He was fighting a rising panic now himself, half convinced she would change her mind at the last minute.

She nodded, her throat too tight to speak, and pushed the

handkerchief into her reticule. Then a figure on the beach caught her eye, waving wildly at her to stop. Margaret hesitated, feeling the vibration of the rough wooden planks as passengers pushed around her.

She clutched Ian's arm. "It's Morag."

"All the more reason to hurry," Ian said in a clipped voice, still furious at the woman's destructive influence. "I'll be willing to bet you won't be plagued by any more peculiar occurrences, either, as soon as we're out of Morag's reach."

Margaret smiled at him, reassured by the warm concern in his eyes. "All right. Let's go."

But as they turned, Morag finally reached them, laughing breathlessly as she lifted a black velvet-bound book to Margaret. "It's a wedding gift, ye ken. I've been saving it for ye for a very long time now."

Ian stared at her in disgust. "What is it, *How to Start a Coven Aboard a Steamer?*"

Morag's hazel eyes glittered with humor. "Aye, there's a spell or two in it, Doctor, I'll admit. But it's mostly healing receipts for Margaret." She gave Margaret the heavy book, closing her fingers around the younger woman's hand. "Be careful, Margaret. Be so very careful, my dear."

Ian snorted. "What for? She's leaving you behind, isn't she?"

Morag backed away, then turned to hurry down the gangway to the beach.

"What just happened was very much like a dream I used to have," Margaret said in a low voice.

"Was it?" Ian asked distractedly, motioning to the steward that everything was all right. He wouldn't relax until he and Margaret were miles from the island. "Tell me about it in the cabin."

"There were several differences though," Margaret continued reflectively.

The steward came forward to greet them. Ian frowned at the tension in his wife's voice and said, "What was different?"

She glanced down at the sea, then looked up at Ian with a remote smile that made his heart constrict. "In my dream I was walking up the gangway just as we are now. Then suddenly my father came up behind me. He pushed me and I fell."

"Your father pushed you into the water?" Ian asked quietly. "To drown, you mean?"

"Yes. In the dream."

"It wasn't real, Margaret."

"I know."

Fiercely he gathered her against him, murmuring into her hair, "There's another difference, too. I'm holding you, Margaret, and as long as you're in my care, I'll never let you fall."

"Oh, Ian—"

"But you have to let me hold you. You have to learn to trust me, love."

In her secret heart Margaret suspected she would come to look back on the short steamer voyage as the quiet before the storm, the last magical interlude she and Ian would enjoy before the outside world claimed them.

Her deepest fear was that everything would change once they reached Aberdeen. Ian's work would absorb him, and sooner or later he'd come into contact with his former fiancée. After all, it was less than a year ago that he'd been planning to marry Jean, and just because he'd married Margaret instead didn't mean that all his feelings for Jean were dead.

Actually, Margaret was even more afraid that *she* would change once they reached Aberdeen, that all the confidence she'd gained on the island would disintegrate like a shell, leaving exposed the frightened, unwanted child she had been when her father had sent her away five years ago.

And these were fears she could never admit to Ian, opening

herself to a greater vulnerability than she dared risk. Yet she wanted so much to trust him, had no real reason, in truth, to doubt his commitment to her.

"Do you regret our impulsive marriage?" she asked him half teasingly on the second evening of their voyage as they shared a light supper of soup, fresh crusty bread, and chablis in their cabin. "I mean, you were virtually honor-bound to marry me after parliament burst into the manse that afternoon, weren't you?"

Ian looked up from his bowl of oxtail soup, aware of the undercurrent of insecurity beneath her lighthearted question. "I've wanted you forever," he said, his gaze holding hers for a burning interval, and even now, he couldn't believe that this sweet, intelligent, deliciously sensual young woman was his wife. She was so beautiful, he loved her so much, that he'd selfishly prefer to stay on this ship with her forever than to reintroduce her into a society that might steal her from him. She had after all been raised in a slightly higher social circle than had he, and the Rose reputation had a certain allure.

"How long?" she whispered, her face warm as their eyes met.

"Since I saw you dangling out of that drunken rogue's carriage on Union Street."

Her eyes narrowed. "Now wait a minute—didn't you predict that I'd come to a bad end because of my behavior?"

He laughed softly. "Aye, and just look at you now."

Smiling, she got up from the table and walked to the porthole where silver-green waves washed the moonlit horizon. He followed her with his gaze, noting how her beige lace dress outlined her softly rounded hips, the curve of her breasts.

"Would you like a glass of sherry?" he asked, his appetite for food suddenly diminished. This was his honeymoon, and he intended to make the best of it.

"No," she murmured. "Oh, all right, if you're having one."

He poured two drinks from the decanter on the sideboard

and took them to the dressing table where he unbuttoned his gray velvet waistcoat and removed his cravat. From his vantage point he could see Margaret's reflection, her face to the sea.

She's mine, he thought, arousal pounding in his blood.

"Do you want to change into your nightclothes before we have our drinks?" he asked casually.

She swung around, her face so shadowed he almost missed her beguiling smile. "Are you trying to seduce me?"

"Unashamedly." He took a sip of sherry and put down his glass, leaning back to watch her with a roguish grin. "Now hurry up. I've been lusting after you since lunch."

"It was the oysters," Margaret teased. "They're a well-known aphrodisiac."

"It wasn't the oysters because I didn't have any." He removed his shirt and waistcoat, then hung them in the armoire that was bolted to the bulkhead behind him. "You made quite an impression on that Edinburgh merchant in the stateroom. I might have been jealous had he been several decades younger."

Her face amused, Margaret disappeared behind the dressing screen. As he finished his sherry, Ian could hear that intriguing female business of struggling with hooks and petticoats, then an unabashed sigh of relief as she was released from her stays. In his imagination he saw her standing in her lacy camisole, stockings, and silk drawers.

He picked up her glass of sherry and drank it, but it did nothing to subdue his desire.

She stepped out from behind the screen, tying the sash of a dark blue velveteen dressing robe, her hair in soft disarray down her back. He stared in fascination at the slope of her breast where the robe did not quite meet, her skin the texture of soft bisque silk. It was going to be a memorable evening.

"It was the Rose name that impressed him," Margaret said, raising her eyebrows at the two empty sherry glasses on the table. "I forgot how influential my father had become throughout Scotland. He's planning to open a new branch in Dundee."

She leveled an accusing gaze on Ian. "In spite of the fact you told me he was dying."

He didn't want to discuss Douglas Rose, aware that his precious time alone with Margaret, three fleeting days, was almost over. "Rose is no longer your surname. You shouldn't have mentioned it if you don't want the association known." He moved toward her, his face dark as he drew her against his bare chest. "Don't wriggle away from me, Margaret. I'm dying to know if you're naked under that robe."

She shivered as she felt his hands loosening the sash at her waist, his subsequent groan of approval at having his question answered. "It seems so strange," she murmured, her breasts pressed to his chest, "to think of myself as Margaret Mac-Neill."

He slid his hands down her back to the lush curve of her buttocks. "I mean it to last a lifetime."

"Not longer?" she asked with a mischievous smile, and then her eyes fluttered closed, a delicious sense of anticipation flooded her senses as he drew the dressing robe from her shoulders.

"All right. Even longer," he said agreeably, taking her hands to draw her back to the bed.

"You're only saying that to seduce me," she accused him, laughing softly at the guilty grin that instantly appeared on his face. "You don't even believe in an afterlife."

"Yes, I do," he said, his body aching for a deliverance that had nothing to do with spiritual salvation. "I'm very hopeful that within a few minutes, I'll be in my own private heaven."

He fell back heavily onto the bed, dragging her down against him, both of them laughing helplessly at his irreverent silliness.

"Don't worry." His face suddenly intense, he rolled her over beneath him. "If there is an afterlife, we'll be together. I guarantee it."

He leaned back to pull off his trousers and Margaret watched him, her breath trapped in her throat, her blue-gray eyes darkening with desire at the sight of his nude body, its suppressed power and grace.

His own eyes heavy-lidded, Ian stretched out alongside her and ran his fingers down the curve of her belly, smiling at the tiny shiver she gave. "Do you think they do this sort of thing in the otherworld?" he asked softly.

She smiled and snuggled against him, lifting her face for a kiss. "I hope so." Then, "Oh, Ian, do we really have to go to Aberdeen?"

"It won't be bad as long as we're together."

"But what if . . . what if it wasn't Morag? What if there's something else . . . something your logic can't explain, and it means to hurt us?"

There was silence then, as his mouth covered hers, except for the steady thrum of the ship through the sea. Yet Ian could still feel the subtle tension emanating from her as she awaited his response. "Why do you worry so?" he asked huskily. "Everything bad is behind us . . ."

Two hours from Aberdeen Harbour, Margaret fell prey to an unexpected attack of anxiety that had her pacing the cabin like a caged tigress. At first Ian was amused and then alarmed when he found himself unable to reason with her.

"Why do we have to go to Aberdeen anyway?" she demanded, twisting in her hands the slouch hat he had bought her in Skye until it looked like a pathetic velvet pancake. "Why can't you practice in a quiet country village?"

He walked toward her, resisting the temptation to rescue the hat from her hands, but instead he gathered her against him. "Please don't ask me to see my father," she said quietly.

He kissed her forehead. "I promise. Anyway, you'll be too busy helping me."

She brightened. "With your patients?"

"With the social functions we'll be forced to attend."

"What social functions?" she asked suspiciously.

"Nothing grand." He thought she looked interested, so he indulged in a little exaggeration. "A supper for a professor now and then, perhaps a ball given by some wealthy milord I'm hoping to wangle research money from. Enough to keep my young wife busy."

"How exciting," she said with a sarcastic edge to her voice that should have warned him he'd made a tactical error.

He smiled uncertainly. "Did I say something wrong?"

She gave a little shrug. "No. But to be honest I'll probably be quite busy getting my own practice started. I've brought some cuttings from my garden, if they survive, and some seeds I saved from last year."

"Margaret, you aren't serious." He walked back to the dressing table, shaking his head as if to dismiss the very notion. "If your kind heart needs to help others, there are numerous charities and organizations in Aberdeen that can use your compassion—the soup kitchens and the Female Benefit Society, for instance."

"But I enjoy healing with herbs, Ian. I'm good at it." She came up behind him. "I really am."

"And charms?" He grinned at her in the mirror, tying his cravat. "The old raven's egg and rowan branch cure, eh?"

She flushed, gripping the slouch hat in her hands. She could have cheerfully clobbered him with it for his patronizing grin. "Charms and prayer," she added with mounting irritation. "Faith is the ultimate healer, according to Morag, and if a charm helps—"

He rolled his eyes. "Look, love, we'll discuss this later, shall we? But please don't start talking about burnt snail shells the moment you meet my friends. They're intolerant of such nonsense."

She gave him a brittle smile. "I'm not liking you very much right now, Ian."

A knock sounded at the door, and the steward politely identified himself. Margaret simmered with a slow-rising resentment as Ian went to answer it, giving her an impudent wink on the way. Until this moment she hadn't realized how she'd come to define herself through her healing practice on Maryhead, gradually replacing her father's tarnished image of the incorrigible hellion she had been with the competent young woman she'd become who gave herself to the needs of others. Her work had been as healing to Margaret as to her patients. And now Ian, with his offhanded male arrogance, expected her to abandon the one endeavor that brought her a sense of personal satisfaction.

"Doctor, husband, be damned," she grumbled with quiet determination. "I will *not* give up the work I love any more than I'd expect you to stop experimenting with your goldfish and gas."

He turned halfway to the door, trying to suppress a smile. "There's a slight difference between what you and I do."

Not the way Margaret saw it. She drew an enormous breath, preparing to do battle. "I'm not going with you."

The knock at the door grew more insistent. Shaking his head in exasperation, Ian strode across the cabin to answer it.

"Your wife's cat, sir," the wiry white-haired steward said, smiling as he held aloft the large hamper used to contain Cyclops in the hold. "Little dickens is chewing away in there, eager to be out and catch a nice mousie, I expect."

"Margaret," Ian said firmly, his eyes troubled, "get your cloak on."

She went to the door, giving Ian a resentful look as she took the hamper from the steward. "I expect he's frightened by all the confinement." She looked up pointedly at Ian. "It's a cruel trick to play, caging him when he was used to the freedom of the island."

Ian followed after her, catching the sympathetic look the

steward gave him. What did she need with freedom anyway when she'd be busy running his home and raising his children?

He glanced back into the room, checking he'd left nothing behind. "You've forgotten your hat, Margaret."

"You wear it," she said from the deck. "I hate the damned silly thing anyway."

He smiled at the steward. "In the event I've left anything behind, you can reach me in Aberdeen in Union Square."

"I understand, sir."

"I wish I could say the same," Ian muttered as he followed Margaret onto the breezy deck where the sight of Walter and Sybil Armstrong waiting did not improve his mood. His honeymoon was apparently threatened, if not over, because of Margaret's stubborn insistence on practicing her outdated arts. Like it or not, she would have to learn that magic and medicine did not mix in the real world.

Thirty-seven

It was dark when they disembarked at Trinity Quay. Walter had found a carriage to take Ian and Margaret away from the waterfront where the taverns had begun to teem with evening life.

"Everything will be all right," Ian said hopefully, studying his wife in the darkness of the carriage interior as the driver pulled away from the wharves. "Maybe we're both just a little on edge at returning to the city."

Margaret was silent as the carriage wheels jounced over the cobbled street, having decided she wasn't ever going to speak to Ian again.

He stretched forward to take her hands. "Come and sit beside me."

"No, thank you," she said coolly. "I'm not sitting beside you either."

He leaned back, sighing in resignation, and closed his eyes.

"Will we have a back garden in the house you've let?" she asked, waiting to speak until it looked as if he was almost asleep.

"I expect so," he said without opening his eyes. "Why? Do you fancy growing some spring flowers?"

"Not exactly. I told you, I've brought a few herb cuttings in a jar and want to plant them right away. Not that my tyrant of a husband will allow me to use them for any medicinal purposes."

Having conveniently forgotten their argument in the cabin, Ian said the first thing that came into his mind. "Margaret, this is a big city, not a backward island. My colleagues will laugh me out of town if it's found I married a wee witch, though once they get a look at what a beauty she is, I'll be the envy of the entire Royal College."

Margaret sat forward. "You're a pompous ass, Ian MacNeill. I almost wish my teeth would fall out overnight, and I'd sprout warts on my nose, just to spite you when you woke up and saw the 'beauty' you'd married."

He opened his eyes and looked at her in surprise. "We're both tired, Margaret," he said cautiously. "I think you'll feel better in the morning."

"Only if you change your pig-headed mind."

He laughed softly at the insult and swung onto the seat beside her, attempting to take her into his arms. She went deliberately stiff, swearing she would not give in. But when he began nibbling at her earlobe and unbuttoning her bodice, it became more difficult to resist him, even though she was deeply hurt at his ridiculous scientific prejudices—and *determined* to change his mind.

He trailed a string of warm feathery kisses down her throat, his voice husky. "Are we going to quarrel then, on our honeymoon?"

She swallowed, her insides quivering, although she managed to sound quite normal as she replied, "Are you going to seduce me then, in a hired carriage? Think of the scandal if your colleagues found out."

He chuckled unwillingly, his fingers slipping inside her loosened bodice to fondle her breasts. "Oh, I'll take the chance."

She drew a sharp breath and leaned back, her breasts tingling where he had stroked them. "What about nursing? Why can't I work at a hospital?"

"Do you have any idea what sort of women become nurses

in our society? Runaway daughters, dismissed servants, and wives abandoned by their husbands."

"Misfits, you mean. Well, that certainly includes me."

Ian's face softened; it hurt him so much that she saw herself that way. "I'm sorry. Nursing should be an honorable profession, but it isn't."

"And it's never likely to change with an attitude like *that*," Margaret said under her breath.

The carriage slowed before a three-story graystone house in a posh residential district in Union Square. A light flared to life from a window in the servants' basement, as if someone had been awaiting their arrival.

"We're home," Ian said with a relieved sigh as he reached down to lift the hamper.

The cat gave a low angry growl.

Margaret grinned. "My sentiments exactly, Cyclops."

Ian leaned over the hamper, the cat hissing, and lightly kissed his wife on the lips. "My father said the house has running water."

"You're trying to placate me."

"Absolutely. It will make it easier to seduce you later on."

Ian's father Colin had found the house and hired, for immediate purposes, a young chambermaid, a footman, Ian's former coachman Donald, and a short, trim, auburn-haired Welshwoman in her forties named Blodwen Jones. Margaret and Mrs. Jones took to each other like long-lost relatives, for no overt reason Ian could perceive. But he was secretly relieved that his wife had found a sort of motherly guidance in the warm Welshwoman. He also hoped, naively, that perhaps Mrs. Jones could divert Margaret's interest from folk healing to safer domestic pursuits.

"Now, Mrs. MacNeill, it's too late at night to discuss kitchen matters," Mrs. Jones began, already scooping Cyclops into her sturdy arms and escorting Margaret down the hallway. "You can approve the menus in the morning, but I've a lovely pot of chamomile tea on the hob, and some hyssop wine for the doctor to help you both sleep."

Margaret's face lit up. Ian, standing alone in the unlit hallway, felt a foreboding in his vitals.

"You have an herb garden, Mrs. Jones?" he heard his wife ask in an exuberant voice that was definitely meant for his ears.

"Oh, indeed I do," Mrs. Jones answered, giving Cyclops a friendly cuddle. "And I've taken the liberty of converting the wine cellar into a still-room. I realize your husband is a doctor, but there's no replacement for the old ways, madam. Don't you agree?"

"Oh, I do, Mrs. Jones. I truly do."

"This still-room wouldn't be the room my father mentioned would serve as an excellent laboratory?" Ian interrupted.

Mrs. Jones gave a dignified sniff. "We've three empty rooms belowstairs, sir. Your father gave me permission to take over the southeast portion as I saw fit. You will agree, sir, that even to a doctor, laundry is more important than laboratories."

"Yes, he would," Margaret said.

"No, he wouldn't," Ian countered.

Those three empty rooms, he realized, were probably situated in the chilliest, darkest bowels of the basement, where on cold mornings, he'd grow icicles on his nose and have to spend a fortune in lights.

Margaret removed her cloak, frowning down in embarrassment at the hastily buttoned bodice of her gown. Ian watched her, wanting nothing more than to get her upstairs and resume the seduction he'd started in the carriage. "Oh, hell," he said. "Do what you like, Mrs. Jones, if my wife approves, but mind that the consulting room is to be abovestairs and my laboratory is off limits to *everyone.*"

Victory sparkling in her gentle brown eyes, the middle-aged

woman inclined her head in gracious assent. "I'll see to madam's tea. I expect that the cab just stopping outside is your domestic couple arriving with the rest of your luggage."

Ian did not bother to glance around, his gaze riveted on Margaret as she nervously peered up the long wooden staircase to the bedroom they would share.

"Leave my wife's tea on a tray outside the door," he quietly instructed the cook before she moved away. "She's tired and may be asleep before you return."

"I'll send Bridget up to light the fire and bring you a warming pan for the bed."

Ian shook his head and began to remove his bulky black overcoat. "No warming pan tonight, Mrs. Jones. We're still on honeymoon."

Mrs. Jones blushed and whisked down the hall, apparently wise enough to recognize when she could not press a point.

Margaret stared down into the quiet street several moments later, so deep in thought she barely heard Ian light the coal fire and turn down the lavender-scented sheets on the big four-poster with mohair bed hangings. There was a cab on the corner with what looked like a woman passenger in it, and since the vehicle hadn't moved, she assumed Walter was carting Ian's books and trunks into the house while Sybil waited.

A sense of unease crept along Margaret's nerve endings, a disturbing sensation of being observed. Indignant, she imagined Sybil watching through her husband's field glasses . . . but then suddenly the cab took off, and Margaret caught a fleeting glimpse of a veiled female face that definitely did not belong to Sybil Armstrong. Probably a neighbor, she thought, dismissing the incident from her mind.

She turned at a rattling noise behind her and saw Ian place a silver tea tray on the table between the loveseat and wing chair that faced the struggling coal fire.

"Have your tea and get ready for bed," he said. "I promise my parents will be here first thing in the morning to inspect the new member of the family."

He was teasing her, but Margaret's stomach clenched at the prospect, the years of social isolation on Maryhead making her uncomfortable around strangers. "Were they fond of Jean?" she asked, sitting in the chair opposite the loveseat while the coal fire cast shadows on the flocked wallpaper.

Ian glanced up at her from beneath his brows. "Yes," he admitted, a trifle resentfully. "And they took her side when she married my brother, too. They told me I'd neglected her, and what did I expect."

Margaret sipped the sweet herbal tea, easily picturing Ian as an eager young medical student absorbed in his studies. "Did you neglect her?"

He looked down at his hands. "I was busy trying to get my practice started, but I assumed she'd understand."

"And she had an affair with your brother?"

"Which led to the conception of a child."

The warm beverage failed to counteract the sudden coldness that gripped Margaret. "If she hadn't gotten pregnant, Ian," she asked quietly, setting down her cup, "would you have forgiven the affair?"

"I don't know," he answered honestly. He got up from the loveseat and pulled her by the hands against him, holding her tight. "But what I felt for Jean is a pale shadow of my feelings for you."

He led her to their bed, his face intense as he undressed her and then himself, their naked bodies huddling together beneath the unwarmed sheets. They made love slowly before drifting off to sleep, and in the back of his mind, Ian realized that remnants of their unresolved argument still hung between them. He wasn't really worried, though. There was time to sort things out, and he was hopeful he could convince Margaret to leave her former life behind.

* * *

Gareth Rose looked up from his easel at the sound of the carriage stopping outside the villa, the rushed footsteps on the entrance stairs. He threw a canvas over his work and wiped his hands on an oil-soaked rag, expecting Lucy to burst into the studio as was her disturbing habit.

When after several minutes she did not appear, he grew suspicious. Gareth knew what had lured her out this late at night, the expected arrival of that doctor and the bride he'd brought back to Aberdeen, Gareth's estranged sister Margaret. Christ, he'd known MacNeill was trouble from the moment he'd met him.

He lowered the lamps and left the room. Until tonight, he'd been praying Margaret would stay on Maryhead. Only she could threaten the uneasy closeness between him and his father. Only Margaret, with the unleashing of a single memory, could label Gareth the murderer he secretly believed himself to be.

He was shaking with nerves by the time he traced Lucy to her late husband's consulting room. He heard the low burr of unfamiliar voices, and he stood in the hallway, listening. She was talking to several young boys, offering them money, and only after they'd left quietly by the street door did he go into the darkened room to see her.

She turned slowly from the window. Gareth saw that she was smiling, and he felt an unwilling surge of sexual excitement as their eyes met.

"I saw them," Lucy said, her voice taut. "I followed them to their town house and watched your new brother-in-law carry his wife over the threshold. Very touching."

Gareth swallowed over the knot of anxiety in his throat. "What if they saw you? What if—"

"They didn't," she snapped. "They won't know anything unless *you* make a mistake."

He leaned against the wall. "How did my sister look? Was she well?"

"I didn't exactly pay a social call, Gareth."

He fell silent as she turned to draw the drapes across the window, the four boys she'd spoken with moments before moving down the gaslit street, sinister little shadows. "You said Margaret wouldn't come back." He was having trouble breathing now. "You said the Armstrongs would take care of her."

"We're not finished yet, are we?"

"But my father asks about her every day." His voice was rising, and even though he knew Lucy hated it when he got upset, he couldn't help himself. "He'll insist on seeing her."

"It doesn't matter, Gareth. We'll take care of them." She moved toward him, the scent of her perfume overpowering in the unventilated room. With her luminous green eyes and spun-gold hair, he'd often thought she looked like an angel. "Are you coming to bed or not?"

Despite the anxiety that churned in his stomach, his fear, he desired her. "She's my sister, Lucy," he said in an undertone. "I don't want to hurt her. You promised me you'd only scare her enough to keep her away from Aberdeen."

She shrugged, her voice innocent. "Margaret could have an accident. It would make her husband so very sad. And perhaps the 'Devil Doctor' would even be implicated . . ."

He looked at her in horror. "She's my *sister*. What were you doing with those boys in here earlier?"

"Do you really want to know?"

He shook his head slowly. She was a dangerous woman, and his every instinct urged him to break off with her while he still could. "Don't tell me anything," he said hoarsely.

"Show me your sketches?"

Her smile sweet, she held out her hand and the weak-natured part of Gareth that his father abhorred went to her without a care for his certain damnation and Margaret's downfall.

Thirty-eight

Colin MacNeill, his youngest daughter, a vivacious brunette named Dara, and her four-year-old son, Malcolm, arrived during breakfast the following morning. If Margaret had been anxious over meeting Ian's family, she was instantly put at ease by the warm hug Dara gave her and the approving twinkle in Colin's eye as Ian introduced her.

"I can't credit it, Ian," Dara commented, helping herself to an enormous plate of kippers and eggs from the chafing dish on the sideboard. "She's far too pretty for you." Her light blue eyes shining with good spirits, she glanced at Margaret. "Did you know your husband was so dark and ugly as a bairn my mother thought he was a brownie?"

Margaret glanced at Ian and started to laugh only to stop herself at the look of embarrassment in his eyes. Her heart went out to him. Didn't he realize that to her he was the most handsome man she'd ever met?

"Come to the club this afternoon, Ian," Colin was saying, sitting back in his chair as the young maid refilled his coffee cup. "Mark Kincardine will be there—they've made him Professor of Obstetrics and Gynecology at the college. He's a good man to have on your side, what with your resuming a practice in town." He sniffed his cup appreciatively. "Mmm. What is this? It smells like chicory."

"It is," Margaret answered. "My cook is partial to using herbs for both cooking and medicinal purposes."

"Aye, well, there's nothing wrong with the old ways," Colin said, sipping his coffee.

"Don't, Dad," Ian warned him. "You're opening up a Pandora's box. My wife really believes in charms and the magical properties of plants."

"And didn't we get digitalis from the foxglove?" Colin smiled at Margaret. "Ian's own grandmother swears she was cured of consumption by taking a midnight dip in Loch Monak."

Ian sighed, drumming his fingers on the table. "Thanks for the support, Dad. You'll not mind if I go to the club for a couple of hours, Margaret?"

Dara spoke up before Margaret had the chance. "I'll keep her company for you. Perhaps she'd like a day at the dressmaker's. I take it Maryhead isn't known for its high fashion."

This was said in such a critical, though not unkind tone, that Margaret couldn't help glancing down self-consciously at her practical gray muslin gown.

Ian shook his head. "You might try a little bluntness in future, Dara."

"Well, honestly," Dara said, "don't you think Margaret would look lovely in turquoise-blue taffeta?"

"Margaret looks lovely in anything," he said quietly.

"Och, I meant no harm, Margaret," Dara said in a totally unapologetic voice. "But if I'm to be blunt, then I'll give your husband a piece of advice right here and now: Don't abandon your bride for your work. She's bonnier than Jean by half, and brighter, too, if those blue-gray eyes give any indication. You've lost one woman to medicine, Ian. I hope you'll not let it happen again."

Colin glared at her over his cup. "Are you quite done with the domestic advice, Dara?"

"Almost," she said calmly.

"I don't want to go to the dressmaker's, Mum," Malcolm

grumbled from under the table where he was feeding Cyclops the remaining kippers.

"Another thing," Dara went on imperturbably, ignoring the boy. "Jean and Andrew have a son, Ian. His name is Kevin. I know his existence is a sore spot, but the child is innocent—"

Ian picked up the morning newspaper, his voice like ice. "I'm fully aware of his existence and do *not* wish to discuss the subject further."

There was a strained hush. To cover her own confused reaction, Margaret began to stack dishes on the sideboard. For a moment she considered leaving the room, to give Ian and his sister a chance for a private conversation. But she was frankly too curious about Ian's feelings for Jean to tear herself away.

"Leave the dishes for the maid, Margaret," Ian said in a low voice.

She froze, turning back to the table to face him, uncertain what she would find when she met his gaze. Regret for the child born to Jean and Andrew that might have been his? An attempt to cover what he felt for Jean? But he was still reading—or pretending to read—the paper, and all at once Aberdeen and all its unpleasant associations became unpleasantly real, and Margaret wasn't sure whether Ian was avoiding her eyes on purpose, afraid of betraying his emotions.

"I'll go with Dara for the afternoon, then?" she said softly.

Ian glanced up, his eyes glittering with humor and love for her, making her ashamed of the fears running rampant in her imagination. "My sister has shockingly extravagant taste."

Margaret grinned. "Unfortunately, so do I."

"Aye," Ian said dryly. "I was afraid you might."

Margaret hadn't really wanted to spend the day with Ian's outspoken sister, planning instead on assessing her own household needs, but as soon as she, Dara, and Malcolm settled into the brougham, she began to enjoy the drive through the poignantly familiar streets of Aberdeen where she had misspent her adolescence—and met Ian. She chuckled at the distant memory of that night.

"I should have held my tongue," Dara confided as the driver slowed for the thundering crush of traffic at the Market Square. "Ian's furious at me, you know."

The brougham stopped, and Dara swept aside her stylish lace-trimmed skirts to alight. Margaret hung back for several moments. Bluntness, she'd decided, called for bluntness.

"Do you think, Dara, that Ian's angry because he still cares for Jean and doesn't want to, or because you brought up the subject in front of me?"

Margaret and Malcolm stepped down onto the pavement. Dara frowned, considering the question. "Jean and Andy are understandably a painful subject for Ian and will probably remain so for a long time," she answered slowly. "But as to whether he still cares for her—why, you've only to see how he behaves with you to realize he's deeply in love. If he'd ever looked at Jean like that, she'd never have left him. You've charmed the beast, my dear. I hope it lasts."

It was a strange compliment, double-edged, in fact, but Margaret took it as reassurance. Yet as they crossed the street onto the arcaded walkway to the dressmaker's shop, she felt a pang of anxiety to realize how much she'd come to care for Ian, how much it mattered that he loved only her.

At the doorway of the exclusive shop, Dara paused again. "You're an asset to Ian, Margaret, and his reputation needs a bit of polish."

Margaret caught her own reflection in the plate-glass mirror, the shabby gray dress, her outmoded cloak. "An asset, you say?"

Dara nodded a greeting at the young aproned clerk who hurried forward to open the door. "The Rose name is a golden link in Aberdeen society. Ian can only be helped by the association. Come along, Malcolm, and don't touch the fabrics with your smelly kipper fingers."

Margaret followed Dara into the shop. It took considerable restraint not to remark that Ian needn't look for any help from Douglas Rose, since she had no intention of reestablishing any ties with her father. Then as she gazed at the bolts of fabric on the counter, the rich brocades and tartans, the shimmering silks, as her cloak was whisked from her shoulders by a pair of cheerful shopgirls who showed her to a chair, she decided she would momentarily sacrifice her worries and force herself to enjoy one of the sheer feminine experiences which she had been for so long deprived of on Maryhead.

Thoughts of Jean, her father, even Ian receded, replaced by the deliciously elegant images she glimpsed in the fashion journals heaped on her lap—*Le Bon Ton, Ladies' Gazette of Fashion, The Scottish Mode.*

Long dormant, Margaret's sense of female vanity was reawakened—by the peacock-blue brocade held up for her inspection, the ivory tarlatan embroidered with lavender lover's knots, an apricot silk that made her mouth water.

Standing before the looking-glass in her plain linen chemise and pantalettes, she shook her head in delighted confusion. "I can't decide. Something simple, I suppose."

"No," Dara said emphatically. "You'll be receiving patients, attending lectures and luncheons. What would everyone think, to meet the doctor's beautiful young bride dressed in those—" She waved her hand at the unremarkable gown and cloak a shopgirl had draped over a dressing screen.

Mrs. Bailie, the stout silver-haired dressmaker, joined forces with the persuasive Dara, an avaricious gleam in her eye. "The Islands are horribly out of touch with the rest of the world, Mrs. MacNeill. I haven't seen a primitive red cloak like yours in five years."

"Primitive?" Margaret repeated, remembering in amusement

how overdressed she had been considered on the island in that same cloak.

"It predates druidic times," Dara said flatly.

Margaret burst into laughter.

"Jean was a dressmaker herself when Ian was courting her," Dara added slyly. "Always stylishly turned out, wouldn't you agree, Mrs. Bailie? Even when she went to the water closet, Jean Drummond was the picture of Paris style."

"Oh, indeed," Mrs. Bailie said heartily. "And stiff competition she was, too. Quite frankly, I was never so relieved as when Jean closed shop and went to the country."

Fully aware she'd been cleverly manipulated by a pair of old professionals, Margaret smiled grimly and raised her chin. "I surrender. Do your damndest, Mrs. Bailie, but mind none of those sable boas—"

Her opinions were swept away in the flurry of activity that followed, the passionate arguments between Dara, the dressmaker, and her assistants, on color, style, and cost. Malcolm fell asleep on the floor. Margaret's head began to ache.

"She'll have the blue cashmere cloak—the Oriental influence is all in vogue."

"And the black maltese lace shawl."

"The bronze taffeta gown is overpriced, but so perfect for a ball with that beaded bodice—"

"She could use a nursing corset, too."

Margaret's brows shot up. "I could?"

"Eventually, Margaret," Dara said patiently.

Three hours later, Margaret emerged from the shop in a happy daze. "I'm famished," she announced. "Dara, is Barclay's Tea Room still in business? I haven't had a cream slice in years."

"Oh, please, Mum," Malcolm begged, yawning into his palm.

"The Tea Room's moved to James Street," Dara said, motioning away the driver who waited for them in the brougham.

"But there's a wee grocery shop on the corner, where Auntie Margaret can buy herself a broonie and you some almond-rock to hold you a while. I've just got to pop into the milliner's shop a moment—if you don't mind watching him, Margaret."

Margaret took the boy's hand. "Not at all."

As Dara scurried off, Margaret and Malcolm began to stroll down the pilastered pavement toward the corner, Margaret wondering how she could have survived so long on Maryhead without the pleasure of shopping.

"Good God," a man said behind her. "I'm having a vision."

She swung around toward the street at the sound of that vaguely familiar male voice, her eyes widening in astonished delight at the sight of her old cohort Daniel Munro stepping onto the pavement. There was a young blond woman clinging to his arm, but he swiftly whispered something in her ear and pried loose her hand, giving her a gentle shove in the direction of the dressmaker's.

"Margaret Rose." Daniel looked older, thinner, but his dark eyes gleamed with warmth and poignant memories as he studied Margaret; for all his weakness of character, his profligate ways, he had cared for her very much, she'd been his best friend in the world, and he had never quite forgiven her for suddenly vanishing from his life.

"Daniel," she said over the knot of emotion in her throat, dropping Malcolm's hand to embrace her old friend. "You wicked rake," she whispered tearfully in his ear even as she teased, "Was that pretty wee thing on your arm your daughter?"

He pulled back with a grin, drinking in the sight of her— Margaret matured, all mystery and mischief, still so lovely it hurt to look at her. "She's nothing, darling," he said with a gallantry that was more sincere than he could admit. "She's no one, now that *you're* back in town—"

"I'm married," she said quickly, forcing a smile. "To a doctor, so mind you behave yourself."

"A doctor? Well, if I'd known you were on the market—"

"You might have written."

"I wrote you dozens of letters, all of them returned or un-answered. But they spirited you away in so much secrecy. . . ." For a moment his face reflected his own pain and shock on discovering what her father had done, his regret, suddenly, that he hadn't had the moral fortitude to go after her.

"A doctor," he said with a patronizing sniff. "Do I know him?"

"Ian MacNeill."

"Ian—" He roared in delight. "Well, damn me." He glanced past her to where Malcolm stood gazing at the lollipops in the grocery-shop window. "And that's your bairn, is it?"

"Ian's nephew."

"Oh." He looked back at Margaret, his amusement dying. "You never wrote me, did you?"

She looked down at the pavement. "No."

The confession brought the conversation to a halt, and they stood for a minute in awkward silence. Then Margaret glanced around at the grocery shop, her voice rising.

"Where did Malcolm go?"

"Inside to examine the sweets, I expect," Daniel said, a frown darkening his face. "I didn't notice."

Margaret swung around, trying to suppress the mild panic welling up in her as she hurried toward the grocery. She pushed the door open, the shopbell tinkling in the gaslight atmosphere that exuded the pleasing smells of gingerbread, fresh vegetables, and sweets.

"Malcolm?" she whispered anxiously, glancing in every corner for the boy's pale face. She strode past the counter, catching the eye of the elderly woman who stood measuring sweets into a bag for a customer. "The wee laddie in the brown velvet jacket—"

"He never came inside, madam," the woman replied, not looking up. "He went off around the corner while you and the gentleman were talking."

Margaret felt suddenly cold all over. How could she have been so engrossed in conversation that she hadn't noticed the child? And to vanish, with the harbor and all its potential dangers two minutes away.

Daniel, who had entered the shop moments after Margaret, quickly led the way back outside. "He can't have gone far, Margaret. We'll take my carriage to look."

Margaret scarcely heard him, looking past the pilasters to scour the crowded street for the boy.

"Making friends already, Margaret?" Dara called out cheerfully behind her on the pavement, her face half hidden behind the hatbox she carried. "Introduce us, won't you?" And in the next breath, her keen blue eyes lifted from Margaret's worried face to Daniel. "Malcolm's broken something in the shop, hasn't he?"

The sky had darkened, rainclouds gathering above the sea and moving inland in a purple-gray mass. Margaret felt sick with worry and guilt, imagining the child lost and frightened or even worse. And Ian's reaction—telling him she'd lost his nephew because she was flirting with an old friend.

"I thought he might have run back after you," Margaret said, her last hope dying as Dara quickly shook her head and bit her lip against tears.

"I'll find a constable and have the carriage brought round," Daniel said. "You two should split up and search the arcade in the meanwhile."

"Perhaps our driver noticed where he went," Dara suggested, but as the three of them turned in unison, it was to see the elderly coachman sound asleep on the box, his chin tucked into his chest.

"The lad's just wandered off," Daniel said over his shoulder, slipping off the pavement. "Children do that."

Margaret nodded and turned away, hurrying down the arcade toward the harbor. She told herself Daniel was probably right, but suddenly the sense of evil that had been haunting her for months seemed to have taken a terrifying form, so palpable that she could feel its oppressive threat in the air.

And Ian had been wrong—it had nothing to do with Morag. In fact, in leaving Maryhead, Margaret had not escaped the evil at all. It had followed her, a mocking presence she could feel in the shadows of the arcade.

Thirty-nine

Malcolm hung back in the secluded corner of the arcade, staring at the lady in a veiled hat who spoke softly to him and held out a bag of almond-rock and assorted sweets. The lady had told him that Uncle Ian was an old friend of hers and had sent her to take Malcolm back to the house. But the boy was confused, aware he'd disobeyed his mother's instructions to stay with Auntie Margaret.

He wanted to run back and find his mother now, but he wasn't sure which way to go. And the lady frightened him, standing so close now he couldn't move around her.

Although she was pretty in her black dress, with her golden hair, she didn't smile, and Malcolm pressed harder against the wall, the heavy floral perfume she wore unpleasant to him.

"Is that your mother?" she'd asked earlier when Malcolm had first wandered to the toy shop while still in view of Auntie Margaret and her friend.

He'd turned from the window, answering, "It's Auntie Margaret."

"She's very lovely," the lady had said, and he hadn't been afraid then, not with so many people still in sight. "Your Uncle Ian must love her very much," the lady added in a soft, almost sad voice. "And I'll bet he loves *you,* too. In fact, he's told me so, and he also told me I was to give you the special present I have waiting in my carriage.

"Well?" she said, her voice sharper now. "Are you coming

for your present? If you hurry, we can drive around the harbor before it rains and see the ships."

Malcolm looked at the bag of sweets in the lady's hand and very slowly took a step.

Margaret and Dara had covered half the arcade before a shopkeeper told them where he'd last seen the boy. And seconds later they spotted him, pelting toward them with a relieved grin on his small freckled face.

"Thank God," Margaret said, letting Dara overtake her.

Malcolm slowed to a walk on seeing his mother's angry face, her upraised hand as she dropped the hatbox onto the pavement. "Little demon," she said, her voice shaking. "Did I not tell you to bide with your Auntie Margaret?"

"I—I only went to look at the toys, Mum, and then there was a lady in a white dress who asked about Uncle—"

The conclusion of his defense ended in a sliding yelp as Dara pitched him over her knee and whacked him on the rump, her face empurpled with the effort. "Do you want to be carried off by gypsies or kidnapped into a press gang?" she shouted. "Do you not remember the wee laddie's body they found last year in the links—that foolish boy who disobeyed his mother?"

Daniel pulled Margaret aside, waving away the constable who had come up behind them. "Well, welcome back to Aberdeen, Margaret Rose," he said with a grin. "It's good to know you can still cause a scene in the street, isn't it?"

Much later that same night, after she'd gone to bed and briefly discussed her eventful afternoon with Ian, Margaret stirred, disturbed by a noise from the garden beyond the servants' quarters. She sat up, instantly awake. It wasn't a *normal* sound: the cat, a servant using the water closet.

She nudged Ian in the back, but he merely rolled over with

a grunt, leaving her to tiptoe to the window, which she managed to open without a sound.

At first she didn't see anything, but as her eyes adjusted to the garden's midnight glow, she slowly perceived four or five ragged shadows carrying sacks and shovels, young boys of the street-urchin variety skulking about like goblins. Clearly they had mischief in mind—burglary, perhaps? But strangely it looked as if they'd begun to dig along the garden wall.

Furious, Margaret thought of her tender transplanted cuttings.

"What's the matter?" Ian whispered in her ear, his unshaven jaw nuzzling her neck.

She nearly fell out of the window, so upset at what she was watching that she hadn't heard him leave the bed. He gathered her back against his warm chest, his arms encircling her waist. "Look over there by the wall," she whispered. "There are four or five boys digging for something."

Ian didn't seem upset. "They're probably trying to pry open the cesspools. I understand they have contests to see who can uncover the most by morning." His hands pressed upward against her ribcage to cup her breasts. "Close the window, and get back into bed."

"They're ruining my garden," she retorted with a shiver that was part sexual desire, part reaction to the cold night air. "I'm going down to chase them away."

"No, you're not." She tried to wriggle loose, but his arms only gripped her harder, holding her immobile while he leaned them both toward the window to shout in a voice as explosive as a cannonball: "Get off my property, you miserable little sods! If you ruin my wife's garden, she'll turn you into tiny black tadpoles!"

A door shot open from the servants' quarters. Several lights flared, spreading bright circles into the dark reaches of the garden. The boys threw down their shovels and scrambled back up the wall like squirrels, their pounding footsteps echoing into the evening.

"There," Ian said with a grin. "That took care of that."

Margaret lingered for a moment at the window after he'd closed it, not entirely convinced the disturbance could be put down to a childish prank. And after she had followed Ian back to bed, she could not fall asleep again, sighing and staring up at the tester. Finally Ian hoisted himself up on his elbow to frown at her.

"Now what is it?"

"I miss the sound of the sea. It helps me sleep."

"Margaret, you could walk to the harbor from here."

"It's not the same. The waves here have been tamed, spoiled somehow."

"Give it time," he said gently. "Give us time." He settled back into bed, his voice slurred. "You had a nice day with Dara, didn't you?"

"Partly, until Malcolm got lost."

"That was just a boy's misbehavior. The same as we witnessed a few minutes ago in the garden. Relax, Margaret." He closed his eyes, drawing her back into his arms. "Who knows?" he said drowsily. "Within a year we could have a son of our own."

She closed her eyes and grinned, picturing a miniature black-haired Ian running around the house with a stethoscope instead of toy soldiers. And then she opened her eyes, sitting up again to stare at the window. "I thought the cesspools were outside the kitchen," she said with a sudden recollection of Mrs. Jones complaining about the smell. But Ian had already drifted off, the subject closed, and Margaret did not think it worthy of waking him. Still, in the deep silence of the night, with her husband asleep beside her, she was uneasy.

Forty

Two days later Margaret came to learn exactly why those boys had been digging in her garden, and it was not a pleasant discovery. She was having tea at the breakfast table with Ian's mother, Grace MacNeill, a diminutive blue-eyed brunette who did not look strong enough to have borne six strapping children. But there was steel beneath that fragile bone structure, and for all her ethereal appearance, Grace had the comfortable down-to-earth disposition that Ian had inherited.

"You're white as a ghost, Margaret," she observed, setting down her cup. "What is that thing you're reading anyway?"

"It's called a Penny Dreadful," Margaret said quietly. "I found it on the front steps just before you came—when I was letting out the cat." She pushed the illustrated pamphlet across the table. "Read it."

Grace put on her spectacles and had just finished the article when Ian entered—actually exploded—into the sunlit parlor, his appearance so bizarre that both women gaped at him in wordless astonishment. There was an inhaler tube hanging out of his mouth, attached to the canister he had hooked onto his waistcoat pocket. Several pencils protruded from behind his ears like insect antennae. His shirt was stained with some chemical and only half tucked in. His blue eyes were so dilated as to appear black.

"That's you, Mother?" He squinted in surprise, his voice like gravel.

Grace put down the paper. "I know who I am, but I'm not sure you're my son." She glanced at Margaret over her spectacles. "Does he take these spells often?"

Ian walked unsteadily to the table to pour himself a cup of tea, which he quickly drank. "I'm lecturing tonight at the Surgeon's Hall. I can't get this damned experiment to repeat. I can't find my notes. And"—he looked across the table with an engaging smile—"I need someone to volunteer to test the ether. My frog got away."

"Don't look at me," Margaret said in genuine horror.

"I have an appointment with the draper in a half hour," Grace hastily said, then lifted a delicate hand to the Penny Dreadful. "Have you read this?"

He frowned. "I can't read anything until my vision clears. Does it mention the lecture I'm supposed to give?"

"It mentions you," Grace replied wryly, "but not in reference to anything so innocuous as a lecture. It—well, a group of young boys claim they were playing pirates' treasure and that they dug up . . . human remains, a skeleton, in your garden, and—"

Ian pulled off the inhaler and stared at Margaret. "So that's how the bloody skeleton got into the neighbor's garden."

"And," Grace continued, "it goes on to say that the recently returned Dr. MacNeill has brought with him a wife who served as a folk healer on the remote island of Maryhead, known for its adherence to heathen religions. 'Could the doctor and his wife have combined medicine and magic to revive a pagan cult in the very flower beds of civilization?' "

She snorted and glanced up over her spectacles. " 'The very flower beds of civilization.' Ye Gods."

Ian sat down on the edge of the table, his face furious. "I used that skeleton for my anatomy lectures and it came from the university. What shit—excuse me, Mother, Margaret. But I can't believe this sort of nonsense is starting up again."

Grace frowned and poured them three fresh cups of tea.

"There's a cartoon above the caption, depicting you in a cemetery with a wolf's head and gravedigger's spade. How did your skeleton get into the yard in the first place?"

"It's my fault," Margaret answered in a small voice. "I had Bridget sweep the floor and clean the grate in your laboratory, Ian, but she fainted dead away when she saw the skeleton, and I had Walter lay it on the garden bench while she worked. I suppose he forgot to replace it."

Ian sighed in exasperation. "I wonder if the silly bint tossed my notes in the dustbin then. For God's sake, Margaret, I thought I made it clear I wanted that room left alone."

"Your wife didn't bring those boys into your garden," Grace said pensively. "Nor did she sell the story to the press. Could your old enemies have decided to renew the feud?"

He shoved his hand through his hair, inadvertently knocking the pencils to the carpet. "Christ, I got into it again at the Institute with that old bastard Abernathy about the dangers of inhalation, but I can't believe he'd have the imagination for this. They'll be calling me a bodysnatcher in the streets again."

He slid off the table, shaking his head, and walked out of the room, pausing at the door to ask: "Are you sure neither one of you would like to volunteer for an experiment that might make medical history?"

The two women pretended not to hear him. Then when he'd gone, Margaret got up from the table, her face troubled. "I'll find Bridget and question her about his notes. You don't really think, Grace, that Ian's professional rivals could play such a nasty trick on him, do you?"

Grace frowned. "Medicine is a highly competitive business, my dear, as much as is trade or even banking. It can bring glory, money, and power. Ian is participating in possibly the greatest medical discovery to benefit humanity. Men and women have committed murder for much, much less."

"I don't know how to help him," Margaret said with a sigh.

Grace grinned at her. "Don't let him experiment on you for

a start. One of you is obviously going to need to keep your wits about you."

Within the hour Margaret had recovered the lost notes from the dustbin, said goodbye to Grace, and left Ian to prepare for his important evening. He gave her a distracted kiss and assured her he didn't blame her in the least for the article in the Penny Dreadful, but in her heart she feared she might be a millstone around the neck of her brilliant husband. After all, he was risking his life, his reputation to save the world. All Margaret could claim from her modest repertoire of medical successes, as recent certified cures, were the chicken-pox rashes of Maryhead's children and Bridget the maid's indigestion.

Dejected, Margaret wandered out into the high-walled garden and presently the early March sun, the green smell of new growth in the freshly turned earth, lifted her spirits. She sat in the rose arbor on the same bench where that wretched skeleton had laid and touched her abdomen, wondering if Ian could be right about their making a child. She thought of all the tonics and teas for encouraging fertility, for assuring a healthy pregnancy: milk-thistle tea, seaweed, sleeping with an eel skin under the mattress.

And as she was seriously debating whether she should give nature a helping hand, an amused male voice spoke behind her.

"I'd frown too if I'd married a man as ugly as Ian."

Margaret started, the mood of the peaceful morning interrupted. She turned her head to see a brown-haired young man in tweed knickerbockers standing beneath the budding vine-draped trellis, in a sort of sunlit haze, a stranger to her and yet vaguely familiar.

He took a long draw on his pipe, and although Margaret could swear she saw no smoke, she smelled its pleasant masculine aroma in the air.

"Don't get up," he murmured.

The queer thing was that she *couldn't* seem to move. Her limbs felt leaden, her mind caught in a languorous contentment. Yet her senses were alert. Was she dreaming?

"You're a friend of my husband's?" she guessed.

His smile seemed rueful. "Well, I was. I wanted to say goodbye to him, but he's too engrossed in his work to see me. His mind is too full, ye ken, too cluttered with worldly intellect to understand anything he can't find in a book."

Margaret didn't know why, but the gooseflesh rose suddenly on her forearms. She was afraid and not afraid.

"You understand, Margaret," he said in a hushed voice that made her hold her breath because she knew she hadn't told him her name. "You're willing to look beyond appearances, aren't you?"

Margaret put her hand to her heart, telling herself this *was* a dream, or a trick of sunlight, that he was becoming more and more transparent. "Who are you?" she whispered.

He was staring at the shuttered laboratory window, and she wasn't sure he'd even heard her until at last he glanced back toward her, answering, "Andy. Tell him Andy came to say goodbye and that I'm so very sorry for what happened between us."

"This sounds serious," Margaret said, struggling to shake off her lassitude long enough to rise. "I'll fetch him myself."

"There isn't time. As you can see, I appear to be disappearing." He grinned. "Tell him I don't have the damned limp anymore."

Margaret assumed from that remark that he was a former patient of Ian's. "You had an accident?" she asked.

"Oh, I was born lame," he said casually. "But, yes, I had an accident. Shot myself right after tea while my wife and aunt were playing whist. About twenty minutes ago as the world judges time."

Margaret smiled to conceal her confusion, unaware that Ian had ever worked with the mentally sick.

"I've got to go, lass," he said softly.

At that instant Cyclops bolted up the garden wall from the street and leaped onto the trellis. Margaret glanced up, noticing that the cat had begun to make peculiar mewling noises in his throat at the man in the shadows. But like Margaret, Cyclops did not seem to regard him as a threat.

She looked back to the man who'd called himself Andy, but he had vanished, although he could not have possibly reached the gate or walked past her without her knowledge.

Her eyes wide, she rushed to the spot where he'd stood, but there were no footprints in the freshly churned soil. Nothing to prove his presence but the faint scent of tobacco.

The nerve endings on her nape tingled like a thousand pinpricks. She whirled and ran toward the kitchen, Cyclops dropping onto his feet to follow. She would have to interrupt Ian, risking his anger, to tell him about the visitor he'd been too busy to receive. But Mrs. Jones came out from the scullery door to intercept her, her kindly face perplexed.

"Armstrong has just let a man into the parlor, Mrs. MacNeill. A gentleman who's quite insistent on seeing you."

Margaret thought instantly of Daniel and was annoyed at his audacity in visiting the house. "Did he leave his name?"

"Armstrong didn't say, ma'am, but I took the liberty of having a wee listen from the hall while he and your visitor chatted in the parlor—quite inappropriate behavior for a butler, by the way. But I believe your caller is Gareth Rose."

Forty-one

As close as Margaret and her brother had been in childhood, she was hurt that Gareth had never made more of an effort to communicate with her after she had been sent to Maryhead. But perhaps Uncle Angus had destroyed those letters, too, at her father's request.

Actually, over the years she'd convinced herself that must have been what had happened. She didn't want to believe that Gareth had forgotten their years of affection.

As she closed the parlor door behind her, Gareth turned from the marble fireplace. The expression on his face reminded Margaret of a small boy who'd done something wrong and was waiting for his punishment.

"Hello, Gareth," she said gently.

"Margaret." His voice broke, despite his obvious efforts to control his emotions, and she was both angry at him and so deliriously happy that she rushed into his arms, the years of painful doubt obliterated.

He laughed in surprise and lost his balance, stumbling back against a chair. They fell on it together and held each other tightly. When Walter brought in the whiskey Gareth had apparently ordered, then quietly left the room, Gareth broke away. There were tears in his eyes, and his gaze took in every detail of her happily flushed face.

"The darkest Rose," he said in a rueful voice. "And the best-looking one. You were always a pretty child, Margaret.

I've sketched you often from memory, but I never imagined you'd become so beautiful."

She snorted. "You always said I looked like a monkey."

He grinned. "I must have meant a pretty monkey."

They sat together on the sofa, Gareth pouring himself a drink. "You've pursued your art then?" she asked eagerly.

He sipped the whiskey, shrugging his narrow shoulders. "Not as a career. I've been too busy at the bank. We're amalgamating—taking over a rival bank in Dundee, and Father—"

Margaret got up and pretended to pull the tapestried footstool away from the fire, afraid of how she would react to whatever he was about to tell her about their father.

"He wants to see you, Margaret," he said behind her. "He knows you're back and is waiting for you to call at the house."

"So he still thinks he's Prince Albert?" she joked with a humor she didn't feel.

"More like the Pope actually," Gareth muttered.

He finished his drink and glanced around the room, his gaze critical. "So you've married that doctor. I always hoped you'd do better for yourself with your looks and breeding."

The remark offended her.

"You'd have preferred a lobsterman or a shepherd for a brother-in-law, I suppose?" she couldn't help asking. "That's about the extent of Maryhead's eligible bachelor list."

Gareth put down his glass and rose from the sofa. "You're my sister, and I care about you. There's talk about town that your new husband is a professional eccentric who dabbles in untested theories, that he's broke and has been soliciting donations for his research."

Ian, broke? For a moment Margaret was too shocked to respond, but then what *did* she know of her husband's financial status? As a child of one of Aberdeen's wealthiest citizens, she'd grown up with a casual disregard for such mysteries as how her family could afford their affluent lifestyle. She thought guiltily of the small fortune she'd spent with Dara at the dressmaker's shop. Perhaps she could sneak back and cancel the extravagant wardrobe she'd ordered. Except for the black maltese lace shawl.

Suddenly suspicious of Gareth's motives, wondering if their father was behind this, she demanded, "How do you know about Ian's work anyway?"

He looked uncomfortable. "The hospital he's affiliated with has just applied for an enormous research fund from the bank. And your husband is named as its director."

Margaret's heart sank. What possible reason would Gareth have to lie? And yet she couldn't imagine Ian going behind her back to ask a loan of her father.

"Are you sure?" she asked, her voice strained.

Gareth's face looked so sincere, it was impossible to doubt him. "I could show you the documents at the bank. I'm truly sorry, Margaret, especially after all you've already gone through." He hesitated. "Do you want me to find out about the possibility of having the marriage annulled?"

An annulment. The idea stunned her, and it seemed incredible that only two short weeks ago, she herself had discussed a divorce with Ian.

She swallowed. "I'm sure Ian meant to tell me about the loan later on."

"Men marry women every day for their money, Margaret," he said gently.

"I haven't got a penny to my name."

"You have an inheritance that any man would covet."

She laughed uneasily. "You're suggesting that Ian married me for the fortune I never intend to touch? How ludicrous."

"You're very naive," he said carefully, "and very emotionally vulnerable from the way you've been treated. It would be easy for a man you loved to take advantage of you. Look, I have a flat in Edinburgh which I only use for business purposes. You can stay there to think things over."

She shook her head in amused disbelief. "I wish I'd had

this sort of support from you a few years ago when I needed it."

"I'm trying to help you now."

"Ian and I will work our problems out together," Margaret said firmly, hoping it was the truth.

He nodded, summoning a smile. "Let me know if you do decide to visit Father. I'll arrange to be there to act as a buffer for you." He pulled out his pocket watch. "Damn. I have an appointment at one—"

"A love interest, Gareth?" Margaret teased. "She's not after you for your money, is she?"

He smiled grimly. "She has her own fortune, believe me."

Margaret followed him to the door, her tone deceptively light. "Are you really that eager that I should leave Aberdeen again?"

He turned at the door, and Margaret felt a frisson of unease go through her at the dark intensity on his face. "I care about you, little sister," he said softly. "You've suffered enough, and I think it's time it stopped."

"You're being overprotective," she said quietly. "My husband cares about me very much."

His eyes scanned her face. "I hope so."

"You're cheating," Ian said over Margaret's shoulder, studying the game of patience she was playing in bed on the rose satin quilt.

"I never cheat." She frowned, pretending concentration. "You're in my light."

He sat down beside her, his hands sliding down her shoulders to force her back into his arms. The deck of cards scattered beneath their combined weight, Ian silencing Margaret's protest with a leisurely kiss. The watch passed outside below their window, crying out the hour, one o'clock on a clear

March morning. It had been a week since Margaret had caught the boys digging in the garden.

"How was your important meeting?" she murmured when she could catch her breath.

"Boring compared to this." He untied the insubstantial pink silk ribbons of her nightdress, rubbing his face across her unconfined breasts.

Margaret strained upward in the reaction he never failed to elicit from her, her nipples contracting, sensitive to the light stroking of his tongue. "New nightdress?" he murmured. "It's very pretty."

"And too expensive for you to tear." She sat up, the garment in question slipping down her waist, her dark hair brushing her breasts. Her eyes narrowing mischievously, she retrieved a card from under Ian's kneecap and pressed it to her forehead. "The gypsy Magdalena will read your cards for a silver coin, *gorgio,*" she said in an exotic accent of undefinable origins.

Ian grinned, his craggy face amused, and took off his shirt. His blue eyes openly sexual, he lowered his hand to his waistband. "I already know my future. I'm going to take my wife to bed."

Margaret scooted away from him and squeezed back against the pillows, studying the cards she held. "Ah! I see great fame and fortune in your future."

Ian grunted and fell onto his side, his arms flung over his face. "When?"

"My brother came here today." Margaret's voice was low. "He told me you'd applied for a loan at the bank for your research."

Ian sat up, frowning. "The hospital applied for a fund and may have used my name, but I had nothing personally to do with the transaction. Do you really think I'd do such a thing behind your back, knowing how you'd feel?"

She looked down at her lap, wondering how she'd ever allowed Gareth to place the damaging doubt in her mind. "I suppose there are men who marry women for their wealth or social connection," she murmured.

"I suppose there are," Ian agreed, his smile amused.

"And," Margaret continued slowly, "I suppose those wives are so enamored of their husbands they ignore their relatives' well-meaning warnings."

His smile faded into the sharp planes of his face. "I wish my wife were that enamored of me."

Her heart skipped a beat, the emotions rising inside her so disconcerting she couldn't bear to examine them. "I'm not sure I could ever let myself love anyone that much," she said after a moment.

He sighed and moved away from her to lean back against the headboard, his arms folded behind his head. "You share my bed, my hopes, my dreams, but I want more, Margaret. You cheat us both with your holding back."

"Not on purpose," she said, shaking her head.

"Isn't the life we have enough?" he asked her.

"You're very good to me," she said softly, leaning over him to kiss his chest.

Ian shivered, closing his eyes against the confusion he felt. And Margaret lay quietly, thinking. Trying so hard not to love him was supposed to protect her in case she ever did lose him, and suddenly for the first time she began to understand that all her emotional subterfuge might backfire, driving him away.

"I met a former patient of yours today in the garden," she began tentatively, hoping to lighten the serious mood that had fallen. "I forgot to give you his message."

"Tell me in the morning."

She began to stroke his chest. "His name was Andy, and he said he wanted to tell you goodbye. Oh, and he mentioned that the limp was gone."

Ian frowned, his body, his curiosity, aroused. "I remember no such patient."

"I think . . . I suspect he might have been . . ."

"Been what?" Ian asked.

A ghost.

"A former patient," Margaret said, realizing he would only laugh at her anyway.

"Aye. You already said that."

"He seemed to know you well enough." She traced the outline of his ribs with her forefinger, and Ian sucked in his breath, the muscles of his belly tightening. "He said you were too preoccupied to bother with him."

"He was right. He's a nuisance even now . . ."

He rolled over on top of her, his groin pressed to her belly, his mouth seeking hers. Margaret moaned and ran her hands down his forearms, circling around to his hips. If only for a little while, she was eager to act as if everything was perfect between them. No differences, no doubts.

Yet long after Ian had fallen asleep, Margaret lay curved into the warm contours of his body. She thought of all her problems, that sooner or later she'd have to face her father, that she was deceiving her husband about having given up her folk medicine. And they were broke.

But oddly, although she couldn't claim her life was perfect, there were moments in it of increasing joy, when she and Ian were together, not just making love, but planning their future or talking in bed. And those unexpected moments combined had given her more happiness than she'd known since childhood. If only she could believe the magic would last.

Forty-two

Ian's father arrived unexpectedly after breakfast three days later. Visibly distraught, the older man could hardly speak at first, then when he did it was to haltingly explain that Ian's brother Andrew had been killed in a hunting accident in the hills of Taynaross.

"How do you know?" Ian asked, his face disbelieving.

Dazed, Colin sat down in the chair Margaret pulled out for him. "Your mother just got the letter from Jean's daughter, Alanna. Apparently Jean's not taking it well at all. I suppose she's worried about what will happen to her now, with a bairn to raise by herself in the country."

"I can't believe it," Ian said after a stunned pause. "People like Andrew aren't meant to die in accidents. They grow old borrowing money and bedeviling other people's lives."

Colin put his head back against the chair as a dry sob escaped him. In helpless sympathy, Margaret watched grief transform him into a broken old man, the distinguished mask dropped, never to be worn so well again.

Ian got up from the table, staring at his father in concern. His own emotions were frozen inside him behind a wall of disbelief. Despite his bitterness, he'd loved his brother, and although he hadn't been ready to forgive Andrew, he wasn't prepared to lose him either with so much unresolved between them. It was too unexpected for him to accept.

"How is Mother taking it?" he asked Colin.

"I think she's in shock." Colin took the glass of whiskey Margaret had poured him from the sideboard. "It's good she has Jean and the child to occupy her mind."

Ian nodded slowly, trying not to imagine Jean's reaction when she'd heard the news. "There can't be much trade for a dressmaker of Jean's talents in a little village. She'll have to come home."

"Aye," Colin murmured. "No doubt Andrew's left her without a penny."

"She's a MacNeill," Ian said. "She'll never go hungry."

Margaret looked up at her husband, then swiftly lowered her gaze to the table, her heart lodging in her throat. *She'll have to come home.* How possessive he sounded. How eager to bring Jean back to Aberdeen, under his protection perhaps. And then she told herself to stop being so damned petty, to work on consoling Ian on the loss of his brother rather than worrying about what Jean's reentry into his life would mean.

She pushed in her chair. "What can I do to help, Ian?"

He looked at his father. "I assume there'll be a wake?"

"Aye." Colin rubbed his unshaven face. "But we'll not have time to make it, so I suggest you take a week or two here to settle your affairs if you want to pay your respects at his grave in person. The family will all be visiting Jean."

"Shall I find out about reserving seats on a train?" Margaret asked quietly.

Ian took his jacket from the back of his chair and shook his head, his face somber. "The railroads don't go that far—we'll have to take the Aberdeen Fly. Have Walter make arrangements for about a fortnight from now. I can't get away any earlier without inconveniencing my patients."

"No point in rushing if we're to miss the funeral," Colin said, his voice remote. "Except to comfort Jean."

"Well, she has Alanna," Ian said with a heavy sigh. "Dammit, I'm late for my appointment, and my patient is a duchess whose condition is critical. I don't know how I'll be any good to her when I can't even think straight."

He walked slowly toward the door, pausing to squeeze his father's shoulder and give Margaret an absent-minded kiss. "Dara should be told today and someone needs to sit with my mother."

"I'll visit Dara as soon as you leave," Margaret promised.

"Poor Andy," Colin said with a sigh. "He wanted so much to be friends with you again, Ian. I'm sorry you never met him, Margaret. He was a sensitive soul was Andrew."

But I *did* meet him, she thought, her skin tingling with the realization. "When exactly did he die?" she asked softly.

"Thursday afternoon."

Just after tea and a game of whist, Margaret thought.

She looked up, aware that Ian had stopped at the door to stare at her. This wasn't the time to bring up her strange encounter with Andrew—his *ghost*—in the garden. She could deliver his personal message later, but for the moment it would be too painful, too implausible for Ian to accept.

"Perhaps I should cancel my appointment," Ian said with a frown.

"Go," Colin advised him, his voice stronger now. "Just don't get your hopes up about your duchess. No one from Aberdeen to Edinburgh has been able to help the poor woman. I'm familiar myself with her case."

"Walk me to the door, Margaret?" Ian asked quietly.

She did, and as they reached the entrance steps, Ian turned and gazed down into his wife's face, struck as always by not only her loveliness, but by her kindness, that gentle part of Margaret which never failed to uplift him.

"Thanks for being so good to my father," he said.

"Oh, Ian. I'm so sorry for you all."

He hesitated, his blue eyes troubled. "That man in the garden—you think it was my brother, don't you?"

She nodded slowly, feeling a tug of sadness at the memory

of Andrew's wistful attempt at farewell. "I think he wanted
your forgiveness."

"A ghost," he repeated dubiously.

Then to her disconcertment, Ian closed his eyes for a moment to compose himself, his voice hoarse when he spoke
again. "Be here when I come home this evening."

"Well, yes, unless your mother needs me."

"I need you. Oh, God, my little brother . . . Please, Margaret, be here for me."

It was early evening when Margaret took a light meal of
veal cutlets and salad on a tray, then fell asleep reading on the
loveseat by the bedroom fire. When she awoke, it was eleven
by the clock on the mantel. She got up, yawning, and peered
through the curtains. She could see a faint light in Ian's laboratory. Presumably he'd returned home and, finding her asleep,
had gone to the basement to work.

She put a shawl on over her gown and went downstairs,
noting that Ian hadn't left his walking stick in the hall stand.
A creature of habit, he was usually so particular about such
things that she, untidy by nature, loved to tease him.

To reach the lab, you had to walk around the garden and
past the privy. The garden was quiet, the servants in bed an
hour ago, and Margaret unconsciously hurried along the path,
thinking that ghosts and skeletons and grave robbers seemed
laughable by daylight, but midnight was another matter.

As she descended the three irregular steps to the basement,
she began to feel a little lightheaded, slowing to draw a breath.
No light showed through the shuttered window. Yet the door
was ajar. Ian *never* left his lab unlocked. Unless he'd had an
accident . . .

She pushed open the door and strode into the darkened
room, the waxy scent of a recently extinguished candle still
in the air. Something thumped against the closet door, and as

she glanced up, the door suddenly sprang open and the infamous skeleton swung out toward her, bones shining, clacking together in a macabre dance.

"Oh," she cried, then suddenly the blood rushed from her head, a tall figure moved into her peripheral vision, and she sank to her knees with the smell of oranges coming toward her.

The next thing she knew Ian was leaning over her in the chair where he must have placed her, his face tight with alarm. "It—that—something attacked me," she whispered. "Where did you come from?"

"I was looking for some old papers in the closet. I must have frightened you when I opened the door." He put his hand under her chin to study her face in the moonlight. "You fainted. It crossed my mind you might be pregnant."

She sat still, mentally counting back to the date of her last courses. It seemed to her that something had happened right before she fainted, but her mind was in a fog. Had she imagined that figure, the smell of oranges? "I can't remember my last time . . . so much happened so fast, our marriage, moving here." She looked at the closet door, shuddering at the medical horrors it held.

Ian was silent, and Margaret glanced up in time to see the pleased grin fading from his face at the thought of a possible pregnancy. Could it be true? she wondered with a stab of joyful hope, watching him return to his desk where a bottle of whiskey attested more to his grief over his brother's death than anything he'd said.

"What happened today with your important patient?" she asked quietly. "I was curious about your consultation."

Ian's face clouded over. The shift from the subject of new life to death depressed him. "She's going to die. Nothing I do, not money, not her title, can help her. She's spent the past twenty years founding charities and giving to others, and she'll be dead before the year ends."

"I'm sorry," she whispered. "Can you do anything to make her more comfortable?"

He got his jacket from the wall peg and draped it around her shoulders. "She refuses to take morphia and says she wants to feel every moment of life that she has left." He glanced back over his shoulder, his voice low. "She doesn't believe she's going to die."

"Perhaps she won't."

He gave a rueful laugh. "And perhaps the world needs more people like you to believe in the impossible."

She smiled and huddled into his jacket. "You believed in the impossible or you'd never have begun your research, and look what has come of it, the pain you've saved your patients."

He swallowed hard. "But I've never achieved the glory I'd hoped for. I'll probably end up like poor Roger before I make medical history."

"Roger? The one who—"

"Yes. My old friend and colleague who died during an experiment in my laboratory." Ian sighed heavily. "His wife swore she'd ruin my life."

"But it was an accident," Margaret murmured. "Don't give up. I believe in you."

"But you believe in everything, my love, including fairies and ghosts—my brother's ghost."

"You're in a cynical mood today," she said gently. "I think losing your brother affected you more than you'll admit."

"Perhaps." He took her by the hands and drew her from the chair, still unwilling to discuss Andrew's death, the conflicting guilt, anger, and grief that threatened to overcome him. "It's been a bad day. My practice isn't drawing many new patients. I guess everyone is still afraid of the Devil Doctor."

Margaret stared into his darkly compelling face, understanding how he could frighten people but also aware his fierce looks concealed a deep capacity for caring.

"Don't look at me like that," he warned her softly. "Not if

you want to get any sleep at all tonight." He pulled her against him, his hands closing around her shoulders. "Oh, Margaret, I would like you to have my child so very much."

She only smiled, her heart beating hard at his nearness, and allowed him to lead her to the door. As they walked together through the garden, she racked her mind for a way to lift Ian out of his troubles. And much later, in the middle of the night, she came to the unhappy conclusion that she might even have to ask her father for help, never guessing that what she intended as a loving sacrifice on her part would only drive a wedge between her and her husband.

Forty-three

Blodwen Jones loved people and she lived to blether. Not that you'd call her a gossip of the caliber of a Sybil Armstrong, but Mrs. Jones did enjoy the long-winded chat—with the neighborhood butcher, the grocer, even with the toothless Romany ragman who pushed his wheelbarrow through the streets.

Mrs. Jones also considered it her Christian duty to pass along word that she was now in the employ of a genuine healer—not the dark Dr. MacNeill, of course, for surgery among the lower classes wasn't a common resort. But Blodwen could not help boasting how the pretty Mrs. MacNeill had cured her of the megrims, the chambermaid of leg cramps, and even Alex, the new footman, of a very persistent, painful and embarrassing rash on his bum.

Accordingly, in society's subterranean circle of elite domestics where Blodwen held considerable sway, Margaret's name became rapidly known. Almost overnight, small merchants and servants of other houses began to search her out in the streets when she went shopping. Eventually a few, driven by the lonely desperation of their uncured ailments, summoned the courage to come to the servants' entrance. They never called when Ian was home, and Margaret was at first reluctant to treat them, fearing the damage to his reputation should her secret practice become known.

"Just this last time, Mrs. MacNeill," the compassionate Mrs.

Jones would beg her. "How can you turn away these poor souls when you are their court of last resort?"

In good conscience Margaret couldn't, and she took each patient on the condition he would never reveal the source of his treatment.

She prayed for guidance in each case. She referred often to Morag's book. She helped cure a few completely. She gave relief to many and hurt no one. And her strange fame spread until, by word of mouth, it passed from servant to employer.

And on that Wednesday morning when Mrs. Jones came home from the butcher shop with a nice leg of lamb, she felt so pleased at her latest coup that she broke her personal code of ethics to take a glass of Dr. MacNeill's best sherry. Thus fortified she began to pace in anticipation of her mistress's return.

A Very Important Personage who did not wish her identity known, stricken with a grave disease which no physician had been able to cure, had asked to meet immediately with Margaret. The meeting was to take place in a posh hotel located on the town outskirts.

There was no doubt in the kind and uncomplicated mind of Blodwen Jones that Mrs. MacNeill had the "gift" and now, at last, the world was destined to learn of it.

Two days later, on the morning she was to meet in private with this mysterious patient, the rank of which Mrs. Jones suspected belonged to royalty, Margaret received a note from Gareth that her father's condition had deteriorated.

Douglas Rose asked to see her as soon as possible. Margaret read the note only once and then placed it in the parlor grate, her face deceptively impassive as the paper curled at the corners and burned. So much for *that* royal summons, she thought. But the undeniable pang of sadness she felt, the regret for the years and relationship lost, must have shown in her eyes. When she turned around, Ian was at the door, his troubled gaze moving from her face to the fire.

The emotional turmoil he had seen in her eyes made him instantly imagine the worst. He hadn't been completely unaware of her furtive comings and goings of late, but he had assumed there was an innocent explanation for them.

"If I were the jealous type, I'd suspect an admirer was trying to steal my wife away," he said with an enforced lightness. "What were you burning, and why are you dressed to see the queen?"

"My father wants to see me," she explained quietly. "He's taken a bad turn."

"And you're going to see him?" he asked in surprise and selfish relief. "That's what the pretty dress, the gloves and hat are all about?"

"Not exactly." She avoided his eyes, improvising wildly and hating herself for lying. "I have an appointment in a wee while with a woman in town—about some charity work."

She turned to the tea table and poured herself a cup of lukewarm tea. She hated to lie to Ian, but she knew he disapproved of her practice, and if her conscience had allowed it, she'd have refused the woman's case. Anyway, it was her husband's obstinance that had forced her into the subterfuge. She'd rather have consulted with him on the woman's condition, perhaps suggested a blend of his methods and hers.

"Charity work," he said with such a sigh of approval that Margaret was tempted to blurt out the truth just to shake his male complacency. "That's wonderful, Margaret, but if it's the Female Benefit Society you're joining, I'm afraid you're a little overdressed."

"It's too late to change now."

"And you have no intention of seeing your father?"

"I suppose I have to."

He looked at her in concern. "Would you like me to go with you?"

She turned back to the fire, feeling miserable, awash in memories of the father she'd tried so hard to forget. "Yes," she whispered. "I'd like that very much."

Margaret discreetly sent Mrs. Jones ahead to the hotel to tell the mystery patient that Mrs. MacNeill would be detained until later that afternoon. But as she and Ian were waiting for the brougham to be brought round, a young footman came hurtling out of a cab to stop them. His mistress had gone into an early labor, and could Dr. MacNeill hurry to the house to attend her?

Ian hesitated, torn between professional duty and personal worry over breaking a promise to his young wife. "I'll summon another doctor," he said at last. "Someone from the hospital."

Margaret shook her head. "You'll never rebuild your reputation by putting me before your patients. I'll be all right, Ian. Gareth and Lilian will be there to help me."

He nodded and ran back up the stairs to the house to fetch his bag, leaving her in the street, a slender figure in blue whose sudden show of strength made him feel both proud and afraid for her. He felt vaguely uneasy, too, at the idea of entrusting her to her brother and sister's care. The truth was that he had never reconciled his own unfavorable impression of Gareth and Lilian with the fond memories of them which Margaret seemed to claim.

She might have been a lonely, frightened sixteen-year-old girl again. The five years that had passed since Margaret had last seen her father might never have happened. The self-confidence she'd gained in that interval, the lessons she had learned about life on the island abandoned her with terrifying suddenness.

She was acutely aware of the tension in the air as she entered the grand house that had once been her home. She was an outsider to the three people who were waiting for her in the drawing room.

She was still the darkest Rose.

Despite all efforts to steel herself, she was shocked at her father's appearance, his skin as colorless as clay, his body frail beneath the tasscled woolen blanket. But his gray eyes burned with emotions that were strikingly intense, the most dominant an unmistakable tenderness that took Margaret completely off her guard.

"You came," he said, his smile almost shy. "I wasn't sure you would."

"Yes," she said softly. "I came."

She was astonished at her reaction. The anger, the bitterness, she had so long used as a shield against more painful feelings had crumbled. She felt more numb than anything.

"Hello, Margaret," someone said softly from the chair in the corner, and she recognized Lilian by her pale timorous face and restrained smile.

They had never been as close during childhood as Margaret might have wished. But there must have been a deeper bond between them than she'd realized because Lilian started to cry when she and Margaret moved toward each other to embrace.

Tears stung Margaret's eyes, then both women began to laugh. Lilian was well along in a pregnancy, and the protruding mound of her stomach allowed only the most awkward hug.

"My first," she explained, her face pleased and a little embarrassed.

"I know an excellent doctor," Margaret said mischievously. "In fact, I married him. And I know a few things about midwifery myself."

Lilian looked away. "Yes, I'd heard. Actually my husband Edward would be upset if we didn't use old Dr. Struthers, wouldn't he, Gareth?"

"Very upset."

Margaret took the remark as a personal rejection of her husband and it hurt. Forcing a smile, she glanced over at Gareth. "Ian is a fine doctor, Lilian. Don't let *anyone* tell you otherwise."

There was an awkward pause. Then Gareth, after pouring Douglas a cup of tea, rang for his hat and cloak. "Dad wants to see you alone, Margaret, so I'll take Lilian home and come back later to stay with him."

"Take the afternoon for yourself," Douglas said, his breathing shallow. "Margaret's here now. I'll be all right."

Gareth looked reluctant. "Dad, I think it might help if I stayed. You mustn't get upset."

"For God's sake, Gareth," Douglas said in a tone that instantly cowed his son. "Just go."

Margaret felt a moment of panic. She couldn't face her father by herself.

Douglas was watching her closely—he hadn't taken his eyes off her from the moment she'd walked into the room. "Your brother is meeting his mystery woman, Margaret," he said in a weak attempt at humor. "We've none of us been allowed to meet her yet, and I'm afraid I'm going to learn her identity in the papers when her cuckolded husband sues for divorce."

Gareth's eyes flashed. "Come on, Dad. She's a widow, and doesn't feel like an active social life. Anyway, we're only friends who share an interest in art."

Douglas lifted his hands in a resigned gesture. "I wouldn't have even known she existed if one of Gareth's customers hadn't spotted them in the park and mentioned it to me. I'm beginning to wonder if she's a demimondaine," he added with a little laugh that didn't hide his concern.

"She's from a good family." Gareth followed Lilian to the door. "We'll talk later, Margaret. Don't overtire him."

"Come to supper next week," Lilian called over her shoulder, giving Margaret and Douglas an anxious parting smile.

Margaret's panic flared anew as the door closed. Impulsively she reached for the reticule she had laid on the sideboard.

"Do you hate me so very much that you can't stay alone with me for a few minutes?" Douglas asked, challenging her.

She turned slowly, and for the first time in years, looked him fully in the face. They were father and daughter, more alike than either of them could admit, and yet they were strangers. "I don't hate you."

It was, to her surprise, the truth, although it had taken Ian's love to make her realize that the futile emotion had burned out inside her long ago.

Douglas appraised her in the ensuing silence, and Margaret was reluctantly moved, sensing he saw past her physical appearance to the person she'd been forced to become because he'd exiled her to Maryhead. And suddenly she realized that she had in many ways gained more than she'd lost by being evicted from the Rose family. She had become stronger, self-sufficient. She had learned to care about others.

She had gained Ian, her lover, a friend, and if there were still shadows, ghosts, to contend with, she had the courage to overcome them.

Her father's voice was faint. "Are you happy with your doctor?"

"As happy as anyone is, I suppose."

A pained look came into his eyes. "I could interpret that in many ways."

"You're tiring yourself," she observed, edging away from the sideboard. "Perhaps I should—"

"I've heard that you're something of a healer yourself," he said, and Margaret heard a note of unexpected pride in his voice. "Perhaps you could help me."

"Ian said your heart had been damaged."

Douglas gave her a rueful smile. "He's right. But it isn't

folk medicine I want from you anyway, Margaret. It's forgiveness." His voice broke. "I want my favorite daughter back."

Margaret stared down at her hands, terrified by the strength of her feelings for him. He wanted forgiveness, and she wanted—what? For him to restore the years that the locusts had eaten . . .

"I don't even know if I can forgive myself for what happened to Alan and Mama."

"I haven't helped." His tone was heavy with self-reproach. "But at least you came to see me today."

"I have an appointment," she said softly. "A lady who is very ill."

"I've read about your husband in the papers," he said in concern. "If you're unhappy in this marriage I could help you find a way out."

She bit her lip. "Do you really want to help me?"

He struggled to sit up against the cushions. Without thinking, Margaret leaned down to help him, her heart beating hard as he caught her hand in his, his grip surprisingly strong. "Anything," he said quietly.

She straightened, looking over the settee to the window where a carriage passed outside.

"Restore my husband's reputation," she said, her voice low. "If you want to help me, then use your influence to clear Ian's name."

Douglas stared at her. "It's odd, but the day he examined me, I remember I was impressed by the accuracy of his diagnosis and his forthright manner. I liked him, Margaret."

"Your friends are intelligent," Margaret added. "If you make it known that Ian is more than competent, it could help him get the start he needs."

Douglas smiled slowly. "It's so very little to ask of me, Margaret. Consider it done."

* * *

Margaret's anonymous patient was a pale heavyset woman in her sixties who shuffled with a cane through her hotel suite of adjoining rooms to introduce Margaret to her many cats. "I know what's wrong with me." The woman slowed to catch her breath. "The doctors have all told me it's a disease of the liver, and that I'll be dead by the end of the year."

"This is very serious, ma'am," Margaret murmured.

"I do not intend to die." The woman prodded Margaret with her cane. "By the way, you are to call me Anne."

Margaret smiled and knelt to stroke a kitten, trying to remember how Morag had treated a similar case many years ago. "I'll need to think about this, madam," she said, rising, "and come back in a day or so, before I leave for the country. In the meantime—"

"We'll have a wee bite, first, to fortify ourselves," the woman said with a weary sigh, and reached for the bellcord. "The service here is excellent."

The "wee bite" turned out to be a gargantuan feast of well-roasted beef and turkey, a grilled trout, sausages, and herbed potatoes, with hazelnut pudding for dessert. Margaret, who strongly suspected by the tenderness of her breasts and her recently increased appetite that she was indeed pregnant, ate one of the largest meals of her life.

In fact, she still felt like one of the stuffed sausages she'd sampled several hours later when, alone at home in her bedroom, she took Morag's book out from its hiding place in the wardrobe and began to read.

In those cases of gout, kidney, and liver ailments—
Treat with broom, juniper-berry tea, horseradish, and parsley.
A talisman of fox claws and green acorns should be placed on the abdomen at night.
The patient should abstain from eating meat, fish, and

fowle, preferring boilt vegetables and unseasoned breads—

The bedroom door opened. Automatically Margaret slammed the book shut and shoved it under the covers, lifting her face to Ian in unconscious defiance.

"Consulting your witch's grimoire again, Margaret?" he asked teasingly from the fireplace.

"Maybe. How was your delivery?"

"Very long and successful. A boy." He smiled tiredly and went to the washstand, unbuttoning the cuffs of his rumpled white shirt on the way. "How was your father?"

She sat up on the bed and watched him wash and towel off his face. "Not very well. It—it was a difficult meeting for both of us."

He walked back to the bed, his eyes searching her face for signs of battle wounds. "I wanted to come. In fact, I did stop by his house when I finished the delivery, but you were gone." He paused, his voice low. "I also stopped by the Female Benefit Society, and no one had seen you."

"I was so upset after seeing my father, I decided not to go," she said, soothing her conscience with a half-truth. "And then—oh, Ian, I ate so much food this afternoon, I'm afraid my new wardrobe will have to be altered."

He raised his eyebrows. God knew Ian wasn't stupid, but if he perceived any holes in her explanation, he made no comment.

"Speaking of your wardrobe, I just received the bill from the dressmaker," he said. "My God, Margaret, where did you and Dara think the money was to come from?"

She got up from the bed and went to the dressing table, actually relieved that the dangerous subject of her afternoon had passed. "Well, at the time, I thought all doctors were rich."

He smiled ruefully. "Successful ones are."

She picked up her silver-backed hairbrush. "You'll be successful soon," she said confidently, remembering her last words to her father and hoping he'd keep his promise. "And when you are, I'll see even less of you than I do now, and I'll have to shop even more to fill in my time."

"Or raise my children."

He came up behind the stool and put his hands on her shoulders, his strong fingers massaging away the strain of the day. Margaret smiled to herself, wondering how long she could keep the fragile secret to herself. Sooner or later, he'd recognize the signs, if she were indeed pregnant.

He leaned down to kiss her neck. She closed her eyes briefly and tilted her head back, not merely compliant, but eager, as he drew her to her feet and led her back to their curtained bed. In the warm shadows they undressed each other with tantalizing leisure, letting their clothing fall at their feet. Naked, Ian kissed her where they stood, their bodies barely touching until he had to support her, and they fell, still kissing, onto the bed.

"I think you're very brave to have faced your father alone," he said against her mouth.

"I was terrified," she whispered.

"Poor Margaret," he said with a slow wolfish smile as his hands glided over the satin flesh of her stomach.

She shut her eyes and arched her spine, sighing against his shoulder, his lovely witch, then rolled over onto her side, falling into an immediate sleep. His smile fading, Ian tugged the quilt out from beneath her and covered her with it. Leaning back against the headboard, he found himself unexpectedly unable to sleep.

His rough face reflected a private anguish that he had managed to hide from his wife. He and Margaret were growing closer. No man could ask for a lovelier, more sexually responsive partner. She had faced her father today and emerged apparently unscathed. His own parents adored her. And she had lied to him tonight for the first time that he was aware of. She had lied to him about going to the Female Benefit Society earlier in the day, and the lie, her secret afternoon, made him afraid.

Forty-four

Margaret put down her dessert spoon and stared in surprise at the small velvet box Ian slid across the dinner table toward her. Almost a week had passed since she had seen her father, and in that interval, Ian had been acting a little strange, rushing home from the hospital to have tea with her, returning at unannounced hours as if he expected to uncover some dark secret. Or perhaps he realized her courses were long overdue.

"Open it," he said, leaning back against the chair with a grin. "I had it made just for you."

"Don't tell me," she teased him. "It's a diamond-studded inhalation mask."

He laughed appreciatively. "Only a pearl-studded one. It's all I could afford."

Curious, she took the box and unlatched the lid, arching a brow at the gold initials of a very exclusive jeweler embossed on the blue velvet exterior. "Who did it come from?" she asked suspiciously, snapping the lid shut again. Her father had commissioned this same jeweler for much of her mother's collection. And he had sent Margaret a cashmere cape just this morning, still untouched in its box.

Ian looked insulted. "I bought it. Who did you think it came from?"

"I thought we were broke."

He raised his wine glass, his long elegant fingers cradling the base. "Things have taken a miraculous turn for the better.

Suddenly Dr. MacNeill has become sought-after by the upper classes—not that I'm abandoning my work at the Poor's Hospital, but Margaret, the money is welcome."

She managed a smile, but the nagging guilt she felt overshadowed her happiness at his success. So, her father had kept his promise and apparently kept it well. But how would Ian react if he found out his sudden popularity had less to do with his own skill than Douglas Rose's influence?

"Open the box, Margaret. This is a celebration."

The gift was a strand of baroque pearls interspersed with miniature marquise diamonds. Exquisite. Simple. Extravagant.

"It's beautiful," she said, her eyes shining with guilty pleasure. "Surely you haven't made that much money yet."

"No. Not yet." He got up from the table to take the necklace from its box and place it around her throat, his touch warm, lingering. "But I will. If it hadn't been for Andrew's death, I'd say life was beginning to look good. I only wish we were visiting Taynaross under better conditions. Not seeing my brother there . . ."

"Less than a week away," she murmured.

Warm shivers ran over her skin where his fingers rested. If only he knew how much she herself dreaded making that journey, meeting Jean, the rest of his family. She would be the only outsider in their close-knit warmth. And there were her few but dependent patients to consider, her fledgling herb garden, the fragile life in her womb.

"Wear it tonight for the lecture," Ian said, interrupting her worried thoughts.

"I hadn't planned to attend," she confessed.

There was silence. Margaret could feel him staring down at her; she could feel the tension radiating from his fingertips where they rested on her shoulders. She had, in fact, planned to visit the elderly Anne, to check on her progress.

"Do you have other plans?" he asked quietly.

She rose, twisting around to face him, her heart tightening

at the dark worry on his face. "I'll change my dress. Thank you for the necklace." She kissed his cheek and turned to leave, but he drew her back by the arm. "Ian, we'll be late."

He stared down at her, helpless to fight whatever it was that seemed to still stand between them. "You're hiding something from me."

"That's ridiculous."

He swallowed as she pulled away, staring down at the table after she had left and knowing in his heart she was lying.

Ian's lecture on the use of anesthesia during childbirth had gone well. The surgeons and midwives who'd attended seemed impressed not just by a single doctor's reports of success but by the fact that Queen Victoria herself had taken chloroform to deliver her last child.

Ian was grinning from ear to ear as he finally pushed through the noisy throng to reach Margaret and his father. "Let's get a bottle of champagne and go to Dalrymple's for cheesecake," he said, taking Margaret's arm.

"Mmm." She smiled up at him. "Cheesecake sounds divine."

Arm in arm they emerged onto the semicircular stone steps that faced the street. Margaret was a little tired, but she couldn't bring herself to deflate Ian's good spirits.

"I was very impressed by your talk," she said quietly, jostled up against him by the crowd gathering to await carriages and cabs.

"Impressed enough to use anesthesia yourself when I deliver our child?" he asked in a teasing undertone.

Margaret laughed at his persistence. "We'll see."

"I wonder what's taking Donald so long with the brougham," Colin remarked behind them.

Ian shrugged; nothing was going to spoil his mood. "Perhaps he's caught in traffic. Why don't we start walking and see if we can spot him on the street?"

No sooner had they stepped onto the pavement than a small band of street urchins exploded out from behind a parked carriage, hurling stones and rotten eggs and shrieking insults.

"The Devil Doctor and his witch! She drowned her family and he murders the rich!"

A stone flew across the street and hit Margaret on the shoulder, bringing tears of pain to her eyes. She hadn't heard the abusive epithet screamed at her, but Ian had, and in a rare outburst of rage, he ran after the boys, shouting over his shoulder, "Watch Margaret for me, Dad."

More concerned about Ian's rash show of gallantry than her shoulder, Margaret reluctantly allowed Colin to draw her back onto the steps while Ian caught one of the boys and brought them both crashing down onto the pavement. The carriage parked opposite them rolled slowly away, and a flicker of recognition stirred in Margaret's memory as she watched it, only to fade as Ian's furious voice rose into the night.

"Who paid you to do this, you stinking little bastard?"

The boy, abandoned by his cohorts, twisted frantically beneath Ian in an effort to escape.

"Answer me," Ian said through his teeth, all his pent-up anger rising against this anonymous enemy who'd not only damaged his career but had hurt his wife. "Who, dammit?"

The boy stilled, his voice shaking. " 'Twas a man and woman is all I know."

Ian ignored the voice in his head which told him the child was hungry, a bag of bones who'd do anything for a shilling. "Shall I call the constable?"

"Let him go, Ian."

Ian recognized his father's voice, looked up and saw the crowd of curious onlookers who'd gathered. He relaxed slightly, and the boy popped out of his hold like a champagne cork, vanishing into a warren of unlit back alleyways where he could probably hide undetected for days.

"It would have looked bad if you'd hurt a child," Colin said, reaching down to retrieve his son's lecture notes from the gutter.

Ian straightened, brushing off his black velvet evening jacket as he glanced toward the steps at his wife, reassuring himself that she hadn't been hurt and that she was out of earshot.

"A man and a woman," he said slowly. "Goddamnit, Dad, that could be anyone."

Colin frowned. "What about Lucy Patton? She did this sort of thing before."

"Lucy was always open about her hatred of me," Ian said, his eyes troubled. "Anyway, Dara said she moved back to Glasgow with her family last winter."

"It might not be a bad idea if you moved to another city yourself for a while," Colin suggested as they walked back across the street.

"I've just moved back here," Ian said angrily. "Anyway, I've finally begun to make a good name for myself. I'll be damned if anyone will drive me away again."

Forty-five

The next morning, several days before she and Ian were to leave for Taynaross, Margaret had Donald drive her to the Female Benefit Society, a small vine-draped building on the outskirts of town. Bethia Lambie, the Society's tall gray-haired directress, praised Margaret for her unselfish interest in wanting to help the town's downtrodden women. As Margaret took cold tea in the kind-faced woman's office, she wished she deserved the compliment paid her. But the truth was, her inspiration to volunteer came not from a sense of social conscience but to cover her secret medical practice and placate Ian.

"I won't be able to follow a regular schedule, Mrs. Lambie," she explained. "Not until my husband and I come back from the country."

"That's fine, Mrs. MacNeill," the woman said, offering Margaret a plate of slightly rancid shortbread. "We need every ounce of help we are given."

Margaret nibbled at the edge of the shortbread, feeling her already queasy stomach roil in rebellion. "I'll do whatever I can, although I have to admit, I'm not certain I have any useful experience to help these women."

"You'd be surprised, Mrs. MacNeill," Mrs. Lambie said, "at one's own capacity for charity."

Surprisingly Margaret did begin to feel she could be of genuine service after a few hours of advising, listening, and serving meals to the assortment of women who came to the

Society for help. Unwed mothers whose families had cast them out, homeless wives without skills or money, abandoned by their husbands; cynical young prostitutes who spoke of escaping such horrifying abuse at home that Margaret wanted to weep, vowing that the child she was almost positive she carried would be the most cherished and protected child ever born.

She also felt an unexpected kinship with these unwanted women, a bond. She saw herself as she had once been—in their confusion and self-destructive rebellion. She could have ended up on the streets or in an unhappy marriage herself, but by the grace of God she had not.

When she told Ian after supper that evening what she had done, he looked so relieved that she almost laughed.

"I'm proud of you," he said, putting aside his newspaper. "By the way, your brother came by today to see you."

Margaret did a strange shifting dance in her chair to loosen her corset. "Why do you frown whenever you mention my brother? Don't you like him?"

"I'm not sure yet," Ian replied. "Why are you undressing at the table?"

She lowered her gaze, repressing a grin. "Indigestion, Doctor. What else could it be?"

Within two days Margaret had made a friend at the Society, a well-bred young widow named Lucinda Menzies who, like Margaret, had only recently joined Mrs. Lambie's corps of volunteers. Although Lucinda never mentioned her late husband, Mrs. Lambie quietly confided in Margaret that he had been a young Aberdeen doctor starting out in his own practice. The parallel between Ian and Lucinda's husband made Margaret realize how lost she would be if anything happened to Ian so early in their marriage, with a child on the way.

Lucinda still wore the black bombazine of first mourning,

and several times as they worked Margaret caught the woman studying her, perhaps sadly envious of what she had lost.

By Friday Margaret had confided in Lucinda more than was probably wise for a new friendship, but she missed Agnes's ever-willing ear, and she and Lucinda had more than a few things in common: their affluent upbringing, their interest in social causes, suffering the losses of loved ones.

Lucinda also professed an interest in folk healing, her leaf-green eyes narrowed in absorption as she listened intently to Margaret's secret cases and their treatments. Once or twice, she even offered sound medical suggestions of her own, and it never occurred to Margaret that the fair-skinned face hid anything except a lonely woman's need for friendship.

"Your husband's career could be ruined if word of your unorthodox practice reaches the wrong person," Lucinda remarked once with a reflective frown that Margaret interpreted as concern for her own welfare.

Margaret looked down at the basket of laundry she had just brought in to be folded. "I can't let that happen. My husband is really a good man at heart."

"And yet such dark rumors about him persist," Lucinda murmured.

Margaret felt the fine hairs on her nape rise. "You've heard the rumors too then?"

Lucinda looked up slowly, her light green eyes guileless. "I'm afraid so. Where do you think they could have started?"

"From jealous rivals," Margaret said tightly. "Anyway, I hope they'll die down while we're in the country."

Lucinda stabbed her needle into the sampler she worked on in spare moments, a wall hanging Margaret was not allowed to see because it was to be Lucinda's special gift for when the baby came. "You'll have to be careful in the country in your condition, won't you, Margaret? So far away from everyone. So many things that could go wrong."

"Well, Ian will be there."

"Have you told him yet about the baby?"

Margaret couldn't help smiling. "I'm going to tonight—" She broke off in surprise, recognizing Gareth striding past the window to the front door. "How strange. I never told my brother I was working here."

Lucinda's needle stilled. "Your brother?"

"Gareth Rose. Ian must have told him where to find me."

"I'll leave you in privacy," Lucinda said hastily, stuffing her sewing into her bag. "I can read to the girls in the back parlor over tea."

"But I'd like him to meet you," Margaret said, already romantically matching Lucinda with Gareth. And why not? A well-bred widow had to be a better choice than the secret mistress her father had mentioned.

"Margaret." Gareth stopped cold in the doorway, his gaze moving from her to Lucinda in cautious assessment.

From his reaction Margaret realized he must have passed several prostitutes in the hall and might be afraid Lucinda was one of them, a bad influence on his younger sister.

"I know what you're thinking," Margaret said with a little laugh. "Father would have a fit if he knew I was helping here, but then I've run my own life for a long time now. Oh, this is Lucinda Menzies. She's on the volunteer staff here, too, and she's a perfectly decent person."

Gareth didn't move. "A pleasure, Mrs. Menzies."

Lucinda gave him a cool smile and picked up her veiled hat. "I assume you've come to take Margaret to tea. How nice to have such a solicitous brother."

Gareth flushed, and Margaret wondered whether there was indeed hope for sparking a romance between them. "In fact, I did come to take Margaret out," he said, recovering his composure. "I wanted her to see my paintings at the auction."

Lucinda started toward the door. "Well, take care of her, won't you? And mind you don't discuss anything unpleasant—

it's bad to upset an expectant mother. Goodbye, Margaret. Have a nice time in the country."

Gareth remained silent until the door closed, Lucinda's heavy floral perfume lingering in the silence. Then, "Do you have to work in a place like this, Margaret?" he demanded. "Can't you join a ladies' kirk group instead?"

She laughed, linking her arm with his. "I don't think a church group would take me."

He escorted her outside to his carriage, his face worried in the dim interior. "Are you really expecting?" he asked, and at her nod, he leaned back with a sigh. "What's happened to you—folding laundry for vagrants and whores, marrying a man accused of the lowest crimes?"

Margaret glared at him. "Stop criticizing my husband—and since when did you start believing every filthy broadsheet you read? Don't tell me you've forgotten what was written about *us* after the accident."

He paled. "Your husband is a different matter."

"Ian happens to believe in his work," she said heatedly, "and so do dozens of other prominent doctors."

"He believes in making money," Gareth said baldly. "Marrying *you* was certainly a shrewd enhancement to his professional image."

Margaret laughed. "If you want to know the truth, I'll probably end up doing him more harm than good."

"You know nothing about the real world," Gareth said in a sadly resigned voice. "For your own sake, I almost wish you'd never come home."

"Well, thanks very much," she said crossly.

He grinned. "Since you're here though, I suppose we'll have to make the most of it."

At the time she didn't think much about their odd conversation, attributing Gareth's persistence in encouraging her to leave Aberdeen to his unfounded distrust of Ian. Only much later did she look back on his behavior as a serious warning sign and wish she'd paid closer attention.

Ian wrapped the towel around Margaret's damp naked body as she stepped from the clawed hip bath in their bedroom, holding her close to him for several moments. "Almost two months pregnant," he said with an irrepressible chuckle. "I wondered why the hell there was a nursing corset on the dressmaker's bill."

She tilted her head back, her eyes shining. "I didn't know then."

He grinned, white teeth gleaming in his swarthy face. "Congratulations, Mrs. MacNeill," he said softly.

He picked her up in his arms, the towel slipping to the carpet, and carried her to the bed, gently dropping her in the center.

"Lie very still and close your eyes," he instructed, reaching for the small pot of pure rose oil on the nightstand.

She obeyed, then peered at him through her lowered eyelids. "Don't forget to do my feet."

He smiled and worked the scented oil over her body, her breasts, stomach, and thighs, until her skin began to glow with melting warmth, sensitized to his touch.

"Perhaps," he said reflectively, "you shouldn't be working at the Society at all."

She sighed. "You sound like Gareth. He doesn't want me to live in wicked Aberdeen or work with wicked women or even stay married to my wicked husband."

She could feel the sudden tension emanating from Ian, his strong hands working magic on her calves. "That's strange," he murmured. "I have a similar dislike of him myself."

She opened her eyes. "Why?"

"I'm not sure. Nothing that a prospective mother should worry about. Speaking of which . . . maybe we shouldn't travel to Taynaross, after all. The carriage ride along the coast is tedious, if not uncomfortable."

"Your family is expecting us to go." And Jean, she couldn't help thinking. "Besides, you'll feel guilty about it later if we don't."

His hands splayed across her stomach, caressing the tiny bulge. "We won't go at all if you don't want to."

He lay back against the pillows, pulling the covers over them, fussing to make sure she was warm. She felt secure and protected in his arms, waves of sleep lapping at her fading awareness. Then just as she was drifting off, a voice from earlier in the day broke across her thoughts like a wave of cold wind.

You'll have to be careful in the country in your condition, won't you, Margaret? So far away from everyone. So many things that could go wrong.

"A bad dream?" Ian murmured, his arms unconsciously tightening around her.

"No," she whispered. "Just had a thought about the baby."

"Nothing to worry about, I promise," he said with a smile in his voice. "I'm holding you—*both* of you."

Forty-six

The day before she and Ian were to leave for Taynaross, Margaret received an urgent message from her mysterious patient, Anne, insisting Margaret meet with her and several gentlemen of importance later that afternoon at an as yet unspecified location.

A coach would collect Margaret at noon. The meeting would not take long, but it was in "the interest of humanity and healing" that Margaret attend. It seemed that Anne had shown such a dramatic improvement that a physician called in had said she could possibly live for several years yet.

"Oh, dear," Mrs. Jones said when Margaret read her the letter. "Could be she's having a will drawn up and wants to include you, ma'am."

"A will," Margaret said in consternation. "How am I to explain this to Ian? I'm positive now that 'Anne' is the duchess he failed to help. She mentioned that even the 'Devil Doctor' couldn't help her."

"The doctor isn't going to be in, ma'am. Said he had an important meeting himself today with some colleagues."

"I'll have to go then," Margaret said reluctantly. "Oh, I'll never finish packing this way."

When the gilt-trimmed coach drew up before the house a few hours later, Margaret's eyes widened, recognizing the ducal crest on the lacquered side panels. So Anne *was* Ian's duchess, and there would be hell to pay if he ever found out that Margaret had treated the woman with Morag Strong's cures.

The ride was short, and Margaret was certain the driver had made a mistake as to her destination when he slowed to deposit her on the circular steps of the lecture hall. "Where am I to go?" she asked the footman in confusion. "Is there a solicitor's office inside?"

"Her Grace's secretary will show you the way, ma'am," the footman said, indicating the gray-haired man at the door.

The secretary led Margaret down a side corridor to a door bearing a brass plate inscribed PRIVATE. Puzzled, she allowed him to usher her inside, and before she could even enter the room, the circle of men who had been seated by the crackling fire, the duchess in the center, rose from their chairs.

Their expressions, their muttered remarks, as they studied Margaret, ranged from incredulously amused to outraged.

The duchess spoke in a soft, scornful voice. "This, distinguished gentlemen, is the young woman who has healed me, when all of you said healing was impossible."

"Come now, Your Grace—"

"Professor Abernathy, if you wish to continue receiving my financial support, I suggest you listen carefully to her methods. You stand to learn something beneficial to put in those articles you publish so profusely."

Startled, Margaret scanned the faces of the men assembled, the closed judgmental faces of physicians and professors, masculine superiority, impatient arrogance. All the old curmudgeons of medical convention whom Ian had described to her in humorous detail while they lay in bed.

And, not in the least bit humorous, at the end of the standing circle was Ian himself, his face shocked and furious. "You," he said under his breath, words failing him. Then he sat down, refusing to meet her eyes at all.

"Go ahead, my dear," the duchess urged her. "Don't let them

frighten you. They're only men after all. Explain what you did to heal me."

Margaret moistened her lips and began to speak, so flustered she doubted she made any sense. Then one of the professors peeled off his spectacles and leaned forward in his chair, rudely cutting her off in midsentence.

"By God, that's your wife, MacNeill."

Ian put his hand over his eyes, shrinking in his chair.

"Why, she's practicing without a license," the distinguished surgeon Conall Campbell remarked.

And the representative from the Royal Medical Society, "This is ridiculous, a waste of precious time, gathering us all together to hear some young woman's unproven drivel."

"Honestly, Your Grace! You'll have us studying the gypsies next."

The duchess banged her cane down on the carpet. "Dr. Campbell, you said yourself my condition had improved dramatically."

The surgeon, white hair sticking in tufts from his head like an owl, blinked angrily. "Then perhaps you were misdiagnosed in the first place, Your Grace."

"By twelve different doctors?" The duchess angled her head to address Ian. "Dr. MacNeill, you were the last physician who diagnosed me as a fatal case. Did you make a mistake?"

Ian lowered his hand, his voice clipped. "I stand by my original diagnosis, Your Grace."

"But you said I would be dead by now."

Ian's mouth curled in a sardonic smile. "Obviously you are not."

"Thank you. And will you confirm that this young woman's treatments have healed me?"

Ian stared at his wife. He was torn between wanting to shake her for making a spectacle of him and protecting her from the pack of jackals around him who attacked anything they didn't understand.

"Only time will tell for sure, Your Grace," he said guardedly.

The other men around him began to rise from their chairs, muttering on their way out about the wasted time, scoffing at Margaret's dietary suggestions and charms as having any curative influence.

Margaret stood in the middle of the room, her head bowed in mortification.

Ian sat in his chair, too stunned to move, afraid when he did it would be to take her over his knee and beat the living daylights and defiance out of her.

"This looks very bad, Ian," his old friend, Professor Kincardine said, pausing by Ian's chair. "You'll not make much of an impression where it counts if you can't control your own wife."

Forty-seven

Ian walked unsteadily up the stairs to the bedroom, having sequestered himself in his study all evening with a bottle of whiskey and a mountain of medical treatises from every civilized country in the world.

There *was* mention of the cure Margaret had used on the duchess in medical history, but oddly no one had ever seriously pursued a connection between diet and healing similar ailments to any conclusive degree.

The unpalatable fact remained that his unschooled young wife had saved a life where he had failed. The realization opened exciting intellectual vistas in his mind. Emotionally, however, he was a wreck. He was wildly envious of her success.

When he entered the room, she was sitting on the loveseat by the fire, fully dressed, although it was two o'clock in the morning. She stood hastily at his approach, her eyes red and puffy from crying, and he hardened his heart against a tender urge to console her, refusing to let her ravaged face make him feel guilty. This was all her fault.

They stared at each other. Then Ian noticed the small traveling bag beside the loveseat, and even though he'd forgotten they were leaving early in the morning for Taynaross, he was deeply afraid his wife had other intentions.

But he *was* still furious at her, for going behind his back, to treat a damned duchess, no less, and for humiliating him in front of his colleagues.

"I waited to tell you I was sorry," she said, clasping her hands together.

He walked past her to the fire, his lips compressed into a tight line. "I'll *never* live this one down."

Margaret drew in a shaky breath, her voice faint above the crackling of the fire. "What could I have done, Ian? I couldn't refuse her."

He half turned. His blue eyes raked her. Had this determined, defiant facet of Margaret always existed? "You could have considered the consequences," he said coldly. "What it meant to my career—our marriage—"

"I did."

He regarded her in astonishment, then turned back to the fire, his broad shoulders set in a stiff unyielding line. "I don't know how to interpret that," he said in a low voice. "Do I take it to mean you have so little regard for me you didn't *care* that this might happen?"

She came up slowly behind him. "I have the greatest regard for you," she said softly, "and for that woman's life."

He moved away from her and sat down on the loveseat, staring at her with dark brooding eyes as he struggled to understand. "Do you know you've hurt me more with your one noble act than all of my enemies combined?"

Margaret flinched, tears burning behind her eyelids.

"My own wife," he said, shaking his head. "God, Margaret, didn't it occur to you to come to me first for advice?"

"What for?" she cried, her temper rising at how unfair he was. "So you could forbid me to help her?"

"Possibly." He rubbed his face, tension etching deep creases in his cheeks. "How could you let me talk about her and never let on you were treating her behind my back?"

Color rose to Margaret's face. "I didn't know who the hell she was," she said indignantly. "Do you know what I think—I think you're angry because I succeeded at something and you didn't."

He jumped up from the loveseat. "Och, Margaret, you've made me look so incredibly stupid."

They were standing so close together that Margaret could smell the whiskey on his breath, could see a muscle twitching beneath the stubbly shadow of beard on his jaw.

She was angry at him and she ached for him to hold her.

He was hurt by her deception and had never been more proud of anyone in his life.

He swallowed over the knot in his throat and stepped back before he could weaken by putting his arms around her. "I'm tired," he said hoarsely. "We've got a long journey tomorrow. Let's get ready for bed."

She exhaled and bent stiffly to reach past him for her bag. "I won't subject you to further humiliation in front of your family."

He caught her wrist, his brows drawn into a black scowl. "What the hell does that mean?"

Margaret blinked, more than a little afraid to tell him what she had planned. "I'm going to stay with Lilian," she whispered. "I think you should go to Taynaross alone."

He pulled her back down with him onto the loveseat and roughly hauled her across his lap, so angry he didn't speak for several minutes while she sat at an uncomfortable angle across his thighs. "We are husband and wife," he said at last, his voice deeper than she'd ever heard it. "We aren't going to abandon each other at the first disagreement we have."

"It—it was slightly more than a disagreement, Ian."

"Aye. And there'll be plenty more in the course of our marriage. I guarantee it."

She laid her head on his chest, feeling his heart beat strongly against her cheek. "I thought you might have wanted me to leave," she said in a small anguished voice.

He pushed her hair back from her tear-stained face and frowned. "You'd never make it to the front door."

"Meaning you'd murder me first?" she asked, pulling away from him in alarm.

A reluctant smile lifted the corners of his lips. "Meaning I'd never let you go. I suppose I have to assume some responsibility for knowing what you were like when I married you—impetuous and kind to a fault."

"I did try to warn you," she said with a little sniff.

He started to laugh, a deep rumble in his chest. "It's a damn good thing we're leaving town, isn't it? You realize you can never practice your folk healing here again, or they'll throw you in the clink?"

"Would you let them?" she asked.

"I would have a few hours ago, my wee lawbreaking wife."

She yawned and dropped her face back against his chest, so exhausted her eyelids felt like lead weights. "I'm so glad I don't have to stay with Lilian tonight."

"Aye." He sighed, ruffling her hair. "I'd only have to bring you home in the morning."

As she started to drift off, she felt Ian pick her up and carry her to the bed, his rugged face loving and amused.

"I'm sorry, Ian," she whispered miserably.

"It's all right now, Margaret."

"You're sure?"

"Yes, I'm sure." He hesitated, sitting down beside her on the bed, his mind too overstimulated to sleep. "Will you do me a favor though, Margaret?"

"Anything," she promised extravagantly.

"In the morning I want you to write down everything you did to help the duchess, and then we'll never talk of it again."

She opened her eyes in surprise. "Morag's cures?"

"Everything."

Forty-eight

The Highland stagecoach cost them two guineas apiece and boasted a pair of liveried coachmen and a guard for the protection of its four passengers. As Margaret gazed out across the sea from the window, she thought of Stephen so far away in Siam, and of Agnes, soon to deliver her own child.

She thought of Morag, too, but her feelings for her former mentor were ambivalent. Although Morag had taught her much, she had also tried to hurt her—the rat and the runes, the wee boy on Clootie Hill, the banshee, and turning the island against Ian. Still, if Morag hadn't betrayed her, Margaret would never have begun her new life with Ian, the child growing inside her would never exist. Out of the darkness, she thought philosophically, had come the dawn.

"And what are you looking so pleased about?" Ian whispered, careful not to waken the coach's two other sleeping passengers, a stout retired judge from Ballater and his wife.

"It's a secret," she whispered back.

He took her hand. "You keep too many secrets, my love." His fingers tightened over hers. "Once my family gets ahold of you, there won't be too many moments like this when we can be alone."

The retired judge blew out a resounding snore. Margaret turned her face into Ian's shoulder to smother a giggle. "Alone, you say?"

They didn't discuss the touchy subjects of Jean or Andrew

or Margaret's father or even medicine as the coach rumbled into hilly uplands and green wooded glens, a blue haze of mountains to the west. With Aberdeen behind them and Taynaross yet far away, they began to relax and quietly talk about names for their unborn child.

"I like Adam," Ian said.

Margaret wrinkled her nose. "Silly name for a girl."

"A girl?" He gave a hoot of laughter. "That's a wee laddie in there, my dear. I'm a doctor, don't forget."

"Perhaps I'll have a midwife assist."

"You won't."

"I might," she teased. "And a charmer, for good measure, to make sure my daughter isn't spirited away by the fairies."

On the second night they stopped outside the hamlet of Tuillich, in an old half-timbered coaching inn. Their room overlooked a freshwater lochan which shone like blue silk in the midst of fragrant pine woods. Margaret felt so relaxed in the peaceful setting that she lingered behind when morning came, and Ian went downstairs to settle the bill.

"I wish we could stay," she said as he reached the door.

He gave her a fond smile. He'd been worried about her in Aberdeen, her assertion that she'd seen Andrew's ghost, her secret afternoon. She was a sensitive person, strong in many ways, but too vulnerable in others. "Taynaross is even more beautiful—and secluded."

Yes, she argued silently, it might be. But Jean was also there. Sighing, she took her mug of breakfast tea to the window and stared out at the misty lochan. She still felt a little queasy in the morning and did not look forward to another day in the coach.

Ian could not have been gone two minutes when she noticed three figures emerge from the edge of the woods. At first she thought nothing of them, but as they drew closer to the water, she realized they were a woman and two children. Holding hands, appearing to laugh, they approached the rowboat at the shoreline.

A prickle of apprehension stole down Margaret's spine. She set the mug on the windowsill and rose slowly, mesmerized by the scene unfolding before her. The children, a young girl and a smaller boy, were characters from the darkest day in her life. The woman, her face animated and framed with soft brown hair, could have been Susan Rose.

Could have been.

But she isn't, Margaret told herself fiercely. *She isn't my mother.*

The young boy climbed into the rowboat.

"NO," Margaret whispered, trying to back away from the window. But she couldn't move. She couldn't move even though she knew what would happen to the three people rowing out across the peaceful water.

She knew two of them were going to drown.

She knew they couldn't be real.

"Oh, God," she whispered. "Make it stop."

The young boy in the boat carried a fishing rod. When he rose up on his knees to cast the line into the lochan, Margaret buried her face in her hands and couldn't watch. She could never reach him in time to save him. And the rational part of her mind rebelled, screaming illusion, coincidence. Or was she going mad? Would she see a banshee in the woods if she looked again?

The door opened and she swung around, lowering her hands, so relieved to see Ian she could barely speak. *"Look,"* she cried, rushing forward to drag him over to the window. "Look out across the water and tell me what you see."

He gave her a puzzled smile and obeyed, but his smile faded as Margaret stepped back into the morning light. Her chalk-white skin, the distress on her face, alarmed him.

"Sit down a minute, Margaret."

"No, no, *no*." She pushed his hands away, the gesture violent, desperate. "For God's sake, Ian, *look*."

He did, and saw nothing, the quiet lochan, the dark bristle of pines against the low-lying hills. "It's peaceful," he said hesitantly, drawing her back against his chest, disturbed by the tension in her body. "Does it remind you—"

She twisted around, her head thrown back to stare into his face. He was frightened for her, frightened of a simple countryside scene that had the power to completely unsettle her in a matter of minutes.

"Don't you see them?" she said desperately. "The woman and her children?"

At his blank look, she turned back to the window and stared out at the undisturbed lochan, cold panic gripping her. "Ian, they were there, I swear it. It was my mother and *me*—"

"Margaret." Gently but firmly he guided her away from the window and onto the oak-framed settee by the fire. She twisted her hands in her lap, then looked up at him, her face rebellious and afraid.

"Say it. You think I'm imagining things."

"I'll go and check," he said calmly, kneeling before her. "In the meantime, I don't want you to get any more upset."

She bit her knuckles, giggling nervously. "You think it's because I'm pregnant?"

He shrugged his wide shoulders. "Probably not."

"Do you think I could be . . . mad?"

"Well, you did marry me," he said with a restrained smile. "Wait here."

She jumped up the moment he left and returned to the window. After several minutes, she saw him striding toward the woods. Her heart tightened at the sight of his tall figure swallowed up by the blue-green shadows, and she wanted to call him back, to ask him to pretend nothing had happened.

At the lochan he looked up at her and waved. She imagined what he was thinking, his strange wife and her visions.

There was no rowboat on the shore.

He knelt, apparently examining the sand. Then he turned to mount a hill, his blue-black hair glinting in the sun that had broken through the haze.

When he returned a half-hour later, he kissed Margaret and shook his head. "The lochan is well-stocked with trout. It could have been anyone you saw. A village fisherman."

It hadn't been, but she didn't say that.

"Were there any footprints by the water?"

"Oh, many. But the village women wash their laundry there, too." He glanced around the room. "The coach is waiting, unless you wish to stay here another night."

She shivered at the thought. "No." But, shaken by the incident, feeling suddenly insecure in her pregnancy, her sanity, neither did she wish to meet the woman who had claimed Ian's heart not all that long ago.

Forty-nine

Taynaross stole her breath away, a mansion of weathered blue-gray stones in a wilderness of pine woods that stood against a backdrop of distant purple-crowned mountains. Secluded as Ian had promised, it lay hidden in the hills of Aberdeenshire, the footsteps to the Highlands proper.

The house itself stood on a grassy knoll, and a village cart deposited them at its base, the pine woods virtually the estate's back garden. Ian carried the luggage up the hill and watched Margaret carefully, filled with pride at her reaction to his home. He'd poured every penny he owned into Taynaross, and he wanted her to love it as he did. Grinning, he slowed to let her pick a few harebells and primroses along the way.

"It's perfect," she said breathlessly. "How could you ever bear to be away from here?"

He glanced up at the house. "I'd always planned to live here actually, to raise a family, and practice—"

"Ian!" a young female voice shrieked delightedly from one of the house's dormer windows.

Margaret saw a pretty dark face behind the curtains. Then several more heads appeared at the window, children, aunts, uncles—a mass of sturdy handsome MacNeills.

She stopped, clutching the wildflowers in her hand. "Go on ahead of me," she urged him. "Have your reunion first."

"Nonsense, Margaret, they're family—*our* family."

"Do they know about me?" she asked suddenly, balking at the mossy entrance steps to the house.

He turned, giving her a strange look. "They know we're married and that I love you. The baby will be a surprise. What else is there to know?"

"You know," she whispered. "The accident, the folk healing, my father."

He grabbed her hand and dragged her up the steps, scattering wildflowers around them. "Och, Margaret, you silly goose. Those are the things that have made you what you are, and even if you've led a slightly different life, it only makes you that much more appealing."

MacNeills. Strapping young boys and girls with curly black hair and infectious laughter. Portly bearded uncles and arguing aunts, a house full of friendly noise and love and warmth. Margaret tried to hide in a corner armchair and longed to escape outside, a polite smile on her face while inwardly she was painfully aware that Jean had not made even a token appearance and that Ian had completely disappeared.

But they wouldn't let the newest member of the family remain a wallflower for long, those persistent, charismatic MacNeills. They insisted on including her in their conversations, drawing her, despite her inward resistance, into their powerful family circle of which she had become a link.

Andrew was gone, mourned, and missed.

Margaret was alive, mysterious, and admired.

"My sister says you're a witch, Auntie Margaret. Can you make her disappear, please?"

"I'd have her turn you into a toad except you already are one," the sister in question retorted. "Put the evil eye on him, Auntie Margaret!"

"Can you make the wind rise?"

"Did you put a love spell on Uncle Ian?"

Then, "Och, just look at how bonny she is. 'Tis more like the other way around."

"Please are you *really* a witch, Auntie Margaret?"

Silence dropped like a veil over the room. A witch. Now everyone was interested.

Margaret widened her eyes. "If I were a witch, do you not think I'd have flown here on my broomstick instead of coming in that smelly coach?"

Ancient Aunt Grizel with her bloodshot eyes and whiskery chin raised her whiskey glass in approval. "That's what we needed in this family, a woman who believes in the old ways. Too many newfangled doctors and such. Colin and his hulking boy Thomas."

Dara appeared in the doorway with a tray of fresh warm scones and milk. "It's Ian, not Thomas," she pointed out. "Thomas is Ronald's son, Aunt Grizel. Speaking of which, where has Ian got himself off to anyway?"

"He's out in the garden with Jean," said one of the children drawing a picture by the fire.

"Andrew's widow?" Aunt Grizel said loudly, making a prune face. "What's the overeducated rogue doing with her when his own clever young wife is here by herself?" She leaned forward and looked straight at Margaret, the cold gleam in her faded blue eyes revealing she wasn't as unhinged as she pretended. "There's work to be done in that garden, my girl. Pulling out the weeds and such as doesn't belong."

"Whist your tongue, old woman," Grizel's husband murmured. "You're embarrassing the poor girl."

But Margaret, inspired by the challenge, nodded and resolutely rose from her chair. "You're right, Aunt Grizel. I'll tend to the gardening before the weeds take hold."

Margaret wandered through the old stone house, finally finding her way into the library where a pair of French doors were thrown open onto a delightful unwalled garden to admit the afternoon breeze. There was a young woman sitting in an armchair reading a book, but Margaret didn't notice her until she herself was almost to the garden doors.

"Oh, don't go out there," the girl said, tossing back her straight brown hair. "Ian and my mother are having a *talk*. I'm playing Cupid between them, you see."

"Cupid?"

"Well, I know it's a little early—Mum would probably die if I told her I knew, but I don't think she ever really stopped loving Ian. Even though she loved Andrew, too, and she's still in mourning, she's rather young to give up her life entirely."

Margaret stared into the girl's animated face. "I'm not sure I understand what you're saying."

The girl rose from her chair. "There's the baby to consider, you see. Mum shouldn't have to raise him alone and work for a living, too."

Margaret instinctively glanced out into the garden, trying to find Ian in the colorful jungle of hollyhocks, lupines, and trellises of sweet peas that grew in overcrowded plots. It was a poignantly romantic setting for a lover's reunion, fragrant, secluded, and she wished suddenly she *were* a witch to go flying in circles over Ian's "talk" with Jean.

The girl peered over Margaret's shoulder, a worried look on her thin face. "Oh, by the way, I'm Alanna, Jean's daughter. You must be Cousin Gillian from Glasgow."

"No, I'm Wife Margaret from Aberdeen—*Ian's* wife."

It took several seconds for the announcement to penetrate Alanna's excitement, and then she flushed, her eyes mortified. "But I didn't know—my mother doesn't know he's married."

There was a ripple of softly muted laughter, footsteps shuffling through the gravel of a hidden garden path.

"Well," Margaret said dryly, "I hope Ian hasn't conveniently forgotten the fact himself."

Fifty

As if Ian could forget. The entire time he talked with Jean on the garden bench, he kept thinking of his spirited wife, unable to suppress a feeling of gratitude that it was Margaret he had married, that because of Jean's betrayal his life had been transformed into the unexpected happiness he knew.

"Your nephew Kevin is upstairs asleep," Jean told him, her voice wistful. "He's the image of Andrew."

Ian grinned. "Thank God he doesn't resemble me."

"I always found you terribly attractive." Jean looked down into her lap with a frown. "It was a shock, losing Andrew like that." Her voice quavered. "I can't help . . . I wondered if God w-was punishing me."

"Because you left me?" Ian asked in surprise. "Look, Jean, Andrew's death hurt us all, but God blessed your marriage with a baby. As for me, well, I should let Margaret tell the family herself, but we're going to have our own child soon."

Jean glanced up, her brown eyes shining with the pain that had taken her off guard. How happy Ian looked. Irrationally, selfishly, she'd always assumed he would remain a bachelor, that he would belong to *her,* even after what she'd done to hurt him. She forced a smile. "Oh. Well, congratulations. I never knew you even cared for children, interrupting your work and all."

He glanced toward the house, his craggy face amused. "I think I've changed."

"Obviously." They both heard the regret in her voice and chose to overlook it. Then Jean stood and smoothed down her skirts. "Alanna held childish hopes you and I would . . . well, that one day. . ."

Her voice trailed off, the unsaid hanging between them as they walked back toward the house.

"I'm leaving with your parents," she said softly.

Ian frowned. "I'm not evicting you from Taynaross. You and Andrew had no other home."

"I'll reopen the shop in Aberdeen." She paused at the unkempt privet hedge. "You're a lucky man. Marrying a young woman with all that money. I assume she and her father have reconciled since you're all living happily in Aberdeen?"

"Money?" And then he remembered that Jean's envy of wealthy people had been one of her less attractive traits. "You can't think I'd marry Margaret for her inheritance. You wouldn't if you'd met her."

"No," Jean said with a little sigh. "Of course not. I didn't mean to be insulting. Your practice is improved?"

"I've more cases than I can handle."

"Oh." She moved away from the hedge. "I only asked because the last time I saw you, you mentioned Lucy Patton was trying to destroy your career."

"She was. Fortunately she moved back to Glasgow to be with her family." Ian followed Jean back toward the house. "I've a few old enemies left, though, but none with as much cause to hate me as Lucy. I suppose I should pity her."

Jean frowned. "Glasgow. But I thought—I'm sure Alanna mentioned seeing Lucy in the kirkyard last month placing flowers on her husband's grave."

"Last month?"

"Ask Alanna yourself if you like. That's her at the door now and"—her voice dropped—"oh, that must be your wife beside her."

Ian looked up, his face brightening. "It is. She's gorgeous, isn't she, Jean?"

Jean swallowed. "Lovely." She plucked at his coatsleeve as he moved toward Margaret. "You will remember to contact the solicitor in Aberdeen, Ian?"

He nodded. And if Jean had held any hope at all for another chance with Ian, it died as she caught the unashamedly devoted look that crossed his face as he pulled Margaret forward by the hand to introduce her.

That night as they got ready for bed in their large oak-paneled bedroom, Ian knew something was bothering Margaret, that she'd withdrawn into herself again. He watched her as she sat in the middle of the massive iron bedstead, her slender figure wrapped in his tartan dressing robe while she brushed out her hair.

"Everyone loves you," he said, sitting down behind her, taking the brush from her hand to finish her hair.

Her shoulders tensed. "What is it?" he whispered, pushing aside her heavy hair to kiss her neck.

"They love me. *She* loves you."

He turned her around to face him. "Jean, you mean. She's confused, perhaps unable to accept Andrew's death. I don't think she knows what she feels."

Margaret thought with unexpected affection of Andrew—or at least of her *impression* of him—a lopsided smile and tweed knickerbockers.

"I heard Jean mention at supper she was moving back to Aberdeen," she murmured.

"Yes," Ian said slowly. "It was where she used to live, after all."

"I'll bet if you'd married Jean, she wouldn't have ruined your career like I did."

He had a hard time not smiling at the convoluted workings

of his wife's mind. "You're right. Jean is too predictably dull for anything so daring as saving a duchess's life."

Margaret sniffed. "I'll bet she never sees people drowning in lochs or ghosts in the garden either."

"Probably not. She'd faint if she did."

She bowed her head, her voice a broken whisper. "I don't want to love you like this. I don't want our happiness to be clouded over by worrying all the time that I'll lose you."

He looked incredulous. "Lose me? I'm the one who should worry—or has Aunt Grizel been stirring up trouble again?"

Margaret shook her head, her voice low. "I heard Jean ask you about a solicitor. When she touched your arm."

"It's in regard to Kevin's trust fund." He fell back on the bed, laughing quietly. "Did you actually think—you *couldn't* have thought I intended to leave you?"

Relieved, ashamed at her lack of faith, and deeply embarrassed, she didn't answer. As Ian's laughter died away, she could hear a nightingale in the glen beyond the house, and through the window she saw a scattering of bright stars burning in the sky.

She leaned back against Ian, sighing. "They say that whatever you're doing when you hear the first nightingale in the spring, is what will occupy most of your time the rest of the year."

"She means nothing to me now," Ian said softly.

"You could make me believe anything," she whispered ruefully.

"Believe I love you then. Believe in our marriage—I just realized—you actually admitted that you love me a few moments ago."

"Temporary insanity," she said with a shaky laugh. "I've had several lapses lately."

"Tell me again."

She crawled under the covers and closed her eyes, feigning a loud yawn. "Leave me alone."

"Not until you say it again." He was leaning over her, the big monster, not about to give up. "Look me in the eye this time, too."

Very slowly she opened her eyes and stared up at him, her heart no longer able to resist the admission. "I love you," she said, her voice sweetly solemn. "Oh, I do."

He grinned. "I always knew you did."

She started to laugh. "Get off me, you oaf."

"The oaf you love."

Ian rarely dreamed, but tonight, the culmination of a day fraught with emotional undercurrents, he dreamt of Andrew, that his brother was standing on a bridge trying to call to him. Ian tried to move, but his legs were too heavy to lift.

"You're dead," he told Andrew. "You're dead, and I'm dreaming."

Andrew grinned. "Are you sure?"

Ian awoke with a violent start, disturbing Margaret, who was tangled up in the mound of sheets and blankets. She stared up into his face in drowsy confusion. "What's the matter?"

"I had a dream about Andrew. He wasn't really dead." Realizing how ridiculous it was, that he was starting to sound like *her,* he ran his hands through his hair and got out of bed.

"I've forgotten how peaceful it is here," he said, moving to the window. "I wish we could stay."

Margaret sat up slowly. "What about your practice?"

"I could practice here."

"The people are simple here, Ian, not unlike your patients on Maryhead."

"Then I'll try again," he said calmly. "I've been thinking that I'd like our child to breathe fresh country air, to grow up with a woods and stream for his playground instead of a crowded street and stinking cesspools."

"You *have* been thinking," she said in surprise.

"I want my wife to be happy, too. I know you hated Aberdeen."

He walked back to the bed and got in beside her. "You're a bad influence on me, Margaret. I never dreamt much before I met you."

She looked thoughtful. "Those in the spirit world frequently communicate through dreams because it's the only time our minds are completely receptive."

"Ballocks." He thumped onto his stomach. "Good night."

Insulted, she leaned over him and tickled his bare shoulder with the ends of her hair. "They'll pay you in chickens."

"Hmm?"

"Your patients here will pay you in eggs and chickens."

He snorted, his face crushed into the pillow. "Then Mrs. Jones will have to pay more attention to inventing new fowl dishes than herbal potions."

Margaret brightened. "When can we send for her?"

"Next month, after I talk this over with my father. And the Armstrongs, too."

"Oh, no, Ian. Can't they stay to take care of the town house?"

"This is a large estate, and you'll be getting around less with the baby coming."

She lay back down and tried to get into a comfortable position, but her mind was suddenly not tired. "You know, Ian, I just had a thought. Since this is the country and the people are unfamiliar with brash young doctors, I could help—"

"Absolutely not, Margaret. Absolutely *not*. No charms, potions, nostrums, herbs, snails, or disgusting soups."

Margaret stared up at the ceiling with wide innocent eyes. "Absolutely *nothing.*"

Fifty-one

It was blissfully quiet in the next six weeks at Taynaross. The weather warmed, spring deepening into an early summer. Chaffinches called from the deep foliage of the larch and alders along the burn at the bottom of the knoll. Butterflies hovered above the dog roses and honeysuckle smothering the outbuildings. Margaret grew fat on the wild strawberries she picked in the woods and slathered in fresh cream. Little by little Ian began to take patients from the nearby village, easing the burden of the parish's elderly physician.

Ian sent for his household staff in Aberdeen, leaving Donald, Bridget, her sister, and the new gardener to maintain the town house until the lease ran out next year. If he and Margaret hadn't decided to make a permanent move to Taynaross, they'd at least await the birth of their baby in October.

Somehow word got out that the new doctor's wife was knowledgeable in the old ways of healing. Resolutely Margaret refused to become involved in even the most heartbreaking cases. After nearly destroying Ian's career, she was anxious to make a new start.

Then late one night in July, a village woman came to the door carrying her two-year-old son in her arms. Racked with coughing spasms, the child could barely draw a breath, and his mother blanched at every wheezing paroxysm, helpless tears running down her face.

"Old Dr. Murray says he's going to die, ma'am, but I canna

accept that, do you ken? I know we're not to question that such afflictions are God's will, but I doubt the Creator meant a bairn to suffer so."

"So do I," Margaret said calmly, motioning to the young scullery maid standing in the door. The house operated on a skeletal staff, efficient enough but generally unsupervised by the alcoholic steward Andrew had employed and, just before his death, let go. "Boil some water, Ellie. My husband will be home soon, Mrs. Kerr. I'll do what I can in the meantime."

"But it was *you* I wanted to see, ma'am," the woman whispered.

"Oh, I see," Margaret said quietly. "Well. Has the boy had these spells often?"

"Since he was weaned, ma'am, and each time he has an attack, I nearly die of fright." She lowered her voice. "I tried the usual charm, spiders' webs mixed into milk and swallowed. And even a fortnight on boiled carrots."

"And neither worked?"

"No, ma'am."

Margaret's hands shook as she hunted in the cupboard for the herbs she'd dried and hidden away for an emergency. Ian would be furious. But she couldn't stop herself. Not when there was such an obvious cry for help in her own house.

Soon the room grew warm and fragrant with the herbal steam that escaped the numerous pots and kettles she had put on to boil. With the mother's help, she placed the boy on a stool with his face over a cooling saucepan in which she'd steeped handfuls of mullein and horehound.

"There now. That's better," the woman said as the exhausted child drew a deep, shuddering breath. "Your husband's blessed to have your help, Mrs. MacNeill. I hope he knows it."

"He does," Ian said quietly from the doorway, and Margaret spun about in alarm, her face flushed with guilt and the vaporous heat. "Great God," he muttered. "This place feels like a Turkish bath."

"I—I didn't expect you for another hour at least," Margaret said defensively. "The wee lad is asthmatic and so I did what I could."

Ian inhaled the pungent steam, stripping off his heavy tweed jacket to hang on a peg. "I can see perfectly well what you did. How is he now?"

"Much better, Doctor, thanks to your wife," Mrs. Kerr said. "I'm always so afraid he'll die during one of his spells."

Ian ruffled the boy's damp red curls. "He'll probably outgrow it, but until then, I'd keep him a little less active. For now you should give him daily doses of castor oil and a cup of hot, strong coffee during a mild attack. If he gets very bad, I'll give him an injection of morphia."

"Oh," the woman murmured, more than a little awed by the dark tall doctor.

Margaret smiled. "I'll give you some red clover tea, Mrs. Kerr. If my husband *allows* it."

He shrugged and glanced down at the pot. "What did you use here, Margaret?"

Margaret was suddenly tired herself, with a backache and burning feet, not in a mood to explain her actions. "Mullein and horehound. I didn't have any lungwort."

"And it worked?"

"Like magic," the woman said, unaware that her words made Margaret wince and Ian conceal a resigned smile. "I'll take him home, shall I, so as to let ye both get some rest?"

Ian looked up at his wife. "No, Mrs. Kerr. You can sleep with the lad in the closed bed in the drawing room. I don't want the walk back to the village bringing on another attack. Margaret—could I see you in the hall please?"

Margaret squared her shoulders and glanced at the boy before following Ian down the darkened corridor. It was the end of her marriage. She pictured herself with her pregnant stomach and one-eyed cat sailing back to Maryhead to beg Agnes to take her in. The melodramatic image made her giggle, but the moment of humor quickly faded as she and Ian came face to face in the candlelit hallway.

"Practicing without a license again, Mrs. MacNeill?" he asked softly, his arms folded across his chest.

Her chin lifted. "I know I promised, but I couldn't help myself. And I did no more than any common farmwife would have done."

"A common farmwife you are not," he said quickly, then he shook his head, staring up at the ceiling. "Incorrigible, yes. Defiant, yes. And"—he sighed, lowering his gaze to her face—"and undeniably talented. I'm not going to interfere with your folk healing anymore, Margaret."

She couldn't stop the jubilant grin that broke out on her face.

"Unless we move back to the city," he hastily amended.

She threw her arms around his neck. "Oh, Ian," she whispered, "you dear old thing."

His arms went around her, an awkward prenatal embrace, but he loved her so much.

"I must be losing my mind," he said, laughing helplessly.

And Margaret hugged him back, deliriously happy that a major hurdle between them had been mounted and wishing that their moment of happiness could continue uninterrupted.

But even before they broke apart, the rumble of a pony-led trap stopping below the knoll distracted them, and Ellie came running from the kitchen to summon Ian.

Walter and Sybil Armstrong had arrived from Aberdeen.

Sitting with Sybil a few minutes later in the kitchen over a cup of tea, Margaret was unable to hide her disappointment that Blodwen Jones had not come, especially since the pair of them had been partners in medical crime and could now work out in the open.

But the Welsh cook, Sybil explained, had gotten a severe case of food poisoning on the way to Taynaross and had gone back to Aberdeen to recover with relatives.

Margaret frowned. "You and Mr. Armstrong weren't affected by the food?"

"Oh, no, Mrs. MacNeill. I never touch that fancy French food, and Walter would never eat duck, with his fondness for birds." She glanced round-eyed at the enormous kitchen. "It's a very large estate, isn't it?"

"If it's too large, perhaps you'd prefer to stay on at the Aberdeen town house instead," Margaret said impulsively.

Sybil looked taken aback. "You're surely not thinking of running this house by yourself with the baby coming?"

Actually, Margaret had been, spoiled by the privacy of the past few months. But Sybil had a point—Margaret would soon be busy with a child *and* her work.

"I'm very glad you're here, Mrs. Armstrong," she said, rising to end the conversation.

But she wasn't really glad to see the blowsy Mrs. Armstrong again, and as Margaret went quietly into the parlor to check on her young patient, she fleetingly reflected that something in Sybil's story about Mrs. Jones did not ring true.

Fifty-two

The baby came two weeks early, at the end of September on a starlit evening so still you could hear the peewits calling in the woods. Margaret had been having irregular contractions all day, her water had broken, and Ian had not left her side, following her like a shadow until she wanted to scream.

"Margaret," he said soothingly, leaning over her, Ellie and the village midwife at the foot of the bed. "Let me place the inhaler around your neck just in case."

She sat up, panting, at the peak of a contraction, nodding gratefully as the two other women hurried to the bed to help her push. "I'll . . . tell . . . you where to put that . . . bloody stupid thing . . ."

Then she did.

The midwife, her arms around Margaret's shoulder, gave Ian an amused smile.

Ellie snorted and stared down at her feet.

Ian flushed and drew back from the bed, never having taken a childbed insult so deeply to heart before.

Mairi Susan MacNeill was born one hour later, on Michaelmas morning, a long, lean black-haired girl who suckled lustily the moment her mother put her to the breast. And after Margaret had been washed and changed into a fresh nightdress, she and the newborn slept, nestled together in the big iron bed, a sight that almost brought Ian to his knees in a prayer of gratitude for the goodness bestowed on him. Now for the first time he understood the aching joy, the miracle, that he had so many times participated in as a physician but never as a father.

Margaret stirred and gave him a sleepy smile, his dark unshaven face, the love in his eyes a reassuring sight. "Thank you . . . Doctor," she murmured on a sigh of exhausted contentment.

She closed her eyes; at her weakest moment, she had broken down and asked for chloroform, which had helped more than she would ever admit to Ian.

"Very nice job, sir," the village midwife said behind him, as Ian was staring down at his sleeping daughter, an enraptured expression on his rough face.

"Oh," he murmured with a smile of sublime tenderness, "she's ever so much more than nice. She's perfection incarnate."

"I meant the delivery, sir," the woman said, amused. "But the baby is even nicer, I agree."

By October they were a family, settled into their own secret harmony and rhythm, Mairi adapting happily to her dad's professional comings and goings, to sitting in a willow basket in the garden while her mother sang Gaelic lullabies and gathered cuttings before the first frosts came.

It was the end of the month when Margaret went out on her first medical call since Mairi's birth, an October dusk with the tang of wood smoke in the air. Margaret had just nursed the baby to sleep and was coming down the stairs to oversee supper when she saw Walter in the hall, a pensive look on his face as he closed the door.

"It was a call for you, ma'am," he said, turning to the hallstand to straighten the umbrellas it held. "Your young asthmatic patient has taken a bad turn."

She frowned, watching his bony hands move methodically

around the stand. "That's funny. I saw his mother the other day and she reassured me all was well."

Walter looked up slowly, not saying a word.

"I suppose I'll have to go to him anyway, just in case. I wish Ian weren't staying late at the Campbells' tonight."

"Yes, madam."

"Well, I'll fetch my basket from the parlor," she murmured, wondering how, for the hundredth time, Ian could overlook Walter's funereal character just because he was an excellent laboratory assistant.

She had just packed up her basket in the parlor when the door opened behind her. Ian came in and casually glanced over her shoulder, scaring a little cry from her because she still had Walter on her mind and Ian wasn't due home for hours.

"Oh! I thought you were the butler."

Ian circled her waist with his hands, enjoying the feel of her uncorseted body, the lushness that motherhood had given her. "Disappointed?"

"What do you think?" She pulled away from him and went to the door, listening for Mairi upstairs in the nursery. "I thought you were having supper with the parson—I was just on my way out. Jamie Kerr, the little red-haired boy, has taken another spell."

Ian frowned and took off his tweed jacket, mist still glinting on the gray-purple threads. "He looked fine last week when he made a face at me in kirk. Do you want me to come with you?"

"Well—"

"Well, what?"

"Well, I thought you should stay home with Mairi." She lowered her voice. "You know how I feel about leaving her with Mrs. Armstrong."

"What about Ellie?"

"She's gone to her mother's until the morning."

He threw his jacket across the back of his chair. "It's a damn long walk to the village, Margaret, and at night—"

"I thought I'd take Andrew's horse and have Seamus ride along for company."

Ian was silent, stricken by an inexplicable impulse to forbid her to go. Of course she'd only think he was trying to hinder her work if he tried to stop her. And he supposed it would be safe enough, with the estate's young groom escorting her . . .

"What if I'm called to an emergency?"

"I won't be long, Ian. No more than an hour or two." She moved forward to give him a quick hug. "What's the matter?"

He pulled her harder against him. "I'll go in your place."

"If that's what you want," she said slowly. "I'll pretend I never got the message if it makes you that upset."

He almost took her up on the offer, but foresaw a mountain of resentment to be overcome later if he did. He smiled rue-fully. "Don't be such a damned martyr. Go see your patient, but make sure Seamus never leaves your side on the way."

"It's only four miles or so."

"Aye. In the dark, over a road you're still not entirely fa-miliar with." He frowned. "And tell the little blighter not to make faces at your husband."

She sighed, breaking away from him. "I'd better fetch my cloak."

When she had gone, Ian walked around the parlor and stood in the early gloaming shadows, glancing down without interest at the side table where Margaret had placed his mail. Letters to Andrew mostly from acquaintances who didn't know he'd died, and Ian wasn't in the mood to deal with that right now. He didn't even bother to turn up the lamp.

Fifteen minutes later, he had settled down in an old leather chair with a glass of whiskey. As he took a sip, he heard Margaret and the young groom ride away from the stables, their two mounts whickering in the quiet country twilight.

Don't let her go.

The warning came from out of nowhere. Ian sat forward so abruptly, the whiskey sloshed onto his lap.

"Who is it?" he said suspiciously, getting to his feet to face the door. But of course no one was there.

He rubbed his jaw, feeling very foolish, hearing voices now like Margaret and Ellie and Blodwen Jones. He was simply overtired and uneasy about letting Margaret go, perhaps even a little jealous of how easily people trusted her if the truth be told.

Och, Ian, you're so book-learned, you can't see the forest for the trees.

Oblivious to the other presence in the room, Ian wandered to the window and stared outside. The trouble was, he'd always believed himself too sophisticated to acknowledge the validity of his own intuition or, God forbid, "messages from the other side." But all his reason seemed to crumble when it came to his young wife.

He shook his head. Stupid, staying in a darkened room with a bottle of bad whiskey.

He glanced at the grandfather clock in the corner. He had always felt safer at Taynaross than anywhere else in the world. Why then did this dark feeling about Margaret persist?

Fifty-three

Margaret smiled gratefully at Seamus, the homely tow-haired groom who helped her dismount outside the heather-thatched cottage. The village of Taynaross was a stopping place for travelers about to make the breathtaking journey into the Highlands, but even so, it was considerably out of the way and especially lonely at night.

"With your permission, Mrs. MacNeill," Seamus said, leading their horses to the nearby stream. "I'll wait for ye out here."

"Don't wander off," she called after him, gripping her basket as she turned toward the path.

Why was the cottage so dark and quiet?

After Margaret had knocked for several moments at the door, Alison Kerr answered, looking sleepy and disoriented in her nightrail. "Bless me, Mrs. MacNeill, is ought amiss to bring ye out in the dark?"

Margaret was taken aback, staring down at the three young children crowded around their mother's skirts, Jamie among them and in obvious good health. "Did you not send to the house for me, Mrs. Kerr? I was told Jamie had taken another spell."

"A spell of bad manners is all, ma'am. He's not had a coughing fit for months."

"How strange." Margaret glanced over her shoulder at the

groom standing in the shadows. "I'm sorry to have awakened you and the family. Walter must have misheard the message."

Seamus, waiting at the end of the path, had another explanation. " 'Twas a brownie who came to your house, Mrs. MacNeill. Them wee demons are never so active as in October. It's an enchanted month, ye ken."

Margaret mounted her horse. "Well, it was a wasted evening for certain. I only hope I don't have a poor sick patient waiting for me somewhere, because I simply can't see myself waking up the entire village to ask if I'm needed."

" 'Twas a brownie, Mrs. MacNeill," Seamus reiterated, "jealous of yer healing powers."

"Or a butler," she said grimly, thinking she needed to have a good talk with Walter.

"Aye." Seamus frowned. "He's an odd bird, I canna disagree."

"I wonder if it was the Cairns's little boy. The name sounds similar enough to be mistaken."

"They live on the other side of the hill, Mrs. MacNeill. It's a long ride there."

Margaret bit her lip and stared at the rough road they'd have to travel. "I'll not rest until I know for certain, Seamus. Stay here if you don't want to come."

"No, Mrs. MacNeill," he said reluctantly. "I'll come."

But the Cairns's boy was asleep when Margaret quietly knocked at the door of his home, and the few scattered cotter's huts they passed were quiet, with no distressed mothers waiting at the door for the healer to arrive to help a sick child.

"We've been gone almost three hours, ma'am," Seamus reminded her uneasily.

"Ian will be livid," she muttered, and urging her horse toward the woods, she added, "Hurry up, Seamus, please."

Seamus shook his head apologetically and reached over to grab the reins from her hands. "Forgive me for this, Mrs. MacNeill, but I canna let ye go."

She felt a flash of panic and then anger as she stared down at his hand. "My husband," she said, taking a breath, "will be very upset at this."

"The bridle path through the woods is narrow and irregularly maintained," Seamus explained, then looked past her, lowering his voice. "There's talk in the village that those woods are haunted, ma'am, by yer husband's late brother. It was while riding along a wooded ridge hunting grouse that he accidentally shot himself in the stomach."

Margaret released her breath. For the first time in her life she was more afraid of her husband's human anger than of whatever supernatural entities might be lurking in the wooded path they had to follow. "I don't think we need to be afraid of Andrew MacNeill's spirit, Seamus."

He looked unconvinced. "But if we ride around the village, we can bypass the woods entirely."

"And go another hour out of our way," Margaret said. "If you don't want to ride with me, I certainly won't force you."

"Weel, I'm not about to leave ye alone."

They rode in silence, penetrating the overgrown pine woods where occasional glimmers of moonlight fell upon the path. Seamus was noticeably nervous, balking at every hooting owl and popped twig he heard.

"What was that?" he asked suddenly, slowing his horse.

Margaret shrugged, impatient to reach the open road. "I didn't see anything."

"It was a flash of white over there in the trees, madam. And I thought I heard a cry."

Margaret frowned. "It sounds like a sheep."

They'd come to a fork in the path which led either to the glen road or into the deep gorge that opened into the valley of Taynaross, wooded hills cradling it on each side.

Margaret guided her horse toward the gorge. "I know that sound. A sheep's gone over the hill."

"Someone will find it in the morning, Mrs. MacNeill."

"Not before the hoddy crows blind it." She dismounted and started to climb the hill. "It's a cruelty I can't allow."

Seamus jumped down after her in alarm. "But we'll need help, a rope, to pull it out."

"Can you ride back to the village to fetch someone then?"

"I'll not like leavin' ye alone."

"Well, perhaps we can get it to climb back out itself."

Margaret hoisted up her cloak to descend into the gorge, allowing Seamus to take a steadying hold of her arm. The darkness of the sheltering hills, the quiet, made her uneasy, but as soon as she saw the sheep standing in the stream that traversed the gorge, its legs entangled in a fishing line, she forgot her nervousness.

"We can't bring it up without a rope," Seamus said. "Let's go home, Mrs. MacNeill. I'll come back with my father."

"Oh, all right. Ian wouldn't appreciate this anyway."

He sighed in relief. "Take my arm—och, no."

Margaret looked up to see what had upset him. "What is it?"

"The horses have wandered off. They must have broken their hobble and gotten into the woods again."

"I'll help."

"No. Wait here, Mrs. MacNeill. No point in us both getting winded."

She sighed. "It looks like we're going to be very late after all."

She sat down on a damp tuft of gorse with her cloak pulled down over her knees. But after a few minutes, the quiet began to wear on her nerves again, and she decided she might as well untangle the sheep from the line.

It gave a plaintive bleat as she climbed down toward it.

"Well, you wee dickens, where is your shepherd then, to let you get yourself in such a coil?"

Several loose stones skittered down into the gorge. Startled,

Margaret caught a blurred movement from the corner of her eye and glanced up, expecting to see Seamus.

The white-draped figure that had haunted her since childhood hovered at the crevice's edge. Its robes like a shroud, it spoke in a voice so faint Margaret could barely hear it over the rush of blood into her ears. She could not see the banshee's face at all, and for that was fiercely glad.

"You ignored my warning, Margaret Rose."

Margaret slowly got to her feet.

"You should never have come back," the creature said, its voice quavering. "Go back to the island, or pay a price for the past."

Margaret's mind raced, reason rebelling against what she clearly saw and heard, and in a way it was a relief to confront this evil thing that had haunted her and made her doubt her sanity.

"What price?" she asked, fear constricting her throat.

The creature's hand lifted, and in it hung a child's china doll, Mairi's doll . . . the one Ian had bought for her in Aberdeen, that said "Mama."

Margaret began to shake with anger as much as fear. "Damn you! Damn you! If you're threatening to hurt my child—"

"For heaven's sake, Margaret," a chagrined voice said behind her. "Do you not know cheap theatrics when you see it?"

The masculine voice, rising as it did from the gloomy shadows of the gorge, so startled Margaret that she swung around involuntarily, her heart pounding.

Andrew MacNeill, outlined in a nimbus of green-gold light, began to walk—no, float—toward her.

"Oh, God," she said, stumbling back a step. "You again. I am mad."

"Not mad," Andrew said in irritation. "But you're exceedingly impressionable, and I'm growing quite concerned about you."

Margaret put her hand to her mouth, realizing in half-hysterical amusement that although the nasty white-robed figure above had vanished, she was stranded alone in a gorge with an impertinent ghost and a sheep.

"Listen to me," Andrew said sternly, drawing on his pipe. "I've been waiting for a quiet moment to have a talk with you, and although the setting isn't exactly ideal, it will have to do."

Fifty-four

Ian *was* upset. Mairi had cried inconsolably in his arms for two hours before falling into an exhausted sleep. And after he'd gotten the baby back into her cradle, he'd returned to his vigil at the parlor window, awash in relief when he finally spotted a horse cresting the hill to the house.

He hurried to the back of the house, through the servants' quarters to the stables. Halfway there he almost collided with Sybil Armstrong returning from the washhouse with an armful of linen. She gave an involuntary cry when she stopped; Ian knew she was afraid of him, and perhaps that was the reason he really didn't like her. But as he apologized, he was distracted by the sight of Seamus's father Archie rushing down the drive toward him, leading a riderless horse by the reins.

Ian broke into a run. "What is it, Archie? Where is my wife?"

"I canna say, sir. Looks like my son's mount ran off and left him, though."

Ian stared into the woods. "Then where is my wife's horse?"

The older man shook his head. "I'll take my other son to find out, sir. But Seamus is a responsible lad. He'd not have left yer wife's side unless something happened."

Ian didn't respond.

"Are ye all right, sir?"

"I'm not sure," Ian said, shaking his head. "Saddle a horse for me, too, Archie. I'm coming with you."

* * *

Strangely Margaret was unafraid. Andrew's presence seemed to have a calming effect on the sheep, too, for it had stopped bleating and allowed Margaret to disentangle its leg from the fishing line.

"That's very good," Andrew said, watching her with his crooked grin. "A country man could use a woman of your talents about the house."

She straightened and shook her head as if it would dispel his image. "Actually, I could use a guardian angel myself."

"Not me." He released a rueful sigh. "I don't even want to be here, if you must know the truth."

"But you came to save me from the banshee?"

"Banshee?" He gave an insulting snort. "Where did such a clever girl come to believe in such nonsense?"

"I'm asking myself that same question even as we speak."

She glanced up at the hill, feeling cold again as she remembered the white-draped figure taunting her with Mairi's doll. I'm not mad, she thought. Andrew had seen it, too, except that Andrew wasn't real either. . . .

"Oh, I'm real enough . . . in an otherworldly sort of way." Andrew started to fade away, smiling at the startled gasp she gave as his boots and knickerbockers disappeared. "What did I tell you?"

"Stop doing that! There was a thing in white on the ridge when you appeared. A banshee, and you said something about cheap theatrics."

"It wasn't a banshee," Andrew said confidently. "It wasn't a supernatural being at all, but a horrid human being trying to scare you."

"A person," Margaret said grimly. "Then who?"

"I've no idea. All I could say for certain is that it's part of the dark mass moving in around you and Ian."

In the distance Margaret could hear the approach of riders

in the woods. "Then you didn't come back to protect me?" she asked urgently, sensing that Andrew had heard the riders too and would vanish with all her questions unanswered. "And you saw the banshee, the *person,* and it must mean I'm not mad, except that I'm talking to a ghost—"

He threw back his head and laughed. "I'd be your guardian angel if I could, Margaret, for the sheer amusement of it. But the truth is, I'm here for the most selfish reason. You see, I'm stuck, as it were, between two worlds and I can't go on to my great reward without your help."

She closed her eyes for a moment, overwhelmed. *"My* help?"

"To make peace between me and Ian. I can't leave with this open wound in my brother's heart where there was once so much love and trust. And yet"—Margaret opened one eye in curiosity, to see Andrew had all but faded away—"I can't return to my physical form either. So I need your help."

"Margaret," Ian shouted from the top of the hill. "Where in heaven's name are you?"

Andrew winked at her. "In heaven's name, Margaret."

"But how—" She broke off, disconcerted to find herself addressing the air above the sheep's head.

Then Ian was jumping down beside her, Seamus and his father watching from above with ropes and a canvas sack.

Ian gazed around the gorge, his face wary. "Who were you talking to?"

"You wouldn't believe me if I told you," she said, shivering. "Is Mairi all right?"

"She's fine." Ian swung around to stare at her. "Who were you talking to?" he asked again.

She lowered her gaze. "It was your brother."

"Great Christ, Margaret! What am I supposed to do with you?"

"You could take me home," Margaret suggested wearily. "I've had a very upsetting night."

* * *

They didn't speak again until they were back at Taynaross, and Margaret had checked for herself that Mairi was still sleeping undisturbed in the nursery. Then, sitting alone with Ian in the parlor, everything that had happened earlier in the evening seemed like a bad dream.

"I'm beginning to regret agreeing to let you practice," he said, sitting back to stare at her. He was concerned by her uncharacteristic pallor, the way she kept glancing toward the window as if she expected heaven knew what to appear. "How was your patient anyway?"

Margaret shook her head. "I never found him—Walter must have made a mistake in the name."

His face darkening, Ian rose from his chair to sit beside her. "A mistake? That's not like our annoyingly careful Walter."

She drew a deep breath. "Do you remember seeing Mairi's doll lately, the one you bought her before we left Aberdeen?"

Ian frowned, confused by the shift in topic. "I think I saw it yesterday in the nursery. Why?"

She rose and walked to the window, her voice so soft he could barely hear it. "You'd never believe me anyway."

"Try me."

"I—I saw that creature again tonight. Ian, I'm so afraid." She glanced around, her gaze bright. "Something—someone—wants to hurt us."

He got up and walked toward her. The time had gone for putting down Margaret's fears to her superstitious beliefs. She *wasn't* mad, not with that agile, intuitive mind. And he could no longer ignore the fact that someone had been covertly trying to destroy his career again.

"But not here," he thought aloud. "Not at Taynaross." And because that unknown enemy had dared to invade his home, to threaten his family, he knew he would have to pursue, unmask him no matter what it took.

He slid his hands up her shoulders, his touch unconsciously tense. "Come away from the window. We'll talk to Walter first thing in the morning and see if he can remember anything about who came to the door."

"Ellie will be back tomorrow to help watch the baby," Margaret murmured. "Perhaps it would be a good time to try to find some answers."

"Aye," Ian agreed, but his mind was already working, balancing suspicion against fact. "I'll take care of this, Margaret. It's gone too far."

Fifty-five

By morning it seemed possible that they had both been over-tired, their emotions strained to the point when even a minor disturbance such as losing a cherished doll took on irrational proportions. One of Archie's sons had found the missing doll outside the stables, presumably dragged there by Margaret's cat, and this seemed to put Margaret in a better mood.

Yet watching her at breakfast, his heart brimming with a possessive love that was almost painful, Ian knew he could not pretend the strange sequence of events of the previous evening had never happened.

He'd promised her an answer. He had told her not to worry, and she seemed to be more relieved over finding that doll than anything he'd said. Now, with breakfast over, they were waiting for Walter to finish his morning duties, then explain about the mysterious messenger who had lured Margaret away. Ian knew there had to be a rational explanation for everything, including Margaret's banshee and his brother's ghost. Nothing could make him believe otherwise.

"You look very formidable with that black scowl on your face," Margaret chided him, standing by his chair to refill his coffee cup. "Like an ogre sitting down to a breakfast of children."

He put his arm around her, squeezing her waist. "I was thinking, you insulting woman."

"About your work as usual?"

He smiled and sipped his coffee, but he didn't correct her. Margaret, his wife. Their peaceful home and sweet adorable bairn. He ached with grateful happiness . . . and a fear he could no longer deny.

The post arrived while they were sitting in the parlor. Ian caught up on an appalling number of letters forwarded from Aberdeen while Margaret sewed an herbal sachet of violets and lemon verbena to place under the pillow of some local insomniac patient. It was an intimate domestic scene that brought him a welcome sense of peace after a sleepless night, questions tossing in his mind.

Margaret, too, basked in the intimate warmth they shared, the baby asleep upstairs, the quiet October day easing her anxiety. What had happened last night had left her shaken, but she drew comfort from Ian's support, his promise to find an answer behind the chain of disturbing occurrences that had begun on Maryhead.

As to Andrew and the other apparition, the alleged banshee. Well, she'd given the matter great thought. She'd first sighted the creature at Loch Meirneal almost thirteen years ago, and its appearance had portended two tragic deaths. How could Andrew know it was a human impostor? And who—who had played the part not only here but on Maryhead, and for what reason?

Besides, she only had the opinion of a ghost to go on.

"There has to be an answer," she said aloud, shaking her head.

Ian glanced up from his letter. "Answer to what, love?"

"To—to whether I should add valerian or chamomile or both. Any exciting news from Aberdeen?"

"Not really." Ian looked up, distracted by the sight of Ellie sneaking past the window. The young maid had stopped at the ash tree beside the gatehouse, a spade in her hand. He was afraid to ask Margaret what the girl was doing, suspecting some superstitious ritual, so he didn't.

Frowning, he returned to his letters. "Now here's a ridiculous piece of gossip from my father."

"Oh," Margaret murmured.

He gave a short laugh. "How absurd. He heard at the hospital that the only reason my practice had grown so fast was that *your* father was influencing his clients to come to me. Where do you suppose these rumors start?"

Margaret stared down at the sachet, stitching furiously.

"Well?" Ian said. "It's ridiculous, isn't it, to assume I couldn't attract my own patients? I know my reputation is a little tarnished, but I hope I'm a decent enough doctor that I don't need to rely on my father-in-law's meddling."

Margaret stared down at the sachet in guilty silence, compressing her lips to hold back a gasp as she jabbed the needle into her thumb.

Ian got up slowly from the chair, his voice deep-pitched with realization. "It's true, isn't it?"

She looked up, her face miserable. "I thought I was helping you."

"For God's sake, Margaret! You gave me the distinct impression you'd rather die than ask your father for help."

"Well, I only did it for you," she retorted, hurt that he'd condemn her for what had been such a sacrifice at the time.

"Then I wish to hell you hadn't. God forbid you've kept anything else from me. This invitation from the professor, for instance—was it your father's doing?"

"Not that I'm aware of," she said stiffly.

He strode to the bellcord to summon Walter for a whiskey. "I don't believe you did this to me. The duchess was bad enough."

She flushed, getting angry now herself. "I was trying to help."

He was pacing behind her chair. "What did Daddy do, threaten to call in his customers' notes if they didn't let his son-in-law treat them?"

"I doubt he did anything so drastic. Moreover, I fail to see why you're making such a fuss."

He stopped and stared at her. "You don't? Oh, hell, what's the use? Just call me Margaret Rose's husband. Where is Walter anyway? I told him to come here right after breakfast."

Margaret put down her sewing. "I haven't seen Sybil all morning either."

The new scullery maid from the kitchen entered the room and took Ian's request for whiskey.

"Where are Mr. and Mrs. Armstrong?" he asked as the girl reached the door.

"Why, they've gone, sir. Left early this morning. Did ye not know?"

Ian looked at Margaret. "Do you know anything about this?"

She shook her head, slowly rising from her chair as the door closed. "They can't have just vanished. What if something's happened to them? What if whoever brought that message last night lured them away, too?"

Ian put down his cup, then strode past her to the door. "I have a feeling you needn't concern yourself with the Armstrongs' welfare," he said grimly.

"Where are you going?"

"To their room."

"I'm coming with you." And even though the look on her husband's face filled her with foreboding, she was as anxious as he to learn what was going on.

The Armstrongs' room was a shambles of emptied drawers, containers of half-used cosmetics, and haphazardly strewn papers that were covered with yellow feathers and bird droppings from the pet canaries Walter had often let fly loose from their cage.

Ian entered the room first and knelt to examine a yellowed newspaper on the floor beneath a chair. Before he could read it, a heap of crumpled linen stuffed under the bed caught his eye. He stretched forward and grabbed hold of the lumpy pile: several white sheets, a theatrical mask with an ivory fang.

"Your banshee," he said flatly.

Margaret leaned against the door and closed her eyes, murmuring, "Cheap theatrics. *Oh.* I'll kill them myself."

Ian was silent, fury overwhelming him. Mystical appearances, missing servants . . . Sybil, Walter. From Maryhead to Taynaross. Of course. Of course.

When Margaret opened her eyes again, Ian had unfolded and brushed the newspaper free of debris, reading it with a puzzled frown. "It's about me," she guessed. "The accident at Loch Meirneal?"

"No," he said in a baffled voice. "It's about me—about my early experiments with anesthesia on canaries."

"It was never Morag," Margaret said, her face white. Everything made a warped kind of sense, but she was fiercely glad her old friend had not tried to hurt her. "The rat. The boy on the hill. It was the Armstrongs all along."

Ian looked stunned, his square jaw tight with slowly building rage. "I never checked their letters of character. Walter was so familiar with medical procedures. He even understood anesthesia."

Margaret's mind raced. "Now I wonder whether that woman in the carriage who tried to lure your nephew away could have been Sybil. But why? Why would they want to hurt us?"

"That scene on the lochan," Ian began, then broke off, his face ashen. "Jesus God, when was the last time you checked Mairi?"

"Right after breakfast. She was grumpy, so I nursed her and she took an early nap. But she's all right. After last night, I made Ellie promise not to leave her alone."

Ian started for the door. "Ellie, my dear, is burying God only knows what under the ash tree by the gatehouse."

"The doll," Margaret said in horror, hurrying after him. "It was Sybil who had Mairi's doll. Oh, God, Ian, was it a warning that she intended to steal the baby?"

Fifty-six

They found Mairi still asleep in the nursery under the watchful guard of the young undergroom, Seamus. "Ellie had to run an errand, sir," he said in defense of the young scullery maid who was fiercely proud of her promotion to the nursery.

Ian melted inside as he gazed down at his sleeping daughter, her rosebud mouth pouting in utter relaxation, her softly rhythmic breathing like the singing of angels in the silence.

"What's going on?" Ellie asked moments later from the doorway, mistrustful of so many people intruding upon her domain.

"It's all right," Margaret murmured. "But I wish you hadn't left the baby."

"I went outside to bury her toenail clippings, madam, to protect her from the evil fairy ye said ye saw last night in the woods."

Ian traced his index finger across his daughter's cheek, smiling as Mairi's mouth moved in a reflexive sucking motion. "It's a human threat you and my wife should watch for, Ellie," he said quietly.

"The Armstrongs are gone," Margaret said as if to reassure herself. "This nightmare has to be over."

Ian stood and walked past Margaret to the window, so deep in thought she believed he had forgotten her. "My enemies were obviously more bent on my destruction than I realized, to try to ruin me through my family. One of them must have hired the Armstrongs." He shook his head. "God, I'd not have thought any of the stodgy old bastards had the imagination for this elaborate, this evil, a scheme."

Margaret glanced around the room and shivered. "Why would your rivals have bothered to have you followed to Maryhead if they wanted you out of the way?"

He shrugged. "To make sure my experiments failed? To discredit my name completely?"

"Then why would they have tried to frighten *me* with something from my past before even you or I knew we'd end up together?"

Ian turned, his face so harshly determined that Margaret felt a chill go through her. "Oh, I'll find out," he said softly. "Whoever is behind this is not going to go unpunished. *Nobody* is going to hurt my family."

Margaret moistened her lips. "Perhaps it was me they wanted to frighten. Perhaps they wanted to hurt me by destroying your career. It makes more sense."

"From a mentally sick perspective, I suppose."

Margaret lowered her voice. "I can't imagine anyone I know wanting to hurt me like this, though."

The disturbing memory of Gareth and Lilian Rose that first day Ian had met them flashed into his mind. But until something could be proved, there wasn't much point in subjecting Margaret to further upset. And he could be wrong. In fact, he was convinced that the Armstrongs had been hired by *his* professional rivals. Above all, he wanted to protect his family from these unknown dangerous enemies, who perhaps had not played their last card yet.

"What are you thinking?" Margaret asked, her eyes dark with anxiety.

He glanced over at her. "The answer will be found in Aberdeen."

"No," she said, panic rising. "Go to the authorities."

"And what crimes have the Armstrongs committed that could be proven?"

"I don't know." Her voice was strained. "I don't care. We're safe here now."

"Are we?" Ian turned to the door, his face preoccupied. "I want you and Mairi to go to my sister Shona's house in Mormedie. Seamus and Ellie can go with you. I'll ride you there myself on my way back to Aberdeen."

He opened the door. Margaret followed him outside, her emotions in tumult. "We could go back to Maryhead—"

"The hell we could. Nobody's chasing me from my home again."

"Ian, please. Don't go."

He swung around at the top of the stairs. "My career has been damaged, my wife terrified, and now my daughter is threatened."

"I have a bad feeling about this, Ian," she whispered. "I have a fear in my heart that if you go back to Aberdeen, something will happen to you."

"I'll be fine," he said, curbing his impatience. "In fact, I'll not be fit to live with until I lay this sordid thing to rest."

She gripped the newel post as he started down the stairs. "I've lost too many people in my life, damn you," she said, tears of frustration thickening her voice.

He pivoted and stared up at her, suddenly realizing how deeply rooted her fears were, how profoundly it would affect her if he did not come back. "Margaret, I have to go. Now be a brave girl and pack a bag for you and Mairi. The sooner we leave, the better."

Tall, as bold featured as her older brother with the same intelligent blue eyes, Shona MacNeill Kidd cheerfully ensconced Ellie and Mairi in the family nursery with her own one-year-old son. Then, her long black hair in a braid to her

waist, she took Seamus to the servants' hall and Margaret and
Ian to the spare bedroom, bringing them a few minutes later
a tray of cheese, scones, strawberry jam, and warm milk.

Margaret took a glass of milk to the fire, a brush in her
hand. "Your sister is incredible," she whispered. "We turn up
on her doorstep at midnight like a band of gypsies, and she
doesn't bat an eye."

Ian sat down on the bed and pulled off his flat-heeled boots.
"That's family for you. She won't ask, either, although I daresay she's dying of curiosity."

"What's her husband like?"

"Graeme? A bit peculiar—a portrait painter. He's pleasant
but slightly off."

Margaret smiled, the mention of painting fleetingly reminding her of Gareth, of their last unenjoyable conversation in his
carriage. Her brother had been trying to warn her about something, she recalled. Had he had a premonition that he'd been
unable to put into words?

After she and Ian had eaten, washed, and undressed for bed,
they found, to their mutual dismay, that they couldn't sleep,
too tense from the rushed ride here in Andrew's open trap over
rough country roads. Ian pulled Margaret across his chest, her
face resting on his shoulder while he watched the dying fire.
His wife, warm, sweet, afraid—was it a mistake to leave her?

"Mairi's cutting her first tooth," he said absently. He tugged
on Margaret's hair. "Time for another child soon, do you
think?"

Margaret drew back on her elbow with a deep chuckle.
"Morag said a woman can't get pregnant as long as she's still
nursing."

"And how long do you plan to nurse her then?"

"For a year, at least."

He turned onto his belly, dragging Margaret beneath him.
As they kissed, he untied her white lawn nightgown and pulled

it down to her waist. "Your sister," she whispered, peering over his naked shoulder. "What if she hears us?"

He stared down at her. "There's a good chance you won't get pregnant while you nurse, for nature seems to have designed it so. But there's no guarantee."

"Oh, Ian, you're not even wearing drawers."

He grinned and kissed her breast. "We MacNeills don't waste time."

She sucked in her breath. "It's so late, and——"

"And we don't take no for an answer."

He leaned back on his elbow, his free hand stroking her belly and then moving between her legs. Margaret closed her eyes and felt the familiar pulsing, like a wave surging toward the shore, a deep thrum of pleasurable anticipation in every pore. He knew so well how to seduce her.

He lowered his mouth to her breasts, capturing a nipple between his teeth and tongue. "Just tell me when I should stop," he murmured. "I wouldn't want to deprive you of your rest."

She caught a handful of his crisp black hair in her hand and tugged at his scalp, hearing him laugh painfully against her breasts. Then with a soft moan of amused female aggression, she pushed him onto his back and began to kiss him, her hands lowering past his belly to stroke his erect sex.

Afterward, they lay drowsily in each other's arms, drifting off on a cloud of contentment that would have been the perfect ending to the day had Margaret not known that tomorrow he would leave.

"I'll miss falling asleep with you in my arms," Ian said softly.

"I wish you'd not go," she murmured.

"Don't worry. . . ."

Margaret closed her eyes, weariness so suddenly overwhelming her she had no idea she had even fallen asleep until she awoke several minutes later, feeling a cold draught on her arms and face.

There was a perceptible difference in the room, a change in light and temperature. Disentangling herself from Ian, she sat up on her elbow to listen.

"She's fine," an amused male voice said from the chair by the fire. "I do see a family resemblance—that MacNeill chin, but thank God she favors you and not my brother."

Margaret stared in disbelief at the sight of Andrew MacNeill seated by the fire with a pipe in hand, an amiable lopsided grin on his translucent face. With a soft moan, she started to pull the quilt up over her head.

"Go away!" She pulled the quilt down long enough to glare at him. "How long have you been here anyway?"

He looked insulted, tiny eddies of light colliding around him. "Are you suggesting I've become a voyeur in the after-life? I can assure you, without a physical frame of reference, it wouldn't be worth my trouble. Now, why haven't you talked to my brother about me?"

"He won't believe me." Margaret shook her head. "*I* don't believe me, and by the way, you were right about the banshee. Ian's going to Aberdeen tomorrow to confront her, the woman who pretended to be the bean sith, that is."

Andrew's image seemed to grow mistier, and a coldness filled the room. "No," he said at length. "I don't like it. You'll have to stop him, Margaret. It's a dangerous proposition, hunting down human banshees."

"Look, I've tried to stop him," she retorted, lowering her voice as Ian stirred. "There's no changing his mind once it's made up."

"Oh, well I know."

Andrew's voice had begun to fade. "But try again. There's still something very black and ominous around both of you—"

"Why don't *you* go with him?" Margaret asked, pleased with herself at the suggestion.

"Me?" The lights outlining Andrew were dimming to a colorful haze. "I don't know. The rules on this side are rather explicit about not interfering where one isn't wanted."

"Oh, please—"

Ian sat up with a loud disoriented shout, his hair disheveled. "What is it?" he said, swinging his bare legs over the bed. "What's going on?"

"Pathetic," Andrew murmured, shaking his head.

"It's Andrew," Margaret said, banging Ian in the back to get him to look before it was too late. "Over there by the fire. Oh, *look*. It's your brother."

"My who?" Frowning, his face blank, Ian turned his head a fraction of a second after Andrew had disappeared. "You're dreaming again, Margaret," he said grumpily, falling back into bed. "And you're talking to yourself in your sleep. Jesus, I thought something was wrong with the baby."

She leaned over him, her hair falling in his face. "I wasn't dreaming and Andrew says you can't go to Aberdeen, that there's danger there for you."

Ian opened his eyes and searched her earnestly frightened face. "You really believe all this nonsense, don't you?"

"Yes!"

He frowned and stared past her to the fire. "Go back to sleep, Margaret. Go back to sleep, and everything will be all right."

She lay back down on her shoulder, huddling against him. "Then you won't go?" she asked him in a small voice.

"Margaret," he said after a moment. "You cannot expect me to change my plans because of some phantom you imagined by the fire. It—it isn't normal."

She stiffened. "Does that mean you think *I'm* not normal?"

"I think Morag has filled your head with so much nonsense that you don't know what to believe. Anyway, staying here with Shona will help you. She's the most down-to-earth woman I know. She'll put you straight about ghosts and the like."

Fifty-seven

Ian had a good memory for detail, and he remembered as he reached Aberdeen very late that night that Sybil Armstrong had once mentioned her sister-in-law owned several flats in one of Aberdeen's shabbier wynds near the waterfront. Perfect hideaways, those dark narrow passageways. The perfect place for a pair of rats to hide.

On a hunch, he took an omnibus the next morning to the area and disembarked at Trinity Quay, walking until he reached the undesirable district. The smell of ordure and rotting produce in the gutters assailed him, a pungent reminder of the days when he'd made calls on the poor for free, fatigue and financial gain offset by youthful idealism.

This part of the city depressed him now as it had then, the claustrophobic tenements, poverty, crime, overcrowding. Suddenly he missed Taynaross, the purple hills, the village which had accepted him—and his wife. If he hadn't been so determined to confront the Armstrongs, he would never have been able to leave Margaret in the country.

Luck was with him.

Apparently he had caught Walter Armstrong on his way back from market. A heavy basket over his arm, Walter hurried down a winding passageway to a flight of worn outer stairs, nearly knocking down a water carrier who was walking by.

Ian quickened his pace, his heart pounding with anger. That was the little bird-crazy bastard he had employed and invited into his house, the man who had made Margaret's life a veritable hell.

Rage broke inside him like a tidal wave.

"Stop right there, Walter, before you take another step. I can't tell you how much I'd enjoy killing you with my bare hands if you give me the chance."

Walter turned jerkily, his long face ashen. "Oh, God, sir. It's you." Then, with a panicked look, he threw down his basket and spun to clamber up the stairs.

Ian caught him in one easy lunge, throwing his entire weight on Walter and slamming them both against the stairs. His walking stick bounced on a step and slid into the gutter. Walter's shoulder blades, then his head, hit the stone steps with a thud. From upstairs a tenement window squeaked open and Sybil Armstrong's horrified face emerged, her strawberry-blond hair wrapped in rag curlers.

"Help me!" she called down to the empty street in her strident voice. "He's killing my husband!"

"Don't hurt me, sir," Walter said quietly. "I know I deserve it."

"Oh, yes," Ian agreed, his hands closing around the frayed velvet lapels of Walter's jacket. "Tell me who put you up to it, and why."

Sybil was leaning out the window, frantically pulling out her curlers. "Don't tell him, Walter!"

Ian's face hardened. "I'll take you to the police then, shall I?"

"Oh, no. Oh, no, sir! I'll tell you, but y-you have to understand, when we took the position with you, we thought it would be no more than a few pranks."

"You terrorized my wife," Ian said slowly. "You made her question her sanity. Now tell me why, goddamnit, and who put you up to it."

Walter's throat worked. "The money was so tempting. I'd

never make that much in ten lifetimes, and I thought you were an evil person."

"You thought *I* was evil?"

"I'd read about you in the papers." Walter's thin face was creased into lines of misery. "I'd read about your experiments with the birds, and I—I thought at the time you'd killed them, sir, the canaries. I thought you'd anesthetized them to death. The newspaper implied that the poor creatures had been killed—"

"God help us," Ian said, blinking in disbelief. "You almost killed my wife because I put a few birds to sleep?"

Walter licked his colorless lips. "The money. We were going to retire to the south of France, set up an inn. She promised . . . the ship was to set sail at the end of this week. But—but it all went too far, hiring that village woman and her children outside the inn and staging the drowning. And then b-bringing the wee bairn's doll into it. What would she have us do next, we asked ourselves?"

"She?" Ian's eyes narrowed; the thought of anyone hurting his daughter made him insane.

"Who is 'she,' Walter?" he demanded in a dangerously soft voice. "Lilian Rose?"

A door creaked open, and then Sybil appeared at the top of the stairs, yanking at her curlers, her black eyes desperate. "We never meant any true harm. But Mrs. Patton convinced us you'd all but murdered her husband and stolen his fame."

"Mrs. Patton?" Ian's mind seemed to freeze. "Lucy Patton hired you?"

Walter hoisted himself onto his elbows. "We had just started to work for Dr. Patton when he died, sir. His wife led us to believe we would be doing society a service by ending your career. She said you'd go to any lengths to make a name for yourself in medicine, even if it meant committing murder."

"I didn't kill Roger," Ian said, closing his eyes briefly. "Dear God."

"I disbelieve it now, sir, after watching you work."

The fishy smell of finnan haddie boiling wafted from the opened door behind Sybil. The odor turned Ian's stomach, that and the realization that Lucy Patton's grief had driven her to such deranged behavior.

"But why would Mrs. Patton want you to threaten Margaret?" he asked slowly, thinking back to his first days on Maryhead when Margaret had begun to report the strange disturbances, the banshee, her young brother Alan on the hill. "Lucy couldn't have known then that I would marry Margaret. What possessed you to try to hurt my wife?"

Sybil and Walter exchanged frightened looks. "Mrs. Patton and your wife's brother were in on it, sir," Walter admitted, his voice barely audible. "I—I believe they had become lovers—"

"Oh, they had," Sybil interjected with a certainty that might have made Ian laugh under other circumstances. She drew her cheap calico wrapper around her ample waist. "What a queer pair, him with his horrible paintings, her with her scalpel and scrapbook, cutting out every article she could find about you and Mrs. MacNeill."

"Oh, Jesus," Ian said as cold fear flashed through him. Why had he ignored his instincts for so long? It had to concern the Rose fortune. Douglas Rose, in his guilt, had probably allotted the lion's share to his mistreated daughter. God knew where Gareth would draw the line.

"We wasn't to harm Mrs. MacNeill, mind," Sybil said, chewing the greasy red lip pomade from her mouth. "Just to give her a good scare, so she'd stay away from Aberdeen."

"He said that, sir," Walter agreed. " 'Make her stay away from Aberdeen.' "

"Where are Gareth and Mrs. Patton now?" Ian demanded.

Walter's high forehead creased in a frown of concentration. "Mrs. Patton is still in the city—we were to meet her Friday for our payoff. And Mr. Rose, well, I believe he divides his time between his father and the bank."

"I overheard him mention he was busy opening the new branch in Dundee," Sybil added. "The old man's dying, I understand."

Ian felt a small measure of relief pierce his anxiety. "Dundee is at least days away from my sister's estate. My wife would appear to be safe for the meantime."

"Aye." Sybil knelt then to clasp her husband's hand, her voice quavering. "Are you going to turn us in, Dr. MacNeill?"

"I don't think I have a choice." Ian straightened, backing down the steps into the street. "But right now I'm more concerned with finding Mrs. Patton before irreparable damage is done to my family."

Walter got awkwardly to his feet, his voice hesitant. "Mrs. Patton convinced us you murdered her husband, sir. She swore you deliberately overdosed him in your home with anesthesia and made it look accidental. She said you were afraid Dr. Patton would make a discovery before you."

Ian clenched his jaw. "And you know that now to be the wild fabrication of Mrs. Patton's unbalanced mind?"

Walter nodded. Then Sybil spoke up, tears coming to her eyes. "The last time we saw her, Mrs. Patton offered us a huge sum if we would . . ." Her voice cracked, and she wiped her nose with her sleeve. "She s-said if we'd arrange that . . . if your wife had a fatal accident, we'd never have to worry about money again."

Ian looked away, overcome by disgust and anger, his revulsion at what a man would do for a price. And he was furious at himself for failing to protect his family. His face like granite, he lifted his head and gazed at the tenements that rose along the wynd like overgrown tombstones.

"I've often thought that these buildings should be condemned for the squalor they encourage, sickness of the body and soul."

"Dark places breed dark deeds," Walter said remotely. "So my father claimed."

Ian backed swiftly away from the stairs, so anxious to return to his family he couldn't get away from this stinking street fast enough. He was afraid, so afraid for Margaret and Mairi that he couldn't think straight. But Sybil's voice echoed in his mind. . . .

If your wife had a fatal accident.

If your wife had a fatal accident.

At the end of the wynd he glanced back involuntarily over his shoulder. Walter was still standing on the stairs with his head in his hands, and Sybil, her wrapper hiked up to her garters, had recovered the bread from the gutter and was brushing it off with her hands.

Fifty-eight

The elderly butler at Lucy Patton's sandstone villa on the Ferryhill politely informed Ian that Mrs. Patton was not expected home until late that evening.

"But she is here?" Ian persisted, craning his neck to see around the older man's head into the marble-tiled entry vestibule. "I mean, Mrs. Patton is in town?"

"Oh, yes, sir," the butler replied, glancing back over his shoulder in faint bewilderment. "She left instructions for a late supper."

Ian forced a friendly smile. "Of course. With Mr. Rose probably."

"I don't believe so," the butler replied guardedly. "May I tell Mrs. Patton who called?"

Ian fished a card from his pocket. "Oh, please do. And tell her I'll be back." He flashed the man a cold smile. "With the police."

After Ian strode away from the house, he hailed a hansom at the corner and instructed the cabbie to drive him to Douglas Rose's Broad Street mansion. The ride gave him the time to realize that he couldn't simply turn Gareth in to the authorities on circumstantial evidence—Sybil and Walter would no doubt "disappear" before the case came to trial.

And how could he drag the Rose family name through the mud again, knowing it would devastate Margaret and probably kill her father? He had to discuss it with Margaret in private, but first he had to reassure himself she was safe from her brother and Lucy Patton.

The mansion looked unoccupied, the drapes drawn, when he arrived to knock at the front door. Then, after a brief deliberation, he walked around the high-walled path to the servants' entrance and was surprised when Lilian Rose Doyle answered, her pale face equally astonished to find him standing there.

"Dr. MacNeill—"

"I was looking for your brother," he said hurriedly, dispensing with polite formality. "Do you think I might find him still at the bank?"

She raised a lace handkerchief to her reddened nose. "He isn't in Aberdeen at all. No one is. Father took another attack and asked to go home to die."

"Home?" he said, not at all reassured by the news Gareth had not gone to Dundee.

"To Meirneal House—that horrid place." She sniffed resentfully. "We're all supposed to abandon our busy lives and gather around him like the loving family we've never been. I was, in fact, just checking that the servants had properly closed up the house before I wrote to ask Margaret to come to Meirneal. She won't, of course, but Father insisted."

Ian waited to speak again until she'd blown her nose. "But Gareth *is* with your father? There's no chance he'd leave your dad at a time like this? I know he's a devoted son."

"Devoted or disturbed, I can't decide which," Lilian answered gravely, then paused, her thin voice almost inaudible in the hissing of the gaslight behind them. "Ever since he took up with his 'mystery' woman, he's become so secretive and moody, I scarcely know him."

She hesitated, then impulsively took Ian's arm and drew him into the large kitchen's warming-room, leading him across the brick floor to a rectangular canvas-draped object propped against the unlit fire.

"Look for yourself," she said, drawing the canvas down to reveal an oil-painting. "I found this in Gareth's studio, and the paint is still fresh."

Ian stared, his breathing suspended, at the painting of the accident on Loch Meirneal, Margaret's face twisted in horror as she stared at the white-cloaked figure on the shore. The waters of the loch seethed with hideous water horses, creatures with faces like gargoyles, their pointed teeth bared in a cannibalistic frenzy as they dragged Susan and Alan Rose under.

"Jesus," Ian whispered.

"Why are you here anyway, Dr. MacNeill?" Lilian asked, deliberately not looking at the painting. "It has to concern Margaret."

"I'm afraid Gareth and his lady friend have been trying to hurt her," he explained with a patience that belied the frantic anxiety he felt. "Thank God I left her in Mormedie with my sister."

"Mormedie?" Lilian said in surprise. "But that's only a two-hour ride from Meirneal, faster if one knows the loch path and hills."

Ian started back toward the door. "You know Gareth perhaps better than anyone. Is he capable of hurting your sister?"

"I don't think so." She paused. "But like Margaret, Gareth has been haunted his entire life by that accident, and in all honesty, I can't say what my brother is capable of anymore."

Her gaze drifted down to the disturbing painting. "The answer is there," she said to herself. "The secret, the horror, perhaps even the healing. The answer is at Meirneal."

Ian bounded up the stairs of the Union Square town house to his bedroom, glad that he hadn't bothered to unpack earlier. With luck Donald could still drive him to catch the Highland Fly to Glendrummy and then he'd hire a horse to Mormedie.

He could stop by his father's house on the way and briefly explain what had happened.

The chambermaid gave a start as they almost collided on the landing. She was Bridget's younger sister, both girls now worked for his mother, and they took turns once a week at airing out the town house.

"Good gracious, sir," she exclaimed. "I nearly knocked yer puir wife down in this verra spot just a few moments ago when I was bringing up fresh linens."

Ian frowned. "My wife?"

The girl put a hand over her mouth. "Perhaps it was to be a surprise. She came in all quiet-like, and went upstairs with instructions I was to leave a pot of tea outside the door—"

Ian looked up at the closed door, realizing Margaret must have left Mormedie early last night to have made it to Aberdeen by now. It seemed all rather odd, her traveling at night with the baby in a public coach.

"She didn't want me to wake the bairn," the girl added in a loud whisper.

"The baby's ill?" Ian asked quickly, taking another step up.

"I don't think so, Doctor. Bundled up peacefully in her mother's arms by the look, but yer wife mentioned she wasn't feeling well and wanted nothing more than a cup of chamomile tea."

Ian grinned. Margaret and her herbal tea which tasted like hay. Well, nothing could be too terribly wrong, or perhaps she'd missed him as much as he had her. The thought warmed him, Margaret in an amorous mood waiting in their comfortable bed.

"You'll leave the tea in the hall?" he asked the maid, already three steps above her.

"Your wife's just taken it in, sir. Shall I bring you up a cup—"

But Ian didn't acknowledge her, taking the remaining stairs two at a time to reach the room. He and Margaret had parted rather abruptly, and he was anxious to take her back under his protection until Lucy Patton had been dealt with.

He reached the hall, glancing at the nursery door and deciding he wouldn't disturb his daughter. It would be nice if he and Margaret could enjoy an intimate hour alone first.

Then just as he approached his own room, the light burning in the brass wall sconce flickered, and a cold draught swirled around him.

The oil painting on the wall of a Highland hunting scene began to shake.

The floorboards behind him creaked.

Don't go in there, Ian. Do not go into that room.

He turned slowly and stared down the hall. Had he imagined that distant, disembodied voice?

The long-case clock on the landing began to chime. One. Two. Three. Seven, eleven times, and Ian knew it wasn't quite six o'clock.

He felt a chill go over the flesh of his forearms. There was nothing at the end of the hall except a peculiar shifting outline of smoke that was rapidly dissipating as he stared in disbelief.

The smell of pipe tobacco drifted toward him.

He glanced down at the landing. The girl was gone. And that disembodied voice had held a familiar, masculine ring. . . .

I'm getting as bad as Margaret, he reflected with a grin. Fairy lights and floating voices.

He turned around, putting his hand on the doorknob. A sudden coldness clutched him, the voice so faraway, so indistinct that he could barely make out its warning.

Mistake.

No, no, Ian.

Don't go in.

DON'T—

He twisted the knob.

GO—

Ian opened the door, raising his brow at the extravagant

number of rose-scented candles burning on the dressing-table, his wife's black French lace peignoir draped provocatively over the rosewood screen, the faint rustling as she removed her clothes.

It was a scene set for seduction, and Ian was definitely in a mood to be seduced. Lucy and Gareth could wait another hour now that Ian's mind was free from worry about Margaret and the baby.

"This is a very nice surprise," he said to the figure moving behind the screen.

She tossed a stocking up over the screen, and he caught it, grinning. *"Very* nice. And you're wearing perfume, too."

The bedclothes were turned down invitingly, he noticed, working off his own cravat and jacket, wondering whether he should tell Margaret what he'd learned or wait until they'd relaxed.

"You're quiet," he observed, sitting down on the bed to pull off his boots. "I guess the journey was pretty tiring, alone with the baby—"

He broke off, a flash of movement past the dressing-table mirror registering in his peripheral vision. Something wrong. A veiled hat on the chair. Fair hair in the candlelight, a short, angular body that was not his wife's—

She stopped at the foot of the bed, a shadow behind the curtains, whispering, "The past returns to haunt you. This is for my husband, you bastard."

He twisted around as Lucy threw herself at him, the bed curtains shorn from their rings with the weight of her fall, covering their bodies.

He flung her off him, saw the glint of an upraised surgeon's scalpel in her hand, Lucy's delicate face like a demon's, lips pulled back over her teeth, eyes burning in the candlelit shadows.

She came at him again.

He grunted and rolled to the other side of the bed, but she

was clinging to him like a wildcat, and he felt something warm dripping down his back before the deep burning pain in his shoulder told him she'd managed to stab him. He swore, throwing off her hand as she forced a sponge to his mouth and nose.

Chloroform. He ripped the sponge from Lucy's hand, amazed at her strength, but she had taken him by surprise long enough to weaken his reflexes. They struggled and he hit her in the chest, the impact sending her reeling back against the bedpost. Incredibly she did not stop, her arm lowering again, the scalpel this time slicing across Ian's chest.

And laughing wildly, she pressed the sponge back to his face.

He lunged upward, the movement uncoordinated, and caught the pearl-buttoned cuff on the peignoir instead of her arm.

Lucy stared down at him and slid to the floor, and Ian, suddenly feeling too faint to pursue her, realized she knew anatomy well enough to let him bleed to death in his own bed. He grabbed a pillow and pressed it to his chest, trying to stanch the flow of blood.

"Your wife next," Lucy whispered, wiping the scalpel across Margaret's peignoir. She began to undress before him, reaching behind the screen for her own black mourning dress. She went to the dressing table to brush her hair, Ian's blood staining the blond ends.

He groaned and crawled to the end of the bed, putting his feet to the floor. His head reeled dangerously as if disconnected from his damaged body. The effects of the chloroform, the loss of blood, made him overestimate his strength and power of perception. Before he could take three steps toward Lucy, he stumbled over a stool he hadn't even seen.

And Lucy had reached the door in her black mourning dress, her crazy laughter floating above his head. "Your wife next," she promised, as he sank to his knees and tried to crawl toward her. "Your pretty young wife."

Fifty-nine

Mrs. Blodwen Jones had come back to the Union Square townhouse to leave a message for Dr. and Mrs. MacNeill. She had had a very frightening experience, almost dying alone in that secluded country inn, and after a long discussion with the innkeeper and his cook, she'd come to the conclusion that she hadn't been poisoned by bad food at all but by bad people.

She intended to have a serious talk with Donald, the driver, to ask him to take an urgent message to Dr. and Mrs. MacNeill in Taynaross, warning them about the Armstrongs. Mrs. Jones would have made the journey herself, but she was still weak from the food poisoning that had nearly killed her.

She'd stopped to chat on the corner with the chimney sweep, then let herself in through the MacNeills' garden gate. But after only three brisk steps, she froze beneath the trellis, turning slowly as a man's voice floated out from nowhere.

Help me!

Shivers danced over her skin. "Who is it?" she whispered. "Is that you, Cousin Alex?"

The leaves that were scattered along the flagstone path rose in a flurry at her feet, although there was no breeze that evening. Cousin Alex had been dead two years now, but Mrs. Jones swore he spoke to her every so often.

Go upstairs to my brother!

No, *that* wasn't Alex. Still, Mrs. Jones hadn't the slightest doubt that she was in communication with a troubled spirit. "Show yourself to me," she said boldly.

And when he did, literally materializing out of the gloaming shadows to stand before her, Blodwen gasped and dropped her bag to the ground.

She knew with every fiber of her fiercely beating heart that the nice-looking young man in tweed knickerbockers was a ghost. Why, Lord help her, she could see right through him!

"What do you want me to do?" she asked, deliciously terrified that this dramatic apparition had chosen *her,* of all people, to ask for human assistance.

"Help me. My brother is upstairs bleeding to death."

"Dr. MacNeill?"

"Yes."

She looked up in bewilderment at the doctor's bedroom window, candles blazing behind the tightly drawn curtains like a kitchen fire.

"Oh, dear God," she said, putting her hand to her mouth.

The ghost took her arm, tugging her toward the house. "Please, madam. Hurry before he dies."

"Oh, yes," she said, rising to the call. "Oh, yes!" And Mrs. Jones broke into a heroic run on her sensible square-toed shoes.

The ghost flashed her an engaging grin before he vanished into the walls of the house. "Thank you, madam! I knew the moment I saw you, I could depend on you."

She squared her narrow shoulders, beaming at the compliment. "Oh, of course, sir," she whispered. "Haven't I always believed?"

Sixty

Margaret wandered deeper into the little hazel copse that surrounded Shona and Graeme Kidd's country home. She'd left Mairi in the house with Ellie for her morning nap so she could gather some purslane and dandelion for the supper salad tonight. But she'd been too preoccupied to bother, so concerned about Ian that she couldn't tell a turnip from a toadstool.

She couldn't stand it here another day not knowing what had happened to him. She was so afraid something was wrong, and she ached to hear him teasing her again, telling her all her worries and superstitious fears had been wasted.

He had left on Tuesday morning, and today was Friday.

Something had happened to him. She felt it in every breath she took.

She bit her lip, shaking off the feeling, and stared down at the clump of tansy growing around a boulder.

"Andrew, watch over him," she whispered.

A shadow fell in front of her, and she looked up, surprised delight spreading across her face. "Gareth! Oh, how ever did you find me?"

He grinned, enjoying her exuberant hug, then glanced down at the plants she'd been studying.

"Talking to weeds now, are you?" His smile faded. "Or is it fairies again?"

"I'm hunting for edible herbs, actually. How *did* you find me?"

"I went to Taynaross, and the head groom there said you were staying with Mr. and Mrs. Kidd of Mormedie. I remembered that name from the bank—Graeme Kidd took out a loan a few months ago and put up the estate as collateral. And so—I found you."

Margaret thought there was something sad and haunted in her brother's eyes. "You came here because Father's dead, didn't you?" she asked quietly, her chest aching with a sense of loss that took her by surprise.

"Not yet." Gareth stared past her into the woods. "But he does want to see you. He wants the whole family gathered around him at Meirneal House when he dies. He's asked to be buried next to Mother."

"No." Margaret's reaction was instantaneous, emotional. "I feel badly for him, and I'll go anywhere but there. It isn't fair of him to ask it of me, Gareth. He's such a selfish man."

She began to walk back toward the house, its solid gray a beacon between the skeletal autumn trees.

"You haven't made your peace with the past," he said behind her. "None of us have."

She turned slowly. "I've made a new life for myself. That's peace enough for me."

He walked forward to grip her hand. His eyes glowed with an intensity that made Margaret afraid. "I want you to know exactly what happened at Loch Meirneal. This is for both of us."

"I was there," she cried. "I know what happened."

"You don't," he said quietly. "And the truth is at Meirneal. Come with me, Margaret. You'll be back here before midnight."

She stared at him. "I don't know you. You're a stranger to me suddenly."

"Trust me." He squeezed her hand. "Trust me, and you'll finally be set free."

It was the first time in almost thirteen years that Margaret had looked down at the loch. The wrenching sadness, the sense of loss, returned with such force that she realized she had never emotionally healed at all from the accident, but had kept the pain locked inside. Standing on the castle path where she and Gareth had dismounted, she couldn't move, tears falling slowly down her face onto her cloak.

"Why did you bring me back here?" she asked heavily.

Gareth stared in silence at the pair of swans gliding across the loch to Margaret's fairy island. In his mind he saw his young sister laughing, her beautiful expressive eyes filled with the wonder of childhood things.

"This is the last thing I'll ever ask of you," he said after the swans had reached the island.

They stared at each other. Then as they had so often done as children, they began to run toward the castle, their refuge, place of fiendish games and make-believe, clambering up the slope where heather still refused to grow. Pounding across the ancient drawbridge, over the stagnant water of the moat, and then into the great hall where a hundred cobwebs embraced them, trembling in the musty air.

"Upstairs," Gareth ordered, taking Margaret's hand. "To Lord and Lady Forbes's bedchamber."

"And then no more secrets, Gareth?" she asked, reluctantly allowing him to drag her up the winding stairwell.

"No more secrets," he promised.

His voice had changed, a subtle signal that set off disturbing impulses in Margaret's mind. But Gareth was her brother. How could she be afraid of him?

And yet she was afraid.

"It hasn't changed much," she whispered several moments

later, staring down at the child's wooden bow on the bedchamber floor.

There was an old brass-bound sea chest in a corner of the room. Gareth opened it while Margaret wandered past a wall of moldering tapestries and gazed out the window onto the walkway.

"Gareth," she said, unconsciously lowering her voice, "I thought I heard something in the bailey."

"It's the merlins," he said, his voice sounding muffled. "They've taken over the place. Turn around very slowly now, Margaret, and don't be afraid. . . ."

The banshee.

She pressed back instinctively against the window embrasure to escape him, a white-cloaked figure approaching her with one hand outstretched in an invitation to death.

Her mouth went dry. "You," she said in disbelief. "It was *you* that day."

He wrenched off the white silk hood. "Yes, dammit, it was me. I'm your banshee, the vision from hell you saw that day."

Margaret shook her head, unable to speak.

Gareth whirled and returned to the chest, drawing from it the cork lifebelt that had been missing from the boat that morning. "I took this from the boat in a childish sulk because I didn't want you to go that day. I wanted to play Turkish pirates, and I was angry because you chose to row to your silly island instead."

"The robes," she said dully. "Not a banshee, oh, but a pirate."

"I wasn't trying to frighten you, I swear it. I just decided I'd pretend to attack your boat from the shore and plunder it for treasure. It—it was a game."

"But you never told me—" Her eyes were dark with anger and bewilderment. "You let me live thirteen years believing I was responsible for the accident, that—that I'd even seen a banshee! You've no idea the effect it had on my life. Oh, God, Gareth, why?"

He stared down at the belt, shaking his head slowly, struggling to explain the personal demons he had lived with himself. "You never understood," he said in a distant voice. "It was my fault they drowned."

She stared at him, caught between pity and incredible anger. "Make me understand then."

"Alan recognized me," he said quietly. "He'd seen me putting on the pirate costume earlier that morning, and he'd asked to play with me. He leaned over the boat because he recognized me in the trees. You see, I—I'd taught him a secret little hand signal, and—and . . . he waved his fishing pole at me in answer. That was how he fell."

The ensuing silence, the coldness of the castle bedchamber was so profound, it seemed to reach into Margaret's soul. Only the sound of something moving from deep within the castle roused her from her dark memories of that morning.

She shivered, rubbing her arms. "What was that noise?"

Gareth shrugged, beyond caring. "The wind blowing through the hall, a hare, a badger. What does it matter?"

Slowly Margaret approached him. "All those years, you've lived with the burden of that secret, with the same punishing guilt that I—"

"That wasn't all." He raised his ravaged face to hers. "I watched them drown, Margaret, and I did nothing."

"What could you have done from the shore?"

"I could have tried to save them," he said bitterly. "I was older, a stronger swimmer than you, and I could have possibly saved Mother if not Alan." His voice was remote, exhausted with the emotional strain he had finally begun to release. "I never tried, you see, and that's the difference between you and me. I was paralyzed with fear that morning, and I've lived my life in fear ever since."

Margaret didn't know what to say to console him when she

was so upset herself, her mind could barely function. More than anything she longed for Ian, for his logic and strength. He would help her put this thing into perspective.

"I need time to think about this," she said slowly. "Gareth—does Father know?"

"Don't you understand anything, Margaret?" he cried. "If I'd told Dad, he would have hated me. You were his favorite, and it killed him inside to send you away because he couldn't make himself stop loving you, and—and you always were so much like Mother."

Margaret leaned her head back against the wall and stared up at the lofty ceiling, absorbing his words like physical blows.

"I was relieved when you left for Maryhead," he admitted, not looking at her. "As long as you were far away, there was no chance Dad could learn what really happened."

She looked down slowly, her face shocked. "It was you who hired the Armstrongs—"

"No." But the guilt, the shame and confusion in his eyes was unmistakable.

"Yes," she said slowly, her mind finally grasping the horrible truth. "You who gave them the newspaper clipping about me, the idea of making Alan appear to me on the hill." She began to edge toward the door, so cold, so sick inside she was shivering. "You were so desperate to keep me away from Father, you didn't care if I, if my husband thought I was losing my mind."

He stood shaking his head, the truth etched on his face.

She turned to look out the window over the darkening loch, overwhelmed by what Gareth had told her. "No banshees, no curses," she murmured. "No magic at all. Just a frightened young boy and girl, an accident . . ."

She whirled, hating and pitying him at once. "Why, Gareth? Why? Why did you do this to me—for my portion of Father's inheritance?"

Stricken, he was unable to meet her eyes. "No. I never cared about the money. It was him. I've tried my entire life to please him. And he'll die hating me now."

"He might have forgiven you!"

"Can't you imagine his reaction if he'd learned *I* was the one responsible for the accident—"

"But you weren't," she whispered.

"He blamed you, didn't he? And I let him. If he'd ever found out that it was *me* all along . . . I needed his love, Margaret. I—I know it wasn't natural, but I wanted him to love me so badly . . ."

"The truth might have brought us back together as a family!"

He laughed bitterly. "You know better."

"After today, I'm very afraid I don't know anything."

"There's more," he said, his eyes pleading.

"No. I don't want to hear—" She broke off as she glanced inadvertently at the dark metallic object lying on the floor by the sea chest. It was a gun. She looked up once at the door, gauging the distance, the time it would take to make it safely outside.

He would kill her to keep her silent.

Her own brother would murder her to keep a young boy's shameful secret.

She heard his voice, a low drone of words, over the rush of blood in her ears. She tried to edge from the window to the door. Her legs would not move.

"I met a woman a year ago, and fell in love for the first time in my life," Gareth was quietly explaining, and Margaret listened without wanting to, fear spreading through her system like a paralyzing poison. "She was a widow, and she hated your husband with a passion that I did not at first understand was a sign of her mental derangement."

"Lucy Patton," Margaret said in slow-dawning horror. "Lucinda—"

"—Menzies Patton. Yes."

He paused and caught Margaret staring at the gun.

"I—I want to go now, Gareth."

"She praised my paintings," he continued as if Margaret hadn't spoken, pacing before the chest. "She'd been following your husband's every move, determined to destroy any chance for success or personal happiness he might find. She hired the Armstrongs—"

He bent unexpectedly and picked up the pistol, a sad reminiscent smile on his lips. "We threatened to hang Lilian's doll in this room, do you remember?" He glanced up at the hammer-beam rafter. "Do you suppose the pulley we rigged with the old skeleton would still work if we tried it?"

It was dark outside. The fact registered on Margaret's numb mind, still struggling to digest, to understand what he had told her. She had to find Ian, warn him, protect Mairi. Down the endless spiral staircase, across the drawbridge, back on the lonely country road to Shona's house.

She had to ride past Loch Meirneal, away from the shadows that had followed her for too long.

Gareth cocked the pistol.

"I'm sorry, Margaret," he said, his light hair falling across his forehead. "I never wanted to hurt you. The truth is that like Father, I always loved you best."

She watched him raise the pistol and she went rigid, her heart beating wildly in her chest.

"Go away," he said. "Hurry up. Get out."

She moved toward the door in confusion, thinking, No, he wouldn't hurt me, he's my brother. He wouldn't hurt me, and she glanced back involuntarily, just in time to see him raise the gun to his mouth.

"No, Gareth." She put her hands to her face, shaking her head, the thought entering her mind that they had played out so many childhood dramas in this very room. Murders and suicides. *Oh, God, please don't let this happen.*

He lowered the gun slightly, his hand shaking. "I don't want you to see. It's the only way. I don't want Father to know."

Margaret held out her hand. "You said you didn't want to hurt me."

"Go away . . ."

"You said—"

The door swung slowly open, and Gareth's eyes widened in shock. "Oh, no," he said. "Oh, no. Not you, not you. Why have you come here?"

Sixty-one

Margaret turned her head, staring in disbelief at her father's thin, anguished face. "Oh, Dad," she said, her voice breaking in boundless relief.

Douglas Rose walked slowly into the room, his alert gray eyes moving from his daughter to his son.

"Put down the gun, Gareth," he said softly.

Gareth did, a sound of defeat and despair breaking in his throat. "I never wanted you to know. Goddamnit, why did you have to come?"

Douglas glanced out the window at the dark peaceful loch. "I've known the truth for almost a year now. The old shepherd, Simon MacTear, told me on his deathbed that he'd seen you at the loch that day in your costume. He encouraged the rumors of a banshee because he didn't want any blame to fall on your young shoulders."

Gareth was silent, his eyes squeezed shut as his father spoke.

"But you shouldered the blame anyway, didn't you?" Douglas continued quietly. "You and Margaret took the blame for an accident that neither of you could have prevented. And I let you."

Gareth turned to the wall, silent sobs shaking his body as a lifetime of pain broke inside him. "It's all right now, Gareth," Margaret said as she came up behind him. Her own eyes filled with tears. "He understands, don't you, Dad?"

Douglas stared at his two children, allowing them the close-

ness, the healing, that his emotional shortcomings had interrupted years ago. His face a mask of suffering, he said softly,
"I was the one who broke the heart of this family. You were
too small to understand, and I failed you. I failed Susan's memory."

Margaret turned slowly to look at him, the anguish in her
eyes giving way to a desperate hope. "Then mend us now.
Before it's too late."

He shook his head, suddenly a frightened, frail, old man.
"Tell me how."

Margaret moved away from her brother, the shock of what
he had told her finally beginning to sink in. "Start with
Gareth," she said quietly, pulling her cloak around her.

Her father nodded, studying her pale face in concern. "And
you, Margaret? Are you so strong or so detached from our
family that you need nothing from it? Or from me?"

She frowned. "What I need more than anything is time to
sort everything out. But for now, I'll leave that to you and
Gareth. I'm very worried about my own family—"

She glanced at Gareth, his face exhausted as he slowly removed the white robes that had played such an ugly part in
their lives. "I have to get back to Mormedie and then to Aberdeen," she said, anxiety sharp in her voice. "I'm very afraid
that the woman Gareth was seeing will try to hurt Ian."

Gareth came up beside them, his thin face haggard and re-
solved, but reflecting a sense of peace that Margaret had not
seen on it since before the accident. "I'm going to Aberdeen
to take care of Lucy," he said.

"My carriage, the driver and footmen, are at your disposal,"
Douglas offered, placing his hand on his son's shoulder.

Gareth shook his head. "I'll be faster on horseback, but you
can take Margaret back to Mormedie." He glanced at Margaret,
his voice determined. "I'll make this up to you. I'll do everything I can to protect your husband. Stay with the baby at
Mormedie."

Her voice broke. "If it's not too late."

Douglas took her hand, warming her ice-cold fingers with a reassuring squeeze. "We're wasting time, and I can't wait to meet my granddaughter."

Margaret looked uncertain. "Should you not go home and rest after only recently having another attack?"

His smile was sad and gentle. "If I'm going to die soon anyway, then let it be surrounded by the people I love, helping them, not in a house full of servants."

Margaret was too anxious about Ian and Mairi to disagree, and she hugged her father gratefully with all the love for him that had too long lain dormant.

"Let's go," she said, tears in her voice. "I'm really worried about them."

But as they filed out of the dark castle bedchamber, she hesitated a moment at the door, glancing back once into the shadows of the room with a wistful smile. As a child she had believed the stories about the castle being haunted, the restless ghosts of Lord and Lady Forbes inhabiting the lonely halls.

"Goodbye forever," she softly whispered. "May we all find peace."

Gareth rode into Aberdeen while Margaret and her father took the carriage along the river road to Mormedie. "Relax," Douglas instructed her repeatedly throughout the hurried ride. "They're fine, I know it."

She nodded numbly, her hands twisting in her lap, and stared out the window at the dark blue-green pines that blurred before her troubled gaze. "As soon as I make sure Mairi is safe, I'm going to have your driver take me directly to Aberdeen to find Ian."

Douglas smiled. "He must be a very special man to have earned such concern."

"Oh, he is." Despite her anxiety, Margaret couldn't help a

smile when she thought of the traits that composed her husband's character. "He's brave and brilliant and amusing and"—her voice caught—"he loves me very much."

"Good Lord, Margaret, why should that surprise you?"

She looked into her father's concerned eyes, her answer breaking his heart. "Because until recently, I never really found much reason to love myself."

"And that has changed?" Douglas asked, deeply worried.

Margaret drew in a breath. "I'm learning to stop finding fault with myself. I've had so many loving people in my life to help me—Ian, Mairi, Agnes, Stephen."

Douglas turned his face to the window, trying to hide the raw emotions that ravaged him. "So much time lost. So many years wasted."

Sixty-two

The Mormedie estate was in such confusion when she and Douglas arrived—servants posted in the drive, dogs running about the estate barking—that Margaret knew something was wrong, barely waiting for the carriage to stop before she alighted. The front doors to the manor house flew open, and Shona Kidd hurried down the steps toward Margaret, her face visibly drawn even in the darkness.

"What is it?" Margaret demanded, breaking into a clumsy run to meet her clearly distraught sister-in-law. "Mairi—no. It's Ian, isn't it? What happened? *Where is he?*"

Shona caught Margaret's arm as she rushed by. "He's in the hallway with Father. He's been hurt, Margaret, but he was determined to go back out after you—"

The words dimly penetrated Margaret's mind, her fear so intense the pounding of her own blood in her ears was deafening. It seemed to take forever to climb the stone porch steps, to push through the door to the entrance hall.

He's been hurt. Oh, God, it must be bad if Colin was here, too.

There were several people, too many people obstructing her view—Colin, Graeme and his children, a maidservant nervously holding a silver basin. They parted at Margaret's entrance, allowing her and Ian to see each other from across the wooden bench where he sat awkwardly propped up against the wall.

Their gazes met, gripping together in a relief that brought a sob to Margaret's throat. Then in the next instant she saw the thick padding of bandage beneath the shoulder of his greatcoat.

He rose swiftly to greet her, suppressing the shock of pain in his shoulder. "Oh, thank God," he whispered, closing his eyes briefly to compose himself.

In another second, they were in each other's arms. Together, safe, a family reunited.

"Graeme and I were going to ride to Meirneal to find you," he said, his voice breaking. "I didn't know the way myself— Oh, God, Margaret, are you all right?"

She pulled back slightly, looking him over with an anxious frown. "I'm fine, but obviously you're not. What happened to your shoulder? Was it Walter?"

"No. It was Lucy and a surgeon's scalpel." At the horror in her eyes, he pulled her back toward him, burying his face in her hair. "I *never* want to relive the anxiety I felt when I arrived here and found you had gone with your brother."

Margaret closed her eyes for a moment, feeling physically ill at how close she'd come to losing him. "How did you possibly make it here with a stab wound?"

He smiled grimly. "Morphine, Mrs. Jones and my father, and an understanding coachman."

"Where is Lucy now?" she asked quietly, almost swaying on her feet as the delayed reaction of the day's events took hold.

Ian hesitated, glancing at his father. Then Colin squeezed her arm, guiding her and Ian back to the bench before he gestured the others out of the hall. When Ian finally spoke, his voice was so deep-timbered with fatigue and pain Margaret had to lean forward to hear him.

"I only know what I was told," he said. "After Lucy left me in the town house to bleed to death, she apparently walked out into the street—in front of an omnibus. The driver couldn't stop in time."

"She committed suicide?"

Ian touched his bandaged shoulder, staring past Margaret

toward the door. "I don't know. The driver was very upset, understandably. According to Donald, he said that Lucy had been trying to get away from a man standing on the town-house steps."

Their eyes met. "Who was he?" Margaret asked quietly.

"No one knows. But the driver said he was wearing a hunt-ing cap and tweed knickerbockers—"

"Oh!" Margaret exclaimed, her eyes shining in gratitude. "He kept his promise, after all."

And for once, Ian did not make fun of his wife's allusion to mystical intervention, or even ask what she was talking about.

He was very afraid he knew.

While Margaret nursed and bathed Mairi, Ian examined Douglas and put him to bed upstairs, under protest in one of Shona's unused rooms. Everyone in the house wanted to know exactly what had happened; even the maids lingered in the doorway during a late-night supper of chicken barley soup and cheese scones to hear how Ian had been stabbed and then saved by a cook—one of their own, a domestic heroine.

"Let's sit outside in the garden for a few minutes," Ian sug-gested quietly to Margaret over their sherry.

She looked at him across the table, her heart constricting with love and concern. During that interminable journey from Meirneal, she'd been convinced her worst fear would be real-ized, that she would lose him, and her mind had been para-lyzed, the thought too agonizing to face. Only now could she admit to herself that she had been poised on the edge of the blackest abyss imaginable. She thanked God with all her heart that her husband and child were safe.

She reached across the table to cover his hand with hers. "You said you'd lost a lot of blood yesterday. After everything that's happened, I think I'd rather you rested. We'll talk tomorrow."

"I slept in the coach almost the entire way." He gave her a

playful grin. "And your Mrs. Jones trussed me up like a Christmas goose and made me drink some perfectly godawful potion. Margaret, the taste of it brought back some very tender memories of your nursing me on Maryhead."

Oh, it hurt, to love someone as much as she did Ian and realize how close she had come to losing him. "Fifteen minutes only," she murmured, averting her head so he couldn't see the tears in her eyes.

They didn't talk at first when they went out into Shona's sloping unwalled garden, the bedraggled rose bushes like ghosts of their summer glory. The hazel wood beyond was hazy with wood smoke, and dogs barked in distant farmyards.

They sat on a mossy stone bench, holding hands. "Why is it that everything significant in my life seems to happen in autumn?" Margaret asked, venting a sigh. "Losing my mother and Alan, meeting you in Aberdeen, the shipwreck, Mairi's birth, and then this, today?"

He didn't answer. As a doctor, he knew how clinically close to death he had come earlier, and he wasn't afraid to die, but he wanted to take care of Margaret and Mairi. He would have come back from the grave to protect them, if such a thing were possible. And he was profoundly grateful for the chance to start their lives over, finally free of the past.

"Someone must have been watching over us," he reflected aloud.

Margaret laid her head lightly on his good shoulder, smiling to herself. "A guardian angel, perhaps?"

He smiled reluctantly. "Perhaps. By the way, your father is very concerned about Gareth's mental state. He's afraid your brother isn't emotionally prepared to plunge back into his work at the bank."

"I know a place where he can go to heal," Margaret said softly.

"Maryhead?"

"Yes." She rose from the bench, holding out her hands. "Fifteen minutes. Be a good patient, Doctor, and let me tuck you into bed."

"Give me a little while by myself."

She looked at him with a quizzical expression. Then she leaned down and kissed his craggy, beloved face. "Hurry then," she whispered. "I can't bear to have you out of my sight for long."

He watched her as she ran back to the house, gratitude and love gripping his heart so tightly that it seemed to stop. And when it resumed beating, he got up from the bench and slowly walked to the edge of the garden.

A few yards away an old rope-and-cradle bridge spanned a rocky burn, and as Ian stared a man's figure slowly materialized before his eyes.

Andrew.

You've had me very worried, Ian, you and your enchanting wife.

That was you yesterday at the town house, the picture-banging and broken clock?

He could sense Andrew's amusement.

Aye. I've tried so hard to get through that thick head of yours, Ian. I had to resort to that embarrassing display. . . .

Silence then. The soothing murmur of the burn over smooth brown pebbles.

I have to go now, Ian. Be kind to Jean and my son.

Oh, God, Andrew. Of course.

Andrew's image began to fade like the smoke of an extinguished candle.

I'm sorry, Ian . . . for everything.

So am I.

I love you, you big ugly genius.

"Andrew, wait!" Ian said, hurrying toward the bridge just as the figure vanished.

"I love you, too," he said quietly, staring into the shadows that still vibrated with his brother's presence. "Wherever you are, remember that."

Sixty-three

Ian peeled the medical journal from Margaret's hands and crawled into bed beside her, his naked body still damp from the bath he had just taken.

"Studying for your medical degree, Mrs. MacNeill?" he teased her, bending his head to kiss her, his right hand reaching up to lower the bedside lamp.

"Afraid of a little competition, Doctor?" she murmured against his mouth.

He chuckled, but in a matter of moments, his amusement deepened into urgent desire, as Margaret untied her wrapper and moved against him, her hands stroking first his shoulder, then his hips, arousing him so effortlessly it was almost embarrassing.

With a warm midsummer evening breeze wafting in from the opened windows, they made slow delicious love, Ian kissing his wife's throat, her soft breasts and belly, prolonging the intimate pleasures of foreplay. And he wondered, as he did every night, what he had done in his life to deserve so much happiness that it overflowed his heart.

As he raised himself above her, Margaret reached up and touched his cheek, her breath caught in her throat. She could not see his face in the darkness, but his blue eyes were like flames, burning, intense. "I read your name in the journal— your research was praised by several esteemed professors," she said softly.

"Old news," Ian murmured, glancing briefly toward the window. "There are countless other doctors making greater discoveries than I ever dreamed."

She lowered her hand. "Do you miss it at all? The striving, the recognition?"

He glanced down and smiled, easing slowly into the soft depths of her body. "Not at all," he whispered, his face suddenly taut, his mouth seeking hers in a deep kiss.

And Margaret twined her arms around his shoulders, whispering, "I have a secret," as their bodies joined, inseparable, bound by love and passion and the sense of completion they only found together. She drew him deeper inside, her legs locked around his thrusting hips, her face pressed to his throat.

The breeze stirred the curtains, bringing the resinous fragrance of pine into the room. The great iron bed creaked and Margaret giggled, Ian swearing under his breath that he was going to throw the damned thing out the window. Husband and wife, father and mother, friends and lovers. They had never lost the ability to laugh even at the most intimate of moments.

And over the past few peaceful months they had even worked together, the doctor and the folk healer, a strange marriage if ever there was one. But if a certain patient in the village found Dr. MacNeill's harsh face a little intimidating, his hypodermics and inhalation devices "rare queer," there was always his lovely wife waiting in the background, with her basket of traditional herbal cures, and her knowledge of the fairies and the spirits, their devious ways.

The marriage of medicine to faith, of Margaret Rose to Ian MacNeill, was a happy one.

Ian stirred, brushing Margaret's hair back from her sweetly flushed face. She was fast asleep, and though it was late, he wanted to stay up a while and write in his journal, neglected more and more as his country practice grew.

He kissed Margaret and covered her with the quilt, whispering, "I know your secret, little mother. A Hogmanay baby."

He put on his comfortable tartan robe and lit a candle, sitting at the old cherrywood writing desk by the window. From where he sat he could gaze out into the misty woods of Taynaross.

No more secrets? He didn't count on it.

Still, life was sweet.

Another child on the way. Douglas Rose defying all the doctors to see another birthday. Gareth making a name for himself in artistic circles with his watercolors of a remote Scottish island.

He picked up his pen, but before he could begin to write, he noticed on his desk the book of Far Eastern philosophy that had been a gift from Stephen Rose. Ian had always meant to glance through it, but somehow had never found the time.

He opened it now to a page of Oriental wisdom, a smile slowly spreading across his face as he read.

"All things come out of joy, consist of joy, and return to joy. To prove this, a man has only to believe."

Oh, yes.

For Ian, it was surely so.

Dear Reader,

I guess it was inevitable that a shy child who walked around with her nose buried in a book would turn that passion for reading into a career. I was the pig-tailed girl who hung around the newsstand in our London suburb waiting for the next batch of "thrill-packed" schoolgirl magazines. By the time I'd grown up, my family had resigned itself to the fact that I was happier in a bookstore than just about anywhere else. Reading simply transported me to a magic world I could return to at will.

Speaking of magic . . .

I had wonderful fun exploring this fascinating subject in *A Deeper Magic*. My heroine Margaret Rose believes wholeheartedly in her charms and herbal cures. The hero, Ian Mac-Neill, a sexy traditional doctor who thinks he knows everything, is as exasperated by Margaret's thriving practice as he is enchanted by her. Rebels, outcasts, impossible dreamers. By the end of the book, these two strong-willed characters have discovered together a more powerful magic than anything they'd ever imagined.

Yes, I know there are critics who claim that romantic novels don't portray reality. But I think they've got it all wrong. Life is *meant* to be magic. I hope you enjoy reading how Margaret and Ian learn the secret to proving this.

Warmest regards!

Jillian Hunter

If you'd like to see what Jillian Hunter has waiting in the wings after *A Deeper Magic,* keep reading. *Denise Little Presents* will publish her next book, *Glenlyon's Bride,* in September, 1995. Turn the page and give it a try—I think it's wonderful. . . .

Have fun!

GLENLYON'S BRIDE

By

JILLIAN HUNTER

One

Scotland
1840

Captain Niall Glenlyon had been sitting alone in his host's darkened library for only three minutes or so when the door to the terrace began to rattle. Fortunately, he'd bolted that door to protect his privacy as soon as he had entered the room. For good measure he'd also drawn the drapes to block out the annoying glare of the bright fairy lanterns strung outside. He really hated parties.

The sash windows shook next, glass reverberating against wood.

He scowled and slowly sat forward, tossing his fresh cigar into the unlit fireplace. He'd spent most of his life in Burma and Indonesia, growing up in a jungle mission, then serving in the Queen's Native Infantry before ending up in a privately supported army. He wondered for a moment if this could be an earthquake. It seemed improbable on a brisk autumn evening in Scotland.

The door vibrated again as if a demon were demanding entry. *Dieu,* was he witnessing an attempted burglary? Or had that obnoxious newspaper journalist finally figured out where he was hiding?

The damned radical press had been on his tail for over a fortnight, hoping to sniff out a juicy scandal about the first of the infamous Glenlyon pride to return to civilization. Unfortunately, Niall's reputation, however undeserved or exaggerated, had preceded him.

Even now he cringed at the stories they'd written about him. Seducer of trembling virgins he'd never met. Harem bodyguard. Far Eastern jungle hero and dabbler in dark magic. Louisiana lumberer and priest gone bad. There was just enough truth in the assortment of fairy tales to get him into trouble. In fact, the last Niall had read, in the ludicrous fictionalized version of his life penned by the reporter who persisted in following him, he was purportedly sharing a cave in Bali with a holy man, a deposed Siamese princess, and a dragon lizard.

Well, hell. It sounded better than the social torture he was trying to escape—some pointless engagement party for an aspiring English politician and his fiancée, a young woman who was apparently too spoiled and ill-mannered to have so far bothered making an appearance in her own drawing room. Niall had a private terror of crowds and enclosed places anyway. He'd only been able to tolerate fifteen minutes of pretending he was a polite person before that reporter had arrived at the party.

An intriguing silhouette behind the drapes outside caught his attention. Rising from his comfortable armchair, he walked soundlessly to the window.

"Blast and hell!" a voice whispered on the terrace. "Some nodcock's bolted the door, and the windows are warped tight! Now what am I going to do?"

Being the nodcock in question, Niall stood back between the drapes and looked outside. The irate female had dropped to her knees to struggle with the window. Yes, she was definitely female. Grinning, he stared down at the well-rounded derrière that wriggled directly in his line of vision. The bold creature had evidently hoped to disguise her sex in a pair of baggy tartan trousers, an oversized vest, and a battered velvet bonnet.

Not a burglar. Not a press reporter. Probably just a maid-servant sneaking home from a rendezvous with a neighboring footman. His heavy black eyebrows arched in anticipation, Niall unbolted the door for her and casually returned to his chair.

Far be it from him to thwart the course of true love, or even lust for that matter. This impromptu performance would add a little spice to what promised to be an interminable evening.

The window groaned open. The little adventuress with the shapely behind poked her head through the dark brocade curtains. Apparently she was assisted by some unseen companion lurking out in the garden.

"Hurry up, Elspeth," an anxious male voice whispered. "I left the cart out in de street—"

She—Elspeth—worked half her body into the room only to freeze in apparent horror as a small collie came tearing across the terrace to bark at her rump.

Unnoticed, Niall scooted his chair back against the drapes and sat quietly to analyze this interesting turn of events.

"You idiot, Clootie!" Balancing at an awkward angle on her hipbone, Elspeth swatted her hand at the dog's ears. "It's only *me*—get your miserable hide back into the kitchen before cook hears you and I catch merry hell!"

The kitchen. A scullery maid, Niall thought as the collie reluctantly turned and trotted back to the wrought-iron railing, stopping once to look at Niall watching through the drapes.

"What happened, Elspeth?" that nervous male voice demanded from the darker reaches of the garden.

"Just a stupid old dog." The daring Elspeth had dropped into the room with a muffled *ooof,* and Niall could only hear but not see her as she fought with the drapes to squeeze herself out from between a small piece of furniture.

"Ouch, damn it! I just broke my big toe on that ridiculous rosewood whatnot."

"Rub some spit and crushed comfrey leaves on it." Her companion sounded more afraid than amorous. "I really got to go before de catch-gadjes come. You get me hanged for dis, girl."

"I didn't ask you to see me home in the first place, Samson," she said testily. She straightened and limped past Niall, muttering over her shoulder. "It's not as if I don't know the way, and George is going to kill me if anyone saw us together. Now hurry back to camp before Delilah turns up at the front door demanding to know where you are. And don't forget to give Ali Baba that bran mash."

Samson? *And* Delilah? Niall grinned into the darkness at the odd characters in this young woman's world. George, he guessed, would be her cuckolded husband—the butler or possibly another footman. The poor unsuspecting sod whose young wife sneaked around in trousers having secret trysts with a nervous young man named Samson.

Dejectedly, the woman yanked off her old bonnet and squatted to massage her toe, heedless of the heavy blond braid that fell down her back. She sighed. The sound hinted to Niall of despair that no amount of illicit adventure could lighten. Raising her head, she sniffed the air in disdain.

"Stupid men and their vile cigars. Why anyone would smoke something that smelled like powdered pig manure is beyond me."

Niall swallowed a laugh. Then just as he thought he'd finally get his first good look at the face of this lower-class Venus, she sprang to her feet with such a horrified shriek that he half rose in reaction himself.

She whirled toward the terrace door. "Oh, my God," she whispered. "My bag—Samson, you dim-witted dumpling, you forgot to give me my bag!"

She'd just wrenched the door open when Niall heard footsteps behind him in the interior hall, a key turning in the lock of the library door. Then a man's voice asked in a frantic undertone, "Elspeth, are you in there?"

Panicking at the sound of that voice, she fled out onto the

terrace, down the steps, and into the garden. Niall stood up. Staring after her, he debated how he would explain *his* presence to an angry husband and how it could be used against him, being caught in the middle of a domestic embarrassment.

He didn't exactly have a saint's reputation. Who in his right mind would believe his innocence?

Impulsively he hurried out onto the terrace. Turning down the path the errant Elspeth had chosen, he took refuge on a bench hidden behind a trellis at the end of the rose garden where he'd last seen her. The evening breeze felt refreshing, rustling the fallen leaves at his feet, and he allowed himself to relax.

A few moments later he spotted her again. Crouched behind a moonlit statue, she was tugging off her oversized trousers with one hand, rummaging through an old duffel bag on the ground with the other.

So that explained the bag's importance. It contained her clothing. Realizing she was about to change back into her normal household attire, Niall watched in unabashed fascination. He was only a man, after all, no matter what had been written about him.

Besides, he was curious to know exactly what this Elspeth and Samson had been up to.

Apparently so was her husband. Niall frowned as he noticed a well-dressed man emerge onto the terrace, his voice low and understandably upset.

"Elspeth Victoria, this is absolutely the last straw, do you hear me?"

At that moment Clootie, the old collie chose to return. Racing across the garden, he skidded to a stop and began circling the rose bushes whose straggly branches sheltered Elspeth. The man on the terrace strode to the stairs, his head cocked suspiciously at the dog's behavior. The young woman herself muttered several unrepeatable words and tried to shoo the dog away with her bonnet. It was quite a dilemma.

"Show yourself this instant, Elspeth," the pompous man on the terrace ordered, but to no avail. He only succeeded in temporarily distracting the dog.

He sounded, Niall decided, too damned imperious for a footman—definitely a butler. Elspeth could be the pastry cook, perhaps some temperamental Parisian-trained upstart from the slums whose culinary talents would play a crucial part in tonight's supper party. The passionate creature must have really thrown the household into a uproar.

"I can't believe you're doing this to me, Elspeth." The man on the terrace was pacing now, and Niall began to think he looked disturbingly familiar. "Everyone is waiting for you to perform."

To perform? A performing pastry cook? Niall frowned, perplexed that he'd failed to solve this preposterous mystery. And even though as a rule he disapproved of infidelity, he felt an inexplicable empathy for this misguided young woman and her predicament.

He'd been forced to hide a few times himself in his life. Not in a town garden with a toothless house dog at his heels, it was true. But he *had* run for cover in sweating rain forests with poisonous thorns ripping the rags from his back and native man-traps making every step a life-or-death calculation. He'd never forgotten the black terror of those days. The remembered fear of being caught and tortured rippled in his blood even now. But he wasn't sure why this ridiculous woman should remind him of his earlier trials.

Aware he would probably regret it later, he cupped his fingers around his mouth and emitted the deep mewling growl of a jungle panther. The old dog pricked its ears in alarm and warily backed away from the bushes. The man on the terrace threw up his hands in disgust and spun around, muttering to the slender man who'd come to stand in the library doorway behind him.

"It was only a bloody dog and cat in the bushes. I don't know where the hell she's got to."

She had, Niall noted, taken advantage of the diversion to scuttle like a crab up the low semicircular steps of the dilapidated summerhouse behind her and vanished inside.

He chuckled, silently applauding her audacity. But his amusement soon degenerated into irritation at the appearance at the far end of the garden of the very man he'd been trying himself to escape all evening.

Archie Harper, the persistent pot-bellied press reporter for the *Bon Temps Magazine*. The abrasive pest had been waiting on the docks of Southampton six weeks ago when Niall and his valet had arrived by steamer from Singapore via Marseilles. Undaunted by Niall's refusal to grant him an interview, Harper had followed Niall here after he'd received word his uncle in the Highlands was gravely ill and wished to see him.

Niall had cut short his London stay and traveled north, pausing only the past two days in Dunhaven to finalize business arrangements for his fledgling coffee plantation with the mercantile firm of Kildrummond and Wescott—the hosts of this evening's entertainment. Tomorrow he'd be on the road to the Highlands proper. Within two months he hoped to God to be on his way back to his unknown little island in the Malay Archipelago.

"Captain Glenlyon?" Harper's irritating nasal whine, with a touch of Cockney origins, set Niall's teeth on edge. "I know you're out there 'aving a smoke. Just want a few minutes of your time to set the record straight about poor Rachel. . . ."

Rachel. Poor Rachel. God, not again.

Niall's reaction was instinctive. In one fluid move, he dove behind the screen of fading autumn roses and swung in a semi-crouch into the summerhouse. Reminded of Rachel, his ever-present anxiety over her, he'd failed to take into consideration the other young woman whose furtive antics had so entertained him until he straightened. Turning slowly, he found himself face to face with the misadventurous Elspeth herself.

She'd taken her braid loose, and her hair was the wildest, most sensual mane he'd ever seen on a woman—a waist-length tangle of dark blond pre-Raphelite curls that made her look like a naughty wood nymph. Her face was sweet. Finely drawn, it had a patrician nose, and a ripe soft, red mouth as tempting as a strawberry. Her eyes, however, the luminous golden-green of an enraged tigress, held his imagination at bay before it could get the better of him. Or the worse. His reaction to her was intensely visceral.

Her physical appearance was far from perfect. Those dark scowling eyebrows and cleft chin were too strongly defined for the rest of her face, but Glenlyon doubted any normal man would be able to resist looking at her.

She was standing in a sleeveless chemise and stockings, her petticoats hitched up to her shoulders like a coat of armor. She stared in utter disbelief at Niall for several seconds, then opened her mouth to emit what he suspected would be one earsplitting scream.

"Don't." He moved swiftly behind her, bringing his hand up to her face. "You scream, *chérie,* and I guarantee that your long-suffering husband, who is searching for you even as we stand here, is going to take one look at you half-naked in my arms and assume the worst. Do you understand?"

She jerked her head into a nod, her eyes wide with indignant anger as he lowered his hand and stepped forward to face he again.

In her entire twenty not-uneventful years, Elspeth Kildrummond had never found herself in quite such an embarrassing situation. Caught returning from one of her forbidden escapades by a guest at her own engagement party. In her underwear, to heap shame upon scandal.

Well, she could only blame her own impulsive nature. It wouldn't be the first time she'd brought disaster upon herself.

"Do you mind going outside while I finish dressing?" she snapped when it became clear he had no intention of doing such a socially correct thing on his own.

Niall lifted his broad shoulders in an apologetic shrug that belied the dark mockery in his eyes. "I can't," he said in a stage whisper. "I'm hiding from someone—just like you. And actually, I have to admit I'm very curious to see how we'll get ourselves out of this situation."

Elspeth clutched her petticoats a little tighter, narrowing her eyes to examine him more carefully.

She'd never met a man who exuded such a potent combination of humor, self-confidence, and unabashed sensuality. His gaze drifted over her in a look that categorized all of her physical assets and deficits—and left her uncertain whether she should laugh at his presumption or belt him across the chops.

He was tall, with a muscular frame that shouldn't have looked as elegant in evening clothes as it did. His sun-burnished face reminded Elspeth of one she'd seen stamped on a foreign coin in her father's desk, a face that hinted of exotic lands and dangerous ports-of-call.

Giving him her coldest glare, which unfortunately seemed to have no effect on his composure, she crept sideways to duck behind the fan-backed wicker chair which held her evening gown.

"You don't have to watch me, do you?"

He grinned, his even white teeth an attractive contrast to his dark complexion. "But I've been watching you ever since you broke into the library window. A charming scene."

She scowled. "There's an expression for men like you—men who like to watch people doing private things. My sister read it in a magazine—something that started with a naked woman on a horse."

"I believe you're thinking of Peeping Tom."

"That's it," she said quickly. "That's what you are."

"I certainly am not," he retorted, looking annoyed for the first time, which gave Elspeth a small measure of satisfaction. "Your sister should find a more productive pastime than reading such rubbish."

Elspeth privately agreed, but she wasn't about to tell him that. "Are you going to leave so I can make myself decent?"

"Not yet. But just to prove I'm no Peeping Tom, I promise I won't look."

He smiled and turned to stare outside while she struggled into her dress, his face in all its sardonic amusement burning in her mind. His features were cleanly sculpted, a strong browline and hawkish nose, the firm mouth of a sensualist above a square-hewn chin. But it was his eyes, those sad, soulful gray eyes that saved him from being relegated to the realm of practiced rogues and crass businessman who paraded in and out of her father's house.

She hadn't met him before, even though Duncan Kildrummond was an established shipbuilder and importer of foreign goods who entertained a remarkable mixture of exotic visitors. No, she'd have remembered such an impertinent man, she was sure.

She bit the inside of her cheek, peering out from the curtain of hair that fell across her face. She was well enough versed in etiquette to realize he might be a foreign dignitary—she tried to place his country of origin by his burnished skin and compelling physiognomy, but her boarding-school geography failed.

He'd spoken both in English and French. An ambassador from Morocco, perhaps? Some sultan's arrogant bastard son? Or a mere sea captain from Quebec who sold lumber? Whoever he was, he offended every decent feeling and made her aware of some indecent ones as well.

She finished fastening the hooks at her back, thinking distractedly that if she continued to eat and drink as she had earlier in the evening, she'd never fit into her wedding gown.

"I don't know where you come from, *monsieur,* but in this country, it's exceedingly rude for a man to impose his presence on a woman in the middle of her toilette."

"In my country it's considered so rude for a woman to cuckold her husband that he's justified in throwing her into a live volcano."

Elspeth's mouth dropped open.

Niall pivoted slowly, his eyes widening at the transformation her change of clothing had made. "You're not the pastry cook, are you?"

"The what?" She frowned and stepped out from behind the chair, hastily twisting her dark-gold braid into a knot at her nape.

He studied her in curious silence. Oh, that poor husband of hers. No wonder he couldn't control her behavior. She needed a much firmer hand—Niall had enough experience with wild creatures himself to see that.

She kicked her discarded outfit under the wicker chair and swept barefooted past him with her bag. Her chin was held so high in the air, Niall privately feared she'd step off the uppermost step of the summerhouse and hurt herself.

Instead, he turned deliberately so that she walked right into him. "Wait *chérie,*" he said softly. "There's someone coming."

Elspeth looked up slowly, suppressing a shiver of apprehension. Face to face, he was even more intimidating than when he'd remained at a safe distance in the shadows. Handsome seemed too tame a word to describe the masculine energy he exuded. Once before in her life Elspeth had fallen for another man who looked like a dark angel . . . and extracted a devil's toll from her soul and reputation.

"You're beginning to seriously overstep the boundaries of the invitation extended you this evening, Mr.—" She stepped back in sudden alarm, her voice rising. "Wait a minute. Three houses have been burglarized in this square during the past week. Just what were you doing in the library with the lights out anyway? Who are you?"

"Niall Glenlyon," he said quietly, unoffended that she thought him a thief. "And you?"

"Elspeth—"

From outside the summerhouse came the sound of footsteps, a man calling furiously, "Fergus said he saw you out here, Elspeth. If you make a fool of me tonight . . ."

His voice faded into a whisper of wind, the dry leaves of ivy that embraced the summerhouse shivering lightly.

Niall stared down into the worried face of the young woman he'd detained. "Ah, not a servant at all—you're one of Duncan's daughters, and that's George the fiancé you've got on a goose chase." His gray eyes amused, he plucked a piece of straw from her hair. "Dear, dear. A roll in the hay cart with Samson right before our own engagement party? It doesn't exactly portend well for a lifetime of wedded bliss now, does it, Miss Kildrummond?"